Exist for Now

BOB HOWARD

ISBN:1945754311
ISBN-13: 978-1-945754-31-9

Cover art by Lorena Martin of Premade Ebook Covers

DEDICATION

When I started writing, I found there's much more to it than putting the story on the pages. I found that you have to live it and breathe it. Writing the story means getting into the heads of the characters and walking in their footsteps. That's the really fun part because you get to make up who they are, what they say, and what they do. For some reason I'll never be able to explain, I can't get enough of that part. This book is dedicated to my wife, Dawn, for living and breathing the creation of each book along with me.

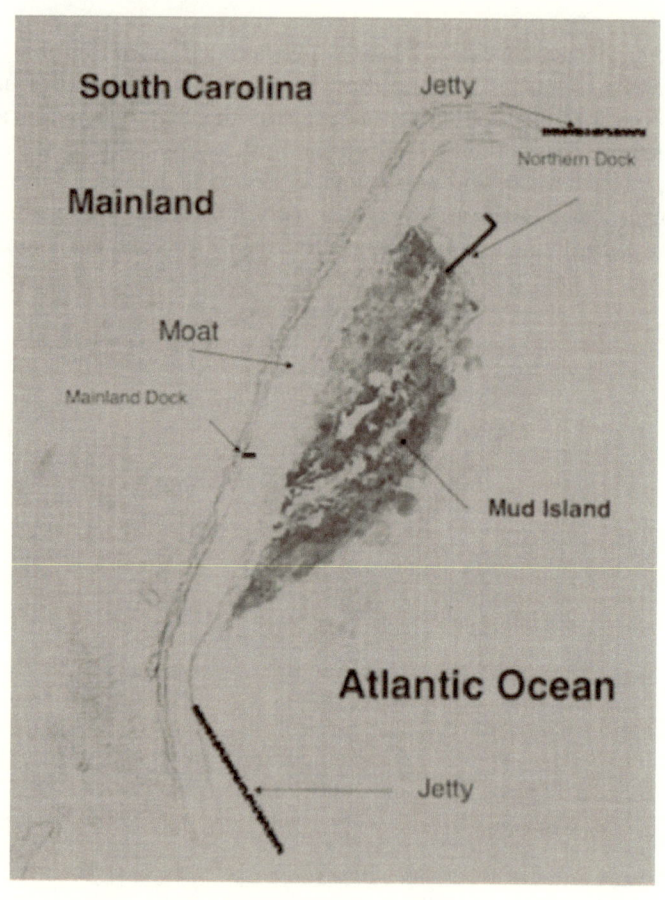

CONTENTS

ACKNOWLEDGMENTS

The work that goes into a book would be much harder without the people who give their time to read it in advance, edit the mistakes, give their reactions and opinions, and sometimes endure the frustration of trying to make me change something. Just ask my wife. I've already dedicated this book to my wife, but she has been more involved with the writing of this book than the first three, so I should mention here that she deserves more credit than ever for her hard work and for being my main advance reader.

As always, my family has given me their support in the form of simply recognizing that this has been a dream come true for me. I can't thank them enough for their encouragement.

This book had three new advance readers who were asked to read the book for various reasons. Stacie Turcotte enjoyed the first three books so much that she immersed herself in the characters. I asked her to read the book to see if she stayed as connected with them as she had in the first three books. It appears that she did, so I hope to have her available for the next book.

Kathi Gibbs was the inspiration for one of the characters, and I had to see if she would read the book with the same excitement as the first three. Believe me when I say she didn't let me down. Her enjoyment of the book was what I needed in order to feel that I had done her character justice.

Tim Harrelson contacted me after reading my books, and he offered me some insights and ideas without really even realizing that was what he was doing. Reading his comments about survival and protecting loved ones during an apocalypse made me realize that we might be able to suspend our beliefs and disbeliefs long enough to accept a book about a zombie apocalypse, but the reality of an apocalypse is something that exists no matter what we suspend. Whether it's a natural disaster or a pandemic, we can't help feeling like something is coming. Everyone I know says we're overdue. Tim and his family will probably be among the survivors.

On a more upbeat note, I discovered the designer of my covers after I decided to put the books in print. That was why the covers changed after the first three were available as ebooks. Lorena Martin of Premade Ebook Covers is very creative and has been a true artist. When I was ready for the cover of this book, I gave her an idea of what I wanted, and she came through for me once again.

1 1969

Standing on the shoreline at the edge of the trees and looking out across the marsh, it didn't look like much more than another overgrown lump of dirt and ugly trees to Titus Andronicus Rush. He had his hands on his hips and his legs spaced evenly with his shoulders. To the small group of men standing behind him, it didn't appear that he had moved a muscle since assuming the stance.

It was warm for March, and the mosquitoes had already begun to swarm and pester the men, but they didn't seem to be bothering Titus. He opened his eyes for a moment and then shut them. The only change on his face was a slightly deeper furrow across his weathered forehead.

"Do you suppose he could hurry this up a bit?" complained one of the men. He was a heavy set bureaucrat of some kind, and his business suit looked out of place against the tall bushes and trees. He was sweating from the humidity and kept mopping at his head with a soaked handkerchief.

His complaint had been addressed to a tall man standing next to him in an Army uniform. He was wearing combat fatigues, or battledress, and was more at home in the coastal wilderness than the other man. He had the close cropped gray hair of a career military type, and he had the hard, chiseled features of a man who had seen rough times. He had a General's insignia on each shoulder, and he appeared to be less interested in the bureaucrat than the man they were watching. He also didn't look like he was as bothered by the mosquitoes, the humidity, or even the rank smell of the mud that appeared above the water when the tide went out. He was wondering more about what Titus Rush was thinking, and he would wait as long as they needed. His job was to make progress with their plans, and they weren't going to make progress without Mr. Rush.

Titus opened his eyes again and looked from left to right. His long hair fell from his left shoulder and crossed to the right as the men watched him move for the first time. He was prematurely gray, and he hadn't bother to shave, so he looked like an aging hippie to them. His head traveled back in the other direction and stopped as he faced the northern end of the marsh. From where they were all standing, they could see an opening and the Atlantic Ocean beyond.

He kept his feet and hands where they were, but he turned at the hips and looked at the General. Titus liked the guy. He was prone to asking questions that he was smart enough to answer for himself, but Titus knew he was just getting things out in the open. An almost imperceptible nod of his head made the General smile slightly, and he stepped away from the others to stand next to Titus. The bureaucrat started to move forward too, but Titus froze him in his tracks with a cold stare.

Titus had made it clear from the start that he didn't like the whining man who had flown with them from Washington down to South Carolina, but he had been enjoying the man's obvious discomfort. Just to mess with him he glanced past the sweating man toward the trees behind the group of waiting men. There were six of them, and they all turned to look at the trees, but Titus knew the desired effect had worked because the only one that didn't turn back toward him was the whiner. They had seen alligators moving through the swamps on the other side of the trees, and it would give the whiner something else to think about while Titus talked with the General.

"What's the verdict, Mr. Rush? Can we make this work?"

Titus grinned at the tall military man. He had given the General a short list of requirements, and the General had come back with his own short list of locations. This was their second stop, and Titus looked pleased.

"General, I don't think we need to visit the other locations. This one will need work, but I can see it. It's not bad as it is, but it can be made perfect."

Titus pointed to the stretch of land that was about two miles long and looked like a bad place to spend the night.

"The island looks like it has a northern entrance and a southern exit. When the tide comes in, of course the water comes in from both ends, but with the right amount of dredging, you could keep the entire marsh flooded and create a current from north to south that would be strong enough to act like a river."

"It sounds like you're talking about a moat, Mr. Rush. How is a moat supposed to make this place safe? People can use a boat to get across."

"Think about layers of safety, General. You said you could finance the construction of a shelter that's impenetrable. That's good, but you can't just put it anywhere you like. It has

3

to have layers outside that at least make it miserable for someone who's trying to take it from you."

The General had heard Titus make his speech before, but he liked the way the unconventional man thought, so he listened to it again.

"The perfect shelter has to protect you from whatever has happened, whether it's a nuclear war, or a natural catastrophe. Let's call it an apocalypse. It also has to be able to meet your basic needs for a very long time, and it should be something you can protect from people who try to take it away from you. Anything else would be temporary."

The General looked back toward the island and said, "Okay, we need a moat. The Army Corps of Engineers can dredge out this marsh until it's deep enough for you. What about keeping it from getting filled back in by sand carried in on the current?"

As soon as he asked the question he knew the answer. Titus didn't bother to say anything.

"Jetties," said the General. "That's a big order, Mr. Rush. Do you know how much that will cost the taxpayers?"

Once again, Titus didn't answer. He already knew he would get whatever he needed. When he and his survivalist group were first approached by the government and asked to make shelters that were guaranteed to protect their occupants, they had agreed to do it on the condition that the financing would be a blank check. Otherwise, they would give no guarantees.

His group had also made it abundantly clear that there couldn't be a total guarantee, but they could be close to perfect if they were given everything and anything they needed. Right now, at this same moment, the other members of his survivalist group were spread out across the country with their teams of Generals, politicians, and money men. All of them were playing out their own personal fantasies about what would work if they could have whatever they needed, and if they had the resources to make their shelters work. Each shelter would stretch the imagination of the planners and builders, as well as the wallets of the government. Besides, Titus knew they were also collecting money from influential people who would be brought along for the ride in the event of an apocalypse.

The General had gotten used to Titus Rush not answering, and he decided it wouldn't do any good to turn down any of his requests no matter how costly they were.

"What else, Mr. Rush?"

"I'll give you the plans for the shelter. I've already drawn them up. This site will be perfect once the moat is in place. I'll also need a dock here on the mainland and one on the island. I'll add them to the drawings so you can see where I want them. I need a boat, and I want the power supply to be permanent, so we'll need to connect the shelter to the mainland by something that crosses the bottom of the moat."

The General started to ask Titus how he could already have the plans drawn when he had just seen this place for the first time, but he decided it was another rhetorical question not likely to be answered by Titus. He reasoned that the smaller man had undoubtedly been picturing this possibility for a long time. If he was really a survivalist, then these ideas of his had been rattling around inside his head just waiting for their chance to come out.

"I need something else, General, and it's something your friends back in DC already agreed to."

"What's that, Mr. Rush?"

"Upgrades. I need to get upgrades as technology makes advances. We're going to start with shortwave radio and TV reception, but there's no way those things are going to remain state of the art. From what I hear, there's going to be a man on the moon this summer. After that, I expect to see technology take off. If it gets invented, I want it in this shelter."

The General turned toward the rest of their group. Two were armed military escorts. The stuffed shirt who was sweating too much was the man who was supposed to make the money move from one place to another without questions, and the others were the engineers who would get the work done. He gave them a nod much like the one he had gotten from Titus, and they all knew the project was begun.

******

The next meeting of the survivalists was the following week, and Titus got to see all of their individual choices. He thought some were questionable, but he had given them free rein when it came to their own plans. He saw that his own choice was going to be far less expensive than a few of the others. His friend, Bus, had chosen to build his shelter on his own property, and he couldn't say that he blamed him. There was something to be said for living close to your shelter. When the bombs fell or the apocalypse began, it would be a good idea to get inside as fast as possible.

Titus had been the unanimous choice when the group had selected a leader. It wasn't that he was the best choice, but his personality was so strong that people stopped talking whenever he started. So it was when they met for the first time to talk over their individual shelters.

Thirty-one people stopped talking as soon as he said his first words.

"Does anybody have a complaint about our government friends? Are they cooperating?"

He looked around at the faces surrounding him, and only one hand had been raised. He pointed at the Vietnam veteran with the serious look on his face and waited for him to speak. He was a tough man because he had already done a couple of tours in the war, so it wasn't like him to complain.

The man stood so everyone could hear him and said, "I was led to believe we would each be taking in a few important people if we ever have to use the shelters. They added to my plans, and now it's going to be big enough to hold an entire army."

"We knew they would have an agenda of their own when we agreed to this, Jerry. Are you saying you wanted something just a bit more cozy?"

That got some scattered laughs, but Titus could get away with it. Not everyone could tease Jerry.

"You know what I mean, Titus. What's to stop them from forgetting who owns the shelters? Remember, that was the deal. They may be paying for it, but we still own it. If I have a battalion living under my roof, they could just chuck me outside."

Jerry said it with just enough humor in his voice to earn his own laughs. Titus got the feeling Jerry was less concerned about it happening than he was with just making sure the point was discussed.

"I can only tell you what we know, Jerry. We are to be treated as royalty in our own shelters, and we have a say in everything. Whether they will honor that promise or not is one of the uncertainties of this little project. Hell, Jerry, what makes you think we're all going to live long enough to ever get to use these shelters, anyway?"

"I'm moving into mine as soon as it's done," said one young man with long hair and a big pair of round, wire framed glasses.

Like most of the people in the room, he was wearing a pair of denim bell bottomed jeans and a colorful tee-shirt. What looked like a roomful of hippies was actually a collection of some of the greatest minds in the country. Most of them had doctoral degrees in some kind of engineering or science, and they would be valuable people to keep alive after an apocalypse.

"That's because you got evicted from your apartment again," said one of the six women in the room. "He keeps asking if he can sleep on my sofa until he gets a new place."

Titus liked the good natured laughing and didn't try to discourage it. He knew they were a close knit group, and no matter what happened, they were getting a leg up on the rest of the population by building the shelters. He just wondered if any of them would actually wind up living in them over the years to come, or if they were really just building them for the government. After all of the major players were dead and gone, whether they were in this room with him or they were people in power in the government, they were going to be replaced just as often as the technology. He looked around and wondered how many of them would be replaced over the years.

"Okay everybody," said Titus. "Let's get down to business. We need to talk about each other's choices. The locations, the construction, second lines of defense, and anything else we can think of. I'll start us off by reading a list of shelter sites. I want each of you to speak up and say what will make the site better."

Titus read the list, and as he did he called out the owner's names. The one that got the most attention as a bad choice was the oil rig in the Gulf of Mexico. The owner was one of their newest members, and he had clearly focused on isolation as a layer of safety.

One by one the other members of the group told why it wasn't such a good choice, but since it was already a done deal, they added how they would improve the plans. One idea was to mine the Gulf for a few miles surrounding the oil rig, but there was no way the government would go for that idea. When all was said and done, the only layers that could be improved upon would be detection and weaponry. It went without saying that the shelter itself would be hardened to be nearly indestructible, but its visibility was going to make it a tempting target.

Titus took the heat off of the young man by putting his own plans on the table. He described a salt water marsh as the perfect place to put a shelter, and the rest of the group started suggesting ways to make it better. One suggestion was to protect the underwater power lines with strong nets. They might catch something in them from time to time, but at least nothing could knock out the power to the island. Titus wrote the idea in a notebook, and in the margin of the page he wrote that it would have to be very strong. He wasn't sure why he thought that, but he was prone to getting hunches, and this felt like a good hunch.

One by one they discussed their locations, and sometimes there were ideas that could be referred back to each previously discussed shelter. Someone came up with the concept that there should be a decoy shelter somewhere nearby. That way people would never suspect there was something bigger and better only a short distance away. That worked for everyone, including the oil rig. It wasn't hard to imagine that plenty of people would try to escape to the rigs. They just had to find ways to keep them from getting inside.

The meeting ended with a plan to return in a month with progress reports. Titus told everyone that he expected to hear that all of the shelters were at least habitable by the end of the year. With the exception of the shelter at Fort Sumter he was sure it could be done.

******

The next time Titus Rush visited his chosen shelter site he was surprised to see the amount of progress the Army Corps of Engineers had made. He had at least half expected to find there had been delays. Money would be tied up by some pending House bill, or some auditor had questioned the manpower and materials. Instead he found they were ahead of schedule. He seriously doubted they could be making the same progress on thirty-one more shelters.

When Titus had selected the site, he had been standing at a tree line on a narrow strip of ground that gently sloped down into marsh grass and mud. As he stepped from the trees he found himself standing on a sandy beach, and about twenty yards in front of him was a cliff. He eased forward and looked over the edge. Wooden framework was holding the beach in place, or it would have all collapsed into a trench that was at least fifty feet deep near the beach.

Toward the middle of the trench it was closer to one hundred feet deep, and at the bottom he could see men working on power cables. The far shoreline looked smooth and metallic, and a second group of men was working on metal fasteners for a pair of the biggest nets he had ever seen. The nets were stretched across the bottom of the trench, ready to be raised into place. The General hadn't balked in the slightest when he had called to suggest the additional layers of protection.

An Army engineer walked up to him and said, "Mr. Rush, you're just in time for the big show. We'll be pulling back the men and equipment in a few minutes and the crews at the dams will be letting the water in from both ends. You might want to be back by the trees when the two waves meet in the middle."

He watched as the crews finished in the deep trench and were hauled to the shore. He realized the only way they could have dug such a deep trench was to dam entrances at the ends of the island, and the nets were too heavy to put in place without cranes, so they would use the water to float them into place.

"Have you guys gotten much done on the shelter?" he asked the engineer.

He smiled proudly and said, "You won't believe it, Sir. As a matter of fact, our crew is competing with the other crews to see who can build the best shelter."

In the distance sirens started to wail, and everyone who was working on the island and the mainland got into position to watch the water fill the moat. It was as impressive as the young Army engineer had expected. The two waves crashed into each other, and for a few moments it looked like a raging sea in the moat. When it finally began to settle, there was a wide river where there had once been nothing but mud and grass.

A boat came around the northern end of the island and was making its way toward the shore where Titus was standing. The officer driving the boat let it turn sideways so it would drift up to the bank where the wooden framework was. He waved for Titus to jump aboard and immediately turned back toward the island.

"We're going to build a dock on the mainland right where you were standing," he shouted over the sound of the twin outboard engines. "The General said he wants the dock rebuilt every ten years. If you ever have to use this place, you'll need the dock with a boat ready for the trip across."

As they approached the northern tip of the island, Titus could see a dock already protruding out from the land, and the officer expertly coasted up to it. Titus was fixated on the stone jetty that sat across from the entrance to the moat, and all he could think was how quickly they had done the work. It crossed his mind that the people in Washington might have been expecting something big.

"Is the jetty already done on the southern end of the island?" he asked.

"Certainly is, Sir. It was better to have them both done before letting in the water. That way neither end would need to be dredged. As you leave the entrances to the moat the bottom gets much more shallow, but it's still deep enough to draft big boats."

Titus followed the man as they left the dock and began hiking along a rough path toward the center of the island. His ankles were a little sore from the constant changes in the ground, and he was just about to ask the officer how much further when they walked into a small clearing. In front of them, set neatly in a recessed wall of earth was the biggest bank vault door he had ever seen.

It was standing open, and the sounds of construction could be heard coming from deep inside the island.

"Can we go in?" he asked.

The officer smiled and made a sweeping gesture toward the door with one hand.

"Make yourself at home, Mr. Rush. It belongs to you."

Titus felt like a kid again. He stepped over the bottom edge of the door sill and looked around. At first he was a little disappointed because the room was so small, but then he realized the construction noises were coming from somewhere below.

"The rooms are far from finished, Mr. Rush, but I'm sure you will appreciate them even more when you know what's underneath the finished product. For now, we'd like for you to see some of the safety features and layouts. We've read your specifications and we think you will like what you see."

For the next hour Titus Andronicus Rush roamed from room to room studying every little detail, thinking the entire time, "Oh yes, I really do like this...even though the master bedroom is in the wrong place."

2 LIFE GOES ON

None of us really knew what it would be like to shut the door and actually have to keep it shut. It had always been an option to go outside, and the promise of fresh air and sunshine had made the shelter inside Mud Island feel like home. When the door was sealed, it felt more like a tomb.

It was too quiet in the first few minutes. We all looked at each other and realized the finality of our situation. We had no way of knowing how bad the nuclear incident was, so we also didn't know how long it would last. We didn't know what would be safe when we went outside, where we could go, and where the contamination would be. There were plenty of questions and very few answers.

No one spoke as we drifted off into our own private pursuits. Jean was experimenting with bread dough again, Kathy was looking through the supply of books, and the Chief had disappeared somewhere below, probably to the armory. Tom had gone in the same direction as he pulled on weight lifting gloves. Molly was sitting at the radio wearing the headphones that always looked too big on her head. Bus had already claimed his right to the computer and was reading an article about radiation exposure.

Not immediately knowing what I wanted to do with my time, I considered putting a video game on the main screen, but somehow I felt like being a little more productive. I switched on the outside video monitors and started scanning the different views. It didn't take me too long to realize there was a reason I had turned to what was happening outside instead of finding something to do inside.

Changes were about to happen again. What the changes would be were unknown, but they were coming. It slowly sank in that I was hoping to see the infected dead fall over and stay dead when the radiation dropped on the coast of South Carolina.

Bus was the one who had the foresight to put radiation monitors in several locations on the dock, all within view of cameras. He had even put one in the houseboat so we could judge how bad it got in a place that had minimal protection. All of them were still reading normal, which was good news. That meant the radiation hadn't arrived before we got inside.

I absentmindedly listened as Molly raised Fort Sumter on her radio. From what I could tell, she was talking with Sam. I remembered having a crush on a girl when I was about the same age, and it seemed to be that much stronger because we couldn't see each other whenever we wanted to. It was a long distance relationship, and the Internet was just beginning to be a way to shorten the distance. I imagined their relationship might be ready to burst by the time they were able to see each other.

My attention was drawn back to the outside views, and I watched a pair of the infected dead walk out of the trees. It slowly dawned on me that I wanted the radiation to arrive. I wanted to see it for myself and to know how the radiation would effect them. I wanted to see them double over and collapse into the sand. I held my breath and waited, but nothing happened. All they did was the usual lurching and stumbling through the sand until they eventually reached the edge of the moat and fell in.

I glanced over at the screen that showed the radiation monitors, and there was still no change. At least it looked like there wasn't. There were two different monitors at each location. One changed colors, and one had a needle that traveled along a calibrated arc. I wasn't entirely sure, but it looked like the needle wasn't sitting on top of the line that meant zero. It was starting.

"Uncle Eddie?"

Molly was holding the headphones away from her ears.

"Captain Miller said to tell you they were reading low levels of radiation. He wants to know if we are too."

"Tell him we are, Molly. Nothing big yet, but it's starting."

Molly nodded at me and turned back to the radio. I went back to scanning the trees on the mainland. There wasn't much breeze blowing, but I could imagine the radiation moving through the air. It would be even more deadly out there than what it had been when the infection started. Now there was just one more thing in the world that would start killing people who had somehow survived the teeth of the infected dead.

Jean came in from the kitchen and sat down next to me.

"Dough has to rise for a while," she said. "What's happening outside?"

I had expected her to say something funny, which is what she probably would have done under normal circumstances, but the gravity of the radiation falling unseen outside was having a sobering effect on everyone.

"It's starting. The radiation monitors are starting to react."

We both looked at the screens and saw the needles had all moved further along their arcs, and the colored monitors were a slight shade of pink. All we could do was sit and watch as if they were going to suddenly reverse direction.

"You know, Eddie, this is what your uncle really had in mind when he built this shelter. Someone was supposed to press a red button somewhere or turn a big key, and everyone who didn't get blown up was supposed to be killed by fallout."

It wasn't like Jean to be so negative, and I wondered what she was thinking. Maybe I was finally starting to grow up because I could see what was bothering her in her expression. It was the way she was looking at the monitors.

"Are you feeling guilty about being safe inside Mud Island?"

"A little. Someone else was supposed to be here, but they didn't make it. Look at the number of times we've managed to stay alive, and some poor slob couldn't even survive once by making it to the shelter."

"Do you think we don't deserve to be here?" I asked.

Jean was so caught up in her feelings, and I was so sorry to see her having a down moment that we almost didn't see the small boat that had pulled up to the dock.

There were at least six people, and if we weren't already feeling guilty enough, there were a couple of toddlers being carried by the adults. They were rushing to get inside the houseboat as if they knew something was wrong outside.

This time Jean read my mind and said, "They must have a radio. That has to be how they know about the radiation, but if they do, then they already know it's too late."

I reached over to the controls and turned off the monitors to the inside of the houseboat. We knew what was going to happen to the people, and there wasn't any sense in watching it happen. Jean squeezed my hand and got up from the sofa.

"I'm going to go do something to keep busy, Eddie. I can't let myself think about what's happening out there."

I couldn't do anything to help Jean or the new arrivals, and there really wasn't anything to be learned from watching them slowly die from the radiation poisoning. I didn't know how wrong I was.

******

We gradually got used to the idea that we were going to be locked inside Mud Island for a long time. Routines began to take shape, and schedules became normal. It wasn't that we sat down and decided what would get done and when. We just started doing the same things at the same times until it became expected.

Kathy started a running club, and within a few weeks we were all doing our time on the treadmills as a group. Even Jean, as pregnant as she was, managed to keep up for a while.

We got daily reports from Fort Sumter, and the Army had the same dismal updates we had for them. As expected, people moved into the fort above the shelter, and someone had taken up residence in the Cormorant, the Coast Guard ship that had saved our lives. It wasn't long before people started to show signs of radiation sickness.

Captain Miller usually took care of the call himself, seeming to draw strength from knowing his rescuers were safe inside their own shelter. I overheard him saying to the Chief that he owed him for his life twice now. If not for the Mud Island group, they would have been stuck outside in the radioactive fallout. Of course the Chief didn't want any part of the credit. He told Captain Miller we didn't do anything they wouldn't have done for us.

Jean started turning out some pretty good fresh baked bread, and the supplies were holding up better than we could have hoped. Time started slipping by without monotony setting in. There just seemed to be enough to keep us busy.

It was over breakfast when the Chief was in the middle of a conversation with Tom, and I was working on a stack of pancakes without much thought for what they were discussing. That was when he decided to have a little fun with me.

Jean was setting Molly up with a fresh glass of her beloved chocolate milk, although it was being poured from a can, and Kathy was having a dispute with Bus over the merits of coffee because Bus preferred tea. The Chief brought the room to a standstill.

"So, Ed, when do you plan to make an honest woman out of Jean?"

True to his usual form, he covered his grin by putting his coffee cup to his mouth. The mischief was still there in the pair of eyes above the steaming coffee.

Not to be outdone, and I have to give myself some credit, I had gotten pretty good at defending myself from the Chief's sense of humor.

"Jean's a very honest woman, Chief. She just happens to be an honest pregnant woman."

Wrong answer.

The last time the topic of marriage came up, I had done a reasonably good job of making myself look good. This time I had focused too much on beating the Chief in the smart remarks department, when I should have just rolled with it.

So began the longest cold shoulder I had ever gotten from Jean, which in its own way served as a distraction from the world outside. It also gave everyone else something to do as they set about trying to repair the damage I had done.

It took about two weeks to set things right again, but the Mud Island family finally got Jean and me to sit down to a candle light dinner for two, and I was able to formally propose to Jean. A date was set for the following weekend, and Kathy presented Jean with a wedding gown artfully crafted from the excess of linen tablecloths we had in storage. It was easily decided that the Chief would perform the ceremony since he was the closest thing to a ship's captain, and Bus would give away the bride. Molly would be the ring bearer and the flower girl, and Tom and Kathy would be the witnesses. We didn't have one more survivor who could be my best man so Tom did double duty. The Chief said it was perfectly legal, and there were no objections from the population of Mud Island.

The wedding was great, considering we were in an underground shelter with a world changing event outside that was threatening the end of the human race. Maybe I'm slow sometimes, but I finally caught on to the Chief's motives. He wanted the group to avoid becoming too scheduled and even complacent. He wanted us to stay a little spontaneous because he knew we would want to leave the shelter sooner or later. He just wanted it to be because we could go back outside, not because we were going crazy being inside.

When I asked the Chief if that was what he had done, he never answered directly, but he explained that people don't live from moment to moment. They live from one big moment to the next. Weddings, births, high school and college graduation, landing a big job, they were all part of living. So much of that had been taken from us that he wanted to give us at least one of those big moments, and it had worked. The birth of our baby was going to be the next big event, but the Chief hadn't wanted us to miss the opportunity for the first one. It had taken our minds off of the world outside, and it had kept our routines from becoming boring.

If not for the fresh new role I had as a husband, I might have become unconcerned about what was happening in the houseboat, but I felt like something had opened my eyes again. I found myself back on the sofa looking at the world outside with the idea that there might be something to learn. I switched on the camera inside the houseboat and looked into the eyes of an infected dead. It was one of the adults I had seen carrying the toddler from the boat.

Others were wandering around inside the houseboat, bumping into each other and the furniture. The door must have been locked because I saw them repeatedly falling against the handle. All of them had sores and had lost their hair. Open mouths revealed that teeth had fallen out or had been broken when they tried to bite each other.

The startling lesson I had learned was that the people had died from radiation poisoning and had become infected dead. The only other alternative was that someone in their group had been bitten before they sought refuge in the houseboat. I wished over and over again that I had watched them at least long enough to know for sure.

The implications were obvious now. If people who had not been bitten died from radiation poisoning, there were going to be a lot more infected dead than living people, because there had been so few places where people could have gone to avoid the radiation.

I ran over to the radio and hailed Fort Sumter. I had to know if they were seeing the same thing. I needed to know if they were seeing what I had stupidly allowed myself to miss.

Captain Miller was paged to come to the control room as soon as I made contact, and he was either nearby, or he hurried from wherever he was to get to the radio.

"Ed, your timing is great. I was just about to contact you."

"Captain, good to hear your voice. Are you seeing anything happening above the shelter?"

"That's why I was about to check in with you. We've been watching everything go down as expected, but there appears to be a new development. The people who die of radiation poisoning are attacking the living."

"Have they been bitten before they die?" I asked.

"I don't think so, but we have a new problem. We don't know if they are getting the infection by being bitten or because they have been eating the seafood."

It hadn't occurred to me even though it was something we had talked about often. There were infected dead out there biting the living to spread the disease. There was radiation falling from the sky that was going to gradually kill most of the people who were still outside and downwind, but there was always that big question about the food chain. I didn't see the people go into the houseboat carrying any supplies, so they must have gone out fishing and crabbing while I had put them out of my mind.

Captain Miller continued, "We've been seeing it all along, but it wasn't that big of a surprise when you get right down to it. We've been fairly certain that not everyone is getting bitten before they die and then come back, and I wouldn't rule out the possibility that everyone we see has been forced to eat the seafood at some time or another. We've been talking about it in our daily updates to you guys, but I don't think anyone was too focused on the obvious."

I considered what he said and realized he was right. The radiation, the bites, and the food chain were all right there in front of us as three obvious ways to die.

The Chief came up behind me when he realized I was talking with someone on the radio.

"Is that Fort Sumter?" asked the Chief.

"Captain Miller's on the line giving me an update about the people above the shelter. The people aren't doing any better than the ones in our houseboat, but he said they've been eating the local seafood, so we still don't know how they're getting the infection."

The Chief took the microphone and keyed it up.

"Captain Miller, any word from the area near the reactor? I've been watching the radiation monitors and talking with Doctor Bus about the levels. It's bad enough to kill over a period of continuous exposure, but he thinks it could be far worse."

"What are you thinking, Chief? You thinking this will be over sooner than we thought?" he asked.

"Bus says one good hurricane could clean this part of the coast pretty nicely."

Captain Miller chuckled and said, "There's a first. Somebody actually hoping for a hurricane to hit."

"Do we have any weather intelligence, or do we have to just sit tight until a hurricane pops up?" I asked.

Captain Miller answered, "We established contact with the shelter on the oil rig in the Gulf of Mexico just about an hour ago. That was the other reason I was going to contact you. He said to pass along his regards to Bus and to Uncle Titus' nephew."

"Who did you talk to?" asked the Chief.

"Some guy named Maybank. He said he's originally from the Charleston area, and he wishes he would have chosen the Fort Sumter site. He also wants to know if we ever heard from Jerry, the guy who was originally supposed to occupy this shelter. We told him the truth, and he said we would have liked Jerry."

"Did Maybank have anything useful to pass along?" I asked.

"Yeah, he said the oil rig had been occupied by survivors from time to time, but they always make the same mistakes. Someone gets the infection, they start biting each other, and the next thing you know, they're falling over the catwalk railings and open decks into the Gulf of Mexico. Sounds like Fort Sumter and your houseboat," he said.

"What about the infection?" asked the Chief. "How does he think it's getting onto the oil rig?"

"Maybank said there's no doubt about it. They're eating the seafood. He said the oil rig only had one occupant for a few weeks, and the guy seemed perfectly fine until one day when he just doubled over, got sick, and died. A few minutes later he got up and started wandering around until he found an open place where he could fall overboard. Maybank said he had considered the possibility of bringing the man inside the shelter, but he wasn't sure about the seafood."

The Chief and I studied each other for a minute, both undoubtedly thinking about the night we had encountered the marina full of people on the Stono River who were surviving on a steady diet of blue crab that had been surviving on a steady diet of infected dead. We finally had our answer. We had considered the possibility of returning to the area to see what had become of almost five hundred people, but in our hearts we had always suspected what we would find.

"What did Maybank have to say about the weather in the Gulf?" asked the Chief.

"That was why he wished he would have selected the Fort Sumter site," said Captain Miller. "He said the oil rig doesn't feel like it's moving, and it isn't moving, but when the whole Gulf looks like one big raging wave after the next, he said watching it can get you seasick."

"The Gulf is having a tropical storm?" I asked. "Isn't it a little early in the year for that?"

The Chief looked at me and grinned, but he spoke into the microphone to Captain Miller.

"Ed may be losing track of time now that he's a married man and getting settled into a responsible life, Captain. He doesn't realize it's the first week of June."

Captain Miller anticipated his next question and said, "Temperatures have been higher than normal, and Maybank said the storm was moving toward the Florida coast around the panhandle. That means we're going to get some heavy rain even if we don't get a hurricane or a tropical storm. He also said he hasn't been getting any radiation down there, so the fallout looks like it's localized."

"That's good news if it washes the radioactive dust off of the coast. Thanks, Captain. Keep us posted on the weather, and try to stay in contact with Maybank. By the way, I've been meaning to ask you a question."

Jean stepped into the living room and caught my attention. When I looked at her, she motioned for me to come to her, and being a newlywed, of course I didn't keep her waiting.

"I'll be right back, Chief."

He took my chair as soon as I left it, and leaned into the microphone, but I didn't catch what he asked the Captain.

******

The rain began the next morning, and it came down hard. After breakfast the Chief told us all it was time to start getting ready to go outside. As soon as the rain ended he wanted to get some fresh readings of the radioactivity near the plane we had tied up near the houseboat. He wanted to take a radiation monitor with him that hadn't been used and see if it measured less than the monitors outside. That would tell us if the rain was lowering the radiation far enough to be safe.

I can't say any of us were too happy with his decision to go outside so soon, but the Chief seemed to have something else on his mind, and he also seemed like he wanted to keep it to himself for the time being.

The Chief had some private discussions with Bus, and when I tried to pry it out of him, he just said Bus was coaching him about radiation safety. Jean told him that we all knew better. The Chief didn't need any coaching on the topic. He acted innocent, but neither Jean nor Kathy could get him to tell us what was really going on.

We all followed the Chief and Bus to the room where we had suits and other outfits that were designed to protect the wearer from radiation. I quit trying to get the Chief to tell me what had built such a fire under him because he seemed determined to go out there. Bus wasn't objecting as much as the rest of us, so he either knew something we didn't, or he wasn't as worried.

I helped the Chief put on one of the suits while the others stood back and watched. Kathy and Jean both had their arms folded across their chests and were standing defiantly between the Chief and the exit. Well, Jean actually was trying to fold her arms across her chest, but they were pretty much resting on top of her belly. She was due in only a few weeks, so she was really out there. I tried to get her to return a smile, but she was busy glaring at the Chief.

Tom had asked Molly to hang back inside and monitor the radio, and for once she didn't seem eager to go. She was sensing that the grown-ups were different toward each other, and she didn't like it. Tom wasn't taking sides, but he looked as concerned as the rest of us.

"So, you're just going out there by yourself?"

Kathy may have meant it as a question, but it came out more like a statement of fact.

"There's something I need to do, and I don't want anyone else taking risks just yet."

That didn't seem to make Kathy feel better. If anything it made her mad because he confirmed there was something going on. She shifted from one hip to the other, and I couldn't say I had ever seen her looking at the Chief with such anger.

The Chief saw it, too. He had everything on except the headpiece, and he looked even bigger wearing the bright yellow suit, but he seemed to visibly get smaller as Kathy confronted him.

He gave in just a little and said, "How about letting it go for now, and I'll tell you when I come back in. There's no sense in discussing some of the issues if the radiation isn't low enough anyway."

Kathy studied him for a minute and then stepped out of his way. He gave her a slight nod and pulled the rest of his radiation suit on. For some reason he picked up one of the extra suits that was still in a sealed plastic bag.

The Chief walked past everyone without a word until he was at the door. When he stopped and faced us, I think everyone expected him to give up something about why it was so important for him to go outside, but he just waited.

Bus was the one who realized what the Chief was waiting for. There was no sense in giving anyone who wasn't dressed in radiation control gear the opportunity to be exposed. Especially since one of them was pregnant.

"Everyone come back inside the shelter," said Bus. "When the Chief opens the door he will let in at least some radioactive dust. Everyone but Jean should bring a RADCON suit back into the shelter. We can suit up in the shelter then come back and decontaminate the room."

We silently gathered up the suits and went back into the shelter. Bus took a moment to place a new radiation detector in the room where the Chief stood waiting by the door, and a second detector was placed on the floor between that room and the door to the stairwell that went to the living quarters. As if by magic, Tom produced a large sheet of plastic and a roll of duct tape. I gave him a hand as we stretched it across the open door between the shower room and the smaller entrance that was more like a foyer. If there wasn't much wind outside, the radioactive dust would probably be limited to the immediate area by the door.

I was the last one to go through the door, and I got one last look at the Chief. I couldn't read the expression on his face because of the plastic sheet, so I just gave him a weak smile and pulled the door shut.

We all got into our radiation suits while Jean went to check the external camera views. As soon as she saw the Chief close the door, she signaled to us that he was clear. We all wanted to get the decontamination done as quickly as possible so we could get back inside and see what the Chief was doing. We finished squirming into our RADCON suits and then opened the hatch from the stairwell into the shower room just far enough for Bus to go through first.

It didn't take more than a moment for him to confirm that there weren't readings of radioactive contamination on either monitor. We had been lucky because the entrance to the shelter faced the ocean instead of the mainland. If there had been contamination, the heavy rains had done a good job rinsing it off. Bus gave us the word that the rooms were safe, but he left the radiation detectors in place just to be sure.

When we finally made it back to Jean, she said the Chief would be coming into view at the dock at any moment unless he ran into some infected dead on the way. Judging by his almost immediate appearance, he must have had a clear path.

Without the slightest pause, the Chief went straight to the houseboat and yanked open the door. The first infected dead fell out so fast, it must have been leaning against it. The Chief stepped back and just let them pile up as they came out and fell over the arms and legs of the first ones. As one of them gained its footing and stumbled toward the Chief, he just calmly brushed the reaching arms to the side and marched the walking corpse over the right side of the dock.

We all had to look away for a moment when the toddlers came through the door. A moment was all it took for the Chief to send them into the water. It couldn't have been more than two minutes before the Chief had dispatched all of them, and he stuck his head through the door of the houseboat. I looked at the camera view that showed the inside, and I saw there was one infected dead moving in the direction of the door. The Chief's massive gloved hand shot into view and grabbed the withered body by a wrist. He pulled so hard that I thought the arm would come out of the socket, and I looked at the outside monitor just in time to see him pull it into view and push it over the side. I didn't notice he was still holding the arm by the wrist until he tossed it into the water where its owner had disappeared. We had seen that happen plenty of times in the past.

The Chief had to know we would be watching, but he didn't even glance toward the camera that was strategically hidden at the end of the dock. We saw him take one of the new radiation detectors out of its package, study it for a minute, and then he placed it on top of one of the dock pilings where we could clearly see that the needle was still resting on the zero line. The rain had apparently done its job.

The Chief didn't waste any time getting into the de Havilland Beaver. The restored seaplane, or float plane, as Bus had called it, roared to life. We couldn't hear it, but we knew what it would sound like. It was a powerful plane, and it was incredibly loud.

I think we all had our mouths hanging open when the Chief started the plane. If not, they certainly were when Molly pointed at the lower part of the monitor.

"Who's that?" she asked.

Another yellow RADCON suit came into view, and the wearer walked up to the plane and stepped easily onto the float next to the dock. The newcomer was exchanging words with the Chief, and at one point stepped off of the float, wrapped the mooring lines around a piling, and then stepped back onto the float. I thought I caught a glimpse of blond hair through the headpiece.

"Where's Kathy?" I asked.

Everyone looked at each other as if we expected to see Kathy standing in the room with us.

"I think we know the answer to that question," said Jean.

"Thank you, Mrs. Obvious, but what's she doing out there?" I regretted the question even as I asked it.

Jean didn't give me the usual teasing scowl when she looked at me, and Bus stifled a laugh. Even Molly was grinning, and Tom was doing a good job faking like he was looking for something on the control panel to the monitors.

"Do you like staying in the doghouse, Mr. Obvious?" Jean emphasized mister.

I decided I would only stick my foot deeper in my mouth, so I turned my attention back to the monitor. We were all just in time to see that Kathy had untied the plane and was climbing into the back door behind the pilot seat of the Beaver. As she did, she gave a hard push with her foot, and the plane was gliding away from the dock.

Under power the plane quickly crossed the bow of the houseboat and then turned toward the northern entrance of the moat. It rushed toward the open sea, and was in the view of the ocean side camera in seconds. All we could do was watch it take off.

It was one thing to not know what the mission was, and it was entirely something else to watch the Chief and Kathy leave as if we had done something wrong. We sat in silence until Jean finally asked what was the last thing I remembered from the night before when the Chief had been talking with Captain Miller.

I told her we had been talking about the weather in the Gulf of Mexico, and that a tropical storm was going to be pushing some heavy winds and rain ahead of it. I thought it meant the winds would shift the fallout from the Oconee Nuclear Reactor more to the north. Then I remembered that the Chief was just about to ask Captain Miller about something else, and Jean had asked me to come help her with something. The Chief was just signing off when I had returned to the room.

We all knew that whatever they had discussed, it had caused the Chief to try to leave on his own, and even though we didn't like being in the dark, it felt much better knowing Kathy was in the plane with him.

"Molly, could you get in contact with Captain Miller?" asked Tom.

Molly immediately started calling Fort Sumter on the shortwave radio, and it only took a minute to get Captain Miller to the microphone. Molly switched him to the speaker so we could all hear what was being said.

"Captain Miller, this is Tom. Most of us are here, and we have a situation. Do you mind if I ask what it was you and the Chief discussed last night?"

"I know it sounds lame, but we talked about the weather. The Chief was happy to hear about the tropical storm coming in from the Gulf of Mexico because it was likely to push most of the radioactive fallout to the north. Why, Tom? What's the situation?"

I described how the Chief had left without explaining to the rest of us where he was going, and that Kathy had forced her way on board the plane at the last minute. Captain Miller listened and then asked if I had heard the question that the Chief had asked him at the end of the call. I told him I had heard the Chief say he was meaning to ask him something, but Jean had called me out of the room.

Captain Miller said, "Yeah, I thought he seemed a bit worked up after I answered his question, but he didn't say why."

"What did he ask you?"

"He wanted to know what happened to our source near Charlotte who had warned us that the Oconee Nuclear Reactor had blown up. He said something about the source being lucky that the normal dispersal pattern for the fallout would be a ten mile radius with a heavy concentration for about fifty miles to the southeast. He said we were only going to get a dusting that would kill people over time if they were caught out in the open, but the Charlotte area wouldn't get anything unless there were strong winds from the south."

We all looked at each other, slowly putting two and two together. The change in the weather, the extra suit, the rush to go. It was all starting to make sense, but we couldn't quite figure out what would make the Chief so worried about the source in Charlotte.

"Tom, are you still there?" asked Captain Miller.

"Yes, just trying to get a handle on everything."

"Well, if you asked me, I would guess that the guy in Charlotte was a friend of his. He acted surprised when I told him the man was named Hampton."

3 GEORGETOWN SURVIVOR

It didn't take us long to sort out the details. When the Chief realized who the contact was and that he was about to catch a heavy dose of radiation, the Chief had asked Captain Miller if he had any details about the man. Captain Miller had told him Hampton had flown out of the Georgetown area and made it as far as the North Carolina border west of Charlotte when he had engine trouble. Hampton told him there were a lot of people trying to make it to the mountains to get away from the infected. He said there were caravans of wagons and trailers being towed by anything that could make it past the logjams of cars and trucks that had been abandoned back at the beginning.

"There are still people on the move?" asked Jean. "I would think the only survivors are the ones who have managed to find permanent shelters."

Captain Miller heard Jean over the microphone and said, "Hampton said people started to abandon their shelters because they didn't have enough supplies, but the one thing they have plenty of is guns. He said they have a small army moving with them, and they're cutting a path through the infected."

"That won't work," I said. "Thousands of people would have tried to make it to their bug-out cabins in the mountains, but most of them would have found one of two things waiting for them when they got there."

"You mean if they got there, don't you?" asked Jean.

I tried to imagine what it was like on I-77 through Charlotte when the infection started to spread. Driving through there toward West Virginia where the mountains would be impossible for the infected to climb was probably a bigger nightmare than Thanksgiving weekend.

"Yes, I mean if they got there, Jean. If they made it to their private shelters and cabins, they were likely to find someone else had already staked a claim to their places, or they were just as likely to find someone with the infection got there ahead of them."

Tom shook his head.

"No, the infection was there ahead of them, and people were running from it back down the mountains straight into the people going the other way. That's what we ran into when we headed west. Thousands of people were trying to go east."

"So," I added, "the ones who lived were the ones who were already somewhere safe, but not safe for long enough. Now, they're going to try to take the mountains from the infected."

"It won't work," said Bus. "It sounds like too many mouths to feed and too many chances for the infection to get behind their lines."

We all agreed because we had seen it happen already. The larger the group, the more likely it was that someone would get bitten by a stray infected dead, and they wouldn't tell the rest of the group. Unless they were stopping from time to time and checking each other for bites the way Captain Miller's soldiers had, someone would cause them to fall apart.

"That doesn't explain why the Chief went out of here like his rear end was on fire," said Tom.

"Maybe I can help with that," said Captain Miller.

We all turned and looked at the shortwave radio as if Captain Miller was inside it.

"Hampton said he was worried about how large the army had become, and that some of the people with guns had started taking supplies from the people they were protecting. He said he was going to try to break away from them to the southwest and make it on his own."

"I don't suppose Hampton gave you a way to contact him, did he?" asked Jean.

"No, he was having to abandon his plane. He has a short range radio, but you would need to know his frequency to talk with him. I gave it to the Chief, but that won't do him much good unless he's practically on top of him."

Captain Miller knew what he was saying even as he said it, and he also knew it would be like finding a needle in a haystack. He felt bad for us and the way the Chief had left on a rescue mission, but before he signed off he said he knew why the Chief had to try. He also understood why the Chief hadn't wanted us to go along. Jean was due to have our baby, and it made sense for me and Doctor Bus to be here. It was a risky trip, so he wanted Kathy to stay with Tom.

Tom wished he had seen Kathy sneak out when the Chief left, but Molly needed some stability and less worry. All we could do was stay in radio contact with the Chief and Kathy for as long as possible.

We signed off from Captain Miller, and Molly immediately began trying to get through to the Chief.

******

Charlotte had been as bad as most cities that were surrounded by a bypass. They were intended to allow travelers to go around the cities rather than through them, but when the interstates became clogged with people trying to leave, I-485 became a prison wall around the city. First responders couldn't get to the fires and accidents, and just like other cities it was too late once they realized there was nothing they could do to help even if they did reach the scene. It didn't take long before traffic came to a complete standstill, and families began fleeing on foot.

Smaller towns fell within minutes as living victims ran straight into the arms of the infected, but the big cities like Charlotte were like a movie on a continuous loop. Traffic came to a grinding halt as the sun rose on thousands of vehicles flowing in from the suburbs during rush hour. To most of the drivers and passengers sipping their Starbucks or munching on a breakfast biscuit, it just seemed like any other miserable day in traffic. There were the mandatory fender benders blocking a lane, and everyone else had to get a good look. There were the drivers with their cell phones at the tops of the steering wheels so they could text, and they undoubtedly thought they were good drivers because they were leaving a five car space between themselves and the person in front of them. A space that was inevitably too great of a temptation for people in other lanes to pass up.

All of it seemed to stop at the same time, and when it did, it wasn't so unusual that anyone thought it would be any different from yesterday. People finished their coffee and their biscuits. The texters enjoyed a few minutes of texting without having to stop and go, and the women who needed an extra minute to finish putting on eye liner didn't really mind the interruption.

People closer to the front of the endless parade started getting out of their cars to see what was happening. Then they joined the tidal wave of people who ran toward them, bleeding and screaming. Some tried to get back into the relative safety of their cars. Some abandoned their passengers who sat helplessly watching as people with purple, bruised looking faces attacked their drivers.

The wave of attacks rolled through the stopped vehicles as thousands of people toward the back of the parade caught on just minutes too late. Even as the new infected dead pushed through the abandoned vehicles looking for new victims, people started honking their horns to get the idiots in front of them to move faster. The horns drew the infected forward, and angry drivers got out of their cars to confront them. Some waved tools in the air at the crazy looking people coming toward them. Others who had always carried a loaded gun under their seats were finally getting the opportunity to exercise their right to defend themselves, but for some reason their targets were getting knocked down by the bullets but getting back up.

That was Charlotte on the day it began, and that was Charlotte as the sun lowered toward the western horizon. People who had been trapped in their cars all day had finally given in to their hunger, thirst, or need to go to the bathroom, tried to sneak from their cars to safety. One by one they found themselves face to face with groaning creatures that used to be humans who, like them, had been simply driving to work.

A charter bus with heavily tinted windows had been the safe haven for a group of forty tourists who were traveling south to a gambling casino. When they came to a stop in the lane closest to the side of the road, most of them were comfortably napping or watching movies on the tiny TV screens above their seats. When they saw the people running toward them, the driver yelled for everyone to get down as low as they could in their seats as he got down on the floor of the center aisle.

The hours went by as the tourists remained hidden. They pooled their homemade lunches and snacks and shared water bottles. The bathroom in the back of the bus gave them extra time to figure out what they were going to do if they ever got the chance. There seemed to be no end to the screams and to the wandering, wrecked bodies that searched for new prey. Most of them had been able to contact relatives and friends, and they all got the same bad news. It was happening everywhere. The news broadcasts were calling them infected, and one bite from them would be fatal. The Emergency Management broadcasts were telling everyone to find a safe place to hide and to stay there.

The driver quietly opened two overhead hatches that let air into the bus, but it was still uncomfortable. There were also new smells that came in with the normally fresh air. Fires were spreading from vehicle to vehicle on the other side of the freeway, and the smoke was heavy with the smells of burning flesh and odors that accompanied violent death.

As darkness began to fall, the driver stood on top of the seats and eased his head slowly through the hatch. All around him he could see something that looked more like a battleground than a highway full of commuters, but as his eyes adjusted to the twilight, he saw that the stumbling creatures moving between the cars were being drawn toward the fires. He looked to his right and saw nothing but woods, and there was no fence or retaining wall to stop them from leaving the road.

He dropped back to the center of the bus and risked the light from his cell phone long enough to check a map of the area. He saw they were sitting on the edge of a large expanse of woods west of the Charlotte Douglas International Airport, and there was nothing but a few miles of woods between them and the Catawba River.

The passengers listened as he explained to them that their only chance of escaping from the bus was to reach the woods and keep going. They had to do it while the infected were gathering close to the fires. He told them he saw the infected literally catching fire when they got too close.

"Why can't we just stay here until they all burn up?" shouted one angry tourist.

Another spoke up and said, "We would have a better chance trying for the airport. We can see it from here, and they're bound to be organized against whatever this is."

"I vote that we stay here and wait to be rescued," said a woman in her fifties. She didn't look like she could outrun any of the infected even though they moved at a slow pace.

Someone asked for everyone to be quiet, and the driver said, "In a couple of minutes I'm going to open that door. By then I want everyone to decide which group they want to be in. I'm heading for the woods. Anyone who wants to join me, just follow my group. Any of you who want to cross the highway and try for the airport, go for it. Those of you who decide to stay on the bus and wait to be rescued, pull the door shut behind you, but take my advice and don't open it for anyone who tries to come back."

He studied the faces he could see in the growing darkness. He wasn't sure how many would go or stay with each group, but he knew they couldn't hang around for a debate. He just turned and went down the aisle to the front door. He opened it far enough to stick his head through and didn't see movement between the bus and the woods. A quick glance to the left and right convinced him that it was all clear.

If Mack Brown, the veteran driver of charter buses, had been able to see an aerial view of the devastating spread of the violence through traffic during the early morning rush hour, he would have thought it looked like someone had scattered a nest of insects. There was no herd mentality as people ran between or climbed over cars. Thousands had small, superficial bites, and they ran off of the roads wherever they could. Some ran for the high fence around the airport, reasoning that the fence would protect them. They were cut badly on the concertina wire at the top of the fence, but they were at least free from their attackers. Many of them would be inside the airport, and most would be dead by the end of the day. So would the population of the airport.

Planes that made it into the sky had nowhere to go, and some of their passengers had concealed bites. Even before dark, planes had begun to attempt emergency landings on congested roads and runways of overrun airports. Some of the biggest fires near the bus had been massive explosions from planes looking for a place to land.

Mack Brown would also have seen how many people had run for the shelter of the woods, disappearing from view. Hundreds would climb trees, and hundreds more would keep going. Those who were bitten were carried along by their friends and families who didn't know they were carrying the infection through the woods. It was almost as if the infection was being spread by a sneeze instead of a bite. The infection carried on the spray of the sneeze was distributed evenly, because some of the commuters would die clinging to tree branches, and some would die as they ran. Then they would bite the people who had tried to save them.

The group that decided to stay in the bus argued that supplies should be left behind with them, and there was random pushing, shoving, and pulling on personal property. Some punches were thrown, but gradually people who wanted off of the bus made it to the door. They split into two groups with only whispers as one group ran down the slope toward the woods with Mack Brown in the lead. The other group ran for the back of the bus and began the long trip between the cars to the other side of the six lane freeway.

As soon as the last person to leave the bus had gone through the door, it was closed behind them. The remaining ten or twelve people ran to the windows to watch the progress of each group and gave reports to the other side of the bus. It was too dark to tell what was happening, but they lost sight of the group that ran toward the airport. They just disappeared between the vehicles. On the other side of the bus, the group led by Mack Brown was also disappearing into the woods. To the remainder of the people on the bus it looked like the woods had been a better choice. To Mack Brown it felt like he had jumped from the frying pan into the fire.

******

Months later and about thirty miles north of where the charter bus ended its journey, a large force of heavily armed men and women moved ahead of hundreds of survivors who had taken their chance to come out of hiding and join the group. As their numbers grew, the new survivors were inspected for bites. If they were bitten or had an injury that could be a bite, they were summarily executed. Hampton heard more than once that it wasn't personal as people were shot.

Some of the survivors were carrying guns, and more than a few times it was a gun carrying bite victim. Sometimes more than the bite victim would get shot, but the force couldn't do any better sorting out the infected when they were still alive. Their primary goal was to target as many of the infected dead as they could while they moved north, and they were very effective with that goal. Staying on the road and keeping an armed cordon around the unarmed survivors allowed them to shoot anything that approached.

The force had stopped moving several times, so progress was slow. Each time, though, there was a good reason to stop. Scouts into neighboring areas would return with reports of heavy concentrations of the infected dead, but sometimes they would return with survivors and reports about locations of sporting goods stores and caches of ammunition. They had to stay resupplied if they were to continue advancing north toward the mountains.

Hampton didn't like what he was seeing. Too many people had joined the exodus, and he looked suspiciously at anyone who appeared as if they didn't feel well. He also looked suspiciously at some of the armed guards who seemed like they were enjoying themselves just a little too much. He wasn't entirely sure of who was in charge because he had always stayed near the outer edge of the group on the western side. If someone stepped out of the heavy woods to the west and waved at them, they were told to come closer. If someone came out of the heavy woods and just shambled toward them, they were shot from a distance. Hampton preferred that job because he was sure of what he was shooting. He hadn't gotten as bad as the rest of them, and he didn't like playing judge, jury, and executioner. He saw one guy get shot who probably only had a head cold.

After almost a year of surviving on his wits and luck, Hampton was amazed to see how many people had survived in the city. He had the chance to talk with some of them, and they all had lost someone or hooked up with someone new. Some had managed to hole up in warehouses full of food. One guy had survived in a grocery store that had a gun store on one side and a liquor store on the other. He said he tunneled through the attic walls, and there were other people trapped in both of the other stores. He said it was pretty good for a while, but there was always someone trying to break into the stores.

There was one family that had a shelter in their backyard. They had gone inside and locked the doors on the first day, and they thought they had made the right decision. The father told Hampton their shelter would have protected them from anything except other people, as they soon discovered. He said it didn't take long for scavengers to locate their air intakes. Once those were covered with dirt, it was only a matter of time before they had to come out.

There were some incredible stories of determination. Some people had just been smart enough to avoid the infected and outwit the scavengers, but they had seen friends and family die too often. When they spotted the army of living people walking defiantly along the middle of the highway, they couldn't resist the call of civilization.

They were passing in and out of the openings between cars, but sometimes it was better to walk right over them. It was good to get a view from on top of the cars whenever possible. Hampton decided it was one of those times, and he stepped onto the high rear bumper of a pickup truck with oversized tires. He walked across the bed and climbed up on the cab of the truck.

From the top of the truck Hampton could see the front of the living army stretching out ahead of him. There were more guns up front where they could punch a hole through the infected dead that were walking along the highway in the opposite direction. They also had more time to reload while others stepped up to replace them. He had to admit, whoever had come up with the idea had at least gotten them out of the city.

There were infected dead coming out of the woods on one side and the buildings on the other. He saw the armed men and women on their perimeters taking aim at infected dead that wandered into the open.

What bothered Hampton was what he saw at the back of their group. He estimated the living army had as many as four to five hundred survivors with about two hundred men and women carrying guns. At the back of the army of living people, trailing by about one hundred yards, was a larger army of infected dead. The living had been out distancing the horde that was following them for the better part of the last two days, but as their living army grew in size, it began to move slower. If they didn't increase their forward speed, they would have to start defending themselves from the rear.

Hampton remembered the horde that had marched down Highway 17 toward Georgetown. He and his fellow citizens had dropped the bridges and watched the infected try to walk on mud and then in the water. It had worked to stop thousands of the infected dead, but nothing could stop the infection that was already on their side of the bridge. He had been warned back then by the foursome he had met on the road. The people had seen things, and they told him there would be someone in his town hiding a loved one who had been bitten. Sooner or later, that person would die, and the infection would spread from within. The four people were trying to go north even though Georgetown was bracing itself against a horde coming from that direction. More than once he had wondered what happened to them, or even if they had made it to wherever it was they were going.

As he stood on the top of the pickup truck, he could see more and more of the infected coming out of the woods and the buildings. The sound of the gunshots and the groaning of the infected dead were both becoming more constant and louder at the same time.

"Hey, Hampton. What's it look like back there?"

One of the other armed guards was looking up at him from the middle of the steady stream of people and pointing toward the rear of the column.

"Not good," said Hampton. "There must be a thousand or more behind us by now. The problem is they don't stop to rest. If we stop, they keep coming. I think we're going to need some guns at the back really soon."

Hampton looked up and saw the sky was clear, but there were some clouds on the horizon toward the southwest. They wouldn't be getting rain today, but the heat was slowing everybody down.

"Can you get to the front?" he asked the other guard. "We need to let them know this parade needs to pick up speed or we need some guns back here picking off the leaders of the infected."

Living people were starting to get nervous when they began to catch on that the infected were closer than before. The pushing started to increase, and from where Hampton stood he could see the rear of their column begin to spread toward the sides and become flat in shape. Some of the people were trying to go around the sides of the living army and were putting themselves between the guards with rifles and the woods. The guards were yelling for them to move because they couldn't shoot at the infected that were coming out of hiding.

He wasn't sure if someone was hit by a shot, but he was sure that someone attacked a guard. Hampton heard the gun go off and saw the guard go down under an angry crowd. Then all hell broke loose when the infected dead got too close to the living people who had been blocked from going forward by the pile up on the guard. First there was angry yelling, then there were screams as teeth found bare skin.

Hampton tried to take careful aim to shoot only the infected, but the crowd started to move around too much. Some of the people who were bitten were running toward the front. He changed targets and started aiming at the horde of infected dead that was behind them. He couldn't miss in that target rich environment.

Several guards joined him in the truck as they began creating a blockade of bodies in the paths between the cars, and he started to yell at people to either run or to climb up onto cars.

He could see that they had slowed the progress of the advancing horde, but they were using a lot of ammunition. If help didn't come from the front soon, they would be running in retreat along with the unarmed people in a few minutes, and they still had to deal with those people who had been bitten and were now hiding among the living.

"This is not going to go well," he said to no one in particular.

"Are you just noticing that?" said a woman who was standing next to him on the cab of the truck. "We need to make a run for it while we still can. These crazy idiots are going to get us all killed."

Hampton looked at her and it occurred to him he hadn't given any thought to who was standing next to him until she spoke. All he knew was there was someone next to him who was a pretty good shot. For a split second he wondered why he had never noticed her before. Her strawberry blonde hair and Irish nose made her look better than anyone he had paid attention to in a long time.

She glanced at him and saw that he was looking at her with obvious appreciation.

"Are you kidding me?" she said. "This isn't the time for speed dating, dude. We have a thousand zombies trying to hook up with half as many living, and you're checking out my freckles and the color of my eyes?"

Hampton was embarrassed because he had been caught in the act.

"Sorry, Miss. I was just surprised," he managed to stammer out like a teenage boy. He took aim with his rifle and fired a shot just to cover up the redness he felt in his face.

Despite it being the wrong time and place, she found herself to be amused and even a little complimented. He looked like a nice guy, and she wasn't meeting many of them lately. He was also kind of cute with short, curly brown hair and broad shoulders.

"My name is Colleen," she shouted over the increasing gunfire and screaming. "What's your name?"

"Everyone calls me Hampton," he yelled back.

She grabbed him just above the elbow of his left arm and pulled.

"Come on, Hampton. I can get your first name later, and I can tell you all about my hobbies. In the meantime we need to find another party. This one isn't looking so good."

Colleen pulled Hampton from the top of the truck, and he wasn't sure why, but he knew instinctively the right thing to do was to follow her. They ran out the back over the tailgate and jumped to the ground. He was surprised to see the approaching horde had closed the gap to about fifty yards, and the man who had started for the front of the living army hadn't made it fifty yards through the crowd of slowly moving people. By the time he would get to the front and alert them to what was happening at the back, there wouldn't be anything they could do about it.

The western slope of the road ran down toward the woods. Hampton knew that somewhere beyond the woods was Lake Norman. It was a massive lake, and Hampton recalled a fishing buddy telling him it was fifty square miles of water, and the shoreline was so long that it would stretch from Charleston to Columbus, Ohio if it was a straight line. Five hundred miles of shoreline meant there would be plenty of places for survivors to have dug in, but there would also have been thousands of people who had found themselves cornered with their backs to the water. He imagined it was the luck of the draw which category someone wound up getting stuck with.

He saw a gap in the trees and pointed at it. Colleen understood, and they moved in that direction. He halfway expected someone to shoot them for leaving, but they all had their hands full. The horde was causing people to scatter even more, and the front of the living army had encountered a barrier of their own.

About a mile ahead of their army was a bridge that crossed a branch of Lake Norman, and the bridge had acted as a funnel for the infected dead. It caused them to come together into an army of their own as the living and the dead were forced to square off with each other. What the living army didn't count on was the infected dead that came up from behind, and if that wasn't bad enough, there were larger numbers coming from the sides than before.

As unarmed men and women began to break away from the protection of the armed guards, it became harder and harder for them to choose their targets. Hampton and Colleen were slipping away by going back past the trailing horde of infected dead, and they were going virtually unnoticed because of the frightened screams of the people who had no defense against the infected. The infected that saw them and tried to turn and follow were pushed from behind and trampled.

Shooting was no longer scattered, and the army of survivors were burning through their supply of ammunition at an alarming rate. They were killing the infected with vicious accuracy, but more and more people were bitten, and that would eventually mean more of the living would die, but not before they were well mixed into the throng of survivors. Even if by some miracle they were to win this battle, the war was already lost.

Hampton and Colleen were into the woods and then surprised by how quickly they were through them. They ran straight into the tall privacy fence that surrounded the backyard of a very large home. They didn't know what was on the other side of the fence, but they knew what was on their side, and they didn't hesitate. Hampton cupped his hands together and held them down for Colleen to use as a step to get over the fence. He practically tossed her over. When he landed on the other side with her, he saw they had made a good choice. The yard was clear of infected dead, and the fence hid them from view on all sides.

Hampton went back to the fence and risked a look back at the battle on the Bill Lee Freeway. He was on low ground, but he could see that the infected dead behind the living army had closed in on the victims in the back, and there weren't likely to be any survivors by sunset. He went back to where Colleen had crouched behind a child's playhouse and just shook his head at her.

"I really thought it would work," she said in a low voice. "I really thought enough people could walk right up the middle of the road and be a match for those things."

"It seemed like a good idea at the time," he answered without a trace of humor in his voice. "What this tells me is there are far more dead than living. We need to hole up for the night and then figure out what we're going to do to get out of this mess. We can't go further up the interstate because there's no way to get across that bridge. Lake Norman is west of here, so that leaves going back the way we came."

"This backyard is pretty secure, so I'm all for checking out the house. If there aren't too many occupants, it would be as good a place as any to spend the night."

Maybe it was her earlier comments about speed dating that had Hampton thinking he already liked Colleen, but he couldn't deny he also found her to be very attractive. Hearing her say the house would be a good place to spend the night made him think that speed dating had never been this fast, and he couldn't stop the small smile before it escaped.

Colleen was quick to pick up on the smile and Hampton's attempt to hide it.

"Does that mansion look like a one bedroom home to you, Hampton?"

Despite the fact that he had been caught, he went ahead and let himself smile like he hadn't smiled in over a year. She could think what she wanted, and he could tell by her reaction to his smile that she had appreciated feeling attractive for the first time in just as long.

There was an instant bond, and they both knew it, but staying alive to live out that bond was going to be a trick. The battle up on the freeway sounded exactly like the war that it was. Screams, groans, gunshots, and people yelling for more ammunition. Sometimes it seemed like they could make out individual shouts about the ammunition or for help, but it was mostly just noise. There was enough noise to draw every infected dead out of the woods and neighborhoods for miles around.

Hampton and Colleen were in the only place they could be if they wanted to stay alive. They were in a place where the infected dead would be passing by for hours, and they had to keep from being seen.

Colleen asked, "How can we get up on that back porch to see if there's anything inside? The deck at the back door is at least three feet above the ground. That means infected dead passing the fence would be able to see us if we go into the house standing up."

"I see what you mean," said Hampton. "If there's anything inside to clear out, it won't be easy going at them from our knees."

Both of them inhaled and let out a heavy sigh. It seemed like that was the way life had become. If you had a choice, you were still faced with a down side. They could stay in the yard until it was dark, but then they would have to go into the house with no light. They could go into the house, but they risked being seen in the daylight. Still, the two choices had one really positive up side. The house was big, and the potential for supplies looked good because it was so big.

"I'm for going in now," said Hampton.

Colleen just nodded. There wasn't much to say.

It was easy to cross the yard because nothing could see over the fence, so they ran in a crouch to the side of the house where the steps to the deck were the closest to the wall. Hampton had a bad moment when he stepped on something metal that was buried in the overgrown grass. His heavy boots kept the pointed prongs of a rake from stabbing him in the foot, but the handle stood up and neatly smacked him in his right ear. Colleen froze where she was and gave him a look that said, "Really?"

"There's no time for that right now, Hampton."

Even as she said it, he had to admit it would have been funny under the right circumstances. He stepped away from the rake and watched the ground closely as he covered the rest of the distance to the house.

They had their backs against the wall as they eased themselves onto the deck. There were four steps that led to a broad landing that still had neatly arranged outdoor furniture evenly spaced around a stone fire pit. The family that lived here had most likely enjoyed many evenings with neighbors over for a visit.

The door into the house was actually a beautiful set of French doors that opened outward. Hampton held up a hand to Colleen then motioned for her to move closer so he could whisper.

"How are we going to pull open that door without the infected outside the fence seeing it move, and what if there are more inside?"

She started to say something, but he got an idea.

"Wait here," he said as he ran back into the tall grass and retrieved the rake.

After he crouched back down beside her he said, "I'm going to play the odds and bet there is something inside. Those things don't really pay attention to each other if there's something bigger attracting them, and the noise up on the road is going to last a while. We have to move fast before everything is done back there."

He didn't wait for her to answer. He went up the steps on all fours and tried the door handle. It was locked. He heard Colleen making a noise to get his attention, and when he looked at her she pointed at the big potted plant next to the door. Hampton leaned it slightly away from him and saw the brass key underneath.

When he picked it up, it crossed his mind that the infection worked its way inside the same way someone got in with a key. It was simple the way it gave the infected dead access to the inside of a house or to the inside of a community.

He nodded at her to acknowledge she had been right but also to see her give him a look that said, "Good luck."

He slid the key into the lock as quietly as he could and turned. When he was sure the door was unlocked, he went back down to where Colleen was crouching and picked up the rake. He held it out at arms length and caught the metal prongs on the handle. The weight of the rake did most of the work pushing down the handle, and as soon as it was down far enough, he started to pull.

The door moved open as slowly as Hampton could make it. If the infected dead walking by outside the fence on their way to the melee on the highway saw it move, it didn't draw their attention away from the bigger attraction. Hampton was guessing Colleen was hoping the same thing that he was. If there was something inside, and it decided to come outside, just let it be quiet about it.

Just as the door was open as far as it would go, an infected dead stumbled onto the landing. It didn't see them because they were not at eye level, but Hampton wanted to remove it from the view of the other infected before it would see them and start to groan.

He freed the rake from the door handle and in one swift move hooked the prongs of the rake through the belt that still circled the emaciated waist. With very little effort he yanked the infected dead from the landing, down the steps, and into the tall grass. He pushed it face down and slid a knife into the base of the skull.

It all happened so fast that he was back at Colleen's side watching the door for more infected before she even knew what he was going to do. There was a wisp of sheer curtains moving slightly inside the door, but nothing else was coming out.

There was no going back, so Hampton crawled up the steps for a second time. From his stomach on the landing he could see under the sheer curtains, and he saw a pair of feet go by. One had a shoe on it, and the other looked like it was mostly bones and shredded flesh. He waited for it to pass by and then dove into the room.

Hampton was ready for more, and Colleen was right behind him, but all he found was the walking remains of what had likely been either the wife or daughter of the man he had dragged into the yard. She never even turned around as he ended her miserable existence.

Colleen helped him move the body just far enough to push it out the door, and they both silently agreed they would wait until dark to move it far enough out of the way to close the door.

The big room they found themselves in was well lit by large skylights. It smelled bad, but everything smelled bad after so many months of the infection, and protection didn't have to smell good. They were both just glad to be inside.

He knew they still had to clear the rest of the big house, but Hampton couldn't resist peeking out through a window that faced the highway. Trees blocked most of the view, but he could see enough. The battle was still in progress, but he could only hear the sounds of the living. He couldn't see them, so there couldn't be many. It wouldn't be much longer.

Colleen asked, "What do we do if someone else gets away and comes over that fence?"

Hampton hadn't thought about that, but he was sure it wasn't going to happen. If anyone was going to live through that mess, they would have needed to do as he and Colleen had done and left early.

"I don't think it will come to that, but I imagine we would have to shoot them," he said. "No one is getting through there without being bitten."

They moved deeper into the house, letting their eyes adjust to the dim light from above. The house had big rooms, and it was obvious that someone had tried to ride out the end of the world in style. In the kitchen there was a Coleman camp stove sitting on top of the stainless steel range.

"Creatures of habit," said Colleen. "The lady of the house was so used to cooking on the stove that she had to put the camp stove in the same place."

"I wonder if they were bitten or if they died of carbon monoxide poisoning because she didn't open a window near the stove," said Hampton.

"That would be a total shame," said Colleen. "You have a place to at least try to be safe, and then you do something really stupid that most kids would know better than to do."

The slight bumping sound from the room above the kitchen froze both of them in their tracks.

"I had hoped for no kids," said Hampton. "I'll take care of it."

Colleen sort of shook her head like she couldn't expect Hampton to take care of it by himself, and she fell in behind him when he located the stairs and started quietly going up. The stairs ended at a large sitting area where guests could relax looking down on the spacious living room. There were two bathrooms standing open near the sitting area, so guests must have been able to wait in comfort when the former residents had a party.

All of the other rooms stood open except one, and it was directly over the kitchen. There was no doubt where the bumping noise had come from because it happened again as they walked slowly toward the door.

"There's no easy way to do this," he said, "so I'm just going to go in with a chair in front of me and try to pin down whatever is in there."

There were plenty of chairs to choose from, and one was exactly what he needed. He looked like a lion tamer like they used to have at the circus, but he didn't feel like one. If anything, he probably wasn't doing a very good job hiding his fear. He had been faced with some bad things since the infected dead had come along, but the uncertainty of what was behind a door was worse than seeing it coming at you.

On his signal Colleen turned the doorknob and pushed it open. He only had to take one step before the chair connected with the first child, or what had been a child, and sent it backward into the second one. He kept pushing until they went down, and he was able to reach around with his knife and finish the job. They had been at the most around nine or ten years old. One was a boy, and one was a girl.

Hampton took a quick look around to be sure they had been the only infected dead in the room, and then he pulled the blanket off of a bed and covered them.

Colleen had stayed in the hall outside the door after catching a glimpse of the first child. Hampton wasn't feeling too well himself, but he was glad he had been able to spare her the job of disposing of them.

"A perfect life in the suburbs," he said as he pulled the door shut behind him. "You get your big job, you get married, you save your money, and you get your boy and girl. Then your worst nightmare happens, and you can't do anything to save your family. It never gets easier, but it's always worse when it's kids."

They both sat down in the sitting area where they could see over the vast living room. They were both hungry, but more than anything, they were both just needing to rest.

4 OCONEE

The de Havilland Beaver rotated into position and then began its mad dash toward open water. Kathy was pinned back in her seat as the Chief brought the plane to full power, and the noise was too deafening for either of them to hear the other. Not to mention the RADCON gear they were still wearing, including the head piece that made her feel claustrophobic.

She felt like making herself useful, so she rummaged through her supply pack until she found a fresh radiation monitor that was still sealed in plastic. She unwrapped it and sat it where she could keep an eye on it, and they were both pleased to see it was reading a very low level of contamination.

"Where are we going, Chief?"

Kathy was acutely aware of the fact that the Chief hadn't started turning toward land yet, and each passing second carried them further out to sea.

The Chief pointed slightly to the right and said, "See that gray area to starboard? That's a nice little rain storm, so we're taking the plane to the carwash. Before we get there let's open the windows and let the wind blow through the plane. Some of our trace radiation readings are because of contamination in the air vents, and some is on our clothing. We can blow the dust out of the plane."

The sound was incredibly louder when they opened the windows, and Kathy reached into the back of the plane to force the cargo door on the passenger side to open for a couple of minutes. She repeated the steps on the port side, and even though she couldn't see or feel radioactive dust, she mentally felt cleaner.

When it was quiet enough again, the Chief continued, "After we wash the plane, I'm going to land so we can jump in for a bath of our own. It should be safe to remove our RADCON suits after that."

Kathy had to admit, even after everything she had seen the Chief do over the months since the apocalypse that had brought civilization to its knees, she was still impressed by the things he thought of. So far he had been handed one challenge after the next, and he always came out of it in one piece.

She thought back to the day she and her friends had watched the Chief crash their first plane into Charleston harbor. She knew he wasn't invincible, but she felt like he was closer to it than anyone she had ever known.

The plane was rushing into the rain storm, and he was right. It was like going into a carwash. The rain slapped at the plane in sheets, and she half expected to see the big brushes appear out of nowhere. Just as quickly, they burst through into the sunlight behind the storm, and the Chief lowered the plane toward the surface of the ocean. The storm was moving away, and the sea beyond it was fairly calm.

As soon as the plane was bobbing on the water, Kathy jumped through the door trailing a safety line behind her. She wasn't likely to need it, but she wanted to be out of the suit and back into the plane as quickly as possible. The Chief leaned out and tossed her a heavy duty plastic bag for her to stow the suit in. Then he stepped onto the float on his side of the plane and dove into the water.

It didn't take five minutes for them to get washed and back into the plane. The cool water felt good to Kathy, and she would have stayed longer, but she had acquired the Chief's sense of urgency. She still didn't know where they were going, but it wasn't hard to tell the Chief wanted to get there fast.

The radiation monitor was reading zero, and as soon as Kathy had her door shut, the Chief began to power up again. He pointed the plane slightly to the north and increased the throttle.

"I don't mean to rush you, Chief, but any time you are ready to tell me why we left the shelter so fast, I'd really like to know."

"There's a good chance Hampton is still alive," said the Chief.

Kathy didn't have a clue what she expected him to say, but that wasn't it.

"How do you know, Chief?"

"You know that source Captain Miller had who told him about the Oconee Nuclear Plant explosion? He said the guy's name was Hampton. What are the odds it's another guy named Hampton?"

Kathy had to admit, if it was the same man, Hampton was worth going after. He had shown them an incredible kindness by escorting them through Georgetown when they had become stranded at a private dock further south. They had been forced to abandon their plane when it had taken a bullet through the engine. The damage was just bad enough to keep the plane from flying, and they were making their way back home in a borrowed car.

What they didn't know until later was that they might not have made it home if not for the fact that Hampton took a chance and not only let them pass through Georgetown, but he did it quickly. North of Georgetown near the road that would take them to their shelter on Mud Island, the infected dead were beginning to break through a tangled road block and head south in large numbers. They made it to that road ahead of a horde that would have swarmed them if they had been too late to reach the road.

"When we were riding through Georgetown with Hampton, I remember that he said he had a private plane stocked and ready to fly out on short notice," said the Chief. "That must be how he managed to reach Charlotte, but I wonder what happened to Georgetown that made him leave, and I wonder how he got separated from his plane."

"I guess we'll find out when we get to Charlotte, but what makes you think we can find him, Chief?"

"He was broadcasting from a radio station in Charlotte that had a generator, according to Captain Miller. He said Hampton told them he was going to be moving on because the station looked like a bad place to stay permanently. It was safe enough, but there was no way to resupply without the risk of getting cornered."

"He also said there was a group of people who had been holed up at the football stadium where the Carolina Panthers played. He said they had a lot of guns, and they were going to try something crazy."

"What does that mean?" asked Kathy.

"Captain Miller was the one who called it crazy, but Hampton said it was better than sitting there waiting to die. He said the people with the guns were running out of supplies they could forage in the immediate area of the stadium, and they decided they could walk right up Interstate 77 all the way to the mountains if they had enough ammunition. He didn't say how many people they had, but Hampton said it was an army."

Kathy looked like she was working through a math problem as she tried to wrap her mind around the idea of confronting the infected dead out in the open.

"Chief, I know none of us have forgotten the horde we saw on Highway 17. The only way they could have stopped that parade was by walking them into the river at Georgetown. If they didn't get stuck in the mud forever, they got washed out to sea with the current. How many guns and how much ammunition would we have needed to stop that many infected?"

"There isn't enough ammunition to do it out in the open, and I'm not sure about how much it would take from a stationary place of safety. Every time you pull the trigger of a gun, you might as well consider it a dinner invitation. The problem is that one bullet, one gunshot, would equal dozens or even hundreds of the infected dropping by for dinner."

"That's what I was thinking," said Kathy. "I wonder why Hampton would even consider going along with such a crazy idea."

"Captain Miller said he had enough time with Hampton to actually say the same thing to him. He said Hampton told him he was tired of doing nothing, and that he wanted to reach the mountains. He said if things didn't go well, he would find a way to break away from the group in time to strike out on his own again."

"So, how does that help us find him, Chief?"

"Hampton has a short range walkie-talkie that will be broadcasting on a specific frequency, and he's going to try to make contact with anyone who is listening every six hours. At noon and six in the evening he's going to stay on the air longer than the other times. I got the frequency from Captain Miller."

"Speaking of which," said Kathy, "It's about time that we checked in with the rest of the gang. Did you even think about how worried everyone else would be when you bailed out of the shelter?"

She gave him a stern look and tried to wither him with a stare, but all he did was smile.

"What? You don't think I'm mad enough at you already, Chief?"

"I don't suppose you took the time to discuss it with everyone else before you snuck out to follow me," said the Chief. He could barely keep himself from laughing.

Kathy looked like a deer stuck in the headlights of a car. She had considered telling them, but she knew what would have happened, and in a flash of understanding, she knew the Chief couldn't have talked it over with them first. There's nothing he could have said to them that would have made a difference, and there was nothing she could think of that she could have said to the others to make them let her follow him.

They both stayed quiet for a few minutes while they each thought it over. When Kathy was a little cooler, she had to admit that checking in with the shelter meant she would at least catch a bit of grief from Tom.

Since the day they had closed the shelter door against the impending death that was drifting in on the wind, Tom and Kathy had started spending more and more time together. Molly missed her mother, but she got a sense of security from Kathy, and she loved seeing her father happy. It wasn't hard for anyone to tell he was happy when he was near Kathy.

They had been sealed inside the shelter at Mud Island far less time than they had expected. By Kathy's best guess, it had only been about two months, and during that time they had a wedding and would soon have a baby born in the shelter. Kathy jerked from her thoughts with a start and even surprised the Chief.

"Chief," she practically yelled, "we can't leave. Jean's going to have her baby in about a week. It could be any day now."

"I think it might be a little too late for us to worry about that. We'll be there in a couple of hours. If Hampton is anywhere near Lake Norman, we'll find him and get back home before Jean even has a chance to get over being mad at us."

"That doesn't help, Chief."

Kathy knew what was going to happen when she keyed the microphone and called back to the shelter, but it was better to get it over with. Besides she planned to say exactly what the Chief had just said. They would be back in no time. What she didn't expect was the answer she got.

Molly had the radio ready for them to check in, and all she said was Aunt Jean wanted to know how long they planned to be gone, and that they didn't need to hurry back. Kathy asked Molly if anyone was mad at them, and all she said was everyone was fine and not to hurry back.

Kathy looked over at the Chief and was just as confused as she was.

"Do you think they knocked Tom out and tied him up?" he asked.

She shook her head and said, "Must have."

Then she remembered one of the rules they had given Molly, and that was to never give information over the radio that would compromise their location. There was always the possibility someone was listening or even on Mud Island. If there was someone on the island, they would need to land somewhere away from the island and scout the area first. The plane was much too loud for them to make a pass to see if it was safe, so they had to do it on foot. They would also have to do it from the other side of the moat.

Kathy took a moment to think of what she could ask Molly when Tom came over the speaker.

"You're going to be seeing an old friend, I hear."

Kathy was sure Tom wanted to be mad, but he was keeping it neutral because there was a situation of some kind.

"Yes, Tom, is there something we can bring back with us?"

Kathy didn't know what to ask, but she hoped he could use her question to give them some idea of how bad the situation was.

"You're going to need to bring a really big flyswatter with you," he said. "The bugs are everywhere out here."

Neither of them were bothering to use radio protocols because it would make them sound too professional. If someone was listening and they followed protocols, it would give them the clue that the Mud Island group was organized and knowledgeable instead of the amateurs they had been less than a year ago. Tom's message accomplished two things. It told her they had unwelcome guests on the island, and if they were listening, they would think he was outside with them instead of inside the island.

"We'll keep that in mind, Tom. Advise when you can if the bug problem gets worse."

What Kathy wanted to say to Tom was that she was sorry she had just run off after the Chief, but that would take too much explanation. Besides, if Tom had talked with Captain Miller, he would already know where they were going.

What Tom wanted to say to Kathy was that he was mad at her for putting her life at risk by leaving the shelter without him, but he was being forced into staying calm, and that was making him less mad at her with each passing minute.

Instead of saying he was mad he said, "Have a safe trip."

Kathy knew they would be out of radio range eventually, but the Beaver could stay in radio contact until then if she wanted. She just couldn't bring herself to stay on the radio with Tom because she knew she had hurt him. She wanted to tell him not to worry, but that was pretty lame when she considered they were flying closer to the nuclear reactor that had released some deadly radiation, and the surrounding area would be swarming with the infected dead.

The Chief helped her out by taking the microphone from her hand and hanging it on its hook. There wasn't much sense in giving away too much information when they didn't know what it was they were missing back at Mud Island.

The first thing they had to do was find Hampton, then they had to figure out a way to pick him up. All the Chief could hope for was that Hampton was near a body of water where he could land. He didn't know if he would be hoping for too much by wanting to just land and pick him up, but the

Chief was sure he would be pressing his luck by also hoping that the radioactive fallout wasn't drifting over Hampton's location yet. Then there were the infected dead to consider. How many would be in the area was anyone's guess, but if someone was shooting guns in the area, it would be crowded.

They flew in silence for a few minutes, but it dawned on Kathy that the Chief always had a plan. As a matter of fact, he always had at least two plans. That must have been why he waited until morning to tell them he was leaving. He took at least one night to think about what he was going to do.

The Chief felt like someone was staring at him and looked over at Kathy. Her long blond hair and naturally good looks made men underestimate her, but the Chief had not been one of those men to make that mistake.

"You figured it out already?" he asked.

"No," she said, "but I'm beginning to. Is there some reason why we had to go quickly besides the fact that it's hard to survive almost anywhere for very long?"

"When we talked with Captain Miller about that guy Maybank, the one riding out the end of the world on an oil rig, he said that tropical storm was going to make landfall somewhere close to the Florida panhandle."

"Is that bad for us?" she asked.

"It would be for Hampton or anyone else in the Charlotte area," he said. "A storm coming in from the south would push the radiation from the Oconee Nuclear Plant in that direction. As a matter of fact, it could already be too late. We won't know until we get a lot closer."

Kathy dug out a pair of binoculars and started scanning the ground for signs of anything moving. She saw groups of the infected dead walking along roads, and more than once she noticed them doing what they tended to do when there was nothing attracting their attention. At those times they just stood around and stared at nothing in particular.

"I wonder what's going on back at Mud Island," she said.

******

It seemed like it had only been minutes since they had watched the Beaver pick up speed as it shot through the northern entrance to the moat and headed for the open sea, but within those few minutes the island had become crowded.

The moat had been a tempting place to hide for a Russian corvette class ship, but they had found it to be a very dangerous place when they had gotten their anchor snagged on a large net that had crossed the moat. The builder of the shelter had two nets stretched across the moat from Mud Island to the mainland to protect the power lines that were running across the floor of the moat. Now those lines had additional protection from the hull of the corvette. They never did find out who had sunk it, but it had gone up in a ball of fire one morning, and it had taken the nets with it.

Once again, the moat had become a place of refuge as a flotilla of private boats in all sizes came around the northern jetty and entered the moat. The lead boat pulled up to the dock, and the Mud Island group watched as they tied up their mooring lines. A steady stream of boats filed in behind it and began filling the moat.

I switched on more cameras, and we saw the moat becoming crowded. The people in the lead boat had already begun inspecting our boat, the houseboat, and the line laying barge. All three were tied up only a matter of feet from where the de Havilland Beaver had been moored just minutes earlier. In an ironic way, the Chief's sudden departure had saved them from possibly losing the plane. Judging by the number of people in the flotilla, someone would probably have tried to fly it out of the moat, whether they were pilots or not.

Tom, Jean, Bus, and Molly gathered around me to watch, and we couldn't help noticing the radiation monitors. We had only gotten a dusting of contamination, but it was enough to kill anyone who stayed exposed. The unseen death was already at work as evidenced by the number of people who looked like they were sick. It was a hot and humid day outside, but people were wrapped in blankets.

Jean said, "When we left Charleston on the cruise liner last year, we didn't know where we were going. All we knew was that we had to leave, or we would die. The crew of the Atlantic Spirit just took her to sea and figured they would think about where to go after we got away from the mobs of infected dead that were filling the streets. Here we are, after all this time, watching people who are still trying to figure out where to go."

We all knew exactly what she meant. When the infection started, some people fled to the sea. Some people got into cars and tried to escape to the west, only to run head on into the people who were escaping to the east. No matter which direction you went, you collided with people who were going the other way, and as the living mixed with the dying or the dead, more and more people were bitten.

When I still had the Internet on Mud Island, I wondered about the people who had expected an apocalypse and built the shelters. One online article I read said there were over one hundred thousand shelters in the United States. The real question was how many people reached their shelters after the infection started. The next question was how many of the shelters were secure enough to stop other, more ruthless survivors from taking shelters away from people. Mud Island was safer than most shelters, and we knew there were over thirty more just as good, but the entire population of the country wouldn't fit in all of them. They had to go somewhere, so they just kept moving and looking for a safe place to be.

Once again we were going to watch as spectators as people tried to survive. We had taken in Tom and Molly, and that was a risk, but there was no way we could help a group this size.

"How many do you think there are?" asked Jean to no one in particular.

"My best guess would be way over five hundred people," said Bus. "So many of them are sick, though. It may be that they have just been looking for a place to shelter the boats, but I have another suspicion. They may be planning to leave the sick behind as they travel south."

"What makes you think that?" I asked

"Look at the beach camera," said Jean. "I think Bus is right. It looks like they're taking the sick to the largest stretch of open beach."

While the apparent leaders of the floating colony of survivors were checking out the houseboat, others were bringing the boats up to the dock and dropping off the sick. They were met by stretcher bearers who would then carry the sick to the beach where they were placed in orderly rows. The beach was filling up fast.

Tom said, "This is going to get ugly in a hurry when they start dying. Haven't they been out there long enough to know what's going to happen?"

Apparently they did know. Whether we thought it was cruel or humane, a small group of men and women began moving through the rows of people wrapped in blankets. Each carried a long, slender blade, and one by one they slipped the blades into the soft spot at the base of the skull. One by one the sick became harmless.

Jean steered Molly away just before they started. She had been there to give the same dignity to people who died on the Atlantic Spirit, so she knew what was coming.

"Did you see that?" asked Tom.

Bus and I looked at him to see what he was pointing at on the monitor. There was something moving in the water that was gently washing up onto the sand and then going back in the other direction. We watched the water come up about six feet, and when it withdrew we were shocked to see hundreds of blue crabs left behind. They were climbing over each other as they headed for the rows of people who were lined up along the beach, and those people were still alive.

We had seen the blue crabs clinging to the infected dead more times than we could count, but we had never seen them attack living people. Another difference was the number of crabs and the way they were attacking so aggressively. It hadn't occurred to me or any of my fellow survivors, but the blue crab population had grown virtually unchecked since the infection had begun. Some people were eating the crabs, but without the former living population actively farming them along the coast, the crabs had multiplied until they were eating more people than the other way around. Now, they were going after the living as well as the dead.

The sick people wrapped in their blankets who were the first to be swarmed by the crabs began screaming and trying to fight them off. The men with the blades instinctively began trying to kick and stomp on the crabs, but the beach was swarming with them.

"When I said this was going to get ugly in a hurry, this wasn't what I had in mind," said Tom.

Watching the drama as it unfolded on the beach reminded me of the first days of the apocalypse. I sat by myself watching TV stations broadcasting the onslaught of the infection. There were no more TV broadcasts, but it seemed like everywhere that people had survived, they still managed to be reduced in numbers by the infected dead, radiation, murderous survivors, poisoned food, and now this. Animals were probably attacking everywhere, but now the creatures that once occupied a much lower status on the food chain had moved to the top.

Word reached the flotilla command center quickly, and on one camera view we watched as men organized to fight back. Tom pointed at one man who was strapping on a rig that looked like SCUBA gear, but this one had a rifle attached to it. When they lit the end of it, we knew it wasn't a rifle. It was a flamethrower.

He led the group back toward the beach, and we followed with every camera we could. The people on the beach were losing the battle against what looked like a solid wall of blue shells. It occurred to me I had also never seen blue crabs get quite that big.

When the flamethrower arrived, the man waved the wand back and forth shooting out a long trail of fire. He ignited everything. The people who had been laid on the beach, the people who were trying to help them, and the crabs all went up in flames and smoke. This group had apparently learned that one man's bad luck didn't have to be everyone's bad luck. By killing everyone, they could stop the crabs quickly, and they wouldn't have to triage survivors.

There were still some of the men who had the blades that managed to escape the fire and the crabs. They retreated behind the flamethrower where they could stop and inspect their wounds. Each of them had bloody arms and legs from the pincers of the crabs. I didn't think blue crabs could actually bite people, but they sure could tear the skin with their pincers.

Bus said, "I don't think things will work out too well for them even though they got out of the way in time. Blood infections can develop from a crab pinch that breaks the skin. Without disinfectant, they can expect to get sick. They also have open wounds with radiation still falling in low doses."

We didn't think it could get much worse on the beach, but we were wrong. The flamethrower had done its job stopping the crabs at the beach, but we didn't expect the people to see it as a windfall. To our surprise, the people appeared with buckets, baskets, and bags to collect the cooked shellfish. Even the men who had been cut by the pincers of the crabs were running around trying to get their share. Some were even eating the meat from the legs as if it was an all-you-can-eat buffet. I was glad Jean had left the room. The thought of eating the blue crabs was one thing that would really make her sick.

As the hours went by, we watched as the boats crowded together in one large mass in the moat, and people from the flotilla set up a picket line of women and children with pointed stakes along the beach. When crabs ventured onto the shore, they were quickly harvested and carried back to the boats. It was risky business to build fires on boats, but they were doing it. Several had big oil drums full of water with fires heating the water, and blue crabs being boiled. Judging by the number of fires and the way the people were eating the crabs, they either didn't know it would kill them, or they had given up and didn't care. Hunger can cause people to take their chances, and maybe they didn't think it was dangerous to everyone.

Some of the boats moved into the area where we knew the oyster beds were the thickest. Men in hip waders stepped into the beds and began digging for the largest oysters. We didn't know if it was safe to eat the oysters, but there were so many infected dead in the moat that oysters were not on our menu either. Besides the obvious exposure to the decaying bodies in the water, it was also the wrong time of year to harvest oysters. If you lived in the South, then you knew that oysters harvested during the warm months from May through August would make you sick whether they had been around the infected dead or not.

We went about our business in the shelter, but we took turns watching the activities in what had become the Mud Island Marina. No one had much of an appetite, so fresh coffee was kept brewing, and Jean's bread was available to anyone who needed something light to eat. As the sun started to dip lower in the west, we saw that sick people were again being carried to the beach, but they were being dispatched with dignity before they arrived, and they were placed on a raging bonfire that lit the area well enough for the picket line to continue harvesting the crabs.

Tom came up and sat next to me, and said, "This scenario has probably been played out up and down the coast, and it will continue until the crabs win."

"Do you think food has become that scarce inland?"

"Sure, and harder to get to. The radiation can't be just a local phenomenon. If any other untended reactors have leaked, then people are being cut off from food in growing numbers," said Tom.

"There have to be food processing plants and warehouses," I said. "People are probably finding them every day. Add to those the number of trucks that were carrying containers of food, and there's going to be food for a long time."

"All true, Ed, but there were people working in those food processing plants and those warehouses. By now they've tried to return to those places, and they've told other people where to look. Those places are either picked clean, or they can't be reached because of the number of infected dead in the area."

Jean was listening to us talk, and she sounded like it was depressing her. Her voice was low and she had a flat tone.

"You make it sound pretty bleak, Tom."

"Sorry, but I think we passed bleak a long time ago. Think of it this way. If you shut your eyes and picture every Walmart you have ever been too, your eyes would be shut for a long time. Now imagine how many other people have been to every one of those same stores. It's the same thing with every grocery store in the country. The only food supplies that will stay intact are the ones inside the network of shelters."

Jean looked openly surprised for a moment.

"I can't believe it, but I forgot about those. I was starting to think about the baby, and I was wondering what we would do without food. As long as we have the other shelters, we won't run out of anything."

Bus walked up with a fresh pot of coffee, and we gratefully accepted a refill.

"I wonder if the Chief has considered making a detour to my old shelter while he's over that way. It would be a good chance to make a supply run," he said.

"He might consider it," I said, "but right now I don't really have a clue about how we can get him and Kathy home again. They may have to hole up at the Guntersville shelter after they find Hampton because one thing is for sure. They can't land here."

Molly had eased back into the room and was watching the monitors from behind us. We hadn't wanted her to see the scene that was unfolding on the beach, but when you came right down to it, she was going to be exposed to the real world whether we liked it or not. She had handled the loss of her mother far better than we had expected, and her birthday was coming up in a few weeks.

Molly said, "Uncle Bus, maybe the Chief and Aunt Kathy will go to one of the other shelters."

There's always something funny about the way people look at each other when they're all surprised. I always think of Eddie Murphy when he looks straight at the camera with that expression that seems to ask if the audience was hearing what his movie character is hearing. The adults all looked at each other that way. Then we looked at Bus.

"Yeah, do you think they may go to another shelter?" asked Jean.

Bus looked a little helpless, but then he regained his composure and said, "That's what I would do."

Tom said, "I think what she was really asking was whether or not there's another shelter in the Charlotte area."

Bus had filled the Chief in on the other locations, but neither of them had found the time to share all of the locations with the rest of us. We all knew about the oil rig in the Gulf of Mexico, and we knew the President was likely to be somewhere under Columbus, Ohio, but there were twenty-seven more shelters out there that Bus knew about. For all he knew, there could be more that the government didn't tell them about.

Bus let out a heavy sigh and said, "There was one guy named Pruitt in our survivalist group who had the idea that surrounding the shelter with water was a great idea, but it was risky to put your back up against a wall the way Titus did."

"What's that mean, Bus?" I asked.

"The Atlantic," he said. "Pruitt felt like there was always going to be the need for escape routes if things went wrong at the shelters, so he wanted to be able to escape in any direction. He didn't see the point in trying to escape to the sea. He preferred to escape to dry land, but he preferred an island in a lake."

"Wait a minute. Are you saying there's a lake near Charlotte that has an island with a shelter in it?" asked Tom.

"Lake Norman," I said. "There's a lake just north of Charlotte that has about five hundred miles of shoreline, but the islands all have houses on them. How could one of them have a shelter in it?"

I knew the answer as soon as I asked. Just as Fort Sumter had tour boats docking at it every day, filled with tourists who never suspected what was really below their feet, the island somewhere on Lake Norman was developed for individual homes after the shelter was built.

"Does the Chief know which island?" I asked Bus.

"I showed him on a map," he answered. "It wouldn't be hard for that old salt to find."

I had an idea of where Tom was going when he got up and went over to a big cardboard box the Chief had stashed behind a recliner in the corner of the living room. He fumbled around in the contents that looked like rolls of Christmas wrapping paper until he found one that had something written near the end. He glanced at the writing, seemed satisfied and brought it over to us. As he walked he slid a large map from the tube and handed it to Bus.

"This is crazy," I said. "I not only wind up owning one of the shelters, there was another one practically in my backyard when I was living in Charlotte."

Bus said, "Remember, we all had our own ideas about what was safe and what wasn't. Pruitt said he knew his island would be overrun with survivors, but the survivors would wipe each other out because they couldn't fortify the island. He said more survivors would keep coming along until there weren't anymore survivors. The last group to move onto the island would have to go to the mainland to resupply, and eventually they wouldn't come back."

"Your friend sounds like he was a real caring type," said Jean.

"Remember what it was like back then, Jean. We were in the Cold War, and the government wanted ideas about how to survive. It wasn't like most of us could build the shelters on our own. When our group was approached by the military, we were busy sinking our own savings into some pretty flimsy shelters that wouldn't have survived more than a few days once the infection got started. We were told to come up with ideas that were meant to protect important people."

"I guess they should have worked on their plans to reach the shelters just a little better," I said. "We don't even know for sure that the President made it to Columbus, and I didn't hear anyone say the important people reached Maybank's oil rig."

"There was one thing Pruitt didn't count on when he picked his location," said Bus.

By now we were all ears. Looking back over the years to the early days of the shelters, we could imagine the group telling the military where they each wanted to be, and we could almost picture the reactions from the people who had to go along with their crazy ideas.

Bus went on, "After Pruitt picked his island, he didn't expect a developer to come along and build a bridge from the mainland to the island. He was so mad. I remember him asking the General from the Army Corps of Engineers why he didn't just build the bridge in the first place. The General told him to get used to the idea, because he couldn't have the bridge bombed in the middle of the night like Pruitt wanted him to do."

We all had to laugh despite the fact that the situation was serious.

"So, do you think Pruitt made it to his shelter?" asked Tom.

"No, I doubt it. Pruitt was pretty good with his tech. If he made it, we would have heard from him. He was always monitoring everything even when the Cold War ended. He didn't think we were wrong about some impending doom, and he would have been way ahead of the spread of the infection. I think he must have been away from the island when it started and wasn't able to make it back."

"Where was his island? Is it far from where the Chief is likely to hook up with Hampton?" asked Jean.

"I know where the island is, Jean, but your guess is as good as mine about where the Chief will find Hampton or even if he will find him."

******

"How close can we get without picking up any contamination?" asked Kathy.

"We don't need to get close. I just want to see how bad it is. If it's on fire, the worst is yet to come."

Kathy could see the Oconee Nuclear Station through her binoculars, but she couldn't see details well enough to know if there was a fire.

The Chief went on, "A fire that goes unchecked can lead to an explosion. An explosion can cause the reactor core to lose containment, and if that happens, we'll get worse fallout than we already have."

"I don't understand it, Chief. If Hampton was relaying information that the reactor had already suffered significant damage, then why did it stop? Why did we get some radioactive fallout but not a lot?"

"The only answer has to be that someone is still alive down there, and they got it stopped in time. Whoever it is saved a lot of people, but there's still a problem."

The problem was visible to the Chief even without binoculars, but Kathy was seeing it too. There was clearly steam or some sort of cloud still rising above the huge, cylindrical buildings at the nuclear station.

"Is that a leak?" asked Kathy.

The Chief had been thinking about what it could be if it wasn't a fire, but he was reasonably sure that it was radioactive. Just to be sure, he increased their altitude and began circling the plant toward the north.

"I think someone is still down there, and they're doing a slow, controlled release of the pressure in the reactor. If they don't, the thing will blow and send everything it has all at one time," said the Chief.

Kathy started to ask the Chief another question, and he held up his hand.

"Save it. I know a lot of things, but I only know the basics about this stuff. I only wanted to get a look because we needed to find out which way the radioactive cloud is moving, and how bad it looks. If the top had blown off of one of those towers, we would be heading back to Mud Island and closing the doors for a few years. It may still happen, but not today."

"Do you at least know if the cloud is going to keep moving south?" she asked.

"No, it won't. That's why we have to get to Hampton in a hurry. The storm that hit Maybank's oil rig is going to push ashore and shove that radioactive cloud to the northeast."

"Right into Charlotte," she finished for him. Kathy automatically looked to the southwest as if she could see the storm.

"Yeah, so let's say a prayer of thanks to whoever it is turning the big wheels down there and keeping that reactor from blowing all at once, and then we need to find Hampton."

The Chief began a long turn toward Charlotte. It was only about one hundred and twenty miles from them, and so far the sky was clear in that direction.

Kathy looked over at the Chief and wanted to ask him what it would mean to them if the reactor lost containment and the storm came inland far enough to push the radioactive cloud to Charlotte. That was one question she didn't need to ask, though. They may get missed by the radiation, but they would never be able to go north again.

The Chief was quick to pick up on the worried look he saw on Kathy's face.

"If the storm pushes the radioactive cloud to the northeast, I expect to see more infected dead moving south, not because the dead will know which way to go, but because survivors are going to become mobile again. It's not like they'll know what's coming or what's making them sick, but they'll know something is happening. As they get sick and die, the infected will start pushing them out of hiding."

"So, all we have to do is find Hampton and get clear of the area before the radiation begins moving in our direction," said Kathy.

"That pretty much sums it up. My plan is to get generally situated somewhere then try to get Hampton to come to us."

Kathy looked at the Chief like he had lost his mind. She could see that his expression was neutral, like he was in a high stakes poker game, and he had a royal flush. She knew that look, and she knew it meant he wasn't telling her something. It also felt like it was something big.

"Well, Chief? Are you going to tell me the plan, or do I have to beat it out of you?"

He couldn't help himself, partially because the only person he knew who had a chance of putting a scratch on him was Kathy. She was pretty and had long blond hair, but her looks had probably gotten men to underestimate her for a long time. He didn't want to find out if she could beat it out of him, even though he knew she was just kidding.

"There's another big shelter near Charlotte," said the Chief.

He looked over at Kathy because she didn't say anything. He saw her mouth was hanging open, and she looked totally stunned.

She finally closed her mouth then immediately asked, "That close to us? We practically flew right by it when we went to the shelter in Guntersville. Where is it? Do you know?"

"It's on an island somewhere on Lake Norman. I've seen a map of the area, and it looks like it would be easy to spot from the air. Its name is Ambassadors Island, and it has a bridge that comes right off the tip of the mainland straight to the island. From the air it will look a little like a boot. You know, like Italy."

"And this is going to help us find Hampton somehow?" asked Kathy.

The Chief looked like he was mulling over how to answer for a few moments. He had a good idea of what he wanted to do, but there were all kinds of things that could go wrong. He also wouldn't know if he was going to have everything at his disposal that he hoped for. So much depended on what they found when they located the shelter.

"Okay, Kathy, this plan has some holes in it, but we have to start somewhere."

"How many holes?"

"You know the houseboat theory, right?"

"Of course I do," she said. "Put the houseboat at the island so people won't even think there might be a better shelter nearby. Build the shelter under a fort so people will feel safe in the fort and not consider the possibility there's a massive shelter fit for royalty right beneath their feet. What does this shelter have, an airport?"

"No, don't be ridiculous, Kathy. That's in Atlanta," said the Chief.

She looked at him to see if the poker face was there again, but this time he was grinning. That usually meant he was kidding around, but after his disclosure of Ambassadors Island, she wasn't completely sure.

Before she could chip away at him to see if he was kidding, he added, "This shelter has a full blown neighborhood built on top of it. According to Bus, the shelter is really big. Not as deep as the one at Fort Sumter, but it covers the entire length of Ambassadors Island."

"I still don't get it, Chief. How's a big shelter going to help Hampton when he doesn't even know it's there?"

"I don't know yet, but Bus told me the guy who built this shelter was really into his technology. He loved his toys, and some of those toys may just help us locate Hampton. When he relayed the word about the Oconee Nuclear Station, Hampton was on a radio. All we have to do is broadcast and monitor at the right frequency, and we should be able to talk with him. If that doesn't work, Bus said the guy who built the shelter wanted a good early warning system, so he had infrared cameras installed miles away. He could literally give you a traffic report on I-77 in real time. If there's someone alive out there, we should be able to find them."

"I hate to rain on your parade, Chief, but what if the houseboat is occupied?"

The Chief got a slightly pained expression and said, "That's one of the holes in the plan, Kathy, but that's where the bridge comes in. If we're lucky the bridge will have been a problem for the inhabitants of the island. I know it sounds bad to hope the people who lived on the island weren't able to survive because of the bridge, but the reality is the water is only a good moat if the infected can't walk right up to your doorstep."

"There's one other problem with the houseboat theory, Chief."

The Chief knew what she was going to say before she could even get started.

He said, "The original inhabitants all became victims a long time ago, most of them on the first day. The new inhabitants would have seen the bridge as a liability by now and either put a big hole in it or found a way to block it. I don't know which would be better for us, but I'm counting on the same thing we've seen before. If the infection got behind their lines onto the island side of the bridge, we may only have to deal with a contained population of the dead."

Kathy could see tall buildings in the distance and asked, "Are we here already?"

The Chief nodded as he corrected his course straight north toward Lake Norman. It was impossible to sneak up on anyone with the de Havilland Beaver. It was about as noisy as a single engine plane could get, so they could only land and hope the one pair of eyes watching them were Hampton's. There was no doubt that every infected dead within miles would hear the plane, but the Chief planned to shut down the engine as quickly as possible once the plane was on the water, and they could anchor long enough for the infected they attracted nearby to walk into the lake.

The biggest difference between fresh water and salt water was the rate of decay. The infected dead that went into a lake became bloated after they were in the water long enough, but they seemed to be able to get around a lot better than the ones that went into salt water. They even seemed to be able to come to the surface and grab at the living better in fresh water. The Chief couldn't do depth soundings, but he could tell brown, shallow water from green, deep water. It would be a serious problem to stop in shallow water and to have the infected dead walk right out of the water onto the floats of the Beaver.

He circled toward the western side of the lake where he estimated Ambassadors Island to be located, and it didn't take him long to pick it out from the other islands. He recalled from the clear satellite photos in the Mud Island shelter that there was a narrow channel at the southern tip of the island, a small grove of trees on a tiny, undeveloped island, and then a long, narrow sandbar that sat just below the surface. It would be easy to approach the island unseen in a small boat by moving along that sandbar straight at the grove of trees, but the plane would be heard by people for miles around. The sandbar was also just the sort of threat from the infected dead that he wanted to avoid. From the pictures and from the air, it looked like the infected could walk along it and be no more than knee deep in water.

The Beaver was bright yellow against a blue sky, and the Chief was well aware that he was flying a slow moving target. Anyone with any skill at all could hit the plane with a rifle. He wanted to get one look at the bridge before he landed to see if the inhabitants of the island had managed to fortify the bridge before the island became overrun. One good look was all he could afford to try, because he could imagine someone was frantically trying to guess where the engine noise was coming from and trying to get into position for a shot before the opportunity was gone.

He approached the bridge from the lake side on the right and dropped his altitude quickly. He told Kathy to hold on, try for a good look, and be ready for some unexpected turns. Kathy quickly slid from her seat up front into the back of the plane and positioned herself behind the Chief at a window. He figured she was just trying for a better view, but Kathy was way ahead of him. She had pulled a cell phone from her backpack and was already getting a good video of the scene below. If they had a chance to study it before going to the island, they would be able to spot details they might have missed.

The yellow Beaver passed over the bridge at almost seventy miles per hour, but the Chief got a good look at the front of the gated community. The bridge was blocked where it touched the mainland by a tangle of cars and boat trailers. Other assorted junk filled in the gaps between the vehicles.

At the entrance to the island, there were two pairs of gates, two for pedestrians and two for vehicles. Three of the gates were blocked in the same way as the other end of the bridge. Whoever had done the work must have realized there would be very little need for a lot of gates.

The Chief banked the plane on its left side and followed the shoreline of the island until he reached the small grove of trees that looked like it was dotting a large letter "i" in the middle of the lake. The channel that separated it from the island was about fifty feet wide, but it must have been deep because there was no brown shading to the water.

The curved end of the island was too sharp for the Chief to make the turn, so he just kept going straight past the trees and along the shallow sandbar. Kathy reached up and tapped him on the shoulder.

"Give me a pass the same way on the right side, Chief. I'm getting some good video on my cell phone."

The Chief brought the plane around and lined it up with the opposite side of Ambassadors Island. This time he was able to hug the shoreline even better because it was a straight run, and the homes seemed to streak by beneath him. He didn't see any movement, and that was more of an indication that there were living people on the island than infected dead. If there were infected, they would be drawn into the open by the sound of his engine. Living people would be hiding.

When the plane reached the bridge for a second time, the Chief banked the plane away from the island and set a course back toward the southeast. He pointed in that direction and told Kathy it looked like the deepest water without a shoreline too close to them would be back toward Charlotte. He told her he was going to stay as far out over the water as possible and then turn northeast to where I-77 crosses part of the lake. He said it would be good to know if the road was passable to the north, but as with many bridges, they were more often death traps.

When they reached their turning point, the Chief made note of three islands on the right and two on the left. It would be so tempting to put a shelter on any of them for the short term, but even without a shelter there had been many people who saw them as the only safe place to be. They didn't have visible shorelines, which meant good fishing from the steep banks under the trees, and deep water that would prevent the infected dead from just strolling into a camp. Two of the islands had small boats tied at spots that had been used by campers over the years, but there were no people moving around, either living or dead.

The Chief pointed to a deep water turn up ahead and said, "That looks like Davidson Creek. About two hundred yards from there we should be able to land and still be able to see the bridge on I-77. It's far enough from land for us to get a good look at the video you did."

As he approached the spot, the Chief came in lower but stayed high enough for them to be able to see the bridge at the same time. Just as he expected, the bridge was jammed with infected dead, and even though they were still far from the bridge, the infected were drawn to the sound of their engine. Before the Chief could sit the plane down on the water and cut off the engine, the infected were falling over the railing into the water.

Even though this particular bridge looked like it had land under its entire length, it was still high enough above the water to allow for the usual spectacular show from the uncoordinated infected dead. It was always a sight that made Kathy think of cliff divers who didn't know how to dive. There was no attempt to enter the water feet first or by extending the arms toward the water for a smooth entry. Some were sideways, some were spinning out of control, and some were doing cartwheels, but none of them knew they were falling. It was probably best described as tumbling into the water.

"What do you suppose happened on that bridge?" she asked the Chief.

"The only thing I can guess is that someone tried to cross it and got cut off before they made it," he answered. "Let me get a look at that video."

Kathy handed him the phone then started scanning the shoreline on all sides for movement. She thought it was a bit odd, but there was no activity until they had reached

Davidson Creek. Then there was movement on both sides of the lake as far as she could see. The Chief had to be right. Something big had happened that had drawn the infected into the open and toward this part of the lake.

On the shoreline nearest to them on the right, Kathy focused her binoculars on one large group of infected dead that were moving toward a circle of homes at the end of a street. They didn't appear to be interested in the homes but were walking in the general direction of the plane. She thought to herself that they must have been drawn to the sound of the plane's engine, but when it cut off, they just kept walking.

The street sign Kathy could see behind the group of infected dead said they were shambling down John Gamble Road, and Kathy wondered what it had looked like before. There were only about a dozen homes on the street, and it looked like it would have been a great place to live. She absently wondered if the dead she saw walking down the street had been the people living in the homes, or if they were invaders who had killed the residents of the peaceful street.

"So much has changed," she thought out loud.

The Chief pushed the video over in front of Kathy and snapped her out of her private thoughts. He had paused it on a spot along the right side of Ambassadors Island where there was a thick growth of trees and no house.

"There are about three dozen houses on the island. Every lakeside piece of property has a house on it except this one. I think it might be door number one."

He moved the video forward a few frames until he reached a house only nine lots further up the island on the right side.

"See anything different about this house?" he asked.

Kathy compared it to the other houses and quickly spotted the difference.

"It's the only house without a private dock," she said. "To live in this neighborhood, you'd better be able to keep up with the Joneses. That means if thirty-five people have private docks and boats, number thirty-six would have one, too. Any chance they haven't gotten around to building it yet?"

"Not a clue," said the Chief, " but where the dock meets the water would be a good place for door number two."

"You think this one has a third door like the others?"

He nodded and ran the video back to the beginning of their pass over the island. He stopped it right as the plane had passed over the barricaded bridge and gates and pointed at the round-about that looked like part of the landscaping at the main entrance. Kathy didn't see it at first, but then she realized what she was looking at. The round-about wasn't paved. It was made of red brick, and from above it looked like the points of a compass, including the midpoints. The points were even aligned with true north.

Kathy looked at the Chief hoping he had a clue which point of the compass was aimed at the door, and he was grinning. She couldn't stop herself from grinning with him, but she still didn't know what he was waiting to tell her.

"Well, are you going to tell me, or do I have to guess?" she asked.

The Chief asked, "Have you ever compared a compass to a combination lock, or the lock on a safe? Combination locks are great for gym lockers, but they have less numbers. Northwest on a combination lock has the number thirty-five, while northwest on a bank vault dial has the number ninety."

"Don't tell me," said Kathy. "The combination for this shelter door wouldn't happen to begin with ninety, would it?"

The Chief gave her a broad smile.

"That's my girl," he said.

5 SUBURBAN LIFE OR DEATH

Hampton had slept with one eye open because the groaning went on all night. The sun was slowly beginning to come through the skylights, and Colleen was still stretched out across the sitting area a few feet away. She had a pillow under her head and a blanket up to her shoulders, but she had chosen the carpeted floor over the beds. There was just something about being caught in a bed. Beds didn't feel safe anymore, and it wasn't because something was hiding under them. It felt like you should be hiding under the bed instead of sleeping in it.

He wasn't sure if he could sneak past Colleen, but he had to use a bathroom and then try to find some food. Somewhere in the craziness on I-77 he had forgotten about getting away with supplies.

Colleen didn't move, and her breathing was even. She was more exhausted than he had realized. The day before had gone well enough at first, but the movement up I-77 had begun early, and like most of the people, sleep had been elusive the night before. Everyone was either afraid or too keyed up on adrenaline to be able to rest. Once the plan was announced to the large group of survivors, there was no debate. They were running out of supplies, and it was too far to go to reach places they hadn't already stripped bare. When the plan started to fall apart, they were already at the edge of their limits, and the only thing keeping them moving forward was fear.

Without his boots on, Hampton was able to make it down the stairs without waking Colleen. He kept his eyes on her as his toes sank into the deep pile of the carpet, and for the second time he wondered why he hadn't noticed her before when they were holed up in the football stadium. She really was pretty, and it occurred to him that he had never known an Irish girl as he grew up in Georgetown, South Carolina. There was probably a lot he had missed growing up in a small town, but he didn't feel like he was ignorant about the world.

He had learned to fly an airplane and had gone to Georgetown Technical College. He played around with degrees in criminology and engineering, finally deciding on the latter because there were more job opportunities. He hunted with his friends and learned to live a peaceful life that in the end kept him alive. He remembered being told by a group of survivors who were traveling north that the infection would kill from within. Someone in the community was already hiding a family member who had been bitten.

Hampton didn't want to believe them, but deep down inside he knew they had been right. He wasn't the only one who made sure there was fuel in his plane and supplies stashed in the cargo section. He started carrying his rifle and a pistol everywhere he went. Not because he worried about the infected getting into Georgetown from another part of the state, but because he was worried about his friends.

He thought back to those last days with friends he had known since childhood, and he remembered how they had begun to be wary of each other. He saw the questioning looks and knew that someone was hiding a loved one. There were fewer children being seen with their parents. People who normally took their families with them everywhere when they were in town were now seen walking alone. Everyone was in a hurry, and people stopped making eye contact.

When the horde of infected dead had arrived at Georgetown on Highway 17, they felt like they were ready because of the warning they had gotten from that group of survivors. They had the high ground with two bridges, and they could shoot from the first bridge for a long time before retreating to the second bridge. They would be cutting off one of their own major arteries out of the city, but as soon as they saw what was coming toward them, they knew they had no choice.

The plan worked as well as they could have hoped, and for the short term they were safe. They began shooting with hunting rifles as the leading edge of the horde approached the bridge. The rows of bodies slowed the approach of what appeared to be thousands of the infected dead, and as the piles of bodies grew, the horde spread to the left and the right sides of the highway. The sheer pressure of that many infected dead caused those in front to be pushed forward as if there was a bulldozer behind them.

Since the trees lined the highway almost all the way to the first bridge, hundreds of the infected on the fringes of the horde were crushed against the trees. They were pinned in place and continued to wave their arms and snap their teeth in the direction of the living who were shooting down at them. Hampton kept yelling at the men not to shoot at the infected that were in the trees and to focus on the ones on the highway. As long as the trees were getting jammed up, the infected would continue to be forced to the outside.

Just as he expected and hoped for, the infected dead that were forced to the outside gradually began appearing around the trees. They pushed each other forward and began stepping off into the soft mudflats that lined the banks of the Waccamaw River. For as far as the eye could see, the brown mud waited to trap anything that dared to walk onto it, and Hampton was convinced they could steer the horde that way.

As he and his friends watched, the infected stumbled out onto the mud and began to get stuck. When they couldn't move forward, they began to be pushed down into the mud by the infected dead that were crawling onto their backs. It wasn't long before there was a solid bridge of struggling infected dead all the way to the river, and the dead that managed to crawl over them were pulled away by the swiftly moving water. They were beyond the beginning of the bridge and were no longer a threat.

Almost thirty minutes after the shooting started, there was still no end in sight. The infected dead were still pushing from behind in unbelievable numbers, and Hampton yelled for everyone to stop firing. An ammunition check was done, and they didn't need a math genius with a calculator to tell them they were going to run out of ammunition long before they ran out of infected dead to shoot.

Hampton and his friends got together for a quick discussion about what they should do, and it was obvious to all of them. The horde couldn't be stopped by bullets, but maybe they could be stopped by the river. It was time to drop the first bridge. The charges were in place, so all they had to do was to pull back and wait for the parade to come to them. They gathered their gear and loaded into waiting pick up trucks. From high ground they could see that a sizable force of the infected had already pushed through the bodies at the base of the bridge and begun the upward climb. They were spread out, but they were coming.

The small army of people trying to stop the infected dead from reaching Georgetown drove from the bridge over the Waccamaw River until they reached the second span. It passed over a narrow strip of land that separated the Waccamaw River from the Great Pee Dee River and was worth saving if it could be done. The bridge over the Great Pee Dee River might be useful if they survived long enough. From there they waited until the horde of infected dead reached the crest of the bridge over the Waccamaw River. Then they began detonating the charges.

The first blast took out a large portion of the bridge and hundreds of the infected dead with it, but something caused the charges to fail along one entire side. Of the four lanes crossing the bridge, two lanes remained intact from one side of the river to the other. The bridge had split right down the middle, and the infected were still falling over the edge, but they still had two lanes to use. Hampton and his friends couldn't believe their eyes as thousands of the infected continued their march toward Georgetown.

For a second time Hampton called everyone together to talk about their next move, and it was an easy decision. They were going to put all of their cards on the table by dropping the second bridge before the horde would have a chance to reach it. If the bridge didn't fall as planned, they would at least have the time they needed to start an evacuation of the city.

Hampton gave the signal to move back, and once again they retreated from the advancing wall of death. This would be their last chance to stop the horde from reaching them, so it had to work better than before. They didn't wait on the bridge to watch. Instead, they drove to the bottom of the bridge and gave the word to the anxious spectators near the city marina to get ready to evacuate if the bridge didn't fall.

Once everyone was in position, the signal was given, and the second set of charges was detonated. There was first a collective sigh of relief, and then a cheer went up from the crowd as the entire bridge over the Great Pee Dee River fell. The only thing left standing was the center span where it crossed the narrow strip of land separating the two rivers.

Hampton sat down to watch as the infected dead continued their march. Once they reached the end of the center span, they just walked right over the edge. There was a pile starting to form at the bottom of the bridge, but anything that managed to crawl off of the pile found itself either going in the wrong direction or walking straight into the swift current of the Great Pee Dee River.

The memories from that day had played over and over again so many times in his mind. They had stayed alive against so many of the infected dead, but they couldn't survive the days that followed. They could fight together against an enemy that they could see, but they couldn't fight against the unseen enemy that was already within their city streets. It began only three days later when there were several incidents at the same time. More than one family had an infected relative or loved one they were hiding, and once it began to spread there was no way to stop it. There was no bridge to drop this time.

Hampton was inspecting his plane when it started. He had gotten in the habit of doing preflight checks two or three times a day before the battle at the bridges, so it wasn't unusual for him to be there again. He had even spent a few nights sleeping in his plane, just as he had done after the battle.

A police car with its blue lights on raced past the fence surrounding the small city airport. Hampton watched it turn the corner a few blocks away and then reached into the cockpit to turn on his radio. He knew what was happening almost immediately. The police dispatcher was asking for everyone available to respond because an officer was down. She said something about a domestic dispute and that deadly force was authorized. He couldn't remember that call ever being made by dispatch.

The next calls from dispatch said it had happened again over by a hardware store near the airport, and that the ambulance driver who responded was being attacked. Hampton could see the hardware store from where his plane was parked, and the ambulance driver was nowhere in sight. What he could see was an infected dead pulling an elderly woman to the ground. Her screams carried to Hampton as the dispatcher went silent. There was only static coming from the radio.

He remembered thinking that they had been warned, but after they were warned, there wasn't anything else they could do. They had to at least try to keep their city together. They had defended it, and then came a time when it would be up to each person to stay alive. He had climbed into his plane with no real thought about where he should go. Once he was in the air, he decided the mountains might be safer than the coast, so he pointed the plane in that direction.

Hampton didn't look back because he was pretty sure of what he would see. No one else was taking off from the airport, and it wasn't likely that anyone else would.

Hampton had almost forgotten why he was in the kitchen of the big house. Then he remembered Colleen upstairs on the floor, and he went back to his search for food. He wondered how long it would be before he quit getting lost in his thoughts about those days when Georgetown fell to the infected dead.

A walk-in pantry turned out to be a major find. It was well stocked with canned foods and boxes of dry goods. Now he just had to find a way to cook it without power and without the fumes from the stove killing them. He took a quick peek through the curtains at the front of the house and saw several infected dead moving across the yards of neighboring homes. He thought it was a little odd that they were moving in the opposite direction as the night before, but you never knew what the infected would be drawn toward. It could be something as simple as the wind blowing a piece of paper down the street.

He almost missed the second closet in the kitchen because he never would have expected to find two in the same kitchen. He wasn't used to the kind of luxury this family had known, and judging by some of the other homes in the area, they had not been among the most affluent. They were just rich enough to live at the edge of the neighborhood.

The second closet looked like a Bass Pro Shop. Shelves of camping, fishing, and hunting gear were neatly arranged from front to back. It only took a moment to locate the Coleman stove fuel. Hampton knew it wasn't a good idea to use a fuel burning stove inside a house, but this house was so big that opening a window a couple of inches should be enough. There was another thing he had learned about the infected dead, and that was they weren't really drawn to smells, just noise. A lot of outdoor cooking would have been interrupted if they were drawn to smells.

As soon as Hampton located the instant coffee, he started looking for the emergency water supply. He noticed that most of the gear in the Bass Pro closet looked new and unused. Either the guy who lived in the house was interested in camping, or he had stocked up for an emergency. Either way, he would have bottled water. He found a case of distilled water in the closet with the canned goods then picked a window that faced the backyard as the place to vent the stove. He looked at his watch to see how long it would take for the smell of coffee to wake Colleen, and as he expected, it was under a minute.

He saw her head appear near the floor of the second floor sitting area. She must have crawled to the edge so she could see him below. Her hair was messed up, and she was wrinkling her nose. He put one finger to his lips and then pointed at the open window. She nodded in understanding and pulled herself to an upright position using the railing that ran across the landing. He motioned that she could stay there, and he would bring the coffee to her. Colleen grinned and pointed at the bathroom.

He was waiting for her when she came out of the bathroom, and she gratefully accepted the hot coffee. When he handed it to her, she leaned closer and surprised him with a small kiss on the cheek.

"Thank you," she said in a low voice. Then she smiled and added, "Do I have to call you by your last name?"

Hampton was caught off guard by both the kiss and the question. He wasn't sure if he had done something else good, or if it was just the coffee.

He kept his voice low just out of caution, but it seemed more like a moment to use a soft voice. He thought he could stare at her green eyes forever.

"Chris. My first name is Chris," he whispered.

She held out her hand so he could shake it, and he asked, "Is it too soon for me to ask your last name?"

She smiled to show she liked playing this little courting game and said, "O'Connor, but it's too soon for me to give you my phone number. How long has it been since you've had a girlfriend, Chris?"

That question really caught him off guard. He didn't realize it was that obvious. He had only been in a couple of relationships, and only one of them had mattered. When it fell apart, he was left with a bunch of hurt feelings and even more confusion. From that time on, he just didn't get close to anyone again.

"Pleased to meet you, Ms. O'Connor."

He shook her hand and made what he considered a smooth recovery, but she didn't let go of his hand when he thought the handshake was over. She also held his eyes with her own.

He finally gave in and said, "It's been a while. I haven't really had a girlfriend for a long time now."

Colleen saw that it was a sore spot with him and knew when to let it go, but to help him past the moment she whispered, "Well, you've got one now, so don't think about ditching me."

Despite everything that was going on outside in the world, Hampton felt good for the first time in almost a year.

He was deathly afraid of something happening to Colleen even before he knew her last name. Now he was going to be worried sick all the time.

"Where did you find the coffee?"

"There's a big pantry and a supply closet, believe it or not. I think there may be guns somewhere around here, too. The closet was full of unused survival gear. Either the guy who lived here had time to go shopping when the infection hit the news, or he was planning on doing some serious camping. He may also have been one of those people who just had to have lots of toys, but he kept them in their boxes."

"Guns would be in a den, but you can bet they would be in a gun cabinet. That means a key would be hidden somewhere in the den where the kids wouldn't be able to find it. Let's go, Chris. We need to search this place and then figure out what we're going to do next. We could stay here for a bit, but it's nothing we could call permanent."

The den turned out to be a very nicely furnished room at the top of a narrow set of stairs. It felt like they were going up into a tower because the stairs made a turn and disappeared at a closed door. It was unlocked, and Hampton opened the door slowly in case there would be another resident waiting for a victim.

The room was well lit by large windows that gave an almost panoramic view of the neighborhood and the lake. At the same time it was high enough above the street that the infected couldn't see if anyone was watching. The room was obviously a man's study, complete with the desk, executive chair, and richly polished wooden book shelves. There was a wet bar in one corner, and Hampton studied the labels on a row of bottles.

"This would be hell to defend because all someone would need to do is set fire to it, and we would be trapped up here," said Hampton, "but it would make a great watch tower for a short time."

"Here's what we came for," said Colleen. She was standing in front of a cabinet that had a row of hunting rifles on the other side of the glass.

"Can we break the glass without anything outside hearing it?" she asked.

As soon as she said it she knew it wasn't going to be hard to find the key. The climb to the man-cave was too far for someone not to have a hidden key. Hampton had grinned at her when she asked, and she turned red. Hampton thought blushing was cute.

Since he was almost a foot taller than her, Hampton started running his hand along the top of every cabinet and sill. He came up empty so he checked through the desk and under the drawers. It occurred to him that he didn't like being too close to the open windows even if it wasn't likely that he would be spotted by the infected dead, but he thought it would be a good idea to slowly close the curtains. It was when he reached for the top edge of the curtains that he saw the key hanging neatly from the mount that held the curtain rod. He took a quick peek through the window to be sure the coast was clear then retrieved the key.

The rifles turned out to be nothing special compared to what they already had, but the supply of ammunition that matched their rifles was something they desperately needed. The bonus was a drawer full of hand guns and spare magazines.

Colleen knew her weapons and how to handle them. Hampton watched with appreciation as she checked each gun before sitting them on the desk. She pulled back the slides, checked the chambers, and checked the safety on each one. She did one dry fire with each to see if they worked, then laid them facing away from her and Hampton on the desk. She was safety conscious as well as a good shot.

She caught him again. He didn't even know she was looking at him because she was handling the guns so efficiently. Without turning her head she asked, "Do you like what you see?"

It was funny to Hampton, but he suddenly realized he had met someone a lot like her before. When the four survivors had met with him on the bridge outside Georgetown, one of them had been a fiery little brunette who seemed to have one of the men off balance the whole time. She teased him in a good-natured way that made Hampton think she liked him. It dawned on him that maybe Colleen was teasing him because she liked him.

Hampton gave her a small dose of her own medicine when he said, "Of course I do. Is there anyone who doesn't like a brand new Glock?"

She kept inspecting the weapon without looking at him, but she couldn't stop the smile that spread across her face. Her quick response showed she was a master at dishing out the full dose of medicine.

"Maybe I'll let you handle it later so you can see if it's to your liking," she said.

He had to laugh, but he knew she was going to be more than a match for him, so he started packing the ammunition into a carrying case with a long shoulder strap. It looked like it was a laptop bag, but it worked well for the boxes of ammunition. There was a closet that had a couple of gym bags on a shelf. He emptied the contents onto the floor and then began filling them with everything that wouldn't fit in the laptop case. They needed all three bags by the time they had taken everything they wanted.

There was one other item in the closet that caught Hampton's eye. It was a decent sized telescope with a tall tripod. The view from the windows in the man-cave was already pretty good, but with the telescope the previous owner of the house would have been able to keep a close eye on his neighbors. Probably a little more than his neighbors would have liked.

Hampton carried the telescope out and set it up by the window. He was careful to stay back far enough from the glass to be sure nothing spotted his motion, and the sun didn't reflect from the lens. He adjusted the eyepiece and was amazed at the quality of the view.

"This will come in handy when we figure out what we're going to do. We can at least come up here and check the amount of activity first."

No sooner had he said it than he saw what they had done by choosing to escape to this particular neighborhood. They had the high ground and the window afforded a large view, so he was able to see all the way across the lake to the opposite side in all directions. He was not happy to find they were in a neighborhood that had water on three sides. The only side not bordered by water was where they had come from the night before, and he had no urge to go back that way any time soon.

"I think we're going to need a plan that includes a boat," he said. "In the meantime, I'm getting hungry."

"Well, now that we have everything we really need from here," said Colleen, "let's see what we can find that's worth cooking in that pantry."

They hauled everything down the narrow stairs and dumped the bags in the sitting area at the top of the stairs. They would be spending more time there than downstairs as they made plans for their escape from the area.

When they got to the kitchen, they spent a couple of minutes taking glimpses from windows all around the first floor. There were a few of the infected wandering around, but since the commotion on the interstate had died down on the previous evening, the infected had stopped flocking to that area.

There was plenty of light for cooking, so it didn't take long for them to put together a decent meal. Spam was never going to replace steak, but it sure tasted good when you were hungry. They boiled some pasta, mixed in a can of peas, and then stirred in diced chunks of pan fried Spam. Since hot water was something they had learned not to waste, Colleen used the water they had used to boil the pasta to cook a box of Stove Top Stuffing. They had plenty of starches in the meal, but it was definitely filling. They hadn't eaten as well in the last couple of weeks at the football stadium, and judging by the amount of food in the pantry, they could eat well for a few months if they wanted to.

Hampton handed Colleen a glass of brandy when they were done eating. She eyed it suspiciously and said she didn't know if they should drink it. He thought she meant they wouldn't be as sharp after drinking, but what she really meant was that they could get used to having too much of a good thing, and they needed to be thinking about moving on.

"I know what you mean," he said. "This place has a lot to offer, but it's not safe. If the infected hear us, they will eventually find a way to get in, and even if they don't, we won't have a way to get out."

"There's one other thing we can't forget," she said. "There's always the possibility of other survivors trying to use this house. Since it's right by the edge of the interstate, it's a likely candidate just as it was for us."

"I think we should search the whole house for things we can use, lay up for a day of two, then start working our way from house to house until we find one that has a boat tied up where we can get to it in a hurry," he said.

"Sounds reasonable, but tell me something, Chris. Don't you think a lot of people headed for the water when this started?"

He nodded and took a sip of the brandy. It was warm going down, and it calmed his nerves a bit. Something he didn't know he needed to do.

"When the infection started to spread, every talking head on the news said stay home. Then they all started saying don't go to the hospital if you get bitten. Then they started saying don't stay home with a family member who's been bitten. People didn't know what to do."

He didn't even notice that he was doing a lot of gesturing with both of his hands. At some point in time he had set his brandy on the floor where they had been eating. Colleen reached over and caught one of his hands in hers.

"Hey, Chris, slow down, You're a little more mad about this than before. What's happening?"

At first he didn't know what she meant, but then it started to sink in. Up until yesterday he had been part of everything that happened around him, but he had not been a part of it with someone else. He had always been a member of the group, a major player on the team, but he didn't have an attachment. Now, there was Colleen. She was a living, breathing extension of him. He felt like he wouldn't survive if something happened to her.

She saw the change in his expression and the way he tried not to look at her, and she understood.

"Chris, when this all started I had a boyfriend. Actually, he was more than that. We were supposed to get married. I was at home when I saw the first reports on the news, and I tried to call him on his cell. He didn't answer because he was with another woman. I got a call from a friend who said they had seen them together. He showed up a few hours later with a huge bite on his side and another on his arm. I wouldn't let him in. He cried, begged, screamed, and tried to break down the door. He made so much noise that a crowd of the infected came right up on the porch to get him. I listened to them rip him apart."

Hampton listened without interrupting, but he didn't really see how that was something related to him. He heard the reports, but Georgetown had somehow stayed outside of the problem. Somehow the infection hadn't arrived the same way as it had everywhere else, and even if it had, there wasn't anyone at home to protect. He lived by himself and only had to be wary of his neighbors. For a passing moment he wondered how his former girlfriend had made out, but he let the thought go as quickly as it had arrived.

Colleen went on, "You didn't have to let go of what you used to be, Chris. You didn't have to tell someone they couldn't come in, so you were spared what you're going through now. You're afraid it will be me out on that porch, and you don't know how you will face it. That cheating jerk did me a favor by getting me mad enough so I would be able to ignore his screams, but he was still someone I had cared about, and I was faced with the decision at the start. I doubt it will make it easier for me if it happens again."

"It doesn't have to be that way, does it?" he asked.

"No, it doesn't. We can cover each other's backs, and if the time comes that one of us is out on the porch screaming to get in, the other one should end the screaming quickly. Now that we know the price for being weak and opening the door, we need to protect ourselves."

Hampton shook his head and said, "That's not what I meant. We can promise that if one of us goes down, both will go down. Commitment will keep us alive longer than self-preservation, and it will give us a reason to stay alive."

Colleen didn't cry easily, but for the first time since she listened to those screams on her front porch, her eyes filled with tears that began to spill down her cheeks. That time she had cried in anger and misery, but this time she was crying from relief. She was relieved that she could care so much about someone again.

They held each other for a long time, both enjoying the comfort they needed. Colleen whispered, "There's something I've been meaning to ask you. When was the last time you took a bath?"

They spent the day searching the huge house. It was really much bigger than they had even realized. Neither wanted to let the other be alone for more than a minute, and they enjoyed the attention they gave each other.

At first they started carrying things up to the designated safe zone in the sitting room, but they gradually realized they were finding far too many useful things in the rooms. They settled on taking inventory and a plan to review the list once they were done. More than once they talked about returning to the house in the future to collect something they couldn't carry, but the goal was to get out of the area permanently.

By nightfall they had narrowed the list down to a couple of oversized backpacks and the bags full of weapons, and they decided to do something about that bath.

******

The following morning was just the beginning of another day, but it felt different to Hampton. He had no more reason to think life was going to get any easier than it had been for almost a year, but having Colleen with him made everything feel worth the effort. When they woke up together, they didn't say much. They just smiled affectionately and began getting ready to go.

They had talked the night before about how they would move down the streets toward the homes with private docks and small boats. If they could find a house with two boats, it would increase their chances of success. Hampton told Colleen he had tried to start too many boats that had not been used for a few months, and there was nothing more frustrating than hearing the engine sputter and stop. Nothing except doing it repeatedly while a horde of infected dead were walking toward you.

What they needed to find was a house that still had its privacy fence intact and had two boats. That would be the best possible scenario they felt like they could hope for. The plan was to use the telescope to study every possible escape route for a couple of hours, spot the home they needed to reach, and then work their way in that direction.

After breakfast on the landing and a second cup of coffee, they carried their backpacks and bags of guns downstairs. Then they made their way back up to the second floor and long, narrow stairs to the man-cave. Colleen teased Hampton about the need for man-caves and asked him to describe what he wanted in his. More and more she made him feel like they had been friends forever, and he couldn't think of a better feeling than to love someone who was also your friend. It felt good to laugh a little.

They got themselves situated in front of the telescope, and using binoculars first, they began making their escape plans. They tried to get an accurate count of the infected that were walking out in the open so they could guess at the number between them and the other houses. It wasn't too hard because they moved so slowly.

They drew a sketch of the streets, sighted in on their names, and drew a decent map of the area. When they looked at the finished product, they saw they were on a large piece of land that was shaped like a leaf from an oak tree. The streets ran down the middle of each part of the leaf that extended out into Lake Norman. From what they could tell, the leaf shaped neighborhood was about two miles long, and they needed to reach one of the many uninhabited islands that dotted the lake. They wouldn't know which one was best until they got there, but the good news was that the majority of the homes had private docks, and over half of them had boats tied up to them. Some were no more than a hundred yards from their house, and if they really wanted to have more than one boat to choose from, there was a marina back toward the interstate.

Looking at the map, Hampton felt like his old self again. He felt like he was being proactive, and he felt like they were going to come up with a good plan. At first he focused on the marina. It was really close, and there were at least two dozen boats in clear view. The problem was the trees. There were large areas of trees that they just couldn't see through. The marina sat near the base of the bridge where their army had run into the horde of infected, so the odds were fairly strong that the horde had spread outward in that direction. They might be jammed up under those trees, just as they had been back by the bridge into Georgetown.

Colleen was looking in the other direction, and she was frowning.

"Is something wrong?" asked Hampton.

"I thought I saw something way out over the water, but I think I was just imagining it."

"Where was it?" he asked.

She pointed to the west, and he aimed his binoculars that way. He didn't see anything, but he wasn't going to ignore any possibilities. As it turned out, it was a good thing she drew his attention that way because he saw something that gave him an idea.

"You just helped me figure this out, Colleen. We need time to get a boat motor to start once we get to a boat, right?"

"Did you find a way to buy us some time?"

Hampton handed her the map they had drawn and pointed at a house only two streets away.

"Look at this dock with your binoculars. What kind of boat is that tied to the dock?"

Colleen found the right house with her binoculars and then located the dock.

"It looks like a pontoon boat," she said.

"Exactly, and pontoon boats can be easily floated away from a dock. Lots of room for our gear, too."

"I don't get it," she said. "How does that buy us more time?"

"Look at the next dock in line with the pontoon," he said.

Colleen saw what he was talking about. The fence that separated the two pieces of property ran right down to the water. There was a dock on one side of the fence, and the pontoon boat was tied to it. Tied to the dock on the other side of the fence were two boats. One was a larger pontoon boat with big twin engines. If even one started, they could get underway. The second boat was a bow-rider that was most likely used for water skiing.

She smiled at him and said, "If anything follows us, we just lead them all into that backyard, then we coast over to the other dock and start one of the boats."

"And if they won't start," added Hampton, "we can cross to the other side to one of those boats on the dock directly across from it. The distance between them is short enough for us to just coast across."

"The worst case scenario is that none of the boats start, but at least we'll be on the water, and I see about six more docks between our target and the lake," said Colleen.

She looked at Hampton, and this time he looked like he was thinking of something else.

"Did you hear that?" he asked.

Colleen cocked her head to one side and listened. At first she was going to say she didn't hear anything, but just as she opened her mouth, there it was. She didn't know what she was hearing or where it was coming from, but it sounded like it was getting louder.

"Is that a boat motor?" she asked.

She started scanning the lake trying to spot the boat, and she almost dropped her binoculars when something yellow came flashing into view from the left side. It wasn't on the water, it was above it.

Hampton spotted it, too. He couldn't believe his eyes, but when he recognized the type of plane that was skimming the surface of the lake, he knew why they were able to hear it from so far away. When he had bought his plane, he toyed with the idea of buying a float plane, but he decided there were more runways, roads, and open fields to land on than water. When he had flown with a pilot in a de Havilland Beaver a few years later, he had enjoyed the ride, but he thought he was going to go deaf from the sound of the engine. Now it was a welcome sound.

They both watched as the plane coasted in for a landing about two miles away. It came to a stop in a direct line with the bridge but at a safe distance from land on all sides. That was when Hampton remembered his short-range radio, and it was downstairs.

He bolted for the stairs and only had the time to shout back up to Colleen that he was getting his radio as he made the turn one flight down. She got behind the telescope so she could get a closer view of the plane. The telescope zoomed it in so close that she passed it going too fast to the left then passed it going too far to the right. She held the telescope still for a moment and told herself to wait. Her patience paid off as the plane coasted right into her area of focus. She was looking at the passenger side of the plane, and there was a woman holding a set of binoculars up to her face. She had really long and attractive blond hair. Colleen watched as the blond pulled the binoculars down, and she saw that the woman was every bit as attractive as her hair.

The plane rotated in the water facing straight at Colleen, but it kept turning.

"No," she said out loud. "Too soon, you're turning away too soon."

Colleen knew Hampton would be searching for his radio, but with all the extra gear they had packed, it was going to be harder to find it. She could see the pilot now, and even though he was wearing headphones, she could see the full head of red hair and thick beard. It looked like the pilot's seat was a tight fit for him. He was showing the blonde something, and both of them were smiling.

The plane completed its turn and immediately began picking up speed. She couldn't track it with the telescope, so she switched to the binoculars again. It was just starting to lift off from the water, and Hampton burst into the room with the radio. He was talking into it frantically and looking at Colleen with the hope that she would say the plane was still there.

"Just took off," she said.

He felt like an idiot because he hadn't been prepared. He was supposed to be broadcasting, but he hadn't bothered. A small part of him knew it was because he had been distracted by his feelings for Colleen, but another part of him knew it was because he didn't expect to see anyone.

"Did you get a look at it through the scope?" he asked.

She nodded.

"The pilot was a great big guy with a red beard. I'm not sure I'd want to run into him on a dark night. The passenger was a drop-dead, gorgeous blond."

Colleen couldn't believe how she sounded. She was jealous of a supermodel she saw in an airplane two miles away for about two minutes.

"Chris? Are you okay?" she asked.

Hampton was standing so still he could be a statue. His mouth was open, but he seemed to be unable to speak until she got worried.

"It can't be," he said. "Was the big guy smiling?"

"Now you're scaring me, Chris. How could you guess that he was smiling? As a matter of fact you could see the smile from here."

Hampton felt like laughing, or cheering, or even crying, and maybe all three at the same time.

"Because it seems like the guy is always smiling about something," he said. "Even when things are a bit rocky. It's like he believes everything will be fine in a few minutes."

Colleen couldn't believe what Hampton was saying.

"You know him? Do you know the blonde, too?" she asked. She cringed, hoping it didn't sound as jealous to Hampton as it did to herself.

"That could only have been the Chief and Kathy McGinley," he said. "It's a long story. I'll fill you in when we're on the water. Right now, we need to get moving. Since that's a seaplane, maybe he'll stay near water long enough for us to make contact with him."

With Hampton in the lead they barreled down the stairs fast enough to be hurt if either of them lost their footing. Once they were on the first floor, they took a quick look out every window to see if there was much movement outside, then loaded the gear on their bodies like a couple of pack mules. Their plan was to drop the gear if they got in trouble, but they had it packed based upon expendability. If it was something they could easily replace, it would get dropped first.

The fastest way to get to the house with the pontoon boat docked behind it was to go straight across the street from the front door of their house. They decided to cut across as many backyards as possible for two reasons. First, they would have to be in plain view if they followed the road. The trees were full, but they didn't look like they were impassable. After almost a year of lawn neglect, the grass was tall everywhere, and hedges needed to be trimmed, but there was a lot of underbrush. The second reason was the infected dead tended to take the path of least resistance. They could be seen walking down the streets and across front yards, so it was at least possible there weren't as many in the trees.

Hampton and Colleen had discussed their escape route from high above where they could see who had privacy fences. There were a couple of places where they knew they would have to do some climbing, but both could easily clear the tallest fences. The plan was to have Hampton go over a fence first, check the yard for infected dead, then Colleen would hand over their packs before climbing the fence herself. That would cut down on the noise.

Their goal was a house on a corner lot just one street away, but to get to it they would have to cross in full view of anything walking near the intersection that held the corner lot. Their advantage was that Crown Lake Drive, the main street at the intersection, was curved where it intersected with Bascom Ridge Drive. That meant the field of vision for anything facing their way was blocked by houses and trees along most of the street.

Once they were on the front porch, reality set in. It would be a race combined with an obstacle course. They could only run at a trot because of their gear, but the good news was that the infected couldn't run at all. It seemed strange, considering the number of infected they had seen since moving into the house, but there were none in view from the porch. Then it dawned on Hampton and Colleen at the same time.

"If we could hear the plane, so could they," said Colleen. "Do you suppose they're all moving in that direction?"

"Could be," said Hampton. "Let's be careful not to run so fast that we catch up with any of them."

"I don't think running too fast is going to be a problem," she answered as she waddled down the steps.

Hampton followed her down the steps but got ahead of her as they crossed Val Circle and cut between the first two houses. Both of them had a machete tucked in their belts, courtesy of the owner of the house they had just left. They also had their Glock handguns where they could get to them in a hurry. As they crossed the yards and passed through the trees, they saw that they had underestimated the amount of brush that had accumulated under the trees, but it wasn't dry, so they weren't being noisy. It was slowing them down though, and the weather was warm. They were sweating before they crossed the first backyard.

Hidden among the trees was a privacy fence, and in front of the fence was a small group of the infected dead. Hampton counted five, and he couldn't see any to the left or right. He eased his packs to the ground and waited for Colleen to do the same. They both moved in from behind the group with their machetes and made quick work of them.

"Impressive," he said to Colleen.

She flashed a cute smile his way and said, "You did okay, yourself."

"Okay? I did okay?"

"We can work on your form when we get the chance. Right now we need to get over this fence."

They climbed over as planned with Hampton having to suppress a grin the entire time. He had experienced a sudden epiphany about why the Chief seemed to be smiling all the time. He had thought it was because he had some inner way of coping with all the bad in the world, but Hampton considered the possibility it was the pleasure he found in the company he kept. Hampton was grinning because he was going through this hell with Colleen.

Colleen dropped over the fence and landed next to him. He helped her reload all of her gear, and then she did what she could to help him. She kept looking at him out of the corner of her eye, probably wondering what he was grinning about.

They set off in the direction of the next side of the yard and opposite privacy fence. The good news about privacy fences was that they kept the infected out of the backyards if the gates were closed. The bad news was that there was seldom a privacy fence on just one side of the yard.

When they reached the other side they found more good news. The people who lived in the pair of houses separated by the fence must have liked each other, because there was a gate. A quick peek through the gate showed that it entered into what had once been a stone garden with a small fish pond. There was an infected dead at the edge of the water looking down at a huge fish.

There was no telling how long this infected had been trapped inside the small garden, but judging by the wet clothing, it had fallen into and climbed out of the fish pond many times. It had been an elderly woman in her seventies, and the garden had been hers. Hampton and Colleen would have felt sorry for her if not for the lips pulling back to show blackened gums and stained teeth.

This infected had moved slowly in life, and being dead hadn't made her faster. Hampton stepped forward and gave her a backward shove, and once again the infected was in the pond trying to find a way back out onto dry ground. In the meantime, Hampton and Colleen were going over a low stone wall on the other side of the yard.

They came out of the backyard facing directly across the intersection down Bascom Ridge Drive. About four houses away there were at least a dozen infected dead, and they were moving in the wrong direction. If they kept going where they were headed, they would go straight across the yard of the house with the two boats tied up behind it. Colleen looked up at Hampton.

There was only one thing they could do, and they knew it without discussion. They ran with their heavy loads straight into the middle of the intersection until they were directly in front of the house with the pontoon boat tied up behind it.

They felt naked standing in the middle of the street at the end of the driveway on their left, but even though they were completely exposed, the small horde continued toward the yard that passed between the houses just two driveways away. Hampton looked at Colleen as if to say, "These must be the blind ones."

"Hey," he yelled. "Are you guys stupid or something?"

Colleen muttered next to him, "Stupid is as stupid does."

He couldn't help himself, and if he had any doubts about his earlier epiphany, she had erased them. Her shout out to one of his favorite movies was more than he could stand. Hampton busted out laughing, and Colleen joined in. The small horde of infected dead made a clumsy turn and began walking toward them. He looked at her and started laughing again.

"In a different time and place, you and I are going to eat popcorn and watch that movie until we have every line memorized," he said.

"It's a date, handsome."

When they were sure the infected were going to follow them down the right side of the fence, they ran up the driveway and crossed the front yard to the left side of the house. Going around that side would give them just a little more time to get the pontoon free from its moorings and across the short distance to the next dock.

They got a pleasant surprise when they reached the gravel path that went to the dock. Before going to the pontoon boat, they had to first go up a set of stairs to a party deck, and then down another steep set of steps to the slip where the pontoon boat was tied up. The infected dead have difficulty going up stairs and no problem at all going downstairs. They would take a long time just getting to the party deck, and if they tried to follow down the steeper steps, gravity would take over. Their already fragile bones would probably keep them piled up in a heap far longer than Hampton and Colleen would need.

Hampton was almost out of breath when he reached the top of the stairs, but he reached back and helped Colleen make it up to the top. They gratefully dropped their gear over the other side and then climbed down the steep steps. The infected still had to cross the gravel path and climb the stairs. At a much slower pace they gathered their gear and carried it to the pontoon boat. They jumped onto the wide boat and untied the lines. Since it was moored in a slip with a dock on both sides, they were able to each take a side, get a running start, and then dive into the silently gliding boat.

It didn't take power for the pontoon boat to slide straight to the other dock. Hampton turned the wheel to the rudder just enough for them to coast into position on the opposite side of the dock from the two boats they wanted.

"Why do we have to take both boats, Chris?"

"We don't know how much fuel we're going to need, and we won't know how much fuel we have until we check them out. I hope we find the Chief on the water not far away, but the other side of the lake in the direction they came from is about five miles away."

"They took off in that same direction. Do you think they stayed around?"

"Colleen, to tell you the truth, there can only be one reason why the Chief would even be here. He knows I'm here somewhere. Yes, I think they'll stay around and keep looking for me. That was the first time we heard their plane, so I don't think they've been here too long."

They had just transferred their gear onto the dock and started loading it into the much larger, twin engine pontoon boat when the first of the infected dead showed up at the top of the party deck. As expected, gravity helped it get to the bottom of the steep steps more quickly than it wanted to, and it landed in a heap. We could hear the bones snap from almost thirty yards away. It started to crawl in the direction of the dock, but the second infected appeared above it. It took one long step out into the air and went into a cartwheel straight down on top of the first infected. The sound of breaking bones must have included a broken neck because the second one didn't try to crawl. It just laid there snapping its jaws at nothing.

The rest of them rained down from the party deck and formed a big pile at the bottom of the steps. The last four were able to crawl free of the twisting arms and legs and found a way to stand again. After taking a few steps in random directions, they resumed their pitiful pursuit.

Hampton had already loaded their gear and untied both boats. One part of their plan was to start the boats while still tied to the dock, but the alternate plan was to push both of them away from the dock and then drop anchor. The backyard of the house next door was heavily wooded, and they wouldn't know until it was too late if there were infected dead near the end of the dock where it touched the ground.

Groaning from that direction made the decision for them. Colleen pushed the ski boat free and jumped aboard. She let it coast while she searched for a paddle. As soon as she found it, she gave a few hard strokes on the starboard side to turn the boat toward deeper water and then moved out of Hampton's way as he did the same with the much larger pontoon boat. Both of them were dropping anchor about ten yards into deep water when the infected stumbled onto the dock. There were far more than they had expected.

With no railings on the sides of the wooden docks, they began falling into the water at random places. Some were still in shallow water, and the bottom was firm, so they stood up and tried to reach the boats again.

"Watch your anchor line, Colleen. They won't be able to climb it, but they can grab it."

It was a good thing Hampton warned her. The words had just left his mouth when Colleen's boat began rocking. One of the infected had grabbed the anchor line first and then managed to get one hand onto a side rail. The rocking was enough to sit Colleen on her rear end in the boat, and that made her mad. She started slapping at the hand on the side rail with the paddle until she realized pain wouldn't make it let go. She slipped her machete from her belt and neatly brought the blade down on the fingers. The infected fell backward into the water while three fingers fell into the boat. Colleen made a mental note to make sure she was in a stable position while she checked the engine.

Hampton had told her not to try to start the engine immediately. He told her to find the oil dipstick first to see if the oil was clean and full, then to check the fuel. He had explained there might be a manual pump or primer to help get fuel flowing.

He had watched as Colleen first kept herself from falling in the water, and then as she disposed of the problem. He was glad she was as capable as she had proven herself to be. When he saw that she had positioned herself safely before checking the engine, he turned to do the same with his boat. He was surprised to see an infected dead pulling itself onto the back between the engines and come to a full standing position. For some reason it made him as mad as Colleen had been, and he closed the distance between himself and the infected in one long stride. His foot connected with the middle of the chest, and the soaking wet body was launched through the air. Hampton pulled in his anchor and paddled over to Colleen's boat. Instead of dropping his anchor again, he tied off to her side rail. He wondered if it reassured her as much as it did him.

Now that they were safely away from the dock, they could give all of their attention to starting the engines. It was a good thing they had time to do it, because the infected dead had begun showing up on the far side of the small waterway they had chosen to escape from.

Hampton looked across at the other side and saw over a dozen of the shambling wrecks walking onto the two docks, and it gave him an idea.

"Let's try something," he said.

Colleen turned in the direction he was looking and saw they would have been in serious trouble if they had coasted over to those docks.

"After we get the engines started, we're going to stay in this spot for a few minutes to let the engines start to run smoothly anyway, so let's stay a couple of minutes longer and see how many of them we can draw into the water. If we have to go ashore for any reason, it would be nice to have as many of them in the water as possible."

Hampton didn't know that his acquaintances from Mud Island had done exactly the same thing many times, even next to bridges and docks, but it seemed like a good idea. The water might not kill them, but it sure did help to contain them. He had a random thought about fishing. He had grown up fishing. Now he wasn't too sure he would ever fish again. Not only was he hesitant about what he might hook, but he wasn't sure that fish weren't being contaminated and dangerous to eat.

The noise was beginning to grow. From four docks and all of the spaces in between them, the dead were emerging, and the louder they got, the more that came. It also increased Hampton and Colleen's sense of urgency to get the motors started.

After a few minutes of what most boaters would have called preventive maintenance, they were both ready to give the engines a try. One engine started up on the first try on the large pontoon boat. The second one and the one on the ski boat were just a little more stubborn, but the pair of survivors were forcing themselves to be patient so they wouldn't flood the engines. Besides slowing them down, a flooded engine would be a waste of fuel.

Their patience paid off as the first stubborn engine roared to life, closely followed by the second. Colleen let out a cheer when hers started, and Hampton joined in by giving her a high five. If he had asked her what that felt like to her, he would have been surprised to find that it meant the world to her to be treated as an equal. He made her feel like a contributor and not a liability that had to be protected by him. The truth was that Hampton felt like someone had his back all the time now that Colleen was with him.

With three engines running, they couldn't hear the frenzy of groaning coming from both banks of the inlet. The infected couldn't run, but they seemed to be capable of showing more excitement when they were closer to a loud noise, and there just happened to be two living people standing by the sources of the loud noise. They began trying even harder to get to the water, and they were practically shoulder to shoulder.

Colleen looked at the incredible number of infected that had come out of the shadows of the trees and asked, "Would we have even tried this if we had known there were so many?"

"Good question," answered Hampton. He had to yell over the sound of the engines. "I wonder why there were so many more on this side of the road than the other. We wouldn't have made it this far if there had been so many on the other side."

"Could it have something to do with where people went back when it started?" she asked. "If I had lived here then, I would've tried to reach the water, too."

"Not likely," he said. "First of all, there's water on both sides, and second there's the parade up on I-77. That should have drawn them up toward the highway and the battle at the bridge."

Not that it really mattered to either of them, but the realization came to them both at the same time. They had been right when they thought of it before. The plane hadn't been out on the lake very long, but its powerful engine must have drawn everything that was dead and capable of walking to go in that direction.

"Remind me to thank your friends for being bait even if it was for just a few minutes," said Colleen.

Their mutual smiles were interrupted by the rocking of both boats. They had the sick feeling that comes with an up and down motion at the same time as the rocking, and Hampton reached across to grab Colleen just in time. He unceremoniously pulled her across from the ski boat to the pontoon boat.

The curved hull of the ski boat was designed for speed, but the increased speed meant it sacrificed stability, while the pontoon boat was a slow but stable platform. It made them both understand just how dangerous their new world was as they watched the ski boat rock so violently that it leaned too far to one side and flipped over away from the pontoon boat. If Hampton hadn't seen it coming, there would have been no way Colleen could have survived.

The white underbelly of the ski boat came into full view with the blade of the engine spinning at high speed in the open air. As the boat upended, it dragged several of the infected with it. They were clinging to the centerline of the hull where it had just enough edge for them to hold. The one closest to the engine reached for it to get a better hold, and the result was one less infected hanging on. Its hand didn't slow the engine, but it did start to sputter and come to a stop. The others were all facing away from the pontoon boat, so they turned to look back at Hampton and Colleen. As soon as they did, they let go of the boat and slid back into the water.

The water was becoming thick with bodies, and it was time to push through to open water. Hampton was also afraid they would foul their outboard engines on the infected if there were too many. Judging by the color of the water as the pontoon began creating a small wake, they were making their fair share of contact with bodies. There were also bits and pieces of the infected that made Hampton decide once and for all that fishing was not going to be the sport it used to be. At least it wouldn't be for him.

Progress was slow at first, but they suddenly burst through to open water and began to move more quickly. Hampton looked behind him and saw that Colleen had once again shown quick thinking. She held up one end of the anchor line as if it was a prize and gave him a big, white smile. He wouldn't blame her if she teased him about it later. Driving away with the anchor in the water was like trolling with a really heavy hook, and it undoubtedly had a few of the infected clinging to it.

They passed between two docks that were straight across from each other, and it was the narrowest point they would have to navigate. The infected were falling off of both docks in numbers too large to count, and Hampton was worried again. They didn't have much choice, though, and they could only hope their trip wasn't already over.

The pontoon glided toward the narrow gap, and the docks were both close enough for water to splash on them as the infected dead unsuccessfully tried to bridge the gap between them and their prey. More than once Hampton and Colleen both felt thankful that the infected couldn't jump or apparently judge distance. If they could, the pontoon boat would have been crawling with them.

The two passengers stayed toward the middle of the pontoon boat and anxiously looked to their left and right to see if any hands grabbed one of the side rails. From time to time there was a slapping sound as a hand would hit the shiny metal of the rail, but none were able to get a grip.

As they cleared the dangerous area between the two docks, Hampton moved to the back to take a quick look and saw what had saved them. The area may have been narrow, but it had been much deeper than expected. He could see the shallows over on the port side and guessed the inlet had been purposely given a deep channel to follow. He took the wheel and steered the pontoon boat slightly to starboard where the water was a darker green color.

As they passed the last two docks on their right before reaching open water, Hampton saw the channel make a left turn, so he followed it out into the lake. The pontoon had plenty of room to maneuver, and they found themselves in something like a bay where two similar inlets converged. Hampton spotted three long docks that were much further from shore than the small docks they had used for their escape.

Each dock would require the infected dead to walk along boardwalks that were at least one hundred feet long, so that would give them the time they needed. All three docks had at least three boats docked next to them, so there were nine chances to find what he was looking for.

"Where are we going?" asked Colleen.

"Those docks over there." He pointed in the general direction, and Colleen saw they were all uninhabited at the moment. The infected dead had been drawn away from those docks by all of their noise before leaving the inlet.

"When you had to abandon ship, we lost some of our supplies. At least one of those nine boats is bound to have a bug-out bag in it that didn't get used. Maybe people got their boats loaded but didn't have the time to use them."

"Don't you mean when you pulled my butt out of there before the boat flipped over?" she asked.

"You would have jumped in time, but you would have tried to do it with the supplies. I didn't want to wind up with more supplies but lose you in the process."

Colleen grinned. She knew he had saved her, and if he had yelled to jump instead of grabbing her, she had to admit, she would have tried to grab the supplies first. She also had to admit, she was grinning, smiling, and actually laughing out loud more in the last few days than she had in a long time.

Hampton coasted up to the first dock, and Colleen was quick to jump over the rail. She loosely circled a mooring line around a cleat on the dock and jumped into the first boat. As Hampton had expected, there were supplies. He idled the engine and jumped onto the dock to receive everything she handed over to him. Now that they weren't going to be running on foot, they needed everything they could carry because they weren't going to be able to rely on fish as a food source. Maybe when they knew if fish could be contaminated by the infection they could begin living off of it, but Hampton wasn't going to be the first person to try it.

The first boat yielded two precious commodities. Not only were there extra cases of bottled water, it had extra fuel containers. Four red plastic containers with five gallons of fuel each were going to help them stay on the water much longer than they could have hoped.

They loaded their pontoon boat with everything they could find that was useful then moved to the second boat.

"Want to consider taking a second boat?" asked Colleen.

"No, after what I saw those things do to a curved hull boat, I think we should abandon that idea. We could take a second pontoon boat, but this one seems like it's in good shape. I think we can trust our luck with it."

Colleen was already into the third boat when Hampton saw the infected dead begin filing out onto the long walkway that led to their dock. It would take several minutes for any to reach them, but he decided to help their own cause.

Once again he employed a tactic that was familiar to anyone who had survived to kill their share of the infected dead. He pulled his scoped rifle from its leather case and carefully sighted on the forehead of the infected dead that was leading the others down the center of the walkway. He watched as the bullet knocked the body of the one in front backward hard enough to take down the next three behind it.

"Nice shot," said Colleen. She had stopped to watch, and was amazed at the logjam the shot had caused. Those that didn't fall down couldn't climb over the pile without rolling off into the water on either side. Those that were still coming up from behind were pushing against the logjam and causing it to get bigger. There was little doubt that they would still be trying to get past that same spot by the time Hampton and Colleen were ready to leave.

Hampton smiled at Colleen in time to see her get surprised by an infected dead that had somehow managed to stay stranded within the confines of the third boat since the beginning of the infection. It was so emaciated, that it had most likely been just decaying in that boat the entire time. Hampton was still trying to bring the rifle around and take aim when he saw Colleen fall over on her back.

When the infected dropped forward to claim its victim, Hampton saw her feet connect with the chest of the infected and shoot outward like a piston. The withered body of the infected flew through the air like a rag doll and disappeared into the water.

Her strawberry blonde hair appeared first, then her freckled face. When she sat up a little higher, he couldn't believe she was smiling again.

"Are you okay?" he called.

"If you mean did it bite me, no it didn't. I'm fine. Just make note somewhere that those stupid things can pop up almost anywhere. I'm just glad I did leg presses at the gym when I worked out."

She stood up and inspected herself, more out of habit than the concern that she had missed the bite or didn't feel it. Hampton watched her and for the first time noticed that he had held his breath for a long time, but now his heart was pounding.

Colleen saw that he was still standing there watching her, and she blew him a kiss. Hampton found himself completely wrapped up in her every move, and he had only known her for a short few days.

"Whoa," she yelled. "It must be the main supply ship. Look what I found."

She held up a Glock for him to see and then checked its chamber.

"There's a bag full of these things and boxes of ammunition," she said. "You sure know how to shop, Chris. Every girl should have a boyfriend like you."

Hampton felt like he was back in high school again. He couldn't believe how much it affected him to hear her say he was her boyfriend. At least that was how he took it.

He thought to himself, "I must have really needed to get out more back before this stuff started. Here I am in the middle of something everyone said couldn't happen, and I've got a crush."

He shook himself out of the pleasant but dangerous standstill the thoughts had caused and checked the progress of the infected trying to come down the dock. He saw that they had made no progress at all, but it was a good thing they had found so many supplies in the first three boats because the walkways to the other two docks were becoming populated. It was time to move on.

Colleen made her way back to their pontoon boat, and they loaded the last of the supplies. She untied the mooring line, and Hampton steered them away from the dock. Open water was up ahead, and his hope was they would see the yellow plane within the next couple of hours.

6 ABOVE EVERY SHELTER

As the plane lifted from the water, the Chief thought for one moment he had heard something on the radio. It was only a burst of static, but he had learned in his long years at sea not to ignore the sound of white noise from a radio. There was too often something to be heard.

The Chief adjusted the dial on the radio to be sure it was on the frequency that he had been given by Captain Miller when he learned that Hampton was still alive and broadcasting from the Charlotte area. He listened for a moment, and he could tell Kathy was doing the same. She had placed her headphones over her ears as soon as she saw the Chief react. She looked over at him and met his eyes then gave a slight shake of the head. She wasn't hearing anything in the static.

The Chief brought his eyes back to the view ahead while Kathy gave the dial a few tries, cycling above and below the frequency and then coming back to it. She heard something too, but it was still just noise. Eventually the plane had traveled too far for them to keep trying to hear what might not have even been there, and Kathy started thinking about how the Chief planned to get them into the shelter on Ambassador Island. They could hardly expect to just land at the front door. For one thing, they had to protect the plane, and they wouldn't know if the area at the entrance was occupied without doing more reconnaissance first. Just because they didn't see anything when they circled the island, it didn't mean it was unoccupied.

"What's the plan, Chief?"

"I think we have to take the long way around," he said. "We can't approach the front entrance and expect to avoid being seen. If you were the average survivor, that's what you would defend the most because that's where you would expect other survivors to come from, as well as the infected."

"So, we leave the plane and try to cross the island from that stand of trees that pops up at the southern tip of the island. How do we get from the plane to the island?"

As soon as Kathy asked the question she knew it was an easy answer. She looked over her shoulder into the cargo hold and saw the big square bundle that would inflate into a raft in seconds.

"Okay, so we raft over. Are we going to try to stay out on the water and raft all the way to the entrance, or are we going to just raft to the tip and then cross the island?"

"Do you have a preference?" laughed the Chief.

"You mean between getting shot in the raft or walking the length of an island that's either crawling with infected dead or is occupied by armed survivors? They might call it Ambassador Island, but I don't expect anyone who lives there is looking to make friends."

The Chief smiled just to keep it light, but he knew this was a deadly serious thing they were just about to do. They were going to be exposed in the open, or they were going to be in the middle of an island that could be a death trap.

"If there were four of us on this mission," he began, "I would cover both options, but I'd still be worried that either way was a bad choice. I think our best chance is to take advantage of the daylight for several reasons."

"I'm all ears," said Kathy.

"We have to consider the concern that the Gulf storm has made landfall by now, and it's going to start pushing the fallout cloud in this direction. We may still have some time before that happens, but we just don't know. If we go in during daylight hours, we can't raft the length of the island because we'll be visible for too long, but if we raft up to the tip of the island we'll only be exposed for a short time. Then we can cross the island with the same visibility the opposition will have. If the island is occupied by survivors, we at least stand a chance of getting to cover first. If it's occupied by the infected, all we have to do is stay quiet and out of sight."

"How do you plan to get close to the island in the first place? Anyone on the island can hear this thing coming."

Kathy had been so caught up in the Chief's plan that she didn't notice he had changed his direction of approach to Ambassador Island. Just as she asked her question, he began descending and she saw that he was coming down on the water in a straight line with another island that was slightly larger than the one with the trees they planned to use as cover. They had approached at such a low angle that they were invisible to Ambassador Island.

"I spotted this island on the way over to the other side of the lake. It's less than fifty yards from the sandbar that leads to that stand of trees. If anyone hears us right now, they can't figure out where the sound is coming from. After we cut off the engine, they're going to listen for a while, and they're going to be on heightened alert, but by the time we need to cross the last piece of water, they will have forgotten about us."

The Chief expertly sat the plane down on the water in a whisper smooth landing, and since the water wasn't like a river or the ocean, there was almost no resistance that would make noise. He cut the engine while they were in a perfect glide straight to the island where they could hide the plane, and at just the right moment he turned the wheel on the steering column to make the plane slide sideways the last few feet. The sideways slide put them at exactly the right spot.

Kathy had watched as her side of the plane drew closer to the trees. She didn't think there was ten feet of space between the wingtip and the trees that reached out over the water. She had seen him do some skillful flying in the past, and had even seen him survive a terrible crash landing in the Charleston harbor, but this landing was as smooth as parking a car.

"We need to drift a few feet back away from the trees and then get a good anchor in the water. We can't have the wind pushing us up to the trees and getting a bent wing," said the Chief.

They could feel the plane starting to drift, and when the Chief felt like it was far enough, both of them opened their doors and dropped anchors. With one anchor from each side, the plane would stay in one spot and wasn't going to rotate with the direction of the wind. Kathy immediately climbed into the back of the plane and dragged the raft to the door.

It didn't take three minutes for them to have the raft in the water, and they were loading it within four. Unlike the bright yellow or orange rafts they were used to, this one was a dark green color that matched the color of the water. When the Chief loaded the plane, he apparently felt like he wasn't going to want the raft to be seen from a distance. This was a covert mission from the start, but Kathy was surprised by how quiet and serene it was on the lake.

"Only weapons, ammunition, and water," said the Chief. "We're not staying any longer than we have to. I'd like to get inside, find whatever tech there is that will help us to locate Hampton, and then get back out."

"Are you that sure we'll be able to find him, Chief?"

"According to Bus, the guy who had this shelter tailored to his own personal needs was really into his high tech detection equipment. If he lived, and if he's in there right now, he not only knows we're here, he knows where Hampton is."

"If he knows we're here, how would he know that we're friendly?" asked Kathy.

"The biggest problem is getting to the front door, but if we can get there and get it open, I don't think he's going to shoot us without warning. First of all, he will want to know how we knew the combination, and second of all, you're going in first. Who would shoot a beautiful blond?"

Kathy looked at him to see if he was kidding and saw that he wasn't. She started to object, but reconsidered. It made sense. To accent the point that no red blooded male would shoot her without warning, she pulled the rubber band from her ponytail and let her hair fall over her shoulders.

The Chief said, "Works for me. I wouldn't shoot you."

Kathy tried not to smile, but it was a losing battle. She dropped from the plane into the raft with the Chief close behind her, and they started paddling around the left side of the island. If they were correct, they would be out in the open for at least one hundred yards, but they would be blocked from view by the trees on the island closer to Ambassador Island.

"Stay low in the raft and use long, slow strokes when we paddle. That way no one will spot us because of motion. Sometimes it's movement that looks out of place even if you're practically invisible," said the Chief.

Kathy knew that the Chief's SEAL training was what would get them through this, and that she wouldn't want to have someone as skilled as him sneaking up on her. She remembered the story about how he became known as The Bear of Kodiak Island when he had braved freezing cold water without a weapon to overcome North Korean soldiers. If he got them onto the island, she had no doubt he would get them into the safety of the shelter.

They covered the distance over the open water much faster than she would have expected, but with the Chief's powerful strokes, they didn't need a motor to do it. They came up on the left side of the long sandbar, and the closer they were to the stand of trees on the small island the less chance there was that they would be seen. When they beached the raft behind the trees they laid down in the bottom and just listened for anything that would indicate they had been spotted.

The Chief moved forward and tapped her on the shoulder.

"Let's move," he said in a voice barely above a whisper.

They climbed out of the raft and slipped in among the trees. They found that the small island was more densely overgrown than they had expected. It made for slower movement through to the other side, but it also meant there was less chance for them to be seen.

"Watch out for snakes," whispered the Chief.

Kathy looked down at her feet and saw that she could barely tell where they were.

She moved into position directly behind the Chief and whispered back, "You watch out for snakes."

Despite the dense brush and tightly packed trees, they were through to the other side in minutes. The last few yards they crawled to the edge of the trees, and both pulled out their binoculars.

It had been a beautiful community. That much was obvious despite the overgrown yards and random bits of debris. The homes were huge, rambling structures that could only have been affordable to people used to the best of everything. In the end, money wasn't going to save them if they didn't have a plan for what happened, and from what they had seen, there were only about thirty-two people who had really been prepared.

The house nearest to them didn't look like it had even been touched by the end of civilization. Other than the neglected landscaping, there were no bodies, no broken windows or doors, and looked otherwise undisturbed.

"I don't know if it's good news or bad news for it to look so empty over there, but we can't wait around here all day."

"I'm going in, Kathy. You stay here and keep watching all three houses that are within our direct line of sight. If I was going to guard the island from the houses, I would have someone in that house on the right. So, pay more attention to it."

The chief pointed at the biggest house. It was also positioned so that it had an unobstructed view of over two hundred and seventy degrees of arc. The only thing that blocked any of the view was the house to the left. The Chief pointed at it next.

"To cover the rest of the island on this end, keep your eyes on the left side of that house. It has some windows up high. Whoever would be watching from up there wouldn't be watching this side of the island as much as he would the big open area to the east." The Chief pointed at a wide open field that led straight to the heart of the island.

"For some reason I'll never be able to explain, people on watch keep closer tabs on places without much cover. Unless we were doing a frontal assault with a few hundred soldiers, I would never take an assault team through there."

Kathy listened without interrupting because she knew the Chief was one of the best the military had ever trained. In her mind, she would be more afraid for anyone on the island than she was for him. Then a thought occurred to her.

"Chief, we haven't seen many good people in our travels, but what if that's what you find? What if there are real survivors on this island with women and children? I mean, all they might be doing is the same thing we are, staying alive."

He thought it over for a minute, and he knew she was right. There were other people who deserved to live too, but they were hardly in a position to do interviews. He was just about to answer when he saw movement across that wide open area. He raised his binoculars in time to see a slow moving vehicle drive by the first house on the left and disappear behind the trees in front of the second house. It was a pickup truck, and it looked like it had at least six armed men and women in the back of it.

"Friendly or not," he said, "this is not going to be easy."

He told Kathy what he had seen, and her only feeling was that they needed to rethink their plan. The Chief wasn't convinced.

He said, "Numbers was never the real issue, Kathy. One thing about them having numbers that may have escaped your attention, and that's the obvious lack of infected walking around. They must have cleared the island."

She saw something in the way he said it that she found hard to believe. The Chief really didn't believe he could lose. She wondered briefly if he was a fan of Star Trek.

He continued, "I just don't know if they should be treated like friendlies or enemies."

"Sorry I brought it up, Chief."

He chuckled a bit and said, "Well, I'm glad you did, and we don't have the right to kill everyone we meet. Even if they're bad guys, they're only in our way. They haven't done anything to us, at least not yet. Now we just have to find a way past them."

They were both quiet for a few minutes while the Chief studied the houses. When he sat up and started taking off his clothes, Kathy knew he had a plan.

"Want to share the plan with me, Chief?"

"Okay, I'm going to go conduct a little interview. I'll let you know if they are good guys or bad guys."

******

Kathy watched the Chief slide gracefully from the trees directly into the water. There was hardly a ripple despite his massive frame. All he told her before going was to stay where she was until she got a signal from him, and that he was going to go for the middle house instead of the biggest one on the right. If someone was on watch from there, he would find out if they were dangerous.

From time to time she saw bubbles appear along the path he had taken, and she worried that those bubbles were from him or something else. They had seen enough of the infected dead on the bottom of lakes to know they could be down there. Fortunately, Lake Norman was big enough that you weren't likely to run into one every few feet.

She spotted something in the water not far from shore and then saw it disappear again. She wasn't sure, but she thought it might be the Chief getting his bearings.

There was a really large dock connected to the house he was going to. It was shaped like the letter H, and it was turned sideways to the shoreline so that either open side could be used as a slip. Boats were moored in each slip, and she wasn't surprised when she saw the Chief surface for a second time at the stern of the boat on the left. Using it for cover, he was able to climb out of the water and sprint to the cover of the trees directly below the windows he had pointed to earlier. There were no gunshots or warning shouts, so Kathy hoped that meant he hadn't been spotted. From there she didn't know where he went.

******

The Chief always went into a different state of mind when his training kicked in. Every sound was important. Everything that moved needed his attention. What he heard first was a woman's voice, and it came from where he wanted to go.

147

He had decided that the back of the house would be more heavily guarded than the front, so he stayed against the wall directly below the windows and headed inland. He knew Kathy wouldn't be able to see him, but no one else would, either.

The side of the house was over two hundred feet long, and judging by the overall shape of the house, it was his guess that it was the garage. The windows above it were probably a furnished guest house. Luckily for him, the side of the house had trees all the way to the front, so he was able to get close enough to hear the voices, and he settled in to listen for as long as he could.

The woman's voice was the closest to him, and the Chief didn't like what he heard. He had been perfectly content with the idea that he and Kathy could help them to survive what he knew was coming their way, but they didn't sound like they would do the same for him.

"The front gate will be opened in about an hour," said the female.

A gravel throated male replied, "How many are going?"

"About twenty this time. The community the scouts found is big, but they don't look like they can handle a real fight. We should be able to take them without losing anybody."

"You going, and what about that plane that buzzed us a while ago?" asked the gravel voice.

"Sure I'm going. I haven't had a moving target to shoot since we cleared the island, and I missed my chance with that plane. I need to kill something."

"That wasn't what I meant. What if they come back? With you guys raiding that settlement, that won't leave but six of us back here while you're gone."

"You afraid of the meatheads?" she laughed. "Don't worry about it. If they land, it'll be like shooting a duck on a pond. You can't miss a plane sitting on water."

Before he could answer, the Chief had eased back away from the front of the house and settled in to wait. There was no way to let Kathy know he would make his move in about an hour, but he knew she would stay where she was until the right time.

From where the Chief was hiding, he gauged the position of the sun against a tree, and was sure the hour had passed. He saw three pickup trucks come around the curve of the one road that seemed to circle the island. They stopped in front of the house and waited. A quick look around the corner was all the Chief needed to see they were getting ready to leave. The fourth pickup truck, the one he and Kathy had seen earlier, started its engine and got in line behind the others. The procession pulled away, and the area was quiet again.

If the front gate was only opened for a group to leave and then return, the Chief reasoned that it was guarded but not heavily fortified. He knew he would have to move quickly, but he was also sure the place they were going to raid had to be far enough away from him to have the time he needed. Six was a very manageable number to him.

He moved back along the wall to the place where he had listened to the conversation and looked around the corner. A heavy and greasy looking man was standing with his back to the Chief smoking a cigarette. He had what appeared to be a vintage AK-47 slung over one shoulder. The Chief could smell him from a distance and wondered why anyone didn't bother to clean himself if he at least had a roof over his head.

The Chief slipped a knife from the waistband of his shorts and stepped up behind the man.

Sometimes you don't hear anything. You just know someone is there, and the man turned around to find his face level with a huge chest. He looked up at the Chief, and then the lights went out.

The Chief pulled the man into the bushes taking the automatic rifle with him, and then went quietly through the door in the end of the garage. Just as he expected, there were five cars lined up in a row. Four were classics, and the fifth was an SUV. He went to the SUV first and pulled the key out of the ignition. He didn't want it to leave without him. There was a set of stairs that disappeared to the floor above, and he moved toward them next.

If there really were only six people left to guard the island, he reasoned that two or more would be at the front gate. That meant there would be at least one more in this house and maybe two next door.

There was a landing at the top of the stairs, so the Chief was able to see into the door of the large room above the garage without the lone guard at the window realizing he wasn't alone. It was still too far away for him to just walk up to the man the way he had outside, so the Chief went down into something close to a sprinter's stance and charged.

The man at the window felt the floor vibrate and looked at his feet first. That gave the Chief the extra seconds he needed. When the man looked up again, all he saw was something blocking his view and getting closer. When the Chief hit him, the impact made a sickening sound because of the number of bones that broke. He was unconscious but not dead, so the Chief finished it.

He went over to the window and lifted it open. When he leaned out, he saw that the man on watch would have seen him if he had been paying attention earlier. Then again, the greasy guy downstairs may have been on watch when he came over from the island. That would explain why he hadn't been spotted.

There was a pair of binoculars on the window sill, and the Chief used them to spot Kathy. She had been watching the window, so she moved into view just enough for him to see her without exposing herself to the larger building. Using hand signals they had used before, he signaled that there were two more bad guys, and then there was a signal that she interpreted to mean ten more minutes. She bagged their equipment into a bundle and got ready to go across.

The Chief wasn't used to making mistakes. He was used to figuring things out and then letting luck be on his side. When his plane was hit by several bullets from a Cuban gunboat, he had crashed into Charleston harbor, and luck had been on his side. He and his passenger, Allison, had both survived the crash. He was still not over the fact that he hadn't been able to protect Allison until they had escaped from the infested city of Charleston. He couldn't get past the fact that he had made a mistake that cost Allison her life. Now, he was getting a bad feeling about Ambassadors Island. Something felt wrong.

He went back down the stairs to the first floor of the garage and found the door that connected the garage to the main part of the house. If he was right, there would be two more people in the house, but something was making him feel like he had missed an important detail. He thought to himself that maybe it just wasn't what he would have done if he was trying to guard the island. Four people at one end and two at the other end just wasn't enough.

The Chief suddenly felt like the missing detail was right in front of him, but he couldn't quite put his finger on it. He started to back away from the door so he could signal Kathy to stay where she was, but as he backed away, the door opened. The man that stepped through the door already had his rifle pointed in front of him in the general direction of the Chief, so he needed to react fast.

Training kicked in again, and the Chief was a half second ahead of the man. He brought his left foot up in a kick that deflected the weapon as it fired, and the bullet went into the ceiling of the garage. His right fist hammered into the lower jaw of the man, and he fell into a heap on the floor. There was nothing the Chief could do about the gunshot, so he quickly used his knife to keep the unconscious man from being a problem, and then he ducked behind the nearest car inside the garage.

Kathy heard the gunshot and knew it wasn't a good sign. The Chief would never give away the element of surprise, much less his position. It could only have been someone shooting at him. The ten minutes weren't up yet, but her instincts were not cooperative with the idea of sitting still and waiting. She dove into the water and started to swim the short distance from her hiding place to the dock.

When the Chief heard the door open again, he was watching from beneath a deep blue Mercedes. He expected to see feet coming carefully into the garage, and he was hoping it would only be one. The first pair of feet came through the door, and they were closely followed by a second and third pair. Then he saw the detail he had been missing. The feet weren't moving like an armed man trying to sneak up on someone. They were shuffling and scraping across the floor of the garage. As soon as they were away from the door, three more pairs of feet appeared. There were now six infected dead in the garage with him.

The Chief never doubted he could handle six infected dead, but he knew that somewhere there was a living person who had let them into the garage with him. He began working his way back toward the door that he had used to enter the garage, but he was also sure the way he would do it if he was the guard would be to cover that door. The Chief didn't have a choice. The infected were between him and the door to the house, and even if he made it by them, he didn't know what would be waiting for him inside. At least he felt like he should only be faced with one guard outside, but he also was worried about getting shot.

While the Chief was weighing his options, the guard that had opened the door to allow the infected to enter the garage started circling the front of the house. He knew that someone had taken out at least two of his three friends, and it wasn't long before he was in a position where he could see the greasy guy that had been guarding the side door to the garage. It was no surprise to him that someone had taken out that idiot, but there was nothing to indicate how many people had gotten by him.

He decided to wait for the meatheads to do their job and flush out whoever was inside the garage. If the intruders didn't come back out through the side door, he knew they would get a nasty surprise if they tried to go in through the house. He had left at least twelve more meatheads trapped inside the first room, and there were almost as many on the other side of every adjoining door. Whoever was in there would have to deal with about thirty sets of snapping teeth.

The door moved just enough for him to know someone was going to come out. Whoever it was, they were being careful, so they must have guessed the door was being covered by now. The small, dark gap got just a little wider, so he raised his rifle and sighted on the dark line that grew slowly as the door opened. The guard knew it wasn't likely that someone would come out standing upright, so he waited patiently for the intruder to show himself. Whoever it was, they had to be dangerous if they had taken out three guards.

The Chief didn't want to just stick his head outside as he eased the door open, but he was running out of options. He had considered opening the door and then sliding under the car parked closest to the door, hoping the infected would be attracted to the daylight outside. When he studied the car he was hiding behind, he decided he didn't have the time to jack up the car and slide under it. The car hugged the ground so closely he doubted that a kid could slide under it. He also knew that whoever was waiting out there, if there was anyone at all, they might be fooled into shooting one of the infected, but not all of them.

So far the infected hadn't noticed the door being opened, but the Chief knew they would see it move when he went out, so he couldn't take his time. He would just have to hope for luck to be on his side as he made a dash for cover. He slipped his fingers back around the lower part of the door and started to pull it open. He heard the infected begin to groan when they saw the shaft of light become wider.

Outside the guard could just make out the shape of someone in the door. As he expected, the shape was lower than a standing position, so he lowered his sights until he was sure he was targeting the head, and his finger began to squeeze the trigger.

He didn't understand what he was feeling. He only knew that his finger wasn't squeezing the trigger the way it should. As a matter of fact, for a split second he couldn't feel the rifle in his hands, and his arms looked like they belonged to someone else because he couldn't feel them at all. He didn't know that's what it feels like when your spinal cord is severed at the neck, and he didn't know that a knife had gone through his neck until it poked out in front. Then he didn't know anything at all.

Kathy pulled the blade back out of the man's neck and then reinserted it a few inches higher. She didn't know if the Chief would come out shooting, so she ducked down and waited. Only a split second later he dove from the door and rolled into hiding behind a tree. It was fast, but she knew it wouldn't have been fast enough, and he didn't have time to pull the door shut behind him.

The first of the infected dead came through the door with the others strung out in a line behind it. Kathy had position and the right angle to the Chief that made her believe he would have time to think before he pulled a trigger, so she calmly step from her hiding place with her machete in clear view.

The Chief had been trained to detect different types of movement. There was darting movement and careful, deliberate movement. It was Kathy's careful deliberate movement that gave him the time to think before reacting, and instead of raising the rifle he had acquired in her direction, he pulled out his own knife and moved along with her toward the door.

Kathy used her machete to slice the back of the first infected's leg right at the knee. It fell over on its side and would be no concern until the rest were dealt with. She let her arm swing with a forehand as soon as it had passed through the leg, and the blade got the second one just below the chin. It fell over backward with the head hanging between its shoulder blades. The Chief stepped in from her right side and used his knife to end the miserable existence of each infected dead as Kathy moved forward. It was over in a matter of seconds.

"Do you know how glad I am to see you?" he said.

"I can imagine," she said. "How did you wind up in there with those things and a live one out here waiting for you?"

The Chief looked over at the bushes where Kathy had emerged and saw the body of a man, and he was stretched out on top of a scoped hunting rifle.

"I guess I was having a bad day," said the Chief, "and from the looks of things, it was just about to get a lot worse. I'll tell you the story when we get a chance to debrief, but for now I think we need to find a safe spot to hide and figure out our next move. Something isn't right, and I'm beginning to get an idea of what it might be."

"Give me the highlights, Chief."

He considered for a moment and knew she was right. What had been tickling at the back of his brain was a warning, and she was better off knowing what it was.

"The shelters always have a plan for the surface, right?"

"Yes," she said. "The shelter on Mud Island has a dock with a houseboat, Fort Sumter has the fort, Guntersville has a village above it..."

Kathy trailed off as the realization came to her. Ambassadors Island had two dozen houses on the surface above the shelter, and they were unprotected by the walls of a fort or the village above the Guntersville shelter. The shelter on the oil rig had the entire Gulf of Mexico around it, and it was hard as hell to climb even if someone reached it by boat. The Mud Island shelter had a moat on one side that was deep, and the current was so swift that anything that walked into it got sucked out to sea through the southern exit.

From where the Chief and Kathy were standing, they could see there was one road on Ambassadors Island. It ran in a long, ragged oval from one end of the island to the other as it circled past incredibly large and beautiful homes. Both of them wondered what kept the island from being overrun with people who had survived the infection.

"Is there another layer of protection?" asked Kathy.

"There must be, and whatever it is, the people who control this place must know about it if they can go off and leave so few people to guard it."

"Where did the people go, and that story you were going to tell me later, Chief, could it have anything to do with another layer of protection? That guy was drawing a bead on you, so he must've known you were stuck in there with the infected, and that means he knew where you were going to come out."

The Chief ran a hand across his beard and turned in a circle taking in the view.

Kathy watched him and asked, "Looking for a realtor's phone number?"

"Cute," he said. "What do you want to bet every house is occupied by infected dead except the ones where the goons live who control the island?"

Kathy said, "Do the math. Six or ten infected in each house, maybe more depending on how many they caught. At least twenty houses filled with them so anyone who sneaks onto the island gets a nasty surprise. Everywhere a survivor goes, they run into teeth. There are probably between one fifty and two hundred infected inside the houses."

The Chief said, "Look at the driveways. Almost every car is outside. I'm going to bet the houses the current residents occupy have the cars inside the garages, but they keep some infected in rooms attached to the garages just in case someone gets inside. The rest of the houses probably have the garages packed with the infected."

Kathy said, "Okay, my estimate might be low. We could be on an island with about three to four hundred infected dead?"

"Or more," said the Chief.

"We need to move fast, Chief, but I have a problem with our plan."

The Chief didn't ask. He just waited for Kathy to tell him.

"So what if we get inside the shelter? So what if we get lucky and actually locate Hampton? If we're still inside when those people get back, how are we getting back to the plane to go collect Hampton? I know this shelter is going to have escape hatches, but just like Fort Sumter, I'll bet they pop up right in the middle of a garage packed with the infected."

It wasn't like Kathy to whine or even sound negative, but the Chief knew she was right.

"You left off the part about communicating with Hampton. This shelter is supposed to be really equipped with the best technology, but I doubt Hampton got the memo. There's no way to know what he's able to do. Hell, he might be able to hear us but not be able to answer, or we might hear him broadcasting, but he might not be able to hear our answer. In other words, we have to try."

Kathy was stuck for a moment. She might have been right about what she said, but the Chief was right, too. If she had whined as much back when the infected first swept across Charleston, thousands of people would not have even made it as far as they did. Because of her efforts on that first day, thousands had lived, and it was all because she had to at least try.

"Chief, the next time I start crying like a baby, please spank me."

He looked like he was going to say something but thought better of it. She saw the pause and said, "Don't say it."

******

The pontoon boat was top-of-the-line, and it made good time across the lake. Hampton wasn't surprised to find charts and maps of Lake Norman in a water-tight compartment on the steering console. He studied them as Colleen steered and spotted more than one good place where they should be able to drop anchor out of sight. If they didn't find the Chief during the daylight hours, he didn't expect the Chief to waste fuel by searching the lake at night. Hampton was especially interested in some of the small, uninhabited islands that dotted the lake.

They could drop anchor behind one that had deep water around it and sleep in the boat. Some of the islands had shallow sand bars around them that he found to be just a little too convenient for the infected to walk on. He didn't plan to park near any of them and have the infected walking right out of the water to their boat. He felt the same way about camping on an island. He didn't plan to get bitten after making it this far, and now that he knew Colleen he was going to be even more careful.

He held up the map where she could see it better and asked, "Do you see any landmarks on shore that would tell you we're anywhere near this island?"

Colleen looked at the spot he was showing her and then at the parts of the map around it. They had just passed a trio of larger islands that weren't developed, and she had wondered why no one had bothered. On the map she was sure she was seeing those same islands. She pointed at the largest of the three.

"Isn't this that island back there to the left of the stern?"

Hampton turned around quickly to catch a look.

"You are so good at this. Do you even need me along for protection?"

"No," she said. "I can take care of myself. I just need you along to help keep up the morale."

She gave him a cute little wink, and he couldn't believe it. She could actually make him blush.

As much as he wanted to continue with the current line of discussion, he had to focus on where they were. He studied the map west of the trio of islands and then compared it to what he could see. There was a long, narrow finger of land with a road down the middle of it. It wasn't as wide as most developed areas around the lake, so it only had a row of houses on one side of the road.

The finger of land almost seemed to be pointing at an island straight out from the end of the road. When he looked straight down their bow, he could see they were heading right for it. As if to confirm it was the same island, he could see something to the right of the island that looked like rocks with trees growing out of them. He hadn't seen anything else like it, so it had to be where they were.

For some reason, knowing where they were on the lake made him feel better. Maybe it was because they had at least accomplished something. The attempt by the armed survivors to march straight through the infected all the way to the mountains may have seemed like a good idea at the time, but maybe the failure had taught them to take baby steps.

Hampton told Colleen to steer straight for the island up ahead, and then to pass it on the right. He wanted to get a better look at the rocks that were sticking out of the water because they appeared to be uncommon in the lake. It also would help him to spot the next island that was going to be their landmark as they turned to the north. The main orientation of Lake Norman was north and south, so they needed to travel in that direction. It seemed logical to him that the Chief would follow a north to south search pattern.

They were passing between the island they had used as a landmark and the finger of land, and Hampton was studying the unusual rocks with binoculars when Colleen said something he didn't quite catch.

He didn't lower his binoculars but asked her to repeat it.

"I don't believe it," she said.

"You don't believe what?" he asked.

He lowered the binoculars and saw she was looking straight ahead, so he turned in that direction.

"I don't believe it," he said.

About two hundred yards ahead of them was the island he had picked as their turning point. It also had deep water on one side with no sand bars, so it would be a safe place to anchor. What they both found hard to believe was the bright yellow seaplane that was already parked there.

Hampton didn't have to say a word to Colleen. He felt the bow rise slightly as she increased their forward speed. He already had his binoculars trained on the plane, and he could see there were two anchor lines in the water. To him that meant the plane was supposed to stay put for a while, but it felt like they couldn't get there fast enough.

Before they even got to the plane Hampton and Colleen both knew there was no one around. Hampton told Colleen that the Chief would have done something to disable the plane so no one could steal it, and he had most likely done the same to the radio. If someone found the plane, they wouldn't know how to fly it, but the radio was worth something if it worked.

"Where are they?" asked Colleen.

"I don't know for sure, but I have an idea which way they went."

Hampton was using his binoculars to get a closer look at the next island. It was hardly more than a place to grow a few trees, but beyond it was a much larger island with huge homes on it.

"The sand bar by that small island over there has footprints on it. I think they parked the plane behind this island and then swam over there."

The words had barely left his mouth when he spotted the camouflaged raft that had been dragged into the trees.

"Forget what I said about swimming over to the island. They came prepared for anything."

Colleen came up beside him with the map of the lake in front of her.

"That has to be Ambassadors Island. On the map it shows that it's one of the biggest islands, and it's connected to the mainland by a bridge. Look at the sizes of those houses."

"I was just thinking the same thing," he said. "Lawyers, stockbrokers, and doctors weren't rich enough to live there."

"My guess would be movie stars and people born into old money," she said. "So, what would make your friends go over there? Did they figure you would try to hole up in a nice place?"

Hampton laughed. "No, they hid the plane first, so they must have spotted something worth investigating. Whatever it was, we can't just go busting up in there, or we might give them away."

"Are we going to just wait here?"

Hampton grinned at her and asked, "Do either of us think that's the best thing to do?"

"I'm glad you feel that way, Chris. I've never been the kind of girl who likes to wait around for someone."

"I'll keep that in mind," said Hampton as he started up the engines and began to steer around the island.

He kept the pontoon boat moving in the general direction of the small island. For some reason he felt like it was a good idea to stay behind the stand of trees that partially blocked the view of Ambassadors Island. He couldn't do anything about the sound of their engines, but they weren't as loud as some.

When they reached the sand bar, he gave it just enough room to keep from running the boat aground, but he was able to get close enough to confirm the impressions in the sand were from at least two people. If they used the raft he wondered why they would have walked onto the sand bar. One set of prints were made by someone big. If the prints were made by an infected dead, he didn't want to meet that one.

Hampton gave the engines a little more power and began circling the small island on the left side. The sand bar extended too far to the right for them to go around, and they would make it to the dock of the nearest house faster on the left. As soon as they rounded the corner, they could see they were no more than twenty or thirty yards from a dock.

"This house first?" asked Colleen.

"It's as good as any place to start," said Hampton. "I don't really like that wide open clearing to the right. There are second floor windows on the first house on that side where someone could shoot from and not miss. The sooner we get behind cover the better."

******

As the Chief got dressed, he filled Kathy in on the rest of the details about the people who were the current residents of Ambassadors Island, and she didn't like what she heard. They sounded ruthless, and they were surviving by killing other survivors.

"So, we pass any house with the cars parked in the driveway, and we use as much cover as possible going by houses with no cars in the driveway because they might be occupied," said Kathy as she was retrieving their gear from the bushes.

The Chief didn't answer immediately, so she looked over at him to see if he was listening. She saw he was looking at one of the high resolution photographs of Ambassadors Island. Their shelter on Mud Island had the satellite photographs of all thirty-two shelters, and the Chief had managed to sneak it past everyone when he tried to leave the shelter without explaining where he was going.

"Chief?"

"We're short on time, so let's go straight down the middle of the island. That way we stay under cover until we get to the front gates and be able to spot the two remaining guards. The last thing they would expect is for someone to come up on them from behind. They're going to be busy watching the road."

The Chief passed the satellite picture over to Kathy so she could get a quick look. The picture was so detailed and so clear that she involuntarily glanced up at the sky. The picture showed that the center of the island was like Central Park in New York. There was some privacy, but it was obvious that the middle of the island was for picnics, walking dogs, and social functions. There was a small boat trailer park toward the middle of the wooded area and something that could be an outdoor theater for live acting and small bands.

Kathy handed the picture back to the Chief and said, "There doesn't look like anybody was planning to build a house in the middle of the island. I guess it was considered common property."

"I forgot I had this with me," said the Chief. "I wish I had talked with Bus about the locations of the emergency entrances and exits."

"You were too busy being a jerk."

The Chief was not someone people tended to insult. If they did, he ignored them because he didn't feel like he had anything to prove. When Kathy said he had been a jerk, he felt genuinely scolded and looked at his feet.

"I thought I said I was sorry for that."

"You did, but I was just pointing out why you didn't talk with Bus about the entrances and exits."

When the Chief looked up from his feet he saw she was just having fun with him. She smiled, and he stood just a little straighter. It amazed him sometimes how close they had become in less than a year.

"Let's get moving," he said.

They set off at a fast pace because they didn't expect to run into any infected or the guards until they reached the front gates. Then they would deal with whatever was there. They could see the houses on either side of them through the trees, but the shade was good cover, and it didn't look like anyone would see them even if they were watching.

Most of the houses had several cars in the driveway. The Chief noticed they were parked in single file and not too close to the garage doors.

"The garage doors must be easy to open and have counterweights on them. That way when someone makes the mistake of opening one of them, the infected can get out before the doors can be closed again."

Kathy knew the Chief was thinking back to the day when they had made the mistake of opening a door that had counterweights on it. Once the door started to go up, there was no stopping it, and inside were some of the meanest dogs she had ever seen. After the dogs had been dealt with, then came a steady parade of infected dead. Kathy swore she would never open another garage door without knowing what was inside first.

"Should we at least check to see if our theory is correct?" she asked as they jogged through the trees.

"Maybe if we have a chance on the way out of here, but we've already lost a lot of time. That raiding party could be back any minute."

"You never did completely fill me in on all of this, Chief. The people who control this island don't sound like they would be much of a match for us if we wanted to put a stop to them."

"To tell the truth, I don't know how bad they are," he said. "I imagine anyone who raids other survivor camps is not someone I would help, but I think our best bet is to find Hampton and clear out of here. We can always come back with some of Captain Miller's men, but remember we also have the radioactive fallout to consider. We need to be out of here before the storm pushes the cloud this way, or we're going to be stuck here for a few years."

Kathy had forgotten about the fallout. Not completely, but she had pushed it to a back burner in her mind. Remembering it and knowing that it meant they couldn't go home to Mud Island if it got to them before they could leave made her run just a little bit faster.

They passed unseen by house after house, but they were always aware that this had been an affluent community, and rich people had some good security. There was nothing to indicate there was electricity anywhere on Ambassador Island, but all it took was one hidden camera. Their own island was covered with cameras, but of course they were controlling them from an underground shelter. If there were cameras here, they were only being used if the shelter below the houses was occupied.

"Chief," whispered Kathy.

She had stopped and then stepped sideways behind a tree. The Chief instinctively did the same. He didn't know if Kathy saw something, but he trusted her.

He looked back at the tree where Kathy was hiding, and he saw her lower her body to the ground. He waited for her to peer around the tree until she could use a hand to signal. She gave him their gestures that indicated she saw someone ahead about twenty yards away, but she also gave him a gesture that said she heard something behind them. The Chief listened carefully, shutting his eyes and absorbing every little sound. He was sure he heard a boat motor. It was coming from somewhere behind them, but it was also far away. That wouldn't be his first concern.

The Chief gave Kathy some gestures that asked if she had eyes on whoever it was she saw up ahead. She took a quick look and then gave him a nod. She held up one finger and then put her hand on the back of her head.

They didn't have a signal like that. The Chief thought over the possible meanings and besides some fairly ridiculous interpretations he reasoned that she meant he was facing away from them.

As if to accent the point, Kathy leaned into the open and putting her thumb to her nose with her fingers pointed upward, she wiggled her fingers.

The Chief remembered that Bus had given him the same salute when he had flown the de Havilland Beaver over his boat. Obviously, Kathy was doing it at someone's back. The Chief leaned around his tree slowly and could see a man standing on a slight rise where the trees ended. There was clear space beyond him, which meant they were either at the little outdoor theater or the boat parking lot.

One other thing he noticed was the smell. The Chief had been around the infected dead enough to know that smell. He pointed at his nose first, then he pointed at his ears and motioned to Kathy that he was confused. A simple shrug of the shoulders did the trick.

Kathy lifted her head and inhaled deeply through her nose. She thought she was going to retch before she could stop herself. It smelled beyond rotten up ahead, and she understood what the Chief had meant. If you could smell them, you could usually hear them, too.

The man was standing where he could see out over the entire outdoor theater, but his rifle was leaning against a tree. He would have been holding the rifle if he felt like he was in any danger, and the smell didn't seem to be bothering him.

The Chief was almost ready to begin advancing toward the man when Kathy held up one hand. The man started to move, and at first the Chief thought they would have to risk shooting him. They couldn't delay much longer. Then the Chief saw Kathy smile and shake her head as if something was really funny. One more peek around the tree, and the Chief started walking straight for the man.

There were times when it was just too easy, and this was one of them. The man was relieving his bladder and was doing so over the edge of a wall. The groaning started somewhere down below. He was also laughing out loud, and that was agitating the infected that were reaching up toward the sound.

The man was lucky the Chief didn't want to advertise their location, or he would have simply given him a little shove from behind. Instead, the Chief grabbed the back of his collar and pulled back as hard as he could, which was a lot more than was needed, and straight at the nearest tree. The man's head hit the bark hard enough to knock a big chunk from the tree. His legs folded as if they were made of Jello.

The Chief felt for a pulse and found one, so he dragged the man up against the tree in a sitting position. Kathy came up to help him, and they wasted precious seconds tying the man's hands behind his back and a gag in his mouth. Kathy kept glancing over her right shoulder down into the pit that formed the outdoor theater. The groaning had subsided for the most part, but the infected had begun to wander around more.

She whispered in a voice so low the Chief could barely hear her.

"How many?"

"At least fifty, maybe closer to seventy-five," he said in the same voice that was hardly louder than a breath.

The outdoor theater that was probably the center of private night life and culture on Ambassadors Island was now a holding pen for a horde of infected dead. They all had burlap bags over their heads, and since they couldn't see motion around them, they were mostly quiet. There was the occasional collision that led to a fall, which led to some groans, but they settled back down quickly. Kathy and the Chief were at least four feet above the heads of the infected, and the theater was only about one hundred feet across, so they could easily go around. There was a barricade across the entrance to the tiered seats, and a fence ran around the perimeter where the seating reached ground level. Since the infected couldn't see where they were going, they tended to fall backward into the lower tiers when they bumped into the fence.

"Why are they here, Chief?"

"My best guess would be an alarm system. Can you imagine making the mistake of coming through here at night? We didn't see this drop over the wall, and it's broad daylight."

Kathy looked around on the ground and pointed at several regularly spaced holes.

"There used to be a fence here," she said. "They must have taken it down so intruders would fall in."

"The burlap bags would keep the infected from biting people when they fall in, but there would be plenty of noise. Most people would start screaming as soon as they went over the edge," said the Chief. "Then they would start trying to find a way out, and in the dark they might not even figure out why they aren't getting bitten."

"Nasty little trap they have here. I'd like to push a few of them into it," said Kathy.

Ever since the beginning of the infection, Kathy had always been for the little guy. She wouldn't really throw the people into the pit with the infected, but she felt like it was what they deserved if they were willing to do it to other people.

"We'd better get moving," said the Chief.

They gathered up their gear and began skirting around the left side of the outdoor theater. They had a long way to go and the delay caused by the guard had the Chief worried. As far as he knew, there was only one guard left on the island. What he didn't know was when the others would be back.

The boat park was their next landmark. The Chief explained to Kathy as they jogged that the center island of trees would end not far after the boat park, and then there would only be one road going out of the gates.

Kathy glanced at the gigantic house to her left. She could only imagine what it must have been like to live in such a beautiful gated community before the end of civilization. This house looked like it had at least six or eight bedrooms. The four car garage had all of its doors closed, and there were three cars in the driveway. Kathy saw the curtains in the front windows moving as something brushed against them. She slowed to a walk and watched as a child squeezed between the curtains and the glass.

Her first instinct was to get the Chief to stop running because they had to help the little boy, but then she saw the way he pushed his face against the glass in her direction, and she knew his chance for help had come and gone a long time ago. Before she could tear her eyes away, another child and an adult woman pushed up to the window with the boy.

Kathy looked in the direction they had been running, and she was surprised to find the Chief waiting patiently for her. He had a sad look on his face, one of the first times she could recall ever seeing him with that look, and she realized it was for her, not them. She felt a lump well up in her throat, and she had to fight back the tears.

"Are you okay?" he asked.

She nodded at him and just started to jog without looking back at the window.

They circled the boat park and crossed through the last of the trees before coming to the two lane road that led to the front gate. There was still no sign of the last guard, but the Chief felt like the temptation to have the guard anywhere except at the front gate was too great to resist. That meant they would be able to get within a house or two of the entrance to the shelter before they would be exposed.

The trees were still full and provided enough cover for them to make it over half way on the road before the front gate was visible. They could only see three houses on their left, and after the gate they only had about thirty yards to the drop off where the shelter door was hidden. That was when they heard the sound they had dreaded. There were vehicles approaching the gate in large numbers, and there would be no reason for them to stop at the gate. Kathy and the Chief knew they were too exposed for no one to see them.

They ran as hard as they could across the wide yard that led to the nearest house on their left, and they almost made it without being spotted. Shouts of surprise were followed by shots from rifles as the caravan of pick up trucks and jeeps rolled up to the gate. The last guard was already rolling the gate open with more than one person yelling at him to hurry. Gunners were sighting over the cabs of the trucks but were hitting the house and the trees. Kathy felt a piece of brick crease the side of her head, and they both heard breaking glass from the nearest windows.

They were faced with few choices. There was no doubt that the armed occupants of Ambassadors Island would outflank them from the front. The Chief knew what he would do if he had the advantage. He would have half of his people cut them off by going in between the second house and the one they had ducked behind. That only left one choice. They had to get to the back of the houses and retreat as fast as possible.

What the Chief was more worried about was the other half of the people. They could stay in vehicles if they were smart, and they could race ahead of the Chief and Kathy to corner them behind the fourth or fifth house.

Luckily for them, that group wasn't so smart. They were well armed, and they had the numbers, but they didn't know how to use what they had. Instead of driving past where the intruders had gone and surrounding them, the second group left their vehicles and rushed straight for the front of the house on foot. As they were reaching the corner of the house and getting ready to slaughter their prey, Kathy and the Chief were already crossing the back yard of the fourth house and well on their way to the fifth.

******

The first house on the left had been a total surprise to Hampton and Colleen. They approached it from the side facing the water and planned to enter it just as they had the house they had stayed in when they escaped the massacre on I-77. The house had a deck that ran across most of the back where guests could admire the view, and at first it had seemed like just another beautiful house until they noticed the black smears on the glass. Colleen had her face up close to the glass trying to see in through the partially tinted window when the first infected dead slammed up against the other side. The glass held, but Colleen's nerves were shot. She fell over onto the deck as one infected after the next hit the glass and bounced backward.

Hampton was quick to get to her side and help her up. He wasn't exactly sure what she was saying, but it was a mixture of angry and scared out of her wits. What amazed him was the way the glass seemed to shake in its large frame but not break.

"Must be some kind of shatterproof glass," he said.

Colleen managed a coherent sentence and shouted, "Is it bulletproof, too? I'm going to shoot every damn one of those things."

Hampton realized just in time that he needed to help Colleen get over it because she really was going to start shooting them through the window.

"Slow down, girl. If they can't get out, it's best just to leave them in there. They can have this house. As a matter of fact, let's take our chances with that big place after all. If the Chief came this way, that's where he would have gone."

Colleen was looking back and forth between Hampton and the large picture window full of infected dead. She had a look like she needed to at least get even with them for scaring the pants off of her. She gradually shook off the embarrassment of landing on her butt and started off in the direction Hampton had pointed.

Hampton didn't like being out in the open, but he felt like he had to get Colleen away from there so she could get her nerve back.

"Did you see how many there were?" she asked between breaths as they ran across the open field between the houses.

"What about it?"

"There were over a dozen at that one window," she said.

"Maybe they had all holed up there as a group when the infection started," he answered.

She was just about to answer when they reached the end of the back of the first house. They had continued to believe that it would be safer to approach the back of the houses, but Colleen caught a glimpse of something up by the far end of the garage just as they were reaching the thick trees on the side of the house.

"I think that's a leg," she said.

Seeing bodies or body parts in this new world was no longer something strange. If it was the first day of the infection, she would have been shocked and unable to move. Now, it was just that the body part was in an unexpected place, and it was the first one they had seen that wasn't shambling around.

"Maybe your friends went that way," she said. "We should check."

Colleen was careful when she rounded the front of the house, but she moved faster than normal. The scene on the back porch of the first house still had her a bit rattled. She was surprised to see several bodies, some with limbs severed that were obviously decayed, but some had fatal injuries that looked fresh.

When Hampton came up beside her she asked, "Does it look to you like a couple of these guys were killed recently?"

"If they ran into the Chief and Kathy and weren't friendly, this is what they would look like," he said. He looked at the pile of bodies and added, "I don't think there's going to be anything worth seeing at this house, but I still can't figure it out. Why did they land behind that island and then come all of the way over here?"

"Maybe they thought they spotted you from the plane, Chris. If they came here looking for you, they must have thought you would be here for a good reason."

The front of the second house on the right side of the island was not far away, so they decided to go to it next. It had a prominent driveway that had a central island of trees in the middle of a sea of concrete. The island was surrounded by eight vehicles ranging from antique to luxury SUV's. Hampton gave up all pretense of stealth and went straight up to the front door. There were two narrow windows, one on each side of the door, and he did as Colleen had done and went right up to the glass to look inside.

The inside of the house was well lit, and Hampton could see the damage caused by the infected dead that had been wandering around in search of prey. Every time one would make noise by knocking over something breakable, the others would all move toward that area. Then something would fall in another room, and they would move that way. They also groaned as they searched for the source of the noise, and that was like ringing the dinner bell for the rest of them. One of them saw Hampton at the window and started toward him.

Hampton took the steps down to the driveway in one leap and caught Colleen by the right arm.

"Just like the first house," he said. "They couldn't be in there."

They went in the direction of the third house, and Colleen started to ask him how many he had seen. They were passing the wide doors to the garage, and for the second time she almost went over on her back as something slammed up against the inside of the door. Hampton caught her and steered her away from the door while he brought one finger up to his lips.

They both found themselves backing away from the big doors as the aluminum panels shook loudly from the continual impact of bodies. The more noise they made hitting the doors, the more noise they made with their groaning.

"Did everybody try to hole up on this island?" she asked.

"I don't know," said Hampton, "but there must be close to a hundred inside the only two houses we've checked. "

He turned around in the direction to the first house they had tried to approach from behind and looked at the front. The driveway was full of cars, too.

"I'm not ready to jump to conclusions yet," he said, "but when the infection started, I would have thought this island was a safe place to be. That is if I had friends or relatives with a place here. All of the cars look expensive, so it's not so strange that there are so many people here. They just weren't the survivor types, and once the infection got inside, they couldn't stop it."

Colleen didn't look convinced. She had a frown on her forehead as she sized up the area around the homes.

"Chris, when we were up in the tower of that first house, how many bodies did we see? I mean, decayed bodies of people who didn't walk away after they died, and maybe some that were put down for a second time."

He thought about it and it suddenly occurred to him that they had been able to see dozens of heaps that could only have been people who didn't survive. He had become so used to seeing them that he seldom even mentioned them. As a matter of fact, when he stepped over them to get from one place to another, the only attention he gave them was to be sure they weren't infected dead that were just very still. He had even become used to the smell and no longer felt the pangs of guilt he used to experience when he thought about why he survived, but they didn't. Then there were the kids. In neighborhoods there were always the bodies of the long dead kids. Somehow, Hampton had learned to look past them instead of at them.

The yard of the homes where they stood had none of the decayed victims. Civilization had ended, and the only places that had no bodies piled on the sidewalks or huddled in corners were places that were somehow under the control of the living.

"Someone lives here," he said in a low voice.

"Where? In this house?" asked Colleen.

"No, I'm talking about this neighborhood. It must be closed off up front, because the houses are full of the infected, but it's clean outside with the exception of back there."

He gestured toward the spot where they had found the bodies.

"I think you're right, Colleen. Where are all the remains? Someone has been picking up the bodies and disposing of them, but they haven't found out about the Chief's handiwork yet. When they do, they won't care who we are or why we're here. They'll think we did it."

"We need to find your friends and get out of here."

"I know, but they could be anywhere. We can't shoot up a flare."

"That only leaves us one choice," said Colleen. "We need to keep moving as fast as we can and check every house."

"You know something," said Hampton. "I almost said it's going to be like finding a needle in a haystack, but they probably said the same about finding me. At least we're all on the same island."

They set off at a trot straight to the next house. Neither of them were surprised when they looked through the windows and saw crowds of the infected wandering through the rooms. Quietly listening at garage doors they could hear the constant shuffling of feet inside. Hampton exchanged a look with Colleen, and he shook his head. Both could tell that the other was sensing there was something wrong with this island.

After the third house they came to a large, wooded lot without a house on it. Since they were away from the homes, they were able to talk as they jogged, and they agreed that the infected dead had most likely been put inside the houses. The one thing they couldn't guess was why. It just didn't make sense to take control of a neighborhood and then stock it with the infected.

Hampton stopped running when he thought he had it figured out.

"This couldn't be someone's warped version of a zoo, could it?"

Colleen looked like the thought made her sick.

"You mean someone comes here to look at them…or worse yet, feed them?"

"Don't be too surprised by the answer to the second part of your question," said Hampton.

After the wooded lot, they picked up speed. They only stopped long enough to look inside a window, nod to the other, and then move on. They knew what they would hear inside the garages if they listened closely, so they didn't slow down. If the Chief and Kathy were somewhere on the island, they weren't going to be inside any of the houses occupied by the dead.

The last six houses were ahead of them, and they saw that the road they had been following was actually an oval shape that went around the island. They had suspected as much by the way it curved across the first two houses they had checked. Now they could see where the two branches met and formed a single, two lane road that went toward a steel gate. That explained the lack of infected walking around, but it didn't mean they were safe.

Colleen came to a sudden stop when she saw someone running through the trees directly in front of where the two roads merged into one. At the same moment there was the sound of vehicles and shouting directly outside the gate. They couldn't see what was happening yet, but the gunshots started and the people Colleen had seen running had disappeared in the general direction of the last few houses on the other side of the road.

"Did you get a look at them?" asked Hampton. Even though he knew the answer, he didn't want to hear it because it was too obvious that the new arrivals were in pursuit of his friends.

"A big guy and a blond? Yeah, I got a good enough look."

"They're flanking them on the right and the left, but the Chief and Kathy are too smart to be behind the third house. They would be moving for the fourth house by the time those people close in."

"How can we help them?" asked Colleen.

Hampton looked around as if there would be someone else to stop the people with the guns from killing his friends. He felt helpless when he came to the instant conclusion that it would be up to them, but just like the Chief, Hampton had survived this long for a reason. He also had the advantage that Colleen gave him. If there was a way to gain the upper hand, they would find it.

The answer crossed his face just as Colleen started to say something.

"One of us just had an idea," he said. "You want to go first?"

Colleen smiled and said, "Knowing you, we just had the same idea."

"The garages?"

Hampton hooked a thumb in the direction of the houses as he said it.

"That's what I was thinking," she said, "but not the ones we already checked. We have to go for the last few on the right and work our way back."

Gunshots were increasing on the other side of the island, and through the trees they could see at least forty or fifty people encircling the third house. Hampton saw what Colleen meant. They had their backs to the right side of the island and were pouring weapons fire into the area around that one house. They were totally exposed from behind. If they could open the garage doors of the houses behind the shooters, the infected would be drawn toward the gunfire.

"Got your running shoes on?"

She smiled up at him and said, "Try to keep up."

"Okay, we run as fast as we can along the backs of the next three houses. There isn't time to go all the way to the first one. We'll circle the house and come around to the garage door. After we get it open, run like hell to the next two, then we'll go behind the fourth house to keep from being spotted."

"What if they're locked?" she asked.

"I don't know, but maybe with both of us lifting we can force the doors to open. We just need to get a little lucky. Let's go before they catch up with Kathy and the Chief."

Months of staying sharp and surviving had been good for both of them. There had been a time when they might have been too winded to do what they had to get done fast, but they were both in good shape. It was an all out sprint, but before they knew it, they were rounding the corner of the third house down the right side. Most of the shooting was coming from men with their backs to them directly across the street. Colleen ran to one garage door, and Hampton ran to the other. They exchanged looks, and both grabbed the handles and yanked as hard as they could.

The last thing they expected was to see the garage doors fly open as easily as a kitchen cabinet. Both had expected resistance in the form of a lock. The best they hoped for was the chains of automatic garage doors frozen in place from lack of use. Neither of them expected to fly upward with the doors.

Letting go quickly was more of a reflex than a decision because each garage bay had about twenty infected dead packed inside. They weren't as quick to react as Hampton and Colleen, so they were just starting to come out of the garage as the two would-be rescuers were running across the front lawn of the house toward the garage of the next house.

The infected dead began streaming out into the driveway, unfazed by the sudden opening of the doors and the brightness of sunshine in their eyes. They were drawn at first toward the two running people, but the gunshots were too tempting, and over three dozen infected moved with a singular purpose toward the men with their backs exposed to them.

As Colleen and Hampton reached the next house, they risked a glance back and saw that the stream of infected was nearing the end of the driveway. They knew they had to hurry if they were going to send more that way in time.

Just as they had at the last house, they each positioned themselves at handles, paused to see that the other was ready, and both pulled at the same time. This time they weren't caught off guard by the doors flying open, and that was a good thing because the infected dead inside had been more agitated than the first group.

As soon as the doors started upward, Hampton and Colleen began running for the third house. The shooting was still in progress, but they heard the first yells from the armed men.

The men were so surprised to find a large horde of infected dead walking right up to them that some of them were yelling at the infected as if they would understand. Hampton heard one voice yelling, "Stop that," and "What are you doing?" Then the questions changed to screams.

The second group of infected had just started reaching the group of men that had tried to outflank the Chief and Kathy on the left side of the house, while the first group of men was thoroughly infiltrated by biting teeth. Some of the bullets meant for the infected were hitting living people.

The third garage doors went up just as easily, and another three dozen infected flowed toward the already overwhelmed shooters. From the looks of things, a fourth house wouldn't be needed. Well over one hundred infected had swarmed into about forty unprepared morons.

Hampton stopped to watch for a moment, and Colleen came back to his side.

"At least when our army tried to march up I-77, we had a plan. It was a bad plan, but these guys just run and shoot," he said.

"What was with those garage doors?" asked Colleen.

"I don't know," he answered. "Even if they were built to be able to open that easy, it was almost like someone worked on them to make it easier. Remind me to ask the Chief. I'm going to bet he's already figured that one out by now."

******

Kathy saw the garage door on the third house across the street fly open. She and the Chief had already crossed behind three houses, circled around the side of the sixth house on the left side of the island, and crossed the street into the woods near the boat park. They knew the men who were shooting at them were trying to outflank them, so the last thing the men would expect was to be outflanked. Soon they would be on the right side of the island, and they could work their way along the backs of the houses back to the place where they had left the plane.

When the door went up, she got a good look at the two people who darted off to the right, and she also saw what had distracted the people who were shooting at them. The trees were blocking much of the action, but she saw the infected swarming in the direction of the third house where they had started their escape.

"Chief, it's Hampton."

The Chief looked across in time to see Hampton and a woman watching the mayhem from the corner of the next house down the line on the right side. They ran diagonally across the boat park, and even though they were out in the open for a short distance, the shooters were far too busy to see them. Hampton and Colleen saw them coming, and they couldn't have been happier. The four of them rushed toward each other, and even though Kathy and the Chief didn't know Colleen, they hugged her as much as they did

Hampton. It was a reunion Hampton didn't think would ever happen.

It seemed like the shooting wouldn't stop, but eventually it tapered down, and then it was quiet. They couldn't tell if it was because the infected had all been killed, or if the shooters had finally been unable to survive the attack. The total quiet was the first clue that the infected had won the battle. There were no sounds of shouting from victorious defenders, but there were some faint cries for help followed by screams. The wounded were going to die anyway, so there wasn't going to be any help that made a difference.

The Chief was the first to remind them it was time to move.

"We can catch up on how we all got here later, but the first thing we need to do is get ourselves into a safe place," he said.

"We can get back to the plane with no trouble if we stay on this side of the island," said Hampton. He had already taken a few steps in that direction, and Colleen had followed.

Kathy said, "Hold up, Hampton. We might have something else in mind. Chief, refresh my memory for me. Are you sure you didn't check for the locations of the secondary entrances and escape hatches? We could use one right now."

"I didn't have time to ask Bus, but I don't think they would be particularly well located," said the Chief. "The guy who designed this shelter probably planned to build a few houses on the island with the secondary entrance and escape hatches inside them. I don't know what kind of apocalypse he was getting ready for, but it wasn't this one. My guess is that we would have to clear all of the infected from the houses to get to the hatches."

Colleen looked back and forth between them and said, "This might not be the best time to discuss this, but you might want to fill in some details for me and Chris."

The Chief and Kathy could see why Hampton and Colleen might be a bit lost. They had never told Hampton about the shelter on Mud Island, and they certainly didn't know about the rest of them.

There was a time when Ed had opened the door to his shelter, and they had all stood in open mouthed awe in the entrance thinking they were looking at something great. They had no idea what was beyond the first room.

Mud Island had been designed by Ed's uncle Titus, and it was one of the smallest shelters. His location for the shelter limited its size a bit, but the Fort Sumter shelter was built on a smaller piece of land and was massive. Titus just hadn't felt the need to build a shelter that could be used as a small town. As it turned out, Mud Island was perfect for their small group, and Fort Sumter was perfect for the Army.

In a few minutes, if they were lucky, Hampton and Colleen would get their first look at the shelter below their feet. Kathy and the Chief didn't doubt the new pair would feel like they had fallen down the rabbit hole.

The Chief said, "Okay, we're not going back to the plane just yet. We need to work our way around to the front gate because there's a place there where we can be safe. If we're correct, it's also a place that has everything we need to be able to contact Mud Island and Fort Sumter."

"Mud Island...Fort Sumter?" asked Colleen. "There are survivors?"

The hopeful look of relief on her face was almost more than Kathy or the Chief could stand. For people who had survived outside the shelters, life had become a daily question, not a given. There was no certainty of food, water, or even being alive when the day ended. Nights were sleepless and long, and if you were in a group, it wasn't unusual to find someone gone in the morning. The worst part was finding out the person you had been sleeping only a few feet away from had been bitten but didn't say anything. Fellow survivors were always waking up to the screams of new victims because someone had died during the night.

Kathy wrapped an arm around the shorter woman's shoulders and pulled her closer. She could see that Colleen had been putting on a brave face for Hampton, but she was in bad need of a break from the daily grind of survival.

The Chief gave them a moment, and Hampton seemed like he needed to catch his breath, but he reminded them for a second time that they needed to get moving.

"We're going to go behind the houses on the right side of Ambassadors Island in order to reach the front entrance. The infected all crossed over to the shooting on the left side, so we should be able to get there with no resistance. If we do run into strays, everyone use blades. When we get to the front entrance, we need to cross the road quickly and drop over toward the water on the other side. There should be a hidden entrance to a shelter there."

Hampton had felt trust for this pair of people from the first moment he had met them, even though it hadn't been under the best of circumstances. Despite that trust, he was looking at the Chief as if he was just going along with a joke, and the Chief would deliver the punch line at any moment. Then they could all have a good laugh while they slapped each other on the backs, and someone said something like, "I had you going there for a moment."

Then Hampton felt like he understood. There had to be a fallout shelter under the first house, and somehow the Chief found out about it.

"Is the shelter big enough for all of us?" asked Hampton. "We could clear one of the houses and make it safe, too."

"Let's go," said Kathy. "It's time to get these two inside so they'll feel like tomorrow may be a bit better than today."

"I couldn't agree more," said the Chief. He gave Hampton a friendly slap on the arm and took off running between the houses toward the water.

There were only nine rambling houses between them and the front entrance to Ambassadors Island. The infected dead had been liberated from the garages of the middle three, so they stayed close to the water's edge to keep the infected trapped inside number seven, eight, and nine from spotting them and getting agitated. The noise would be muted, but on a quiet day like this one, sound might carry too far. They were too close to their goal to take a chance now.

The first three houses all had large pools on their back lawns, and they were all surrounded by plenty of patio space for lawn chairs. Fortunately, the owners of the homes must have all had the same ideas about privacy, because there were rows of hedges along the patios where they faced the water. They had been neatly trimmed and boxed during the previous year, but they had grown considerably taller since then. Even the Chief was well hidden when they passed behind the first three homes.

They were all tempted to take quick looks to see if there were infected dead pushing up against the windows, but there was no longer curiosity about them. It was safe to assume that they would be there, and there wasn't anything new to be seen.

The fourth house was going to be the first test for them as they ran in a stooped over position. There was no pool, and there were no shrubs to hide behind. Their best bet was to run like hell for the next house where the shrubs began again. It had been the last house that Hampton and Colleen had emptied, so they had to watch for infected that had either strayed from the fighting or had been late in leaving the house.

It might have been the breeze that was always coming off of the lake and rustling the leaves, or it could have just been the sound of the water lapping against the docks and boats. Whatever it was that was drawing their attention, there were infected dead streaming between the fourth and fifth houses.

"There are too many for us to take by hand, Chief," said Kathy.

"No guns yet," he answered. "There are ten times as many out front that could come our way."

"Did we let out that many?" asked Colleen

"I don't know if those people in the pick up trucks killed many before they were overrun, but add their numbers to the infected," said Hampton.

The Chief said, "I think those dummies also shot out all of the windows and doors on the houses across the street. If the infected inside those homes got out, we could have about three hundred infected running loose out there. We have to retreat while we can."

"I have an idea," said Kathy. "Let's go two houses back and go out on the dock. There's a boat out there."

"What if the boat doesn't start?" asked Colleen. "We'll be stuck out there."

That was the first time she saw the Chief's famous smile up close. The smile that said, "Everything is going to be just fine."

The Chief had immediately looked toward the dock to houses back the way they had come, and he understood why Kathy had picked that dock. The house closer to them had a dock with a boat tied to it, but he knew if Kathy picked the second dock it had to be because one was over three times the length of the other.

The short dock that was close to them was so short that the infected dead could practically board the boat as soon as they reached the dock. The other dock was about sixty yards long and was shaped like a big letter Z. Kathy didn't just intend to get away from the infected that had begun moving in their direction, she wanted to eliminate them.

As they ran past the first house, Kathy ran out onto the short dock, looked around the inside of the boat for a moment, and grabbed the anchor. She used her machete to chop through the heavy nylon line and brought it back to the Chief. She had cut the line right where it was tied to the boat, so she brought a lot of rope with her.

"You know what to do with this, right Chief?"

Kathy was getting just like the Chief, and she flashed him a smile to equal his own.

"Yes, ma'am, I sure do," he said.

Colleen tugged on Hampton's shirt sleeve and said, "Your friends are crazy…I like them."

Anyone else might have been running like maniacs and screaming for help, but the small group of friends jogged toward the second dock, all wearing smiles and even laughing a bit. Kathy led the way and gestured for Colleen to follow her to the boat. Hampton stopped when the Chief did, waiting to see what he was going to do with the anchor.

The Chief handed his gear to Hampton and told him to give him just a little room. Hampton backed off and watched as the Chief played out a bit of anchor line, then he lifted the anchor free of the dock and started swinging it in a forward and backward motion. When he had it moving in a long enough arc, he gave it a little more power to carry it from its backswing into a full overhead swing. The thirty pound anchor crashed through the first two boards of the dock, destroying them both and lodging itself under the third.

Hampton caught on in a hurry and sat the gear down far enough away before running back to help the Chief. He grabbed the anchor line near the Chief's hands, and together they pulled. The board creaked and the deck screws screamed as they were pulled from the wood, but the next two boards came up with the first two.

"Damn, Chief. Four boards with one swing?" said Hampton.

The Chief laughed and said, "Give Kathy the credit. Whether it's four people or five thousand, she sees a way to buy you time."

He started the pendulum motion with the anchor for a second time, and Hampton stepped back to make room. The swing wasn't as perfect as the first one, so it only took out one board, but the Chief got it moving again and took out another one. Six boards was a long, empty step for the infected dead because they didn't have the ability to take a long step…just a long fall.

"I've got this, Hampton. It sounds like Kathy could use your help with the boat."

"No problem, Chief. Good to be working with a team again."

Hampton gathered up their gear and jogged the length of the dock to where Kathy was ready to start kicking the stubborn motor. Behind him he heard another crash as the Chief widened the gap. The nearest infected were only about ten yards from the dock, but the gap had increased to about five feet. Any of the infected that fell into the gap weren't going to be able to serve as a bridge for the others pushing from behind.

The water at the gap was only about waist deep, but the bottom dropped off and disappeared into darker colors in all outward directions. By the time the first of the infected dead reached the dock, the gap was six feet, and if the Chief wasn't having enough fun yet, he really started enjoying himself by throwing the anchor at them. The thirty pound piece of metal hit the lead infected dead squarely in the middle of the chest, and its feet flew up in the air as it collided with six more that were too close behind it.

Colleen had stopped to watch the Chief as Hampton worked on the motor, and she was amazed at how devastating he was to the horde of infected. What she didn't know was that he was mentally seeking redemption for the one time he failed to bring someone back alive.

The Chief had been forced to abandon ship when he and Kathy had escaped from the cruise liner, and they couldn't save five thousand people, but when he had tried to protect Allison, she had died when he had forgotten to be careful just once. That one lost life meant more to him than the thousands on the ship, because he had let down a friend. This time he was getting some payback. The Chief had found Hampton, and he was going to see to it that they all made it home safely.

The boat motor began to sputter to life, shook violently, and then settled into a steady roar. Kathy let out a cheer, and the Chief gave the anchor one last throw. It looked like he was bowling because he always took down more than one.

When the Chief jumped into the boat, he looked like he was ready for more fun, but it had still been business as usual. It was still all about staying alive.

He shouted over the sound of the motor to Kathy who had taken her place at the steering wheel, "It's too far to go all the way back around the island to get to the entrance. We need to stay with the plan and go for the front gate. If the bridge over to the island is too low to go under, we can beach at the road and cross."

Kathy gave the Chief a thumbs-up as she turned sharply around the end of the dock and increased speed. It seemed like only seconds had gone by as they sped past the front gate of Ambassadors Island and closed the distance to the bridge. Just as they had feared, the bridge wasn't intended to be a shortcut from one side to the other. A fisherman in a Bass boat would be able to slide under the bridge if he ducked, but not a ski boat.

The Chief shook his head at Kathy when she looked at him, so she peeled off sharply to the right and skimmed the boat along the edge of the road back to the sloping gravel. She smoothly beached them right where the road met the brick. It was close to where the Chief had spotted the pattern that pointed to the entrance.

As the Chief went over the bow he called back, "Leave everything but weapons. We'll have everything we need once we're inside."

Hampton looked longingly at the backpacks they had prepared for the long term. He was expecting the Chief to take them down through something like a manhole into the safety of a bunker about the size of a camper, so every can of beans was worth its weight in gold. He looked at Colleen and saw the doubt written on her face, too.

"Let's go, people," she yelled. "If you haven't noticed, we have company."

On the other side of the bridge where it connected to the mainland, there was a horde of infected that had been drawn toward the gunfire on Ambassadors Island. They were still far enough away to be of any real concern.

The problem was in front of them. The people in the pick up trucks didn't bother to close the front gates when they had returned, and the army of infected dead that had destroyed them was moving toward the opening. Some were on the road moving directly toward the gates, and some had already reached the brick walls that kept people from going around the gates. They were moving in from the sides to join those already on the road. Where they converged there would be a brief logjam, but not enough to stop them.

None of them needed to be warned again that they needed to move faster, and they all scrambled over the bow and up the bank of gravel to the road. The Chief was in the lead, and he cleared the road in four long strides. He disappeared over the opposite side before Colleen even reached the road. Hampton reached back and grabbed her hand to pull her up more quickly, and then they followed Kathy as she jumped over behind the Chief.

They were still visible to the infected dead that were straying close to the side of the road, and at any moment they would begin to fall over the edge toward the four survivors. The Chief ran to the place where the brick wall came down to the water like a small jetty, wondering where the door was. He knew it wouldn't be too obvious, but he didn't have time to play games that involved clues.

The others ran up beside him, all breathing heavily, more from concern than exertion. The brick had bright, gold lettering on it that said Ambassadors Island. It stood out as if it was embossed onto the brick. There was something that looked like a broach in the middle of the letter "o", and the Chief saw it was a miniature version of the pattern inlaid into the brick entrance driveway at the front gates. He touched it hopefully, and it moved.

Each point represented a number, and each number was the combination that would open the door. He carefully spun the dial of the combination lock, stopping where he estimated the numbers would be. There was no handle, but a dark line appeared where the sloping gravel met with the equally sloping wall. He shoved his big fingers into the dark line and got a grip, and just as the first of the infected dead began falling over the edge from above, he slid a section of the slope out of the way to the left. A pitch black opening appeared that was big enough to go through. Hampton pulled Colleen into the opening, and as the Chief and Kathy pushed the falling bodies away into piles, they backed into the darkness of the outer room of the shelter. Kathy found the handle on the sliding door and pushed it closed in front of the reaching hands and biting faces of the infected dead.

7 AMBASSADORS ISLAND

"Does anybody have a flashlight?" asked Hampton. "Mine was in my backpack."

"There's a light switch around here somewhere," said Kathy.

"A what?"

"A light switch. You know, the thing that turns on the lights."

Coming from the bright light into the totally dark room caused all of them to be just a bit more blind than they would have been if they had time to adjust. Despite their close call, the Chief was almost in tears over the verbal exchange in the dark room. They couldn't see his face, and he already had a hand over his mouth.

"Why would there be working lights in here?" asked Colleen from somewhere behind him.

The Chief felt Colleen bump into him.

"My God, I hope that was you, Chief."

What they didn't know was that they weren't even standing in a tiny little room. They were so sure that the room would be small that they just stayed close together.

Hampton said, "Did anyone notice that our voices almost seem to echo in here?"

The Chief felt Colleen against his back again and said, "I don't think we were properly introduced, Miss, so I don't think I know you well enough for you to be doing that."

If blushing could make you glow in the dark, Colleen would have lit up the room.

"Chief, Kathy, meet Colleen," said Hampton.

They both said hello to Colleen, and everyone started to laugh. Kathy leaned forward and put her left hand out in front of her. It landed squarely on top of a light switch, and she flipped it upward out of reflex. She had a split second fear that it would open the door again, but in that split second when the lights came on, that fear was gone. They all turned as one to face a wide open room that was situated like a balcony looking down over an immense cavernous shelter.

They were about twenty feet from a safety railing, and they walked over to it to look down at what they had found. There was a metal plate attached to the top of the railing, and they could see it was engraved. Colleen walked over and read it out loud.

"Welcome to Ambassadors Island Shelter."

From their vantage point, they could see that the shelter stretched the entire length of the island. The ceiling of the shelter gave the feeling that it was the sky over their heads, and it was painted a powder blue to look more like the sky. There was a stairwell on the left that descended from a height of about forty feet, but there was also a freight elevator against the wall to the right.

There were a variety of work spaces separated by walls, but there were no ceilings over most of the spaces. It was like looking down over a cardboard reproduction of a building without the roof on it. The rooms were painted in a variety of colors that made it look relaxing and comfortable, just like homes should be. From above they could see wall decorations such as pictures, mirrors, posters, and signs. It all looked very welcoming.

"I wonder what's inside the areas with roofs on them," said Colleen.

"Let's go find out," said the Chief.

He didn't wait for the others to agree. He started for the stairs while he kept his head turned toward the shelter.

"Wait a minute, Chief. Don't we have to think about whether or not it's safe?" asked Kathy.

Hampton and Colleen both wanted to ask the Chief the same thing, but to Kathy and the Chief there was a special meaning. They had lost a member of their group, a young boy, because they didn't take the time to make sure the bottom floors of the shelter at Fort Sumter were clear of the infected.

The Chief stopped and waited for them to get to him.

"Okay, so we go down as a group, and we move as if we know something is here. The thing is, we're also pressed for time. When we find out where the communication room is, we'll be able to figure out how much time we have."

"Hang on a second, Chief. Why are we pressed for time?" asked Hampton.

"Hampton, we're so pressed for time that I don't have time to explain it to you until we get more information. Let's get going so we can at least locate the communications room."

The steps going down were solid metal, and they felt like they were made to last forever. It was obvious that they had not been used by the number of people this shelter could hold because they looked so new. It was also as quiet as a tomb.

When they reached the bottom, they were in a main corridor that ran between the rooms. It was immediately apparent why the ceilings were left off of the rooms. The blue simulated sky above gave them the feeling like they were outside in city streets instead of below a neighborhood on an island. The well decorated rooms of the various work spaces would make inhabitants feel less claustrophobic.

It was all new to Kathy and the Chief, but it was breathtaking to Hampton and Colleen. To them the world was a place where you fought to stay alive. This was a safe haven beyond their wildest dreams.

As if someone had read their minds, the first large room they came to was a dining area. The tables were set restaurant style. Table cloths and silverware were neatly placed on tables, on one end of the room there was a completely stocked bar.

"Remember how to get here," Colleen whispered into Hampton's ear.

There were other dining areas along the main corridor, as well as rooms that were set up as different shops. One had racks of clothing, one was a shoe store, and one was a store Kathy and the Chief couldn't wait to tell Ed about. It was loaded with video games.

One thing the group noticed was that all of the stores were stocked as if they were in a mall, and malls had become a reflection of the variety of tastes and diversity. Whoever designed this shelter wanted the illusion that everything was normal inside, even if it was far from normal outside.

Kathy said, "My guess is there would have been some sort of currency exchange so people could earn their supplies. You couldn't just walk in and pick out your new shoes or order a steak in one of the restaurants. You had to work in one of the businesses too."

"I agree," said the Chief. "They were trying to establish routine here so people wouldn't get bored."

"Oh, my God," said Kathy.

She sounded so horrified that the others drew their weapons and formed a loose circle. They all glanced in every direction trying to see what it was that had Kathy so shocked.

"What is it Kathy?" the Chief asked in a low voice.

"I know who this shelter was supposed to be for. We had a clue all along. It was right in front of us the whole time."

Hampton and Colleen were totally clueless because they didn't know how the shelters came into existence. The Chief had wondered about the name of the island and if it possibly had something to do with the occupants, but he thought it was a little too obvious.

Kathy explained, "I think if we find some records of who was supposed to be here and who owned those homes up there, we would find they were all summer homes for ambassadors. I mean, think about it. They lived overseas in foreign countries, but when they would come back to the United States, they had to go somewhere. Some of their families may even have been full time residents of Ambassadors Island."

"So, where are they?" asked Colleen.

"Maybe they couldn't get in because whoever had the combination for the lock out front didn't make it back," said Kathy.

"Okay, Kathy. We've been down this road before," said the Chief. "No sense in dwelling on it right now. Let's find that high tech stuff we need."

They continued their search for half an hour until they came to a sign that had an arrow on it and said Central Control. It was one of the rooms that had a ceiling on it, and the next sign pointed down more stairs. In front of the stairs was a security station with a metal detector.

"Everyone step around the metal detector," said the Chief. "We don't need to waste time trying to figure out how to turn it off."

The steps only went down one flight, but they went exactly where the Chief had hoped. The room looked like a NASA launch control center. He started looking through the maze of consoles for something to indicate which one would give them radio contact with the outside world. It took almost ten minutes, but the Chief found a terminal that had a headset attached to it, so he hit the power button and waited for it to boot up.

If he didn't have to worry about a login ID or password, he was in business, but he looked under the keyboard just to be sure. Just as he guessed, there was a note taped to the keyboard with a string of letters and numbers, and under that was Betty123.

"How original," said the Chief, "you give people the instructions on protecting passwords, and they do this anyway."

Kathy was looking around the rest of the room and came to a door that was unlocked. The sign on the wall said it was access to the storage and living quarters.

"Chief, I'm going to check out the rest of this level."

The Chief knew they had to at least know what was in the shelter, but he was worried about getting away from the area before the wind shifted and started blowing radioactive fallout their way.

"Okay, but take Colleen with you for backup, and leave a trail of some kind. I'll have Hampton come looking for you if we need to get out of here fast."

Kathy found a black Sharpie next to a computer and pulled off the cap. She checked to see if it had gone dry and found it to be usable.

"I'll draw arrows at every turn. If the ink runs dry, I'll come back."

Kathy and Colleen disappeared through the door, and Hampton started exploring the rest of the equipment. The Chief was busy logging into the computer and looking for communications software.

It didn't take long for the Chief to find what he was looking for, and he opened a program labeled Shelter Communications Network. He immediately saw that the only shelters displayed were those that he expected to be online. That was disappointing because he had hoped to find other shelters were occupied.

Their goal had become more than survival. They planned to occupy all thirty-two of the shelters and then to begin to fight back. It would take years, but they hoped to eventually eliminate the infected dead. Of course there were the living survivors who were making it difficult. If everyone with a gun was on the same side, they could have rolled right up to Ambassadors Island, told the occupants why they were dropping by, and turned the shelter over to them.

"Chief, I found the closed circuit TV system. I have Kathy and Colleen on a monitor and about twenty other areas."

"That's great, Hampton. Try to keep an eye on them. Is there interior communications available with that?"

The shelter at Fort Sumter had lacked that capability or they might not have lost Perry, the young boy who had accidentally stumbled into the only infected dead inside the shelter.

"Here it is, Chief."

Before the Chief could warn him, Hampton keyed the switch and asked Kathy and Colleen if they could hear him. The moment he did it he felt stupid because he had always been so careful. It was the newness of the shelter and the unbelievable feeling of security that made him slip.

Hampton's voice boomed throughout the entire shelter. On the monitor he saw Kathy and Colleen get low to the floor, one facing in each direction with weapons drawn. Everyone waited, holding their collective breath to see if there was an unwanted response to the broadcast. The silence continued for several minutes, and Kathy held up a thumb on one hand.

"You don't have to say it, Chief. I'll keep my finger off that button."

"That's okay, Hampton, but I would have suggested you only tap twice on the microphone without speaking. Kathy would hold up one, two, or three fingers, and you would have tapped that number of times. It's something we worked out a long time ago."

The Chief finally found the control panel in his program that would open contact with the other two shelters. He selected Mud Island, the oil rig in the Gulf of Mexico, and Fort Sumter from a menu and decided to keep it set on the function that would let him send a text message. There was always a chance that an audio signal could be intercepted and less chance of a text message being seen by someone above. Besides, after the mental mistake by Hampton, the Chief felt like keeping it quiet for a few minutes.

All three lights next to Mud Island, Fort Sumter, and one labeled GOMEX turned green, which he hoped meant someone was at their monitors ready for a message.

He typed, "Ambassadors Island shelter is online. Have located Hampton and a friend. What's the word from GOMEX?"

Text messages popped up immediately from Mud Island and Fort Sumter. Both had similar questions about their safety.

The message from GOMEX said, "Cat 4 and increasing. Turning northeast at fifteen knots. Expect heavy rain ahead of storm. Winds should begin influencing Oconee within twelve hours. Would advise a safety window and vacate area of Ambassadors Island within ten hours."

The Chief drew a sigh of relief. Ten hours was better than he had hoped for, and the hurricane was also going to bring enough rain into the area to force the fallout to the ground faster. The water table was in serious trouble, and fishing would be a bad idea, but the fallout itself would be spread out over a smaller area.

The Chief typed back to all of them, "Everyone is safe. We copy your message. What is the radiation level in your areas?"

He was relieved to see the answer, "Negligible." The word appeared on both screens.

The Chief had to know one more thing, and that was what kind of threats could they expect in the area of Mud Island. He wasn't worried about Fort Sumter because of the sizable force of soldiers under the command of Captain

Miller, but if they couldn't land the plane safely near Mud Island, they would have to be guests at Fort Sumter until they figured out what to do about the threat.

He typed the message, "Surface threat assessment for Mud Island approach."

The response was not what he hoped for. It just said, "Unfriendly."

He answered, "Surface assessment for alternate site."

Fort Sumter responded, "Under control."

The Chief knew Captain Miller would send men topside to clear the area within the next six hours. He would probably find that someone else had set up an armed camp inside the fort and on board the Cormorant, but his well trained men would deal with both. There had been far less activity in the Charleston harbor since the fallout began. Survivors had become sick and died, while the population of the infected dead flourished.

Another message came from Fort Sumter that the Chief didn't expect.

"Yorktown questionable for approach."

The Chief took that to mean it would be safer to approach Fort Sumter from the south, and that wouldn't be a problem. He just had to figure out what they were going to do about whatever it was that was happening on Mud Island.

******

Kathy and Colleen were making fast progress through the second level of the shelter. It was far more functional than the first level which was geared more towards day time activities and socializing.

They found the living quarters, and they were as well furnished as the rooms had been at Fort Sumter. They were obviously intended for people who were used to living in luxury. Each room had the latest in technology, from the entertainment systems to the computers. Kathy powered on a computer and found they were on a wireless network, and she was shocked when it said she had an Internet connection.

A voice from a speaker near the computer said, "Shut it down, Kathy. IP addresses can still be traced to approximate locations."

The Chief had seen his own terminal register the IP address as active as soon as Kathy had turned it on. He saw it disconnect, but there was a record that was still displaying that it had come from a location north of Charlotte. What made him feel good about the discovery was the rest of the display. The list had hundreds of locations on it, which meant other survivors had managed to connect to the satellites that still orbited the Earth.

Then came the realization that deflated his discovery. There were plenty of automated signals being sent over a network that was slowly dying. He checked the logs of previous activity and saw they were decreasing in number every day.

Colleen stuck her head through the door of a nearby room and called out to Kathy, "There's hot water in the bathrooms."

Kathy had to smile despite herself. She had been spoiled by what they had on Mud Island, but a hot bath or shower had been a rarity for Colleen.

"Okay, you have fifteen minutes. I'll stand guard for you and give you some answers to your questions at the same time."

She didn't have to say it twice. Hampton saw Colleen on a monitor running across a bedroom shedding clothes as she ran. At first he was confused, but then he heard the sound of the water and saw the steam coming through the door.

Kathy got comfortable on a vanity next to a sink and began telling the story of the Mud Island group. She had to give the highlights, but she explained enough in fifteen minutes for Colleen to understand why Hampton thought so highly of them. She updated her on the status of the Oconee Nuclear Plant and told her the Chief was trying to find out how much time they had. When it came to the loss of Allison, she gave the version Tom had been given. Allison died in the plane crash, not after being bitten by an infected dead the Chief had missed.

When the shower turned off, Colleen only asked Kathy one question.

"Aside from rescuing Hampton, which I'm glad you did, could you tell me again why you guys keep leaving your shelter?"

Kathy said, "Everyone always asks that, but it isn't enough to just survive. We've had to leave to try to fix problems, but the big picture is the shelters. We have to find them, secure them, and then try to populate them. As far as we can tell, the guy in the Gulf of Mexico is the only other shelter builder to survive besides Doctor Bus."

"And the shelter built by Doctor Bus is empty?" asked Colleen.

"At the time we made the decision to all move to Mud Island together, it was for practical reasons, and there wasn't a grand plan. That all changed when we secured Fort Sumter and gave it to the US Army," said Kathy.

Colleen was beginning to see why Hampton wanted to be part of the group with Kathy and the Chief. She was a bit relieved when she heard the story about Tom and Molly joining the group because she had wondered if Hampton had a thing for Kathy. She felt strangely more saddened for the Chief about Allison being killed than for Allison herself, but Colleen knew it was because she wanted Allison out of the way so Kathy could be with Tom.

Hampton kept himself busy at his console by surfing all of the camera views throughout the shelter. It was a convenient way to explore without having to take any risks, and it was faster. He would have preferred to be seeing it for himself, but he had to stand guard for the Chief as he did the things he had to do.

The Chief had exchanged a few more discreet texts with the other shelters about their plans to leave Ambassadors Island, but he also wanted to spend some time reviewing the inventory of the shelter. He hadn't discovered anything they didn't have at Mud Island or Fort Sumter with the exception of some really good shortwave equipment. They would need to take that with them to improve their communications.

He also found that there had really been what he would have needed to locate Hampton if they had not been found by him first. There was a closed circuit camera network around Lake Norman that would give anyone a strategic advantage. He flipped from one screen to the next and found that there were signal boosters everywhere. They were battery powered, so they wouldn't last forever, but apparently there had been very little drainage from the batteries because they had been powered off.

One camera gave him a good view of I-77 where it crossed Lake Norman on a bridge. It was still heavily congested with the infected dead, and it looked like it had been a real battle. The sloped sides of the interstate were covered with bodies, many that were still moving.

"When we get a chance, Hampton, I'd like to hear more about what you guys were trying to accomplish when you met the infected dead horde head on."

"It wasn't our finest hour," said Hampton, "but it seemed like a good idea at the time."

"Well, like I said, I want the details when we get time. What worked? Why didn't it work? I have to admit, I've wondered if they could be eliminated by force."

Hampton sighed and said, "At this point, I don't know how to beat them except one on one."

"I do have one idea," answered the Chief, "but we're in the wrong part of the country to try it."

"I'm all ears, Chief. We lost a lot of people up on the interstate. Colleen and I saw our chance to break away from the group and took it. I think we saw the writing on the wall a long time before everyone else because we were near the back. The people up front didn't stand a chance."

"Winter is a long way off," the Chief began, "but maybe we can use the time to get ready. When it freezes, we need to be in position to go hunting."

"Do they freeze?" asked Hampton.

"I don't really know. I know it got cold outside our shelter, but we just hunkered down and kept warm. Now that we have a US Army contingent at Fort Sumter, we can go hunting when it gets cold. I figure we can travel north to a colder climate, dispose of a few thousand frozen infected dead, and travel back to our shelters before it gets warm again. Wash, rinse, and repeat the following winter. In between cold seasons we can carefully eliminate the infected around Charleston from a distance with snipers."

"It sounds like a good plan," said Hampton, "but what about all the renegades? They seem to be everywhere, and face it, they seem to be a supply source for the infected. We've both added to their numbers in the last few days."

The Chief had to admit, every time they ran into renegade groups, they seemed to leave behind more infected dead. They would need to find a way to negotiate with survivor groups that were willing to cooperate. Some of them were families that were just trying to make it another day. The problem was that they seemed to be outnumbered by the misfits who were enjoying this new world that had less rules.

Hampton thought he saw a shadow in the corner of a room monitor that wasn't there before, but he wasn't sure. It was the room next door to the one where Colleen was in the bathroom. He imagined Kathy was standing guard for Colleen, but the cameras didn't show the insides of the bathrooms.

"Chief, I think something is in the living quarters with the women."

The Chief was at his side by the time the last word was out of his mouth. They both saw the shadow move, and then an infected dead came into view, followed by two more.

"We'll never get there in time," said the Chief. "We have to trust Kathy, but it wouldn't hurt for her to know they're coming."

The Chief tapped the microphone twice, and he was rewarded with the smartest thing Kathy could do. He had to laugh as she gently shut the door and locked it.

"Let's get down there, Hampton. Watch for the arrows at the turns, and close any open doors we have to pass. I don't want anything coming out behind us."

They hurried through the door Kathy had used and started following the arrows to the living quarters. As the Chief had expected, Kathy had made good time checking the rooms, so they had a long way to go. She apparently had seen enough rooms in enough shelters that she didn't find things as interesting as Colleen would.

They made five turns and closed dozens of doors before they came to the room where they had seen the infected dead on camera. They were up ahead in the corridor and being drawn toward the sounds of Kathy and Colleen one door down, but when Kathy had shut the bathroom door, she and Colleen had both become as still and quiet as possible. When the room went quiet, the infected kept moving toward the door of their room, but they did not move with the same interest they would normally have shown.

"Save your bullets, Hampton. There may be more, and we'd rather not give away our location."

Three infected dead were no match for the Chief. It reminded him of the night he had to clear a grocery store in downtown Charleston. He had encountered groups of infected in the aisles, and it was easy to make them fall all over each other. This time wasn't much different. He gave the first one a hard shove back into the other two, and the three went down like bowling pins. It was always that way with the Chief, and Hampton took notes.

The Chief stepped into the pile up and used a long knife to finish each of them. Then he grabbed them by the ankles and dragged them back into the room. When he pulled the door shut, he used his knife to cut a big X on the door.

Hampton went cautiously into the next room and tapped on the bathroom door. The door opened immediately, but Kathy was poised to strike if necessary. Colleen was dressed and standing off to one side with her knife in case she was needed.

"What happened?" asked Kathy.

"The room next door had three unexpected guests," said Hampton.

"But we looked in that room," said Colleen.

The women looked at each other as if to confirm what they were both thinking, and they shared a look of disbelief. Kathy was particularly disturbed because she felt like she could have gotten them killed, but Colleen felt guilty because she had asked for a few minutes of luxury.

They were just about to say something else when the Chief stuck his head in the door.

"No time to worry about what could have happened, ladies. We need to check out the rest of this place and begin working our way back to the plane. We have less than ten hours, but eight is our goal. We'll do it as a group. There's an inventory of the entire shelter on the main computer. I found some flash drives and copied it all, so we won't have to inspect it all like we did at Fort Sumter. All we're going to do is check all of the rooms for either survivors or infected. If it's empty, let's grab the radio gear and head for the plane."

The shelter was large, but they were done in an hour. They had moved quickly and without much talking, but they were deadly serious. The only time they slowed down was when they came to the armory. Everyone restocked their personal ammunition, and each of them added at least one handgun.

They still had eight hours left when they returned to the control room with MRE's they had found in a kitchen, and they settled in for a quick meal. It had been a long day, and they hadn't given much thought to food until they were done searching the shelter. Each of them had something different, and there were the usual jokes about how closely they resembled something other than what the name was.

Kathy tasted hers and made the observation that whatever it was made of, it wasn't real meat. Then she followed with a second observation that she was going to pretend it was real meat. Otherwise she would keep wondering what it was made of.

The Chief was already opening his second container of sweet and sour chicken when a chime sounded. It was one simple note, soft and clear. They all looked at each other trying to decide where the sound had come from.

"Anyone know where that came from?" asked Kathy.

Colleen pointed with her fork at the main console where the Chief had been talking into the microphone. She was sitting closest to it, so it seemed to come from behind her. The computer monitor had its back to them, so they didn't see the screen had become illuminated, and a camera view of the outside had activated. The Chief walked around her and looked at it.

"It seems Ambassador Island has visitors, and the current occupants are expressing their desire to have them over for lunch," he said.

"That's gross, Chief," said Kathy, but she had a hard time not laughing. She walked around to get a look at what he was seeing.

The view on the screen was back toward the mainland, and there was a line of men and women with rifles carefully taking aim at the infected dead that had managed to stay on the road without falling into the water. The men and women fired on a command from a tall woman who raised her hand and then let it drop. Every shot hit its mark, and the crowd of infected was far smaller. The arm went up again, and when it dropped, so did the infected dead.

"Gee Chief, if I didn't know better, I would say that was the female version of you," said Kathy. "She's better looking, though."

The Chief gave her a sideways look that made her focus on her simulated meat again, but she loved the fact that she got him to react at all.

The Chief said, "I'm going to tell her you said she has a beard."

Kathy faked a shocked expression, and then she finally laughed out loud.

"Look how well organized they are," said Hampton. He and Colleen had moved to where they could both see the monitor. As he said it, another volley of shots dropped more of the infected, but this time the shooters stood up and advanced together.

Within minutes the bridge was clear, and the shooters were taking aim at the infected dead that were inside the open gates. The Chief rotated a camera located on the mainland behind the firing line, and he got a closer look at the woman who was leading the assault on Ambassadors Island. She wasn't muscular, but she had a tall, wiry frame that made her athletic enough for track and field or basketball. Her silver hair was long and seemed to shine in the sunlight. He had to admit, he found her to be attractive.

It was her demeanor that really set her apart from the ordinary, and the fact that she was commanding such a well organized group made her even more different. He watched as she advanced with her firing line, and he saw there was a small smile on her face.

Then she did something even more extraordinary. She had the firing line retreat to their original spot. They waited there until the infected dead once again came out through the gates and filled the bridge. Then they went back to work.

Kathy looked over at the Chief and saw him watching the woman closely. He had to be attracted to her, but she knew him well enough to know something else was happening. She could always tell when he was planning something.

The Chief felt her eyes on him and looked her way. He definitely had something going on if he could manage to do it. He motioned to her to join him off in one corner of the room. They had been together long enough that he trusted her opinion. If she said no to his plan, he would listen.

"How can we get her attention without getting shot?"

"I knew it. You're thinking of giving her the shelter, aren't you?"

He looked into Kathy's eyes and said, "It's a risk, but in ten hours or so they're all going to die. There's something different about them. She reminds me of you and even me, both rolled up into one. They could keep clearing the island, and in an hour or so the outside areas will be free of the infected, but then they would have to start working on almost two dozen houses packed with those things. They would probably stop for the night, set guards, and start dying when the fallout arrives."

"All I can think of is to walk outside and pop a flare, but what about the infection? Don't you think it will be like everywhere else? Someone in a group that size has to be hiding a bite."

He looked like he was going to say something, but then he changed his mind and said something else.

"I could spend all day trying to argue that she's different, but I have nothing to base my beliefs on except the control she seems to command."

Kathy gave him a half smile and said, "I think you're trying to tell me not to lose faith, Chief. If we stop believing there are good people out there who are also realistic, then we're no different from the others who wouldn't let us in. Remember the Naval Weapons Station? They wouldn't let us land because they thought we would be bringing in the infection. I guess this would be a leap of faith, Chief."

He returned her smile then motioned for Hampton and Colleen to join them.

"We're going to turn the shelter over to them if we can find a way to communicate with the leader without getting shot. Any ideas?"

Hampton said, "I think that PA system I found may have speakers on the surface."

"You mean the one you used earlier? You think it broadcasts to the surface? No wonder those things are so worked up," said the Chief.

The Chief walked over to the microphone and started to press the talk key, but something crossed his mind at the last second, and he looked at Kathy.

"You're up," he said.

He turned the microphone in her direction. Kathy didn't need to ask why. Whoever this lady was, she had already seen her share of groups led by men who had used the infection outbreak as a means to gain power. She might be more receptive to a female voice.

Kathy paused long enough to grin at the Chief and said, "Women rule."

The Chief rolled his eyes enough to hurt, but he couldn't say he didn't expect it.

Kathy keyed the microphone and said, "Welcome to Ambassadors Island. Will you honor a flag of truce?"

"That's kind of old fashioned, isn't it?" asked Colleen.

"Yes," said Kathy, "but some of the old rules apply now. Honoring a truce dates back centuries, and this infection has turned back the pages on the calendar. Most of the surviving world is probably using the barter system while the rest of it is functioning like those jackasses who were in charge of the island until we got here."

On the monitor the uncertainty was obvious. Everyone on the firing line had dropped to the ground. The tall woman had taken cover behind an abandoned car. It was easy to see that she was coordinating with people throughout the ranks, and they were trying to determine where the voice had come from. No one knew.

Rather than giving them too much to think about, Kathy simply repeated her first broadcast. She waited a moment and then added they could signal the affirmative by the leader raising her right fist in the air.

There were some exchanges between several of the people who may have been officers, and one of the men raised his right fist in the air.

Kathy keyed the microphone and asked, "Will you indicate that you will honor a flag of truce by having the tall woman with the silver hair raise her right fist in the air?"

Instead of raising her fist, the woman stood up straight and walked out from behind her cover. It didn't take a rocket scientist for her to understand that someone who had them at a visible disadvantage was also asking them not to shoot. They couldn't even see them, so they certainly couldn't shoot them. They may or may not have the capability to wipe them out from a place of hiding, but she didn't want to find out.

Kathy immediately keyed the microphone and said, "Please indicate that you will honor a truce. Time is short, and we need to talk."

The tall woman looked a bit disturbed by being vulnerable, but the Chief covered the microphone and told Kathy she was doing a good job.

"The lady is an experienced diplomat. She's not giving in or even conceding. She's establishing an equality between us. If she was dealing with those cretins who were here on the island when we got here, she would have to appear strong. Since she doesn't know we're the good guys, she has to make us work for the truce."

"Chief, would you believe they teach street cops the same thing? It's called a control situation," said Kathy.

Colleen added, "They teach the same thing to school teachers and parents about dealing with five-year-olds. It's all about testing limits and equal giving and taking."

None of them knew much about Colleen, even Hampton, but the observation won her a measure of respect. The biggest reason the Mud Island group had survived from the start was likely to be luck, but sometimes luck was a byproduct of intelligence.

When they looked back at the monitor, they saw that the woman had raised her right hand in a fist.

Kathy said, "You have infected coming your way. After you clear them, please approach the brick wall on the right side down by the water. You may bring an armed escort, but I assure you weapons will not be necessary."

They saw the woman look toward the infected dead that continued to crowd through the open gates, and then she glanced toward the brick wall. She gave the signal to fire again, and her firing line did its job. She walked back and spoke with a man who seemed to be acknowledging her orders and then selected two other men to come with her. The Chief pointed out that the three empty positions on the firing line were filled by three women as soon as the men left.

"Equality in the ranks," said the Chief. "My guess would be she has a military background."

The camera view showed the trio approaching the edge of the road where it dropped down to the hidden entrance to the shelter. Kathy had to hurry if she wanted to open the door without keeping them waiting for too long.

The Chief said, "Remember, Kathy. It's a leap of faith. They could take it from us after we let them in, but I don't think that's what's happening here."

"Me either, Chief."

Kathy hurried away toward the stairs up to the surface. Keeping them waiting was a good idea to some extent, but too long might make them nervous. The Chief was right that they could take the shelter once they were inside, but it seemed that they would willingly accept it as a gift. They were too disciplined to see it as a trick.

The tall woman and her escort dropped over the edge toward the water and waited. They kept their weapons aimed back toward the entrance to Ambassadors Island just in case any infected appeared at the top of the steep gravel bank.

When the brick wall in front of them began to move, and there was the sound of brick rubbing against brick, they forgot about the road above them and aimed their rifles at the dark gap that had opened. None of them expected the pretty blond who stuck her head out into the light.

"Step inside, and I'll close the door behind you. As a sign of good faith, you may keep your weapons. Please don't make me regret it."

Iris Mason didn't believe there was much left in the world that would surprise her. Only a few nights before she had a discussion with some of her officers along those same lines. She told them when they lost the capacity to be surprised, that was when they were likely to lose their lives to the unexpected. She was glad to learn she could still be surprised, and she saw by the looks on the faces of her security detail that she was not alone in her feelings.

When they stepped into the darkness she saw the door was much more than brick. It was as thick as a bank vault, and would have been impenetrable if they had tried to break in. There wasn't much light at first, but as her eyes adjusted, she saw the landing was just the beginning.

"What is this place?" she asked.

"You'll have plenty of explanations in the next few minutes. More than you'll believe."

No matter how many times Kathy got to see the look on someone else's face when they saw the inside of a shelter, it was still a treat. As the lights were brought back up to normal level by the Chief down below, Kathy saw the looks on their faces.

After Kathy had gone to the door, the Chief had darkened the interior of the shelter as much as possible. It was a better idea not to have backlighting behind Kathy that would make her an easy target.

When the lights were back to normal, the tall woman reached out with both hands and put them on the rifles held by her security detail. She gently pressed downward to get them to lower their weapons. She saw that Kathy was unarmed and waiting for her to make the next move, so she did.

She didn't speak even though she hadn't gotten an answer to her first question, but she stepped past Kathy and walked calmly to the railing. She saw three more people approaching the stairs below. The man in the lead looked familiar. He was wearing blue coveralls, but in her mind she saw him wearing a white uniform. By the time he reached the top of the stairs, she knew why he looked so familiar.

"Chief Joshua Barnes, I presume," she said.

Even though she was as tall as the Chief, her wiry frame made her appear smaller.

He did his best to not show surprise because he didn't recognize her. He didn't want to embarrass her by saying so.

"Yes, Ma'am," he said as he held out his hand offering to shake hers.

"Iris Mason, Chief. Don't worry, we don't know each other. I just recognize you. I was Chief of Security on the sister ship of the Atlantic Spirit."

Kathy let out a sigh of relief.

"This is going to be a whole lot easier than I thought it would be if you two are already acquainted. We're short on time, and we need to get down to the explanations, but first we're going to give you a quick tour. You might find some of it more believable if you see it with your own eyes."

Kathy said, "I'm Kathy McGinley of the Charleston Police Department."

They shook hands, and Iris introduced her security detail. There was an awkward moment when she started to introduce Hampton and Colleen, but it broke the remaining tension for everyone.

"For some reason," she said, "I know his last name and her first name."

"Hi, I'm Chris Hampton, and this is Colleen O'Connor."

Hampton stepped forward and shook their hands and then made room for Colleen to do the same.

"Iris, Colleen and I just saw this place for the first time just a short while ago. Apparently the Chief and Kathy are used to this stuff. I know how this must all look to you, but if you've ever trusted anyone in your life, believe me when I say they weren't more trustworthy than these people are."

"I think we're well on our way to trust, Chris, but I sure would like to know what's going on."

"I have an idea," said Kathy. "Since we're short on time, and since your people outside are still in danger, maybe we should start by getting them all inside. How many are there?"

Iris looked like she had a moment when she was considering whether or not to give too much information, but she snapped out of it.

"What was I thinking?" she said. "You said we should start bringing everyone inside, and I almost lied to you about our numbers. You really are offering to make everyone safer."

"More than that," said Kathy.

"There are about eighty adults and about thirty children," said Iris.

Kathy, the Chief, Hampton, and Colleen all reacted the same way when they heard there were that many children. They hadn't seen many in the months since the infection began, and most of the ones they had seen were lost to a bite from someone they knew.

Kathy asked Hampton to go back to the monitors and let her know if the outside cameras showed it was all clear outside the hidden door. He ran down the stairs and jogged to the communications room and then came over the PA system.

"All clear."

"Let's get moving," said Kathy. "Chief, if you and Colleen can lead the way, we can start by having everyone go to the first big dining room. It should be more than big enough. Then we can talk with Iris about how they've controlled bite victims."

The Chief was a bit amused because this was the way he saw Kathy take charge on his cruise ship. He had been the senior enlisted person on board when Kathy was asked to take over security, and he never once resented being ordered to defer to her. It was good to see her in action again.

Kathy opened the outer door again, and led Iris back outside. Her two men immediately scrambled up the steep bank to cover her, and they had to open fire as soon as they reached the top. The infected had started to increase their numbers on the road again, so Iris shouted an order for her firing line to resume shooting and to advance at the same time. She gave an order to one of them. He nodded in understanding and ran toward the people watching from the firing line.

Iris had some really good people with her, and Kathy recognized training when she saw it. Some of the men and women must have been police officers and military. They came forward along the side of the road that was in a straight line to the door, setting up a protective wall for the children and the adults who were watching them. Kathy was fascinated by their efficiency and the way they focused their fire to direct the infected to move toward the firing line.

On a signal Kathy didn't see, the children began running behind the protective wall in her direction. She was surprised by the size of the lump in her own throat. As they reached her and ran inside the shelter, she felt like she had to touch each of them to be sure they were real.

The children were followed by women, a few older people, and some younger adults. Then the firing line and the protective wall of shooters collapsed around toward the entrance to the shelter. They fired their rifles and handguns with efficiency until the last of them backed into the shelter entrance, and Kathy pulled the door shut.

The Chief was busy escorting people to the stairs and carrying children down on his shoulders. They were laughing as they clung to his neck, but otherwise there were only whispers and confused murmuring. Everyone was acting as if they had walked into a library or a church, and they weren't supposed to talk out loud.

"They've had months to get used to the idea that talking in an unknown environment will get you killed," said Iris. "Once they realize what's happened, they'll be loud enough."

"I'll tell you the truth," said Kathy. "We haven't even finished making a really thorough search of this shelter ourselves, and we found three infected in a lower level. We don't know how they got in, but it was probably back when all this began. We can brief you while your men are helping get the search done."

"I heard what you said about controlling bite victims. Is that why you had everyone go to one large room?"

"Like it or not," Kathy began, "undisclosed bites will be the undoing of any group that doesn't make checking for bites a routine."

"I agree, and we have a system that keeps parents from hiding that their kids were bitten and from husbands and wife doing the same for each other."

"Good," said Kathy. "Let's get that started. While the others are working on clearing up that messy problem, the Chief and I can fill you in on the rest."

They all went to the dining room together. The room went silent when they walked in. There was a measure of respect for their leader, but the silence was just as driven by the need for an explanation.

Kathy stepped forward first and introduced herself.

"You're in an underground shelter that cannot be penetrated from the outside. The infected cannot get in. Living people cannot get in. There are large amounts of supplies in the shelter, but we haven't done an inventory yet, so we don't know if they will need to be rationed or if there are already enough for you to live on."

A man spoke up from one of the tables.

"We can always go out for more supplies. We've done pretty well for ourselves."

Other voices started to chime in, but Iris held up her hand to silence them.

"I want everyone to remember we are guests here. Our hosts didn't have to open their doors to us. There must have been a good reason for them to do that, so let's hear them out."

Kathy gave it a moment to sink in, then she continued.

"The first thing I was going to say was that you are completely safe here. There is nothing that can harm you. We will also take a look at the power supply to this island to see if it's permanent. We only need to be sure that you can be self-sustaining here, and we should know that fairly quickly."

Kathy had been trained as a police officer how to speak to people as an authority figure without being threatening. Of course it didn't hurt to have the Chief standing next to her.

"This is Chief Barnes. Besides being an all around good guy, he's a former Navy SEAL and national hero. He's going to work with your leaders to explain very quickly how the shelter works and anything important they need to know. He will need to meet with at least ten people including Ms. Mason, but before they go, we need to follow your process, whatever it is, for identifying any possible bites you may have gotten on your journey to this island."

There were murmurings again from around the room, and Kathy waited for it to settle down again, but before she could resume speaking, a woman stood up at a table off to her left. She was wearing jeans and a sweatshirt, and she had a holster around her waist. When she pulled the gun from her holster, Kathy felt like they had made a serious mistake.

The Chief had been leaning against a wall behind Kathy, and he immediately stood up straight. Hampton and Colleen were off to one side, but both knew it would be too late to defend themselves.

A man at another table near the center of the room calmly walked over to the woman who had stood up, and she handed her gun to him. Before he could walk away, everyone at the table reached out with their weapons, and he collected them. The tables were large enough to seat eight people, and some of them had children on their laps.

As the man walked back to his table, the children and adults who had surrendered their weapons removed the tablecloth and carried it to the corner of the room where the bar ran along one wall. They hung the tablecloth from the glass racks above the bar to create a modest amount of privacy, and then they stepped away to one side.

It was all done with such purpose and acceptance of duties. Iris smiled at Kathy then gestured toward a few of her officers.

One of them announced to the room, "Okay, you all know the drill. Weapons on the tables beginning with this table over here. He pointed to the table nearest to the makeshift privacy curtain."

Kathy leaned closer to Iris and whispered, "What stops people from trying to make a break for it or from drawing their guns at the start?"

"Everyone is assigned to watch three other people. If anyone even looks worried, someone will say something, but just to be sure, there is overlap. Someone may be watching three other people, but three people are watching one person. We can do that because one person can watch more children at one time. They don't hide their bites as well. We've also done this many times, and everyone knows why we do it."

The table that was picked to go first lined up at the curtain and the first person walked behind it. One of the officers walked behind it from the other side, and the inspection began. When they announced they were free of bites, they were joined by two people from the table who had hung the curtain. When they were done being inspected, they inspected the original two who had begun.

With four people done the process began to move more quickly. Those four people inspected four more, and in minutes there were eight people checking eight other people, and then sixteen people checking sixteen more. The children were checked by a group of people other than the children's own parents.

"I'm so impressed," said the Chief.

"As I said, Chief, this isn't our first rodeo," said Iris. "We learned from the beginning that people will hide bites, especially if their children are bitten. Some of the hardcore members of our group were all for firing squads for families that hid bites, thinking that would motivate people to be honest, but some of us understood that family bonds are so strong that some families preferred to die together rather than to give up one of their own."

"So, how did you find the proper motivation? It's hard to get a group this size to care enough to rat themselves out if they get bitten," said Colleen.

"For one thing, you have to inspect several times a day. We started with three but went to four when someone was bitten and died between inspections. We almost lost more people that day. We also talked out this system where family members aren't inspected by anyone related to them. Anyone who didn't agree was told to leave the group. We also had to account for the weapons. You may have braced yourselves when Macey stood up and drew her gun, but she's supposed to go first. She's one of my most trusted people, and she would eat a bullet before she would hide a bite. Plus, she was being watched by three other people."

"We have people like that in our group," said the Chief. "If things go as planned, you'll be able to cut back on your bite inspections."

With the inspections done, it was time to start the searches of the remaining rooms, the inventory of supplies, and above all the explanations. It was announced that everyone would be fed as soon as they knew the extent of their food supplies and all rooms were searched, but it was obvious that the newcomers were all more curious about their surroundings than the food. They were ready to begin exploring.

Iris divided up the men and women to assign specific tasks. One group she sent off to a kitchen with the instructions to prepare the first meal from the supplies they had carried in with them. If they found they could have a second meal later from the shelter supplies, they would make it.

Kathy took Iris and a couple of her officers to the control room and showed them what was happening outside. Iris stared at the monitor with her mouth open watching as infected dead stumbled over the bodies left behind on the bridge outside the gates of Ambassadors Island. Some even stumbled enough to fall over the railings into the water below.

Hampton and Colleen were just as new to the shelter as the group of newcomers, so they stayed with Kathy and Iris to hear explanations they didn't have the time to receive before. The Chief had taken a detail to the power plant to assess whether or not it was as sustainable as the one on Mud Island. Other groups were quickly briefed about doing a fast but thorough search. They were told not to let themselves become so fascinated by what they saw that they couldn't move on to the next room. Colleen gave Kathy a guilty look when she thought about stopping for a shower before getting the job done.

"Iris, the most important thing for you to know at this moment is that the four of us will be leaving as soon as we get you and your people situated, and the reason we will leave soon is because a few hours from now it won't be safe to leave for years."

"How many years, and why?" asked Iris.

"The second part of your question is the easy part. The Oconee Nuclear Plant is releasing a cloud of radioactive material. There's no real answer to how much, but it's enough that it reached the coast. It's manageable, but only if you take precautions."

"We heard it was leaking," said Iris, "but not in this direction."

"That's about to change," said Kathy. "There's a hurricane making landfall on the Gulf coast. It's going to shift the radioactive fallout to this area, and it might be heavy. We just don't know enough to say how heavy."

"I see," said Iris. "If it's heavy, we'll be in here for years. If it's light, we just monitor levels until they're low enough. Of course no one has any idea how hurricane force rains will dilute the fallout. The water table might be screwed. There will be a lot of survivor pockets that will die, and there's also no data on how radiation will effect the infected dead."

Kathy continued, "Our expectation is that the infected won't be stopped by radiation poisoning, but they will be contaminated by it. We think the water table will definitely be unsafe for years, but that will depend upon annual rainfall and snow. Pray for a bad winter and a rainy season from hell."

"You didn't expect us to show up, did you?" asked Iris.

Hampton answered for Kathy.

"They didn't know you were here. As a matter of fact, we didn't either. They came here looking for me. I haven't even had a chance to thank them."

Colleen walked over and put her arm around Hampton's waist and leaned into him. The smile she gave Kathy was thanks enough.

"Why did you show up, Iris? Your timing was perfect," said Kathy.

"We were coming for the scum that lived on this island," said Iris. "They tried to raid our camp a few miles from here. We knew they were over here all along, and we were keeping an eye on them. When they came at us, they turned around and ran, but we knew they would come back, so we followed them."

"My God, Iris, you didn't leave anybody behind when you came after them, did you?"

"No, Kathy, we know better. When we mobilize, we all move as a group. Plus we had plans for Ambassadors Island. It looked like a safe place to defend. Those scum forced us to move on them sooner than we had planned."

"Did you know they had packed the houses full of the infected as a means of defense?"

"Our scouts saw them capturing the infected and bringing them back to the island, but we didn't know why. We were thinking they were using them as a food source. You said they were filling the houses with them?"

"The Chief and I noticed too many of the driveways had cars in them instead of inside the garages. Apparently, Hampton and Colleen noticed the same thing and used the captured infected against the people who attacked you."

"That explains why there were so many," said Iris. "I imagine we would still be clearing the homes when the fallout arrives. So, how do you guys fit in?"

******

Needless to say, Iris was really stunned by some of the things she was told. She was particularly interested in what happened to the Atlantic Spirit. Her ship, the Atlantic Mystic, had docked at the North Carolina State Port at Wilmington. The passengers had disembarked on shuttle buses to do a tour of Wilmington, and when the attack began she had been stranded too far from the ship to make it back. As it turned out, the Mystic had not even made it out of port.

She had been working her way west toward Atlanta in hopes of locating her family, but when she saw Charlotte, she realized there was little hope that Atlanta had been much better. There were too many people dead, which meant too many infected dead.

Kathy told her they had flown over Atlanta, and it had been worse than Charlotte. Iris told her it was okay. She had given up hope for her family long ago. If they were alive, there wasn't much chance of finding them. She said it also wasn't fair to the men and women who had tagged along with her because they had families, too. Now that was all beyond their control.

"Iris, you have a big group of people. Some of them may choose to take their chances outside. They're going to die if that's what they choose, but at least it will be their choice. We should get them all back together and tell them what their options are, but you have to tell them it's a one-way ticket. You won't be able to let them back in if they leave."

"I know. They should all have a choice. Could you fill me in about all of this electronics? I imagine we can have them assemble in the dining room for supper and give their reports, then we can break the news."

It didn't take long to explain the control room to Iris because she took her turns standing watch on the bridge of the cruise ship. She was a fast learner, and she was delighted to find that she would be able to communicate with Kathy whenever she wanted. She would also be able to talk with Captain Miller in Charleston and some guy who had a shelter in the Gulf of Mexico on an oil rig. There was an unmanned shelter in a place she had heard of but never visited named Guntersville, Alabama. Kathy told her they considered it a fall back plan if they ever had to leave their shelter on Mud Island.

By the time they finished, the survey of the shelter was also done. The groups were returning, and everyone was eager to share what they had learned. Each group was told to go to the dining room and await the return of the last groups.

They were a different looking crowd from when they assembled the first time. They were hard-faced and determined before. Now they were overjoyed and hopeful. Some of them were joking around with Hampton and Colleen about something, and the children were lining up for rides on the Chief's shoulders. As dangerous as he was to enemies, he was equally safe to anyone who wanted to be his friend.

Kathy and Iris stood next to each other at a speaker's podium someone had dragged in from one of the small auditoriums they had found. Iris had collected some notes from some of the groups as they had returned, and she was smiling as she reviewed them.

"Did you know much about this shelter before we came along, Kathy? It seems this was supposed to be one of the showpieces for that old survivor's club. Every room has some sort of amenities that rival the others. It's like people were trying to outdo each other."

"The shelters are all like this. They aren't all the same design, but each one seems to be like its own little resort. Our shelter on Mud Island is the most practical I've seen so far. It has less amenities, but it's by far the safest. Even though you are underground, there will be times when you'll feel less safe."

"Well, if you're right about the radiation coming this way, we'll have less problems with people trying to break into the shelter," said Iris.

Iris held up her right hand, and the chatter that had made it seem like a crowded restaurant died down quickly. She held such respect from her group that Kathy couldn't help wondering how much more she would have when she washed her long, silver hair and was dressed in something other than the worn and dirty clothes she was wearing.

"I'll make some announcements first," she began in a clear voice, "and then we'll take reports from each group. When we're done with the reports I'll answer all of your questions. Anything I can't answer, maybe our hosts can answer for me."

"I'm going to start with the bad news because it will help everyone here understand that we are short on time, and we have to make decisions quickly."

Iris surveyed their anxious faces, knowing that she had to get the first decision done with. If anyone wanted to leave, they had to leave soon.

"Our hosts have information that the nuclear power plant in Oconee, South Carolina is going to be sending its fallout in this direction. A Gulf hurricane is making landfall at this time, and the prevailing winds will be to this area. For that reason, anyone inside this shelter a few hours from now will have to remain here until the radioactivity levels outside drop to safe levels."

"How long will that be?" shouted a voice from somewhere in the dining room. It wasn't difficult to spot the man who uncharacteristically interrupted Iris because everyone looked at him.

Iris had never doled out corporal punishment, and she wasn't planning to start now. She understood and even expected the question.

"Years," she said.

No one bothered to ask how many years. The meaning of her one word answer was clear enough.

"Because no one has been forced to be in this group, anyone who would rather take their chances above ground must do so now. Once the door is sealed against the radiation, we will not be opening it for a long time. No one will be allowed to leave or return."

The same man stood, but it wasn't in defiance.

"Ma'am, how can we all survive down here for years?"

"That's a good question, and I'm glad you asked. Now that I've laid the options on the table, I would like for each group to give a summary of what they found in the shelter. Let's start with the group that did an inventory of the food and water."

Iris gestured for the leader of that group to take the podium. A woman who had introduced herself to Kathy earlier as Marina cleared her throat and began.

"If there's anyone here who doesn't like chipped beef, you might want to take your chances with the radiation."

There was generally good natured laughter from the crowd and even some applause, but the audience was still a little nervous about the situation, and some just wanted to hear the reports. It shouldn't really come as a surprise if a few people couldn't stand the idea of being stuck underground for a few years.

Marina waited for everyone to settle down again then continued.

"My estimate is that the food supplies were intended to last for at least ten years if one hundred people were being fed."

There was a general outburst this time because the sheer volume of food she was talking about would fill a warehouse.

Iris held up a hand for silence and said, "We won't get through the reports fast enough this way. Let's wait until we have all reports completed before we start with questions."

"As I was saying," said Marina, "there is a tremendous storehouse beneath this shelter. Food will never be a problem. As for water, there is a filtration system that draws its water from the deepest part of Lake Norman. I have been in contact by radio with a doctor and an Army engineer, with the help of our hosts, and they will be giving us the assistance we need to monitor the safety of the water."

"Ma'am," it was the lone man again who had interrupted earlier. "I'm sorry because I know you said we are short on time, but those infected things walking around up there have been falling, stumbling, and sometimes getting thrown into the lake. We've been avoiding lake water. How are we supposed to start drinking it now?"

Iris waited before answering this time. It was a legitimate question, but she didn't need one person identifying potential barriers to their survival.

"Mr. Dawson, you sit among a group of eighty peers. Why is it that you alone are the only person here smart enough to think of these things? How long will we be sealed in here? How will you make the food last long enough? How will the water be safe enough to drink?"

The man had already made up his mind that he wanted to stay, but he was afraid. Either decision, whether it was staying or going, was a one way ticket, and he was sure which one was for the longest ride, but he was still afraid.

He sat down slowly, but he managed to croak out, "I'm sorry, Ma'am."

Marina explained that there would never be a shortage of water as long as the filtration system worked, and the engineer she spoke with had assured her that the system was state of the art. He told her it would last over a hundred years if they needed. She told everyone that the purity of the water was beyond anything they had ever drank because it was distilled as it was pumped in. The steam was converted into drinking water and used as part of a self-sustaining power source.

That was where Marina turned it over to another former member of the Mystic's crew. His job had been in the ship's power plant, and he gave a quick description of the system in the shelter. Because his explanation was a bit technical, some of the people became bored, but when he said they would have hot showers as often as they wanted, he got their full attention.

A former security officer was next, and he told them about the well-stocked armory under the shelter. As he explained on Iris' instructions, there would be a minimum of armed residents in the shelter. They would maintain a small police force to handle civil disputes, but their primary goal was to be ready in the event that someone was able to breach the shelter. He was quick to add that he had personally inspected the shelter for safety, and he found it to be completely unlikely that anyone could force their way into the shelter.

Iris took over and explained some of what she had been told about the shelter, its origin, and its electronic capabilities. She told the people that the Chief, Kathy, and all of their friends were fighting back against the infected dead by populating the shelters. Eventually, they would all play their part in reclaiming the world from the infected dead.

Then she told them the really good news. There were enough rooms for all of the families with some vacancies left over. She said it was inevitable that their children would grow up in the shelter. There would be marriages, births, and unfortunately deaths, but if they needed the room to expand, it would be available.

"That brings me to the issue of jobs. I've already picked my police force. They are people who have experience in the military and security on the cruise ship. We'll need people to cook, clean, and to operate the critical systems, such as water and electricity. We definitely need to know if anyone has had even basic first aid training so we can set up a hospital."

"You may have noticed there are stores around the shelter. The builders wanted to create an illusion of normalcy, and we would be crazy to ignore the concept. As a matter of fact, it will keep us from going crazy. I'll meet with the leaders of the different groups after our friends leave, and we'll discuss implementation of a system of currency."

"Now, if there is anyone who would like to leave, please let me know quickly. Our hosts will be departing within the hour. Once the doors are closed behind them, they won't be opened again. As for those of you who already plan to stay, dinner is served."

It started with some cheers and random applause, but it spread quickly, and it was aimed at the Mud Island group. They had been skeptical when they had first entered the vault door, but for the first time in a long time, they felt safe. The applause increased when the kitchen doors opened and group members who had volunteered to cook the first meal began setting up a buffet.

"Ladies and gentlemen, could I have your attention, please?"

The Chief was at the podium with his hand raised, and the room gave him the same respect they showed Iris.

"I know some of you are still skeptical, but trust me. This is all real. You will be safe here, and you would not be safe out there. Now, while your friends are setting up the food, Iris has agreed that it wouldn't hurt if each of you had one drink at the bar."

It was only one drink, but it would be the first in a long time any of them had enjoyed without worrying about being attacked, and every adult that could reach the bar was trying to do so. It was good natured, though, and the gratitude was obvious.

"Will you be staying for supper, Chief?" asked Iris.

Kathy, Hampton, and Colleen came up to join them.

"I'm afraid not, Iris. The winds are unpredictable, so we're going to go while we can. We did a good thing when we decided to take a leap of faith and give you the shelter. It will keep you alive, and it will give us one more outpost of humanity for when we're ready to start taking the world back."

"Even without the radiation, do you think we are ever going to see that day, Chief? Do you have a plan?"

"The Chief always has a plan," said Kathy. "As a matter of fact, he most likely has one or two that he hasn't shared with me yet."

The Chief tried to look innocent, something he could never quite accomplish, but it was one of his endearing qualities.

"Winter," he said. "I think we can at least chip away at the number of infected dead by traveling to frozen climates and eliminating as many as we can. They have to be easy to kill when they're frozen, but that's a plan for another time."

Kathy rolled her eyes.

"Did you just say that?" she asked.

"Say what?"

"Chip away. You said we can chip away at the number. We're going to use ice picks, too. Right?"

The Chief was trying to look innocent again, but was having a hard time hiding his grin.

Iris came to his rescue by asking if they had everything they needed for the trip back, and he told her they didn't need much, but they wanted to check in with the others back at Mud Island before leaving. They needed to know what their approach needed to be if the conditions on Mud Island were still "unfriendly".

"There's another thing I don't understand," said Iris. "How do you plan to get from one end of Ambassadors Island to the other? The place is literally crawling with the infected."

"You didn't tell her about the emergency exits?"

Kathy looked a bit sheepish. She had been so caught up with explaining the high tech gear that she had forgotten to tell her that every shelter had back doors.

"Iris, if you check the floor plans for the shelter, you'll find that there are several ways to leave besides the main vault door," said the Chief. "One of the exits is located in the middle of a small copse of trees at the southern tip of Ambassadors Island. Kathy and I actually hid in those trees when we first arrived. From what I heard talking to Hampton, he and Colleen hid there, too. That's the exit we'll use to leave."

Kathy added, "There are other exits. Several are located among the houses, and some are inside the houses. I don't expect those will do you much good. One of the best exits to keep in mind besides the one that we're going to use is one that comes out on the mainland not far from the end of the bridge. When the day comes to go back outside, that's going to be one of your best bets. You can check the area around each exit using remote controlled cameras before you go outside."

"I imagine the emergency exits will be low on our priority list once the radiation begins to fall," said Iris, "but I'm not complaining. You saved our lives, so you have friends and allies forever. When the time comes to fight back, we'll be ready."

The walk to the exit from the Ambassadors Island shelter seemed to be over in no time, even though the foursome exchanged handshakes and waves with the new occupants almost every step of the way. They had made a quick stop at the control center and radioed the shelter at Mud Island. The news on their end still wasn't so good. The squatters were converting the moat into a marina, and there was a tent city on the beach where Captain Miller's men had camped. They decided they would have to talk through a plan on the way back because they needed to get out of the area soon.

Before long they were at a cylindrical stairwell that was encased by the same shiny alloy they had seen in the other shelters. It didn't look like you could scratch it with a chainsaw. The bottom of the stairwell had a coded door that slid silently out of the way when the Chief punched in the combination.

The surface was about four stories above them, and when they opened the hatch they found it was right near the gear they had left behind before they had slipped into the water and crossed over to the island.

The Chief looked through the trees, and he saw they had left it a real mess. There were infected dead everywhere, and some were walking dangerously close to the edges of docks.

"Heads up, everyone. The sides of this little island are too steep for the infected to climb, but that sandbar behind the island is practically a sidewalk. Keep an eye out for infected that are already in the water."

Even though they hadn't been inside the shelter for long, it felt unreal to be back outside where the real dangers were. The three infected that had been inside the shelter had been identified by shelter records as a minimum maintenance crew hired by the builder. How they had become infected would remain a secret forever, but it felt different knowing who they were and that there were no more inside. Outside there were hundreds of them within shouting distance, but they were all unknowns. They were all hostile with only one thing in mind.

When they came out of the trees onto the sandbar, the Chief saw they were right to be worried about the infected in the water. There were more tracks in the soft sand than there should have been, and their raft was gone. Survivors may have discovered it and taken it for themselves, but it seemed more likely that it had been bumped by infected dead until it slid into the water and drifted away on the mild current.

"I never asked you two, but how did you get to Ambassadors Island in the first place? Please tell me you have a boat around here somewhere," said the Chief.

Colleen turned and pointed back the way they had come.

"First house on the left, Chief. Tied to a dock."

He studied her expression for a minute then looked at Kathy.

"Oh, no. She's another Jean."

Kathy said, "You guys just rode right up to the island and knocked on the door?"

Before they could answer she said, "Never mind, but you guys won't believe it when we tell you how lucky you were. So, Chief, which one of us is going for a swim?"

The Chief was already starting to walk out on the sandbar. He looked back at Kathy and said, "Unless you've suddenly learned how to fly a plane, I think I should go get it. I'll pick you guys up in a few minutes, but just to be on the safe side, everyone keep your rifles ready and your eyes on the water as I swim. I don't really want to know if it's as bad on the bottom of the lake as I think it is."

8 MERCY MISSION SHIP

While Ed Jackson was standing inside a video game store in Surfside, South Carolina watching the world unravel before his eyes, people across the world were trying to piece together bits of information about what was happening to them. Ed was watching the parking lot of a fast food restaurant where people were attacking other people and biting them. For no apparent reason, people were trying to kill each other, while some were just trying to get away.

The scene shifted from the police trying to control a handful of people who looked more like rabid animals than people, to a scene of rescue. Emergency Medical Technicians who responded to the scene became victims as they tried to help the injured. When it started, there was far less blood on the ground than when it ended. The police were forced to shoot the rabid attackers because they wouldn't stop. As a matter of fact, it became obvious to everyone that they wouldn't stay on the ground until they were shot in the head.

The Atlantic Spirit was docked at the Charleston, South Carolina cruise ship terminal and was taking aboard supplies along with the scheduled passengers. Chief Barnes was going about his routine duties supervising several assignments at the same time. Being the senior enlisted crew member carried more responsibility than any officer on board had to shoulder, but the Chief had the shoulders for it. He stood over six and a half feet tall, and was nothing but solid muscle. He was a former Navy SEAL, and he had seen plenty of things in his life that the average person would never see, but from his vantage point on a high deck of the Atlantic Spirit, even he was surprised by the chaos he was watching through binoculars.

The streets of the beautiful old city of Charleston were foreign to him as he watched families dragged to the ground by crowds of people who appeared to be dead themselves. He had seen so much in his life that he was able to understand, no matter how brutal it was, but his mind could not come up with an answer for what he was seeing. They were slow. They moved in groups that seemed to grow in size by the minute. They grabbed anyone who was trying to get away from them and sank their teeth into the flesh of their captives. The Chief couldn't make sense of it, and he couldn't hear the screams of the people he was watching, but he could hear closer screams that fit perfectly with what he was seeing at a distance.

It was happening everywhere he looked, and when he looked down toward the parking area of the cruise ship terminal, he saw a police officer who had lost her hat but was running ahead of a group of men pointing at cars and trucks. They were making a blockade along the end of the dock where it met the shoreline, and they were doing a good job of stopping the big groups of the slow moving attackers that were trying to reach the terminal. Below him, Chief

Barnes could see that the pier was standing room only as passengers tried to board quickly. None of it made sense.

The medical crew of the Atlantic Spirit was at the bottom of the loading ramp checking for passengers who had been bitten. They had been quick to assess the situation, and they didn't know why, but they knew once you were bitten you were definitely going to die. They had been given orders by a ship's doctor who was noticeably absent from the frantic crowd in the medical tent. When asked by one bite victim if there was a doctor on board the ship, a nurse wearing a name tag on her blue scrubs that had JEAN engraved on it almost said no, but she told the worried person she would try to get the doctor to come to the tent. She knew it would be a cold day in hell before he let himself get close to a real illness.

Jean was trying to understand why people were being bitten, but she didn't have the time to give it much thought. She had been told that the police were trying to blockade the terminal so they could finish boarding and get underway, but it was going to be close.

Not far north of where Ed stood in the video store watching people tear into other people with their teeth while the police were shooting them, Tom and his young daughter Molly had started trying to figure out what to do. Stuck in a hotel room in Myrtle Beach, they seemed only to be able to sit and watch the news on TV as they were told first to go to hospitals if they were bitten, then they were told to stay home. Staying home was fine with Tom, but they didn't have any supplies. The little refrigerator in their room had a few bottles of water and soda, but the only thing they had plenty of was a supply of tiny bottles of liquor.

Almost as far to the south of Ed Jackson, Chris Hampton watched the news reports and called friends. Georgetown, South Carolina seemed like the perfect place to stay put. Its location on the coast made it a place of refuge for its citizens because they could isolate themselves from the rest of the world. Hampton began organizing friends to close off and defend Georgetown from what he knew was coming. What amazed him the most was the people who left to find relatives up and down the coast. Some headed for Charleston, and some headed for Myrtle Beach or points in between. What worried Hampton the most was the number of people who got into Georgetown before they were able to close the bridges and roads. Any of them could be carrying the infection into their town.

Across the Atlantic along the coast of Africa, a Mercy Mission ship had just left the country of Cameroon. At over sixteen thousand tons and room for a crew of four hundred and fifty, it was the largest civilian hospital ship in the world, and it had been docked at the port of Douala when the attacks began.

For the last year the ship and its volunteer crew of doctors and nurses had been providing medical care to small villages and towns that otherwise would never receive such care. The ship carried an array of vehicles that could transport the medical services to the villages, and when necessary they could bring the villagers back to the ship for treatment and even surgery. The surgical staff was made up of some of the best doctors in the world, and the facilities were modern and well stocked.

When the first reports were radioed in to the ship, the crew didn't know what to believe. In a land where superstition was more prevalent than a first grade education, they were highly skeptical about the dead coming back to life. The crew believed at least for a short time that the people of Cameroon thought the Mercy Mission ship doctors were resurrecting the dead. They thought that local folklore was just making people believe they could bring the dead back to life.

Doula was the largest city in Cameroon with a population of over two million people, and the crowded streets were ripe for spreading the infection quickly. The first cases appeared in the quarantine areas of the Mercy Mission ship. The patients had been brought back to the ship for treatment because nothing the doctors and nurses did for them brought down their raging fevers. Thinking it might be some form of Ebola they hadn't seen before, they were quickly quarantined and restrained.

With a large part of the medical staff still ashore, the Mercy Mission ship had prepared for departure after receiving increasingly alarming reports about the attacks throughout the city. They waited as long as they could and were grateful every time they saw another team arrive at the dock, but it quickly became a dangerous place for them to be. Bitten, sick, dying, and the living were all starting to flood the port, so the Mercy Mission ship had to leave before everyone had returned. They were grief stricken by the loss of each person, but they couldn't wait any longer. A head count revealed they had lost thirty of their young field doctors and nurses.

Doctor Sellers had been traveling through third world countries giving free medical care for over twenty years, and as the large blue and white Mercy Mission ship drifted away from the dock, he was staggered by the desperation of the people who were jumping into the water, but he was even more amazed by the restrained patients in the quarantine areas.

He was standing by an open door that faced the dock. It looked like the dock was moving away from the ship, but his eyes were glued to the patients who had died and then began trying to pull free from their restraints. One of the restrained patients was a young nurse who had instinctively rushed to help the first of the dead when she thought he had shown signs of recovery. The man had bitten her savagely on the arm as if he was trying to eat her. Doctor Sellers hadn't seen anything like it in all of his years in medicine.

A Canadian by birth, Doctor Sellers had moved to America to study medicine, but it had never been about the money. It had always been about a higher calling to heal the sick. Now he was watching people die without knowing the cause, and then he was seeing them come back as incoherent cannibals. For the first time in his career, he felt totally helpless.

His eyes were momentarily pulled from the beds to the screaming crowds on the docks. A small military vessel was coasting between the Mercy Mission ship and dock, and the armed soldiers were trying to shoot at the people who were biting the ones who were trying to get away. Doctor Sellers thought about the number of people they had saved in the last year and wondered if he had already seen a larger number of people die in just this one day.

A ship wide announcement pulled him from his thoughts. All medical staff members were to meet in the large conference room to discuss their plans. There was something in the summons about a pandemic, which was the one thing that scared all doctors and nurses who dealt with infectious diseases. He left the quarantine area and pulled off his mask and gloves.

"Shouldn't you be wearing a biohazard suit in there?"

It was Nurse Brand, the Head Nurse for the surgical unit. She was moving in the same direction as everyone else.

"We've already determined the means of transmission," he said. "It's not airborne, and all indications are that it's caused by being bitten."

"If that's true," she said, "then try to explain the patient who died in surgery this morning. He was pronounced dead at 0900 hours, and he was trying to sit up and bite the surgical staff at 0915 hours. He's strapped to a bed in recovery, and he has no visible bite marks."

Doctor Sellers didn't hear another word that was said on the way to the conference room. All he could think about was what Nurse Brand had told him. If the means of transmission was from being bitten, then how had the patient become infected? He told himself he would need to study the lab results of the patient that were from tests done before the surgery.

The large conference room was crowded with mostly staff members wearing white lab coats, but there were a few in blue scrubs sprinkled throughout the crowd. Most of the faces were tired looking, and absolutely no one was smiling. It was standing room only around the large conference table, but on this occasion most of the staff felt like standing.

The Medical Director called for everyone to give him their attention, and he quickly launched into the description of the pandemic that was sweeping across the world. His report was bleak. Every major city in the world had been overcome by an unidentified viral outbreak that caused victims to die quickly, only to regain some semblance of animation and begin attacking people who had not yet been bitten.

There wasn't a single reported case of a reanimated person trying to bite another person who had died from a bite. They were only drawn to new victims. This had led some infectious disease specialists to assume the reanimated dead were being driven to expedite the spread of the virus, which made them believe the virus recognized itself. An Italian doctor had made the international news quickly when she had given it a name. She had called it the Pensando Virus, which means the Thinking Virus.

Her only explanation for how it could think was pure speculation that the victim's brain functions were reanimated only enough to allow the victim to detect other victims. She was widely criticized because thinking implied consciousness, but the term caught on throughout the world. At least the part about it being an infection was accepted as common knowledge.

The Medical Director explained to the assembled doctors and nurses that the Mercy Mission ship had left Cameroon in order to be more useful in combating the disease. They had received a request to assist an American Navy carrier group that had managed to leave port with substantial resources and personnel. The rendezvous point would be somewhere off the east coast of the United States, and their goal was to provide both care and research capabilities. The Director assured them that they were not being conscripted into military service, and they would play a vital role in identifying and combating the virus.

He opened the floor for questions, and the most prevalent was whether or not the staff members could contact their families. The ship's Captain had been watching the Medical Director give his presentation of the problem, and it was immediately obvious to him that many of the medical staff were not seeing the big picture. Captain Harold Abbott, a former officer in the British Royal Navy stepped forward and asked for quiet. He was known to be fair but firm, and the room went quiet again.

"Ladies and gentlemen," he began, "we are faced with an event of unprecedented proportions. I do not wish to appear uncaring about your families and loved ones, but reports from all corners of the world indicate there was no time for the civilian population of the world to prepare for these events. The likelihood of survivors is slim. We will rendezvous with the American task force to render whatever assistance we can, but any attempts to contact your families would be futile."

There was a general protest from the assembled staff, but the Captain held his right hand in the air, and the room went quiet again.

"The US Navy has informed me there will be missions to American cities in search of survivors. As they are recovered, they will be brought to safety. The military also plans to establish safe zones on the coast, fortify them, and then begin rebuilding. You will be reunited with loved ones if they are recovered, but for the time being, we have a job to do. I think you will find that your work will help you to pass the time. So, please return to your duties, and let's begin doing what a hospital ship does best."

When the Captain and Medical Director left the room, the doctors and nurses felt like they didn't know what to do first. They gradually began to file out of the conference rooms and return to their respective duty stations.

Doctor Sellers arrived at the quarantine unit behind several other doctors and nurses who had already begun tending to the bite victims. As the supervisor of this particular unit, he was prone to observe the staff as they went about their assignments, but he knew he needed to be with them as they encountered the most deadly disease they had ever tried to treat. Even the Ebola cases they had treated had a better chance of survival than the bite victims.

"Wayne, take a look at this bite wound."

It was one of his senior staff who had addressed him. The Nigerian doctor who had been educated in the United Kingdom was known as one of the best infectious disease doctors in the world, which meant he was in the right place to be helping to fight the disease.

Doctor Sellers pulled on a mask and gloves and entered the quarantine tent where Doctor Nkrumah was holding the arm of one of the victims. He had a bright light shining into the wound so they could see the surrounding tissue better. Doctor Sellers studied the bite, but he couldn't see anything unusual about it. It was ragged and looked like the bite left by any carnivore that was using incisors to tear away flesh before chewing it with molars.

"I don't see anything unique about it. Do you?" he asked.

Doctor Nkrumah rotated it slightly under the light and then irrigated the wound. The liquid ran off the arm into a pan, and a nurse immediately pulled it away so the liquid could be examined more closely for whatever pathogens might be involved with this strange virus. She had already removed some tissue and prepared a culture to see if they could grow the virus. Sophisticated lab equipment was trying to isolate the virus from the human cells so they could begin testing to see what would kill the virus without killing the host.

Doctor Sellers thought he saw a change happening in the bite. It was still ragged and ugly, but it looked different. He put a magnifying glass over it and saw the difference. The tissue around the edges of the bite didn't heal, but they didn't look damaged. It was almost as if the wound could be stitched. It would heal and leave a scar, but it would heal. The problem was, the host would be dead long before the wound healed.

Nkrumah said, "This virus is only intended to destroy brain cells, and not just any brain cells. Just the cells involved with higher functions, such as reasoning and thought."

"I don't understand," said Doctor Sellers. "How do the organs and the muscles keep working? It doesn't appear that the heart needs oxygenated blood pumping to the rest of the body, and the brain cells that survive don't need it either."

Both doctors had the same idea at the exact same moment and shared a look of disbelief and horror.

Doctor Sellers said, "The virus produces something that substitutes for all of the body fluids, hormones, and enzymes?"

"And the substitutes are produced in the portion of the brain that is left functioning after death," said Nkrumah. "That's why it takes an injury to the head to kill them."

The patient on the table began to pull at his restraints and snap his teeth at the doctors. There was no concern for their safety, but they backed away out of reflex.

Doctor Sellers said, "There is nothing more we can do for him, but there is much more he can do for us. We need to study the functioning portion of his brain so we can see how and where the substitutes are being manufactured."

The patient was removed to a surgical suite while Sellers and Nkrumah examined each of the remaining patients in the quarantine section. They found one that was snapping at the nurse but had no visible bite marks. They checked for scratches, insect bites, and signs of irritation in the airways and nose, but there was nothing. The discouraging result of their examinations was that there had to be another method of transmission, and they couldn't interview the patients to see what they may have had in common.

Outside the quarantine tent they both took off their masks and gloves and washed in sinks filled with hot, soapy water and chlorine bleach. They both needed rest, but they were puzzled by their patient who hadn't been bitten. He had also been removed to a surgical suite to have his brain removed and compared with the brain of the man who had been bitten. Before going to their cabins for some rest, they decided to stop at the galley to talk over the events of the day.

The galley of the Mercy Mission ship had always been the favorite place of the medical staff to socialize. There were occasional celebratory dinners that featured a special wine or champagne, but for the most part, the staff didn't drink. Coffee was usually given a pass on days when surgery was performed, but it was in good supply when the doctors and nurses were working on a problem.

Today was a coffee day. The medical teams that were involved with the various aspects of the ship's mission were sitting in small groups around the galley trying to come up with answers. There were plenty of theories, but few of them were based in fact.

Doctor Sellers and Doctor Nkrumah sat down heavily into their chairs with big cups of coffee. Neither one spoke for a while as they sat with their heads resting on their hands. Both were experts, but both felt like it was their first day of medical school.

Other doctors and nurses passed their table, saw the far away looks on their faces, and then moved on. They knew the pair were as lost in thought as some of the other doctors who sat alone or in small groups. Entire tables of medical staff sat quietly without saying a word.

"We're supposed to be the ones with the answers," said Sellers. "Everyone else is waiting for us to give them some kind of hope, but the most I can come up with is that there has to be a connection between the patients who have been bitten and the ones that haven't been."

"I have an idea," said Nkrumah, "but I can't seem to put my finger on it. There's something bothering me, but I don't know what it is."

The galley crew saw that the medical staff was gathering in the galley in larger than normal numbers, so the ever accommodating ship's cooks began setting up an array of meals. The Captain had explained to the cooks long ago that the doctors and nurses were somewhat unpredictable about meals. Sometimes the galley was crowded as a meal was being served, and sometimes it was empty. Sometimes it was crowded, like tonight, but no one ate the meals that were prepared. The cooks felt like this was going to be one of those nights when they would put on a display of their skills, but the efforts would be largely ignored.

They were surprised when people began lining up at the serving area and picking out meals rather than just refilling their coffee cups. The cooks always felt good about serving meals that met with widespread approval, so they were replacing the food as quickly as it was eaten. The most popular choices on this evening were the wide variety of seafoods, and Doctor Nkrumah found himself to be a bit fascinated by the number of people who had an appetite. As a matter of fact, he found himself going to the line without giving it much thought.

Doctor Sellers kept sipping at his coffee as he watched his friend walk over to the serving line and pick up a tray. It crossed his mind that he wasn't hungry enough to eat, but the conversations at the other tables began to take on a more spirited tone, and it occurred to him that he might be able to think more clearly on a full stomach rather than a full dose of caffeine.

Nkrumah was several people ahead of him as Sellers got in line, and he focused on the array of choices. The cooks really knew how to make everything look appetizing, so he felt like he was getting more than he should, but he was carrying a full tray of food to the table in only minutes.

As he sat down he said, "I feel like such a pig for getting so much, but everything looked so good."

Doctor Nkrumah laughed when he looked up from his own tray. He said, "If you're a pig, then we have something in common." His tray looked just like Sellers'.

Doctor Sellers was just starting to put his fork in his mouth when he realized Nkrumah was staring at him. Actually, he was staring at his plate.

"We chose the same meals," said Nkrumah.

Given the variety of foods on the serving line, it was a bit odd that they had chosen exactly the same items, but it wasn't exactly the food that Nkrumah was thinking of. It was one of the things they couldn't ask their dead patients who had been taken away to have their brains examined.

"What had the dead patients been eating?" he asked Doctor Sellers.

The question made Doctor Sellers pause with his fork in front of his face.

"The food chain?" asked Doctor Sellers.

"Exactly. If we interviewed them, we would probably find they had eaten different meals in the last days or weeks, but at some point in time, they ate the same thing. This virus must be in the food chain. They might only be able to spread it by biting someone else, but eating something that possibly ate someone else who had the infection could be the other vector."

Both doctors found themselves examining their plates of food. They were particularly fixated upon one of the cook's favorite recipes, African ghost crab minced with mangrove oysters.

Doctor Sellers and Doctor Nkrumah both put their forks down, stared at each other, and then began looking at all of the other tables where the diners were enjoying their meals as they talked. The world was coming to an end, but they were at least for now enjoying a good meal.

"I only have one question," said Doctor Sellers, "how long has it been in the food chain."

"Long enough for all of us to have been exposed," said Nkrumah.

******

The labs on the Mercy Mission ship didn't have the view enjoyed by the medical personnel on the upper decks, but the lab techs who worked there were happy with the modern equipment. Charitable donors who kept the Mercy Mission ships afloat were more than generous, and when doctors wanted answers, they were usually able to give them everything they needed.

The request from Doctor Nkrumah and Doctor Sellers to begin analyzing stomach contents of bite victims as well as non-bite victims wasn't so strange that it caused any speculation, but the manner in which the request was delivered was a bit odd. Both doctors appeared to be almost excited about what they would learn from such tests.

When they burst into the lab together, they looked like they had run to the lab, and when they were informed that stomach contents had already been analyzed, they looked like they had won the lottery. Altogether, there had been twelve autopsies, and the results were complete with the exception of the two that just arrived. The lab techs handed over the files, and the doctors rushed out as they were already thumbing through the pages to the part they wanted to read.

By the time they arrived back at the quarantine ward, they had what they needed. The autopsies of all of the victims contained no surprises. Their diets had been similar, because the mangrove oysters in particular were very common. They were smaller than oysters found in the waters along the coast of North America, but they were plentiful. As for the ghost crabs, they were popular among the people of Cameroon for making broth for soups. They didn't have as much meat on them as blue crabs, but they were big enough to supplement a stew. They also did what any crab would do, and that was to eat anything that fell into the ocean and died. They weren't finding food to be scarce in the last few days.

The last few pages of each autopsy gave a summary of the findings followed by a description of disposal of the remains. On a ship, the most expedient method of disposal was to drop the remains overboard.

"Now it's your turn to speculate. How long do you think this virus has been in the food chain?" asked Doctor Nkrumah.

"When you consider the onset of the attacks, both the frequency and the rapid spread once they started biting people, it could have been a recent phenomenon, but it's such a virulent viral strain that it didn't take long for it to spread."

Doctor Nkrumah opened a desk drawer and pulled out a calculator as he explained what he was thinking.

"About one hundred and fifty-two thousand people die every day," he said. "If no one is born to replace them, it would take almost fifty-thousand days for the Earth to run out of people, but this virus is moving so fast, what if the death rate is faster than the birth rate to such an extreme that we start running out of people?"

"You're referring to a saturation of the food chain that causes the virus to propagate faster than people," said Doctor Sellers.

"What if the food chain reached a saturation point when there were so many people who had eaten food containing the virus, that something triggered the virus to begin propagating? In other words, it contaminated everything first, and then it began to spread."

Doctor Sellers thought about what his friend might be saying, understanding that he wasn't talking about a normal virus, and he wasn't just talking about contaminated food. He was talking about a contaminated environment. The entire planet was contaminated by this virus, and it had been dormant until something caused it to become active. Since practically everything people ate was tied together in the food chain, there was only one thing he could think of that could have triggered the virus to cause people to start coming back from the dead and biting other people.

"Doctor Nkrumah, are you saying that the virus was dormant until someone introduced human tissue into their diet?"

"Yes, but not necessarily through cannibalism," he said. "It could have been from eating seafood that had eaten human tissue."

Doctor Nkrumah was tapping on his calculator as he thought of how quickly the virus could have spread once it began. When he finished, he couldn't believe the numbers himself. He held it out for Doctor Sellers to see.

By his calculations, if everyone who died on the first day had the chance to bite ten people, and those victims all had the opportunity to bite just ten people, and each of those victims bit ten people, then the population of the Earth would be gone in about forty-six days.

"Of course that number wouldn't include the survivors who would be killing other survivors," said Doctor Nkrumah. "There is always going to be attrition due to natural deaths or death by another cause, so it could be as little as forty days."

Doctor Sellers felt his knees become weak, and he had to find a chair.

"We have to tell someone," he said. "We have to warn the carrier group that we are meeting with. There are thousands of men and women on those ships, so we need to warn them that anyone who dies of natural causes or through accidents should be treated as if they died from a bite."

"Good luck convincing the Captain," said Nkrumah.

"We're a hospital ship, Nkrumah. It's our job to convince the Captain of such things. Why wouldn't he believe us?"

"We're going to tell him that mankind will be extinct in just over a month, and you think he will listen?"

Doctor Sellers knew that his friend was right. The best thing they could do was tell the Captain what their lab results revealed and allow him to come to his own conclusions. If he asked for an interpretation, they would give him one.

The two doctors found the Captain in his stateroom instead of the bridge. He offered them each a seat, and then he explained that he was trying to decide whether they should continue across the Atlantic to rendezvous with the US Navy carrier group, or if they should go north to the United Kingdom.

"I thought we were already committed to the rendezvous," said Doctor Sellers.

"We are, but we're receiving distress calls from home, as well. In any case, we have a few days to decide. What was it you wanted to see me about?"

They took their time explaining the results of the lab tests. It was clear that the Captain was distressed to hear that it wasn't necessary to be bitten in order to become reanimated. It was also clear that he was able to draw the conclusions from the news.

"At what rate will the world population decrease?" he asked.

Doctor Sellers tried to remain noncommittal so the Captain could make his own decisions, so he just said, "It could reach near extinction levels in less than two months, Sir."

The Captain studied the two doctors, understanding that it was bad enough to keep them from giving him the direct answer he had asked for.

"Thank you for your assessment, doctor, but at what rate will the population likely be eliminated by this pandemic?"

Doctor Nkrumah answered for Doctor Sellers, "From two and a half to three percent of the population will die per day, Sir."

The Captain stood and walked over to a cabinet where he kept his private stock of liquor and poured three glasses. He didn't ask either doctor if they wanted a drink. He just figured they could use one.

"If we rendezvous with the Americans, how many men and women will they have on their ships?" asked Doctor Sellers.

"There will be five thousand on the carrier alone," he answered. "I know why you asked, Doctor Sellers. They are bound to have some crewmen die, but it is even more likely there is someone on board one of their ships who has already been bitten. Unless they have been screening their crews since the moment this began, someone is going to spread the disease."

Nkrumah cleared his throat to get the Captain's attention and said, "They have good medical facilities on their ships. Why do they need a hospital ship unless they already plan to try to save people who have been bitten?"

"That's what I was wondering," said the Captain. "My guess would be they are also thinking about using our Mercy Mission ship as a research vessel, which means they will want us to take bite victims on board for study."

"That wouldn't be my first choice," said Doctor Sellers.

"Mine either," said the Captain, "so keeping the rendezvous will have its risks. Still, I believe we are responding to an international request for assistance that we cannot decline. It would be much the same as ignoring a Mayday signal from another ship."

The Captain appeared to have made up his mind that they would be keeping their promise to meet with the American Navy, but he also had to think about the safety of his doctors.

"You need to have a bodyguard with you at all times," said the Captain. "When we meet with the Americans I will communicate to them that we are already a quarantine ship, and we will assist with research, but we will take no new patients. We could easily be overwhelmed."

"Why do we need a bodyguard?" asked Sellers.

His tone wasn't dismissive because he was speaking to the Captain, but he conveyed just enough doubt for the Captain to consider it an argument. He held up one hand, which was his trademark signal telling the crew to stop talking.

To both of them he said, "I don't need to tell you what can happen next. If this thing…this virus gets loose on the ship, we will all be dead before we can even reach the middle of the Atlantic. We won't have to worry about what the Americans want from us."

Both doctors knew when they were getting a lecture that meant they didn't need to talk, so they waited for the Captain to continue.

The Captain picked up the phone on his desk and spoke with his personal yeoman. It wasn't a full minute after he had placed the phone back on its cradle before there was a knock on the door. He opened it, and a familiar dark skinned woman dressed in what was known as the Navy Working Uniform Type One snapped to attention. The Captain stepped aside and motioned for the woman to enter. Her uniform was a US Navy version of camouflage, and she was wearing a Glock at her waist.

The doctors had seen Cassandra Gibbs around the ship many times but had never gotten to know her. She was an African American woman who had been in the United States Army until a bullet had disqualified her from further combat duty. When she had seen the ad about volunteers needed to serve on Mercy Mission ships, she was happy to see that they also had openings for security personnel. It had been an easy choice for her. It would give her the opportunity to do what she enjoyed most, and she understood military life.

When the door to the Captain's office opened, she didn't really know why she had been summoned, but she had been told to bring her sidearm. She was prepared to transfer it from the holster into a targeting position in one smooth motion if the Captain gave the order, so she was wound as tight as a coiled spring. She didn't expect to see the two doctors sitting comfortably in front of the Captain's desk holding glasses of what could only be liquor.

"You sent for me, Captain?"

When he motioned for her to step into the room, she looked around as if she expected to see some form of threat in the room, but all she saw was the three men.

"Petty Officer Gibbs, I'm sure you know two of our finest doctors, Sellers and Nkrumah."

Both doctors stood out of reflex. They had been raised as gentlemen, and despite her military appearance and demeanor, she was still a woman. A woman most men would notice when she walked into a room because she was also very attractive. She had her jet black hair in a ponytail that swayed from side to side when she turned her head.

They exchanged introductions and Cassandra relaxed. Whatever the Captain wanted, it didn't involve a threat in his office.

Captain Abbott circled around to the other side of his desk and motioned with one hand for Cassandra to sit in one of the vacant chairs next to the two doctors. Petty Officer Gibbs took a chair to the right of the doctors and shifted uncomfortably. She wasn't used to being seated in the company of doctors, who carried officer rank on any ship, and the Captain.

"Relax, Petty Officer Gibbs. I have an assignment for you. For the remainder of this cruise, however long it may be, you are the personal bodyguard of these two doctors. You are authorized to use deadly force at any time you feel one or both of them are in danger. Pick a detail of security officers you trust to fill in for you when you are sleeping or otherwise indisposed. Any questions?"

"Yessir, is there a perceived threat? I assume you have something in mind if you are so concerned that you are willing to assign personal protection."

Cassandra eyed the two doctors as if she could read whatever it was they were needing protection from.

"You saw what was happening on the docks as we left Douala?"

"Yessir. Is there reason to believe we have bite victims on board?" she asked.

"We already had patients under quarantine with the symptoms. We just didn't know it yet."

Cassandra's eyes got bigger at the news. She had heard the crew talking about what it would be like on the ship if the strange infection had come on board with the crew.

The Captain continued, "Of course we would probably have tried to save people at first because we wouldn't have known how dangerous the disease could be. As it stands, we brought people to our isolation ward not knowing that the dead would come back to life and attack so viciously. We lost a very good nurse before we knew to restrain the victims of this disease before they died. Your assignment is to shoot anyone who even looks like they are afflicted if they are not restrained."

Cassandra continued to study the doctors' faces as if she was committing them to memory, but the truth was that she was wondering if either of them was infected. They had been the closest to the infection when it was brought onto the ship. She made a mental note to never let one of them get behind her.

Doctor Sellers cleared his throat to get her attention and said, "The infected can only be permanently terminated by head trauma, Petty Officer Gibbs. If any are free from restraints, please do not hesitate to use your sidearm."

She looked at the Captain to see if he would confirm that order, and he gave her a silent nod.

"I'll need thirty minutes to organize my detail," said Cassandra as she stood again. "Could the doctors be so kind as to remain here until I return for them?"

All three men stood quickly, and they all nodded their agreement. Cassandra waited for the Captain to officially dismiss her, then she left the room. The two doctors and the Captain all exchanged looks, and they each noticed they were wearing the same expressions.

"Is it just my imagination," asked Doctor Nkrumah, "or do you two gentlemen feel like the authority in the room was the young lady who just left?"

"I thought I was in charge up until a few minutes ago," said Captain Abbott.

The three of them laughed and settled back with their drinks. They had thirty minutes more to spend on planning the next steps.

In the end, thirty minutes was more than they needed. A communication had arrived from the British Royal Navy instructing all ships to remain at sea, and any ship approaching the coast of Europe or the United Kingdom within one hundred miles of shore would be sunk. The Americans were taking it seriously, but they were at least operating within twenty miles of their own shores, so the Captain assumed they had possibly established some form of control of the situation.

Petty Officer Gibbs returned in almost exactly thirty minutes with her detail of two men and two women. She introduced the four security officers to the doctors. They were all carrying Glock sidearms, but each was also equipped with M4 rifles. They had collapsable stocks for easier carrying in the corridors of the ship, but if they needed more firepower, they could easily be brought to the shoulder. Gibbs had also added an M4 to her arsenal.

"Doctors, may I ask that you remain together at all times within reason, and could you please inform us of your destination whenever you leave one area to move to another? If we get separated, it will be useful to know where you plan to be."

"Certainly," said Nkrumah. "The first thing we plan to do is organize an examination of all members of the crew. We will use the large examining room near the isolation ward. If we find someone who has been bitten, we will move them to isolation and place them in restraints."

Doctor Sellers added, "We'll need the entire crew manifest. I understand it has already been completed by the Chief of Security?"

"Yessir, and he distributed it to all of his Petty Officers. I already have my copy."

She pulled a small binder from one of the broad utility pockets on her uniform pants and handed it to Doctor Sellers. He was impressed by her efficiency, and this would save them a lot of time.

The Captain made another call from his desk and informed the Chief of Security that he wanted the examinations to begin immediately. He didn't want to interfere with ship's operations, but it had to happen fast if they were to believe they were not at risk.

After being dismissed by the Captain, the doctors and their security detail returned to the medical area where they would conduct the examinations. Cassandra and her detail eyed the sheets of plastic dividing the isolation ward from the rest of the compartment. They could see the vague shapes in rows of beds on the other side, and the plastic hardly seemed like enough protection from the deadly disease. Some of the shapes on the beds were still, but some were obviously trying to escape from their restraints.

"Don't worry about them," said Doctor Sellers. "We know they are infected, but they can't harm anyone. It's the ones we don't know about that worry me."

"The crew?" she asked.

"We boarded so quickly that no one had a chance to even think about it."

Cassandra bit her lower lip and said, "Surely they would tell someone."

"No, they wouldn't tell anyone at first," he said. "This is a hospital ship. Anyone who was bitten would think, "I can get treatment, so I'll wait until we leave port, and then I'll tell someone."

Doctor Nkrumah had been listening to the discussion and stepped over to add the bad news.

"But word will have spread quickly throughout the ship that a bite was a death sentence. Somewhere on this ship there must be at least one person who is silently hoping that no one finds out about their wound."

Petty Officer Gibbs called together her detail and exchanged a few words. They acknowledged her orders and spread out around the medical bay. The Captain had intended for them to cover for her while she got some rest, but she didn't see rest in her near future.

The Chief of Security arrived fifteen minutes later with a larger detail and the first group of crewmen to be examined. The nurses and doctors had placed partitions strategically to allow for enough privacy, but they also had to be visible to the security personnel.

The ship wide announcement informed the crew to assume port and starboard duty sections, and the port section would report for examinations first. In the terminology of the men and women at sea, that meant half the crew would run shipboard duties, while the other half reported to the medical bay. The roster provided by Petty Officer Gibbs showed that four hundred and eight people were on board. Two hundred and four were on their way to be examined.

It seemed reasonable to expect that crewmen who hadn't been bitten would arrive first, happy to be examined and then get as far away from the medical bay as possible. It seemed reasonable, but that wasn't what they got.

The very first crewman to walk between the partitions was sweating and immediately began trying to negotiate with the medical staff. He kept promising that he felt fine, and all he needed was antiseptic and a few stitches. He couldn't have been much older than twenty, and his accent was South American. He was afraid, and from what he had seen in Cameroon, he had a right to be.

When the nurse tried to get him to go with an armed escort to the isolation ward, the young sailor tried to go back the way he had come. He kept insisting it was all a mistake. The men and women in line behind him began scattering away from him, and the entire security detail had its weapons drawn.

The man turned and ran toward the only opening he saw, and it just happened to be where Doctor Nkrumah was standing. Only one shot was fired, but everyone except the security officers dropped to the deck. Cassandra Gibbs had been given the job of keeping Doctor Sellers and Doctor Nkrumah alive, and the job had officially started.

The bullet from her Glock was a perfect shot that hit the young man about an inch above his right ear. He was no longer a threat, but everyone stayed where they were.

"Okay, everyone. Listen up."

Petty Officer Gibbs knew she had to keep control over the situation, or it could become chaos in a hurry.

"Everyone stay on the floor. Do not try to exit this room. If you do, it will be assumed you are infected, and you will be shot. The medical staff will rearrange the partitions, and you will be directed to stand when it is your turn to be examined."

Doctor Nkrumah could tell why Captain Abbott had selected Petty Officer Gibbs to be their bodyguard. She hadn't hesitated when the sailor had run toward him, and it was a good thing because he had been frozen in his tracks.

Once the partitions were rearranged and the body had been removed, the medical exams continued. A second bite victim was identified after almost one hundred crewmen had been checked, but unlike the previous victim, this sailor faced Petty Officer Gibbs and respectfully snapped off a crisp salute. She returned it with equal enthusiasm and appreciation. The man knew he was going to die, but he chose to do so with dignity.

The port duty section finished their examinations, and another ship wide announcement was made for them to relieve the starboard section so they could report to the medical bay. The process took no more than thirty minutes, and the starboard duty section began arriving. Word had spread about the first bite victim, so the crew arrived without much conversation between them. They were somber and well aware of the security detail that was now holding weapons at the ready.

Doctor Sellers motioned for Doctor Nkrumah to join him as he approached Petty Officer Gibbs.

"We might not find more bite victims in this section," said Doctor Sellers. "We need to have someone check the roster to see who did not report for inspection."

Gibbs had kept a close count on the roster as the port section had come through, and she was surprised to find they had all been accounted for. A quick count of the number of people in line to be inspected showed there were four crewmen missing from the starboard section.

"It looks like we're going to have to do some hunting," said Gibbs.

Her ponytail bounced as she quickly went around the room picking out a few of her best security officers. Normally she would have left that to the Chief of Security, but when Gibbs had been forced to shoot the bitten crewman, he had done what he was supposed to do and gone to see that the Captain was safe.

Gibbs couldn't leave her two charges while the inspections were still being done, so she instructed one of her detail to lead the others. Their orders were shoot to kill anyone who refused to be inspected, and they were reminded that it had to be a head shot. It was a grim group of men and women that left in search of their shipmates.

The examinations went ahead without further incidents, but the security detail returned with three of the missing crewmen. Two had been bitten, and the third had flu symptoms. He had decided not to report for the examinations because he was afraid someone would think he was infected. He regretted that decision when he was almost shot by the security detail.

The fourth crewman had been found hiding in one of the vehicles the Mercy Mission ship used to carry medical teams inland, and he was armed. A standoff began, but it didn't last long. The order had been given to shoot to kill, so the order had been followed. The security detail radioed in to Cassandra that the fourth missing crewman had been shot, and she instructed them to cover the vehicle with a tarp and to paint a biohazard warning on all sides.

As a precaution, the crewman with the flu symptoms was put in a separate isolation ward. Until they were sure about how the infection that caused reanimation of the dead was transmitted, it would be better than having him return to the quarters he shared with two dozen shipmates. The other two bite victims were led away to join the man who had saluted Cassandra, and they cried when they were restrained in their beds.

9 RETURN TO MUD ISLAND

The Chief didn't waste any time swimming back to the plane. The water was a deep green, and he couldn't see what was below him, but he imagined it wasn't something he wanted to see with his own eyes.

Thousands of people lived along the banks of Lake Norman, and a large part of the population from Charlotte had evacuated toward the lake. Many had died on land, but countless numbers had either tried to swim to the little islands or had taken boats. Judging by the number of boats that were still tied to their docks, most of the population must have tried to swim.

The last minutes of their lives had been frantic attempts to swim faster than their pursuers, and when most of them did manage to reach the islands, they were stranded without food, fresh water, or shelter, but worst of all with bite victims.

When the Chief climbed onto the passenger side float of the Beaver, he saw that an infected dead was trying to pull itself over the float on the pilot side. It didn't have the reasoning power to pull itself around or under it, so it just kept trying to go over it. The thing was swallowing so much water as it struggled against the float that it was about to become a moot point, but the Chief didn't want to stay where he was to watch.

He climbed through the passenger side door and crossed over to the pilot's seat. The bobbing of the plane in the water shook the infected dead loose from the port side float, and it sank out of sight. The Chief did his preflight checks before climbing back out to stand on the float and retrieve the first anchor. He stowed it before crossing back through the plane to pull in the second anchor. That was when he noticed the sky had darkened toward the south. It was time to get out of the path of the coming storm that would blanket the area with radiation.

He started the engine and let it run until the sound became a smooth roar, then he started driving the plane like a boat. He brought the plane to the tip of the sandbar as slowly as possible. Bumping against it could do just enough damage to keep them from taking off. If that happened, they would only be able to abandon the plane and return to the shelter for what could be years, depending upon the amount of radiation that was dropped over Ambassadors Island.

Kathy hopped from the sandbar onto the float and pulled open the passenger compartment door for Colleen and Hampton. Then she took a couple of steps forward along the float and climbed through the front door into the passenger seat. She was pulling on a headset even before Colleen and Hampton made the jump to the float and climbed inside.

The Chief pointed to the south, and he didn't need to explain what they were seeing. The sky was as dark as night as the massive storm was moving across Georgia toward the northwest corner of South Carolina.

When the Beaver rotated to point northeast, the sky was so bright that it was hard to believe what was behind them. The Chief knew that direction had the longest stretch of open water the Beaver would need to take off. He powered up, and the plane began to gain enough speed for them to leave Lake Norman behind. As usual, the Chief lifted the plane into the air effortlessly and then banked toward the southeast.

"I want to take one more look at the Oconee Nuclear Power Plant if we can get close enough," said the Chief. "Kathy, you can start hailing Fort Sumter and Mud Island even though we're out of range. We need to see if things at home have changed. When you get him on the radio, ask Doctor Bus for radiation readings on the surface."

Hampton couldn't believe he was in the air again, and even though he and Colleen had been with the Chief and Kathy on Ambassadors Island, it felt unreal to be heading back to the place where he had lived his entire life.

"How many HAZMAT suits do we have back here?" he yelled over the roar of the big engine. The plane had been comfortably refinished inside, but there was no way to eliminate that much sound.

Kathy was busy trying to make radio contact with either Mud Island or Fort Sumter, but the Chief heard the question and held up three fingers.

"It won't be a problem," he yelled over his shoulder. "Someone can go into the shelter and bring another one out, or we can have Tom bring some out in a boat. Either way, radiation levels were already dropping due to the rain when we left. The only reason we picked up any radiation was because we stirred it up leaving the shelter."

"You know I've got about a thousand more questions," yelled Hampton, "and Colleen will have a thousand more."

The Chief didn't answer immediately, but a broad smile crossed his face.

"I'll tell you this much now," he yelled back, "I want to see how the Oconee Plant looks, and then we're going to make top speed for the coast. Our shelter is only a few miles north of Georgetown, but the last we heard it had become crowded by survivors. We don't even know if we can land there."

"And if we can't?"

"Then we'll fly down to Fort Sumter. There's an even bigger shelter there, and it's occupied by friends of ours."

"You make friends everywhere you go?" asked Hampton. "You just made a lot of people happy back there on Ambassadors Island."

"I had a lot of help from my blond friend here, but mostly it's just being in the right place at the right time."

The Chief approached the Oconee Nuclear Power plant from the east and saw what he had hoped for. The trees were clearly leaning toward the north as the storm came in from the south. It wasn't the best news for Iris and her band of survivors, but they would be safe inside their shelter. If they had stayed outside, they would have all died within a few days.

Satisfied that Mud Island had been spared for the time being, the Chief put the Beaver into a steep bank to the southeast and then leveled out for the flight home. The power plant would continue to leak long after the storm went by, but the worst of the radiation would be local or pushed to the north.

The bad news came only a few minutes later when Kathy managed to finally raise Mud Island by radio. Molly's voice came through her headset, and the young girl was ecstatic.

She dropped all pretense of radio protocol and was shouting. Kathy couldn't even get her to calm down long enough to find out what was happening back at Mud Island.

******

I heard Molly practically screaming into the microphone as I walked into the living room where the radio was set up. Molly had the headset on, so I couldn't hear who she was talking to, but judging by her behavior, it had to be our missing friends.

"Uncle Eddy, it's aunt Kathy," shrieked Molly.

I had to carefully get Molly to turn the microphone and headset over to me, because I needed to warn the Chief and Kathy that it wasn't safe to land.

"Mud Island to Beaver. Be advised situation is unfriendly."

"Where are they?" asked Tom.

Tom and the others were filing into the living room. We had plenty of privacy when we needed it, but our little family was feeling the need to be near each other until our friends were back home.

"I don't know. Molly just made contact, and I don't want the current surface inhabitants to guess this is Mud Island."

So far there had been no indication that the people living in the houseboat or anyone in their armada of smaller boats had a clue that the shelter was on the island, but as I answered Tom, we all saw the door of the houseboat fly open. It was prominently displayed on the main monitor that showed the surface.

A man we all had come to recognize as the leader burst out onto the dock, and his head was rotating left and right as his eyes searched the sky. He canted his head to the left and cupped a hand behind his right ear as if he could hear something but couldn't identify its source.

"Beaver, you're noisy," I said into the microphone.

"Roger, Mud Island."

We didn't know if Kathy and the Chief had a visual on the fleet of boats that had filled the moat, but the amount of noise coming from that many boats was probably good cover for the sound of the Beaver. We saw the leader looking at the boat city with open distain as he gave up on the hope of identifying the source of the radio call he had heard and headed back to the open door of the houseboat.

Before he could get back inside to his radio, I keyed the microphone one last time and just said, "Radio silence."

There were two clicks through my headset, and then it was quiet.

"How do we help them get home?" asked Jean.

"A better question might be how we can get this flotilla of survivors to move on," I said.

We had all been trying to think of a way to get them motivated to move, but the island had proven to be the safest thing they had found along the coast. Ironically, it was the moat that was making them stay. The infected continued to emerge from the dense trees along the beach of the mainland, but the water was so deep close to shore that they just disappeared from view as soon as they took one step from the beach into the moat.

The people who filled the hundreds of boats were still sick from the radioactive fallout, but they weren't dying fast enough to be a threat to the living. When they died, they were usually just dumped over the edge of the boat to disappear along with the infected dead, but whenever possible they were carried to the beach on the Atlantic side of the island and used as bait for the blue crabs. It seemed to become everyone else's good fortune when someone else died.

I had noticed that some of the boats tried to keep themselves separated by a little more distance from the main body of boats, and after a while I began to understand that they were family groups that were trying to protect each other. So, there was dissension among the people of the boat city, but it appeared that open conflict was a fast way to bring on the inevitable.

One group used some long poles to push another boat away from them when they had come a little too close for comfort. The response was frighteningly swift. The boat that had encroached on the first group closed the gap quickly, and men jumped across like pirates after the crew of a fat merchant ship.

Within a minute, the family had been killed, and the men who had started the battle were dragging the lifeless bodies into their boats. I was horrified when I saw that no one, not even the children, were spared. Now they not only had bait for the blue crabs, they had another boat.

Of course they were just as likely to turn on each other as they were families, and I was still watching when they started fighting over the boat. Two different groups of people watched as the first groups exterminated each other, and then they happily moved in to take possession of their boats.

So it went from sunrise to sunset, and they still didn't appear to be inclined to move on.

We considered the possibility that Captain Miller could bring the Cormorant from Fort Sumter to Mud Island. The Coast Guard vessel had proven itself to be quite capable of causing destruction, and it would be devastating to the smaller boats if it entered the moat with its deck guns blazing. The problem was the radioactive fallout. As minimal as it was, they couldn't risk the lives of any of Captain Miller's men.

They had also heard the radio broadcast from Fort Sumter when they had informed the Chief and Kathy that Mud Island was unfriendly. Captain Miller had also warned them that there were possibly hostiles on board the Yorktown.

The World War II aircraft carrier sat just far enough from Fort Sumter to keep them from feeling like it was a threat, but if the hostiles saw the Cormorant leave Fort Sumter, it might cause the ship to draw fire from the Yorktown. No one knew the extent of the hostile force's weaponry, but they didn't want to find out what they could do the hard way.

Doctor Bus brought everyone back to the present when he asked, "Has anyone looked at the main monitor lately?"

Molly said, "There's a big ship coming right at us."

She was right. All of us looked at the view on the monitor that showed the Atlantic Ocean, and there was a big, blue and white ship driving through the waves on a course that appeared to be straight at Mud Island.

I put the camera on zoom, and the markings became just clear enough for Bus to tell us all he thought it might be a hospital ship.

******

The Mercy Mission ship had spent months at sea and had only been resupplied once by a United States Navy carrier group that was headed south. They were not invited to join the group and were not given any information other than to avoid making port in any populated areas.

Captain Abbott had placed the ship on a rationing program as they tried to establish contact with other friendly forces, but European ships were not responding, and they had lost contact with the US forces with whom they had hoped to rendezvous.

There had also been very little contact with the Royal British Navy, but bits and pieces of messages were intercepted that indicated Russian ships were seen trying to make port along the coast of England. It seemed that the Russians were trying to acquire territory while it was unprotected. The British Navy was strangely quiet, but Captain Abbot had been a man of the sea for many years, and he knew they were strategically allowing the Russians to think they were going to grab major ports without opposition. When the infection got on board the Russian ships that were foolish enough to dock in major ports, there would soon be less Russian ships to fight.

What Captain Abbott would never know was that United States Navy fast attack submarines were assisting the Royal Navy and had positioned themselves near those same ports to engage any of the Russian ships that managed to make it back out to sea. Mankind was being pushed to the brink of extinction by the infection, but as Sellers and Nkrumah had predicted, mankind would hurry the process along even more quickly by killing each other.

The carrier group had not been unfriendly. As a matter of fact, they had transferred enough supplies to the Mercy Mission ship to ensure they could avoid a dangerous port for a very long time, but they were on a mission of their own, and they were as concerned as everyone else about having a ship near them that was carrying the infection. They sincerely hoped one of the brilliant doctors on the crew of the Mercy Mission ship would find a cure or even a vaccine to prevent the infection, but they were eager to put as much distance between them and the infected dead that were restrained in the isolation ward.

It had been a difficult trip across the Atlantic with more unexpected deaths. Even though they had done exhaustive inspections for bites, there seemed to be new ways for the infection to get into the crew.

The first outbreak began when Cassandra Gibbs had gone to get a couple hours of much needed sleep. She had pushed herself to the breaking point, worried that something would happen to the doctors while she was away. It seemed like her head had just sunk into her pillow when the screaming started. The fatigue was gone instantly as she strapped on her sidearm and went out into the corridor with the barrel of her M4 leading the way.

"Remember your training," she thought. "Doors and corners…doors and corners."

The screaming hadn't come from far away, and the big smear of blood on the deck was an easy trail to follow. When the trail ended, it began again as footprints, and she reasoned that there were at least six sets of prints. Up ahead she could hear the groaning of the small horde as they moved along the passageway.

At the next corner, Gibbs put her back against the wall and listened. If she was close enough, she could single target fire more accurately with her Glock. The groaning was only about six feet away, so she let the rifle down against the strap and made a smooth transition to the sidearm. She was targeting even as she rounded the corner, and since they were moving away from her, the first three went to the floor before the others even turned around. Three more rounds disposed of them before they had a chance to step in her direction.

Petty Officer Gibbs did a quick inspection of each body to be sure they were dead, then she started checking them for their crew identification cards. She was surprised to find that two of them weren't carrying ID's.

A security detail arrived within a few seconds being led by the Chief of Security. When he saw the bodies, he was furious with himself. They had inspected the crew for bites, but even when they had searched the ship for crewmen who were hiding, they had failed to detect stowaways. As a matter of fact, they had never given the problem a thought. Gibbs told herself she would have thought to check for stowaways if she hadn't been assigned to be a celebrity bodyguard. It wasn't that she blamed anyone. It was more that she considered it the job of the Chief of Security to think of everything else. She promised herself she wouldn't make that mistake again.

It was a little too late for the four dead crewmen, but if there were two stowaways, there could certainly be more. As much as he wanted them shot on sight, the Chief of Security gave orders to search the ship and to restrain anyone who was not a member of the crew.

The second outbreak was only a few days later on the midnight shift when a patient managed to free himself from his restraints. At first the nurse thought he had unbuckled the strap on his wrist. When she tried to pull the patient's arm back to the straps, she saw that the hand was still in the restraints. In the split second before she was savagely bitten, she understood that the patient had died and then had pulled so hard at the restraints that the hand had detached at the wrist. She was so surprised she didn't even bother to scream.

Because of the late hour, there were no doctors in the medical bay. During the day, there would be a dozen or more doctors running their tests, trying to isolate the virus, and observing the patients who were dying right before their eyes only to become reanimated minutes later. This was the last patient still alive, and since the others needed no medical care, there had only been one nurse on duty. One nurse to watch the patient, and one security guard at the door.

When the door to the isolation ward began to swing open, the security guard thought the nurse was just coming out to socialize for a few minutes. Boredom on the midnight shift was how most mistakes were made, and that was how it had always been, even before the infection.

The security guard didn't have a chance to draw his weapon. His M4 was leaning against the bulkhead, and even if he had pulled his sidearm from the holster, he wouldn't have had the opportunity to switch off the safety and aim a shot to the head. In that last split second of thought he remembered Glocks don't have a manual safety, and he should have at least tried to pull it from the holster.

The bite hurt worse than he could believe, and shock made him react more with disbelief than to let his training take over. First he asked her what she was doing, then he went to his knees looking at all of the blood as she bit him again on the face.

The nurse moved past the body toward the distant sounds ahead, and she didn't look back when the security guard pushed himself to a standing position. Dead eyes that looked like red rimmed cataracts turned in the same direction as the first infected dead. The sound of her movements down the passageway were enough to make the second infected dead choose to go in that direction.

Unlike most ships, hospital ships have wheelchair ramps in large numbers. One such ramp needed to go directly to the medical bay so emergencies could be treated more quickly. If the two infected dead had made a right turn at the next passageway, they would have fallen to the bottom of a ladder over twenty feet high, but they made a left and began stumbling down the long curve of the wheelchair ramp. The bottom of the ramp came to an end at the port side emergency door where a gangplank could be lowered to a dock. It stood open because the seas were calm, and the two infected dead were drawn to the sound of the ship moving through the water.

A rope railing stopped them from tumbling over the side of the ship, and the bow was riding slightly higher than the stern, so they turned toward the rear of the ship. The port side crewman who was standing watch at the bow glanced down the length of the ship, but all he saw was two people taking a slow walk toward the stern. He continued on his rounds toward the starboard side of the bow.

The stern had been a favorite place for sailors since the beginning of sailing ships. Standing at the stern watching the wake of the ship seemed to make the world better, and on this particular night there were several groups of crewmen who had been unable to sleep. They were lined up along the aft railing smoking cigarettes and cigars. They were a long way from home with no idea of what was happening to their families and friends, and this was the closest thing they could find to give them peace.

One of the men who was leaning on the top rope and had one foot up on the bottom rope noticed the arrival of a nurse and a security guard. At first they were nothing to him except two new arrivals on a calm night. Then they crossed over one of the sections of the deck that was under a light, and he saw they were infected. If not for his warning shout, the group nearest to them would have joined the list of victims.

Everyone scattered away from the approaching pair of infected, and someone was screaming for the stern watch to shoot them. The watch was just taking aim when Doctor Sellers looked over the railing from above and shouted to stop.

"Get a net over them. We need them for tests."

The crew was beginning to hate the doctors. All they ever wanted to do was run their tests, but that meant keeping these things on board. Now two more were dead, and the crew was losing its patience.

A heavy net was thrown over the pair of infected dead, and they were unceremoniously dragged back to the medical bay. Doctor Sellers came down from the upper level of the ship and met the crewmen who were returning the nurse and the guard to the medical bay. As soon as they were strapped into place, he was drawing blood for his tests. He had learned that their blood tended to clot quickly because their hearts were no longer pumping. The blood just sat inside their veins and turned to mud.

This pair of victims hadn't been dead very long, so he was able to draw some good samples, and he rushed them to his lab. He had also learned that the blood tended to congeal even after it had been drawn. It became as thick as maple syrup before he was able to run any meaningful tests.

Doctor Sellers prepared some slides and was beginning to study the samples when he became aware that someone else was in the room with him. He was shocked when he turned and saw the physical shapes of men moving toward him. Before he could say a word or yell for help, a big hand covered his mouth. He was easily lifted from the floor, and someone grabbed him by the ankles. He struggled, but he was being roughly carried from his lab by at least six men.

The lab was on the same side of the ship as the emergency medical bay, and the men switched from his feet to his shoulders to get him through an open door. The cool night air hit him, and it didn't seem real, but he could feel himself being lifted higher as the men got ready to drop him over the rope railing into the ocean.

"You doctors and scientists in your white smocks are always messing around with things you don't understand," said one of the assailants. Doctor Sellers wasn't sure of the accent, but he was fairly sure it was one of the cooks.

"We're all going to die on this ship, and all you do is keep strapping people down and taking their blood," shouted one of the crew. "If we don't stop you, all of us are going to wind up strapped to your tables."

They all heard the familiar sound of someone putting a round into the chamber of an automatic. Doctor Sellers was suspended over the railing by several pairs of hands ready to let go, just as a voice said, "If he goes over the side, all of you will go with him."

Cassandra was mostly in the shadows, but there was no mistaking the deadly serious tone of her voice. They had all seen her in action, and there was no doubt she could shoot every one of them before they got to her.

"I've been given the job of ensuring the personal safety of Doctor Sellers and Doctor Nkrumah, and you people are making me look bad."

Sellers could feel the hands around his arms and ankles grip tighter as each of the men started to understand the need to keep him from slipping out of their grasp. Accidentally dropping him would have the same effect as throwing him. He couldn't see Cassandra Gibbs because he was facing upward toward the night sky, but he had been able to hear the deadly menace in her voice and expected to hear a gunshot at any moment.

He felt himself being eased back toward the ship, and his feet lowered to the deck. There were apologetic voices pleading with Petty Officer Gibbs, and Sellers could hear the men saying they were afraid the doctors were going to bring the sickness to them all.

"The Captain didn't say anything to me about keeping you guys alive," said Cassandra. Each word was said slowly, and Sellers could see that the men were showing her their hands.

More than one was saying they were sorry, and Cassandra gradually began rotating around the group until she was between them and Doctor Sellers. When they had the open door behind them, the men took it as their reprieve and began backing through it. Then they ran.

"Thank you, Miss. I would be well on my way to drowning if not for you."

Petty Officer Gibbs holstered her sidearm and faced Sellers. She hadn't really paid much attention to his appearance before, but in the shadows outside along the railing, she could see why the crewmen had treated him as if he was a monster. Slightly stooped from too much time looking through a microscope, and the white jacket…always the white jacket. Gibbs realized that somewhere in the world there was someone like him, someone in a white jacket who probably gave birth to this disease that was wiping out the population in the worst possible way.

"We'd better get you back inside, and while we're at it, we should locate Doctor Nkrumah to be sure he's okay."

She pointed at the door but stepped ahead of him as he started for it.

"I'll lead. Just in case one of those guys has a change of heart."

On the way back to the lab, a quick radio call to the security team confirmed that Doctor Nkrumah was asleep in his quarters. Gibbs spoke with the Chief of Security and he agreed to place extra guards in the corridors that led to the cabins belonging to the medical staff.

After she saw Doctor Sellers back to his microscope, Gibbs found a chair and placed it where she could see the corridor, the lab, and the plastic curtains that surrounded the beds where the dead had been restrained. It worked on her nerves a bit to see movement where there shouldn't be any, but the dark shapes were in constant motion. There was also that sound. It wasn't quite a groan or a moan. It was just something that escaped from them when they opened their mouths.

Doctor Sellers was peering through his microscope, and it startled her when he sat bolt upright on his lab stool. It looked like he had seen something, and it was coming through the microscope after him. He had been pale skinned before, but now he looked like he had been drained of blood.

"Did I hear you say Doctor Nkrumah was asleep?"

"Yes," she answered. It came out sounding more like she had answered his question with a question.

"Can you radio your security people and have him brought to the lab?"

Gibbs nodded at the doctor as she raised her radio to her face and said a few words. She heard an affirmative and said, "He's on his way."

They heard Doctor Nkrumah coming long before they saw him, and he burst into the lab with his security guards following right behind.

"What is it, Sellers? What did you find?"

Nkrumah was almost out of breath even though it hadn't been that long of a run from his cabin to the lab.

"The sample I prepared on the slide. It's changing."

Sellers pointed at the microscope as he moved out of the way to let his colleague take a look.

Nkrumah took Sellers' place on the stool and seemed to stare through the lens forever. Gibbs didn't even realize she had stood up and was watching the doctors instead of the corridor. The two security guards who had followed Nkrumah into the room were also watching intently.

When he looked at Sellers, the expression of shock was obvious on Nkrumah's face.

"What am I seeing here, Sellers? What's different about this sample?"

"Did you see it too?" asked Sellers. "Did you see the cells attacking each other?"

"I saw it, but how was this sample prepared? Can it be replicated?"

Sellers was ecstatic, but he managed to explain that he had never tried mixing the blood of two victims. It had occurred to him that the infected never bit each other, but that didn't mean they were immune to the infection. Before he had been grabbed by the crewmen and dragged outside, he had mixed the blood of both victims on the same slide. The cells from one victim had dominated the cells of the other.

"What does that mean?" asked Gibbs.

Both doctors looked at the security officer as if they had just noticed her for the first time.

"I'm not entirely sure," said Sellers, "but it's something we didn't know before."

Gibbs blinked her eyes as if she was trying to clear her vision.

"Wait a minute," she said. "Are you saying you got all excited about a discovery, and that was all there was to it?"

She didn't know why it made her so mad, but it did. Maybe it was because she thought for a moment that it had meant a cure was within reach. Whatever it she had thought, she didn't expect to see so much excitement over nothing.

Sellers explained just a little too patiently that any new information was worth getting excited about. As a matter of fact, he was speaking as if she wouldn't understand if he spoke too fast, and that didn't help.

"Doctor Sellers, if I had not received orders from the Captain to protect you, I'd call the crewmen back up here and ask them how far they could throw you."

Petty Officer Gibbs motioned for the security team to follow her, and she stormed out of the lab.

Unfazed by the comment, Nkrumah asked his friend a second time, "Can this be replicated?"

"I don't know, but I'm going to try."

The two doctors spent the rest of the night mixing the blood from the infected dead that were restrained on the beds of the isolation ward. First they tried mixing the blood from the same two infected that had just been returned to the ward, but there was no activity in the blood. The cells were dormant.

The disappointed doctors understood the discovery was related to the length of time the infected had been dead. As the blood had congealed in their veins, it had died along with the victims. The heart needed to be pumping in order for the blood cells to be alive, and they had never had the opportunity to closely examine the vital signs of patients that had just died. What they learned was essentially that the heart kept beating for a brief period of time after the victims came back as infected dead.

"Nkrumah, we will need to study the vital signs of the next victim as he comes back from the dead."

Nkrumah stared at Sellers with his mouth slightly open. If he had just heard his colleague correctly, he was saying they needed someone else to die from this awful disease. The only way they could study the discovery they had just made was to be there when a victim died, and then study everything as fast as they could before the heart stopped.

Sellers saw the expression on Nkrumah's face but didn't understand at first, then it dawned on him that he must have sounded as heartless as the crew had thought him to be. He had dedicated his life to giving free medical care in needy countries, and now he sounded like a Nazi doctor in a concentration camp. He felt ashamed that he had forgotten the victims were people too.

"I'm sorry, Nkrumah. We should focus our efforts on finding a way to reanimate the blood cells and hope there are no more victims. I won't hesitate to gather information as quickly as we can if there is another victim, but I think we should help the Captain find a way to keep this from spreading to the rest of the crew."

Nkrumah was glad to see his friend come to his senses, but at the same time he dreaded the possibility that his friend had been right in a terrible way.

"We will have more victims, won't we?"

Doctor Sellers didn't answer, but he nodded slowly.

"We should talk with the Captain about finding a way to isolate the crew into separate groups. If we have an outbreak, we might be able to contain it," said Nkrumah.

******

As the sun came up on the horizon, the Mercy Mission ship sailed across a calm ocean toward North America. The security teams had separated the crew and begun a process of examinations to ensure there was no infection coming from another source, and that the means of transmission was still just from being bitten.

Cassandra Gibbs rotated between protecting the doctors and patrolling the ship. She always had her M4 ready as she checked the different levels, watching for signs of infection. There was no doubt in her mind that she would shoot anyone that looked like they had a head cold, and she was much more jumpy than usual.

She was checking the vehicle deck when she saw a crewman getting sick into a bucket. She had been looking inside the rows of jeeps to be sure no one was hiding even this far out to sea, and there was a retching sound. There was always the chance it was one of the volunteers who couldn't get his sea legs under him, and it was nothing more than sea sickness, but that was usually gone by the time they had been at sea for a week or two.

Petty Officer Gibbs switched from her M4 to her Glock and eased around a Jeep to get a better look. The crewman had all of the symptoms of someone who was better off staying on land, but he was just a little too sick. He had his back to her, so she couldn't see his face, but she expected him to have a bite mark.

"Don't turn around," she said in a low, even voice. "Do exactly as I say, and I won't have to put a bullet in you."

The man was too sick to be startled, so he hardly reacted at all, but he didn't want the owner of the voice behind him to shoot him when he knew he hadn't been bitten. He turned around despite her warning, and when he saw it really was a security officer with a Glock pointed at his head, he dropped to his knees and began to beg.

Cassandra could see how sick he was, but she couldn't see a bite anywhere. He was only wearing a pair of jeans and a short sleeved tee shirt, so he had likely places for bite marks clearly exposed. As if he knew she was looking him over for the telltale death mark, he held his arms out where she could see them.

There were tears streaming down his cheeks, but he looked like he had a fever besides the problem with his stomach.

"Please, officer. I haven't been bitten," he managed to croak out through a raw throat. "I don't know why I'm so sick, but I haven't been bitten, and I haven't seen any of my friends looking sick."

Cassandra wasn't sure what she was going to do, but she couldn't bring herself to just shoot him despite her earlier thoughts. In the end she knew the best thing to do was get him examined by the doctors.

"You're sweating a lot," she said. "Do you have a fever?"

The man's answer surprised her a bit because she hadn't given much thought to her own appearance lately. She was attractive, and she took pride in her smooth, dark skin. She liked wearing the security officer uniform because she had been told more than once it fit her like a glove, so she wasn't ready for him to respond with anything about her.

"You're sweating a lot, too. Are you sick?"

She kept the gun pointed in his general direction, but she glanced down at herself and realized he was right. She hadn't been getting much sleep, so she certainly hadn't been showering or doing her hair as often as usual.

She snapped out of her thoughts and locked her aim on the crewman again. He put his hands up out of reflex and was sure she was going to shoot him.

"Keep your hands where I can see them, and start walking toward the port side gangway down to the medical bay. I need for the doctors to take a look at you."

The man got an even more frightened look on his face.

"The doctors...they will think I was bitten. I don't want to be strapped to a table in the same room with those things. Please just let me go back to my bunk and let me get some rest. I'm just a little sick."

Gibbs didn't answer. She just gestured with the Glock toward the gangway down to the next level. The look on her face must have been serious because he started moving. She followed as he accepted his fate and went down to the next level. The medical bay was below them at the next gangway, and he kept looking back at her as if he could think of something to change her mind. His hair was wet and matted to his head, and the big stain on the back of his shirt made her sure he was burning up.

When they got to the bottom of the second gangway, the medical staff saw them coming and immediately assumed the same thing as Cassandra when she had first seen the man. Every one of them thought he had been bitten.

Even though Cassandra was still behind him with her gun, he focused all of his efforts on them and started pleading, saying that he was just sick. If things had been normal, this highly skilled staff of medical experts would have been rushing to his side to help him, but things were far from normal.

The sick bay doctor on duty took over and started giving orders to the staff as he chided them for treating the man with so little empathy. He directed the crewman into a small examination room and told the nurses to get the man onto an IV as quickly as possible. He was obviously dehydrated and needed help to get his fever down.

Cassandra watched for a few minutes and slowly began to feel foolish about her own behavior. The man was sick, and she had treated him badly. As the nurses got the man into a hospital gown and onto a bed, she relaxed and decided her work was done in sick bay.

She quietly slipped out of the room and crossed over into the part of the medical bay where Doctor Sellers and Doctor Nkrumah were still getting nowhere with there tests. Cassandra glanced once at the plastic curtains and saw the shadows on the beds were still moving. She wondered how the doctors could go in there with those things for tissue and blood samples. Doctor Nkrumah seemed okay to her, but Doctor Sellers had creeped her out when he had gotten so excited about his little discovery.

"Was that a bite victim?" asked Sellers.

"No, just sick. Looked like some kind of flu bug," she said.

"Are you sure?" he pressed her just a bit more than she liked.

Cassandra snapped back at him, "I didn't inspect him for bites. That's your job."

Nkrumah reached over and took Sellers by the arm to stop him from asking another question.

"Thank you for bringing the man to sick bay," said Nkrumah. "I'm sure the staff will let us know if they find a bite mark. People are bound to get sick, and we can't be expecting the worst every time."

"I'll be outside," she said.

Cassandra appreciated the kind voice of Doctor Nkrumah, but she wanted to tell Doctor Sellers to stop looking so eager to find another infected crewman. She stepped out into the corridor and pulled the door shut behind her. It was usually open, but everyone had gotten used to closing doors as a precaution. She immediately felt relieved to have the door between her and those things behind the plastic curtains.

In the sick bay examining room the nurse was still taking the crewman's vital signs, and an IV bag was being connected by another nurse. As they worked, they were asking him routine questions such as when he had first gotten sick, had he eaten something that might have been bad for him, and did he have any allergies. They wrote down all of his answers, and as far as they were concerned, there was nothing remarkable to explain his fever.

The doctor came in and looked at the nurse's notes. He checked the man's eyes with a penlight and saw normal response, but the crewman complained that it made his head hurt. The nurse taking his vital signs showed the doctor the body temperature reading without saying anything, and the doctor could understand why the penlight hurt his eyes. His fever was just under one hundred and five degrees. He told the nurse to pack the man in ice and went to call for assistance.

He was on the phone when the nurse asked him to come back, and he saw that the man had gotten out of bed and was trying to leave sick bay. He had the IV tube dangling from his arm and was pushing to get by the nurse, but the thing that made him most upset was the man's eyes. They had rolled so far back in their sockets that all he could see was white with red rims.

Doctor Sellers and Nkrumah rushed into the room just in time to help gain control of the man as he was about to get by the nurse. They each grabbed an arm and pulled the man back into the small examination room. A nurse's aid appeared with restraints, and they strapped the man down. Cassandra had followed them in, but she stayed back and watched as they got the man under control. She needed room to shoot if it came to that.

There was blood on the patient's hospital gown, and Doctor Nkrumah looked around at the medical staff to see where it had come from. He saw a trickle of blood running down a nurse's arm. Not wanting to cause everyone to panic, he didn't say anything immediately. He watched the nurse as she inspected the source of the blood herself and stepped over to a sink. She poured antiseptic on the wound to rinse it and looked again. She had a confused look on her face and seemed to be trying to remember something.

"Nurse, did he cut you or bite you?"

She hadn't noticed him watching, and it seemed to startle her. Her voice was shaking as she said it was a cut.

"I'm trying to figure out when it could have happened. I think he dug a fingernail into my skin when he grabbed me."

"Let me take a look."

Nkrumah examined her wound and to her relief he agreed it wasn't a bite.

"I would still like for you to stay here in sick bay under observation," he added. "We don't know what this man has, so we don't know if it's contagious."

Everyone looked at the man strapped to the bed as he started making that groaning sound they had all heard in the other room.

"I think that answers your question," said Cassandra.

"But how did he become infected?" asked the nurse in a voice that was begging for them to be wrong. "He hasn't been bitten."

Doctor Sellers had acted quickly to get blood samples. Instead of trying to hit a vein with a needle, he simply cut the intravenous tube that was still connected to the man's arm and had let the blood come from the vein they had been using. He was filling and capping vials as fast as he could. Cassandra Gibbs watched him as if she were watching a real life vampire and wished she had let the crewmen throw him overboard.

The sick bay doctor and Nkrumah worked together to keep control of the rapidly deteriorating situation. The first thing they had to do was isolate the nurse who had begun to cry as she scrubbed at the fingernail cut. They had two other nurses take her to another examination room where they could clean and dress the wound, then they turned back to the crewman.

"Help me with his gown," he said to the other doctor. "We need to inspect him for bite marks." By now he was desperately hoping to find that he had been bitten.

They worked together as Doctor Sellers hurried off to his microscope with a rack full of blood samples. Cassandra held the door for him, but only because she was glad to see him go. When she turned back to the two doctors, she saw they were standing on both sides of the bed just staring at each other.

With concern she didn't try to hide, she said, "Well?"

Doctor Nkrumah didn't look at her as he answered, "No bite marks."

"Does that mean what I think it means?" she asked.

Both men turned their heads to look at her at the same time. They all knew what it meant without saying it. The infection was spread by another means of transmission.

"We still don't want to jump to conclusions," said Nkrumah. "We have no idea how patient zero, the first person to be infected, had contracted the disease. We just know that the infected try to bite the living, and when they do, it's always fatal."

"That doesn't make me feel better," said Cassandra.

Doctor Nkrumah was just about to answer when there was a commotion at the sick bay door. It had burst open with force as several men came in carrying friends who were all showing the same symptoms as the first patient.

For several minutes sick bay was a beehive of activity as nurses and doctors all got the new patients into their beds and restrained. The men who had carried the men into the room were confused by the restraints, but they didn't object. There was too much fear that the infection had somehow spread through the crew.

Once everything began to quiet down, Doctor Nkrumah took Cassandra aside and told her to find the Captain and tell him they had one, and maybe more, confirmed cases of the infection that didn't involve being bitten.

Cassandra left sick bay in search of the Captain, but she made a stop along the way. She stuck her head into the isolation ward and got Doctor Sellers' attention. She had to admit that even he looked afraid when she told him they had five more men strapped to beds who had the same symptoms as the first man.

When she left the medical bay, Cassandra went up to the vehicle deck again and went to a spot that gave her a good view of the ship and the wide expanse of the Atlantic Ocean. She turned in a circle and took in the view. In all of her years at sea, she had never really felt isolated because there was always the crew. This was the first time she had ever felt completely alone with so many people on board.

She found the Captain and the Chief of Security together in the Captain's dining room. Although they generally ate the same meals as the crew, they were never seen eating in the galley with the rest of the crew.

They both looked at Cassandra as if there had to be more to the news she had brought them, but there wasn't anything else to say. Doctor Nkrumah hadn't speculated about how the crewmen had become infected.

The quick tempered Chief of Security knew Petty Officer Gibbs was just the messenger, but he took it out on her anyway.

"Did you even think to ask him how he thought the infection was spreading if it wasn't from bites?"

"No, he just said to tell the Captain, Sir."

Cassandra tacked on the last word as if it wasn't a sincere sign of respect. The Chief of Security didn't miss the sarcastic tone and started to say something else, but the Captain interrupted.

"Did Nkrumah make any recommendations about how we should proceed?"

Cassandra just gave him a shake of her head and said in a low voice, "There was nothing more Doctor Nkrumah asked me to report, Sir. I got the impression he was asking me to tell you that we're in really big trouble, Sir."

"Did the Captain ask you for your opinion, Petty Officer?"

Cassandra was ready to reply with something really sarcastic when she saw the trickle of sweat running down the officer's forehead. His hair looked wet, and his face was red. He was either really angry, or he was running a fever. She glanced at the Captain and saw that he was looking at the man too.

"Petty Officer Gibbs, will you please escort your superior officer to sick bay?"

Cassandra didn't want to touch the man, and she hoped he would take the request as the order it was intended to be. She stepped back out of the dining room doorway to give him room to pass, and when the Chief of Security looked at the Captain, he gestured for the man to go. He took it as an order and followed her from the room.

They were only a few feet from the door when the Captain called her to come back.

"Petty Officer Gibbs, you're in charge of ship security until he's ready to return to duty."

Cassandra Gibbs doubted that would be any time soon.

If she never had to go back to the medical bay again, it would be fine with Cassandra Gibbs, but after she had escorted her former boss to sick bay, and she really did consider him to be a thing of the past, she found herself escorting six other crewmen to the doctors. All of them were restrained, but only the first had died. She decided to check in with her least favorite doctor and found he and Nkrumah both looking at the blood samples.

"Have you made anymore discoveries?"

The question came out more sarcastic sounding than she had intended. It was obvious that they would all be pinning their hopes on these two doctors in the days ahead, and she really prayed they would make some discoveries that were useful.

Doctor Nkrumah answered for both of them.

"We were looking at the wrong things. We were so sure that the only answers would be in the blood that we ignored some lab results. The blood doesn't need to be alive for us to analyze its contents. We were so excited about Doctor Sellers' discovery that blood cells were attacking each other when mixed with the cells of other victims that we forgot about the fact that every victim had been eating mangrove oysters and ghost crabs."

The statement hung in the air almost as if it had a question attached to it. The question they all wanted to ask was who else was going to get sick and turn into an infected dead.

"Are you both saying that anyone who ate mangrove oysters and ghost crabs is infected?"

The doctors looked at each other first and Doctor Sellers nodded at her. It was a sad look on his face, and she knew they had been eating the same meals as the crew. She hadn't, but they had.

"Have you been eating the oysters and crabs, Petty Officer Gibbs?" asked Doctor Sellers.

"Not me. I'm allergic to shellfish, so I stay away from the galley when those are on the menu. I can't stand to be in the same room when they're being served."

"Lucky you," said Sellers. He wanted to be happy for her, but it wasn't easy since he had been a big fan of the shellfish when it was served.

Nkrumah had joined him for those meals, and it was quite possible that Petty Officer Gibbs was the only person on the Mercy Mission ship that hadn't been eating the mangrove oysters and ghost crabs.

She felt her hand tighten its grip on her M4 when the realization hit home. She was on a ship with hundreds of people who were going to start showing signs of infection. It was already starting, and they had run out of beds fast. Pretty soon there wouldn't be anyone left to strap the infected to the beds even if they had enough beds for everyone.

"Any idea how long it takes for the infection to show up in people who've been eating the shellfish?"

"From what we can tell," said Doctor Nkrumah, "it's different for everyone. They've been serving mangrove oysters and ghost crab meals since we arrived in Cameroon. It was one of the main ways that the people found to pay us for our services. Since we don't accept money, the locals donated food."

Cassandra had a horrible thought. Not only was she thinking ahead to the day when she would be the only person who was uninfected on the ship, she was thinking of the past when they had met with the US Navy carrier group. She wasn't sure, but she thought they may have traded some of their large supply of shellfish for fuel. She hoped she was wrong.

******

Petty Officer Cassandra Gibbs never thought she would ever need her training more than she did now. As the days turned into weeks, more and more people became ill, and as she expected, there came a day when there were more infected on board than uninfected. After being violently ill for a day or two, they died and then got back up. When they got up, they would find someone to bite.

The ship became a graveyard and zoo full of vicious creatures, and Cassandra was forced to sneak from one compartment to the next, often killing several of the infected dead as she moved. Sometimes she killed them for a place to hide, and other times she killed them to reach supplies. She found herself killing them because she was very angry, but there were also those times when she killed them because she was on a Mercy Mission ship. If she didn't kill them, they were a danger to the living, but she wasn't so sure there were any more of them on the ship.

Doctor Sellers had become sick while working in his lab, and Doctor Nkrumah had been bitten by his old friend. Sick bay had long since been overcome by the sheer numbers of people they had already brought in, but Nkrumah had gone to sick bay out of reflex, and when he opened the door it had released the contents of the room onto the rest of the ship. People who hadn't gotten sick found themselves face to face with corridors crowded with the infected, and there was nowhere to hide.

Cassandra managed to reach the vehicle deck where she was able to fight a gradual but successful battle with crewmen and women who had gone up for safety. As they had become sick and turned on each other, the spaces between the vehicles had become crowded with the infected. From the top of a jeep she shot them as they made themselves easy targets, and she kept going until she ran out of ammunition. She was forced to go back to the decks below to resupply, and it took a full day for her to work her way back to the vehicle deck, but this time she was able to finish the job.

When she had finally shot the last moving member of the infected crew on the vehicle deck, she walked to the port side railing and looked down. The ship was still under power and plowing through the water. The crew in the engine room wasn't concerned with bringing the ship to a stop. They were too busy trying to stay alive.

She wondered how many people were still alive in the lower decks and was sure someone else had to be because there were sporadic bursts of gunfire, but then again there were the sporadic screams of agony.

She saw the Captain once. He was near the bow, and it looked like he was still uninfected. Cassandra wondered if there was anything she could do to help him, but she had already remembered that last time she had gone to his dining room with the message from the doctors. She remembered seeing the stew the cooks had prepared with the mangrove oysters and ghost crabs. Even if she could rescue him from the bow, he was doomed.

Cassandra watched him as he tried to climb out onto a lifeboat that was hanging from its hooks ready to be lowered. If he tried to launch a lifeboat at the speed the Mercy Mission ship was traveling, it would tear him and the lifeboat to shreds. She wondered if it wouldn't be more merciful for her to help him end it, so she braced her M4 on the hood of a Jeep and took careful aim.

The up and down motion of the ship made her take longer to keep her sights on him, and just as she was about to pull the trigger, he disappeared. She wasn't entirely sure where he had gone, but she thought he went over the railing. If she had her preference, she would rather drown.

Days went by, and Cassandra lived off of the supply packs that had been stored in the Jeeps. Every time a vehicle had returned from a visit inland, it was resupplied for the next time. With one exception, there were enough provisions in each Jeep to last a three person medical team about a week, and there were forty jeeps on the vehicle deck.

Unfortunately that one exception was big. In order to ensure the freshness of the water supply, it wasn't loaded onto a Jeep until it was ready to go, and there were no functioning water spigots on the vehicle deck. The water supply must have been turned off somewhere below. She had found a couple of random six packs of bottled water, but it could only be rationed for a short while. The sun beat down on the vehicle deck, and there were no clouds on the horizon.

Cassandra decided the inevitable truth was that she would have to go back to the source of the water supply and restore power to the pumps that would carry it to the vehicle deck, and there was no sense in putting it off. Besides she would only get weaker after more time without water.

At sunrise she gathered together a light supply pack just in case she had to hole up in a cabin for a while, and climbed quietly down the gangway to the next deck. She knew what it would be like on the port side where the medical bay was, so she went down on the starboard side facing the bow.

She felt exposed out on the gangway, but she hadn't seen any of the infected demonstrate the ability to climb, and if the next deck down was populated, she could still climb back up. Once she was down another deck, climbing back up quickly might mean climbing back up into a crowd.

There was also gravity. The infected couldn't climb a ladder, but they had no problem falling down one. She hoped she wouldn't look up to see one demonstrating that particular ability when she was ready to make her way back up to the vehicle deck.

Six rungs from the deck she stopped again to survey her surroundings. The ladder led down to an open deck, so she still had a pretty fair idea of what was walking around. She had spent some time the day before watching this spot from above and had seen a few of the infected go by. A few of them walked right over the edge of the ship and disappeared into the ocean, and she hoped the others on this deck had done the same thing during the night.

There was one blind corner in front of her as she lowered herself down the last few steps, so she stayed quiet and moved from the bottom of the ladder to the bulkhead where the blind corner was. She knew she had to at least look around that corner before going down to the next level.

She pressed her back against the bulkhead and eased closer to the corner. As she did, it felt almost as if she knew there would be an infected dead standing there without even looking. The question was whether or not she could wait for it to come into view or if she had to be the one to make the move.

The answer was decided for her as it stumbled directly across her path. She didn't even think about how she was going to confront the dead when she ran into them. Her guns were too loud, so she would give away her position if she used them. She had a long knife that was more like a bayonet than a cutting knife, but she knew she would have to stab the infected through the head. That sounded easy enough, but sticking a blade into solid bone would be a mistake.

Without overthinking it, Cassandra just reached out and pushed with both hands. She connected with the already off balance crewman on his right shoulder and launched him over the railing. She watched him hit the water and was busy congratulating herself when she saw the motion out of the corner of her left eye.

In training she had been taught that corners and doors were the two places where people made their mistakes, and she knew she had made one by assuming there would only be one infected dead coming around the corner.

Her Glock was suddenly in her hand, and she pulled the trigger. She didn't miss, but the sound of the gun was like ringing a dinner bell. She didn't have time to stay and watch as the infected crewman was knocked backward by the punch of the bullet to its forehead. As quickly as she could move, she crossed the deck to the next ladder going down. She knew she had to move with less caution, but she had to be clear of the area at the bottom of the ladder before any new arrivals responded to the gunshot.

The ladder ended below decks, but the lights were still working. She was grateful for that small blessing. She couldn't imagine what it would be like if she had to navigate to the engine room through dark corridors.

Cassandra slid down the railings of the gangway without even using the steps, and as her feet hit the deck below they were already moving. She had holstered her Glock to have her hands free, and she was wishing she had a different weapon. She needed something she could swing in a narrow space that caused enough trauma to stop the infected.

"The galley," she whispered.

She knew the ship like the back of her hand, and she didn't hesitate. There would be some very useful kitchen utensils in the galley. Cassandra changed directions and ran back past the gangway she had just descended until she reached the next one going down. She still slid down the rails using her hands, but she put out her feet on the tops of the railing to use them as brakes. She couldn't keep pressing her luck and hoping there was nothing at the bottom of the steps.

When she landed this time, she saw two infected at one end of the corridor and one at the other end. They were moving away from her, but the sound of her feet hitting the metal deck gave off just enough noise to make them turn around. She pulled her knife free from her belt and stepped quickly into the nearest inboard cabin.

Cassandra needed to be lucky in two ways. First, she had chosen an inboard cabin because there would be a chance there was another door leading from the cabin into another corridor. Secondly, she was hoping the cabin was empty.

She was only half lucky this time, but she had entered the cabin so quickly that the infected inhabitant of the cabin wasn't prepared to bite her as soon as she came in. It was on the far side of the cabin standing in front of the door that she had hoped would be there.

Cassandra saw the cabin was actually a small office for someone on the crew. She turned the lock on the door she had entered and advanced toward the groaning creature that was moving in her direction with its mouth open. She brought the tip of the blade up under the jaw as if she was delivering an uppercut punch, and the blade went straight up through the brain until it reached the inside of the skull. She thought she had actually heard the sound of it stopping against the solid bone, but knew that wasn't important as long as she could pull it free and keep moving.

The door exited into the central corridor of the ship, and turning left would take her straight to the galley. She pulled the door shut as quietly as she could and mentally marked the spot just in case she would need to return to the room. At least she knew it was empty now, and so was the corridor for the time being.

She entered the galley and saw that many of the crew had gone there in the final moments of their lives. It was a large room, often used for movies and meetings when food wasn't being served. None of them saw her enter, but there were at least twenty infected dead wandering between the tables.

She dropped low to the floor and waited to see if any of the feet she could see shuffling past the tables were moving in her direction. They were still moving randomly, so Cassandra started crawling in the direction of the serving line. She had to pass by several openings on the way, but she couldn't stop or even spend time waiting to be sure it was clear at each opening. There would be just too many starts and stops along the way.

Her luck ran out at the very last opening between the rows, and a low groan escaped from a woman who had probably been a nurse when she was alive. Now the former nurse was a shell of a human who was alerting the horde of infected that were scattered around the room.

Cassandra was behind the serving line when she stood up straight and started to run. The infected would have to cross the room and go all the way to the same place where she entered and started down the line in order to get to her. There were no openings in the serving line where they could reach far enough to grab her, but since they could see her clearly, they tried to reach her anyway. The infected didn't have the reasoning power to try to get to her by going to the other end of the line, but it wasn't long before the weight of their numbers pushing against the stainless steel food display racks caused the heavy serving line to move.

The serving line was bolted down in half of the sections, but every other section was able to be removed by releasing the brakes on the wheels and rolling them away. The brakes were always set, but the sections could slide if they were pushed hard enough. Cassandra was shocked when she saw the closest section on her left begin to collapse toward her. She had reached the kitchen door, but she had hoped she would at least be able to enter the kitchen at her own speed, not by bursting into the room. She was getting a bit frustrated by not being able to enter corridors and rooms using stealth. She had been lucky too many times, and she knew luck could get you killed just as well as keep you alive.

Once again, the choice was made for her as the serving line fell over. The infected in front were pushed from behind causing them to pile up on top of the racks, but the ones pushing from behind were able to crawl over them more easily than navigating the metal shelves and serving platters that had fallen over with the racks. The infected would still have to fight their way over, but she would only have a few minutes before they would reach her. She saw that ironically the serving platters and pots still held rotten platters of mangrove oysters and ghost crab stew.

Cassandra took a deep breath and pushed through the door that led to the kitchen, and she saw for once she had gotten a big break. There were no crewmen in the large room, and there was a heavy bolt lock on the door. She slid it into place, and for the time being, she was safe. She still had to make it down at least four more levels to reach the engine room, but there was a good chance she would find some water in the kitchen. If not, there would be juice in the refrigerators.

Almost as important as the water was the rack of kitchen utensils she had been hoping for. There was a heavy meat cleaver that looked deadly hanging from a hook. She lifted it free and tested the weight with a couple of swings. It felt like it wanted to keep going on its own once it got started in motion. She liked that. Plus the blade looked like it was razor sharp. She made a mental note not to swing it too hard, or it would be permanently embedded in the head of the first infected dead she hit.

She found a big bottle of apple juice in the first refrigerator and downed the sweet liquid in greedy gulps. The constant adrenaline rush she was getting as she worked her way down to the engine room was going to leave her feeling exhausted, so the big hit of sugar from the juice was what she needed. She was tempted to grab some of the food, but she was a little worried about it slowing her down. She needed to keep moving, and she wasn't even sure where the exit was. She also wasn't sure what would be on the other side of that exit.

Cassandra never would have guessed the kitchen was so big, but she discovered that the food storage portion was like a small warehouse. It had been depleted by the trip across the Atlantic, but she was sure she could stay in the room safely for as long as she wanted to. The problem was, she didn't want to. She kept searching for another exit until she found what she was looking for, but she didn't stop there. She wanted more than one choice in case she had to retreat to the kitchen.

The second door she found was a cargo door that was larger than normal, and she had an idea of where it would lead. It slid open along the bulkhead on wheels, and Cassandra was hit in the face with a blast of fresh air and salt water spray. It was the door where the supplies would be loaded from the dock, and she was only a few yards above the water. She breathed in deeply for a moment and let herself enjoy the wide open view. Up until that moment, she hadn't realized how the Mercy Mission ship smelled. The dead were everywhere, and she had been so focused on reaching her goal that she had ignored the smell. She decided to leave the door open, and if she had no other choice, she would jump from the boat and take her chances at sea. If she had a life raft and supplies, she would do just that.

Reality came back to her when a body passed in front of her eyes and hit the water. Cassandra looked up from the open cargo door and saw the gap in the side railing above. She wondered how many of the crewmen had fallen overboard, and she wondered if she could get more of them off of the ship that way. It was worth giving it some thought, but there were hundreds of people on board when this had all started, and at least half of them were trapped below decks with no way to get out. At least a small part of her also held out hope that there were others alive.

She started to turn away from the open door when she saw something she hadn't seen in a long time. There were seagulls circling the ship. That meant they were near land, and Cassandra tried to remember how long they had been at sea since leaving port in Africa. She asked herself if it was even possible that it had been long enough for them to have crossed the Atlantic, but the memories came back to her like a movie on fast forward.

There had been time to watch the doctors make one discovery after the next, only to find something had contaminated the blood samples. They would try again, and more than once they thought they had found a cure, but each time it failed when it was tested. Before Doctor Sellers had become infected and bitten Doctor Nkrumah, there had been hope, but hope dimmed when the infection had finally broken free throughout the crew.

There had been close calls with the infected, and there had been many deaths, but mostly there had been the waiting. They spent months circling in the Atlantic just trying to establish communications with anyone who could give them some news of a safe harbor. When they did make contact with military forces at sea, they were warned not to approach land or other ships.

She remembered they had sailed along the coast of Africa, and wherever they passed land that had open areas they saw the hordes of infected walking toward the shores. Sometimes they would send out a blast from the ship's horn and watch the reaction of the infected. That was the only way they could be sure they weren't survivors. If they were survivors, they would have waved, but the infected walked into the water as if they could walk all the way to the ship.

Portugal and Spain were promising because there were less infected along the coast, but it was all an illusion. The infected were still there. They just weren't walking into the ocean. The crew was once again encouraged when the coast of France came into view, and they saw a small contingent of soldiers camped on the beach, but a blast from the ship's horn was met with gunfire from the troops. They could understand why when they saw that the sound of the horn drew the infected down upon the soldiers. There was nothing they could do as they watched the camp being overrun.

The only communication established after France was with a Royal Navy destroyer that ordered them to change course. They were given no reason except that they would be sunk if they proceeded toward the United Kingdom. They had eventually turned back to the east in the hope that North America had done what they had hoped and saved their country.

"Yes," Cassandra said out loud. "It has been a long time."

Up until that moment, she had given very little thought to how long it had been. She had just existed and survived for as long as she could, and didn't even remember when the last time was that she had seen another crewman alive. When the memories rushed through her mind, she guessed it had been almost a year.

Cassandra held onto the door and leaned out as far as she could, trying to see if there was land off the starboard bow. From her angle she couldn't see any, but she didn't want to be in the kitchen or anywhere else inside the ship if it hit land while moving at the speed it was going.

She decided it was time to get herself moving again. She went back to the refrigerator and took a few more swallows of juice then went back to the other door leading out of the kitchen. The big meat cleaver felt good in her hand, and she lifted it half way between her hip and shoulder so she would be ready to use it when she had to. One more deep breath, and she was ready to go again.

This time the door opened into a narrow service corridor, and Petty officer Gibbs felt really afraid for the first time since the infection had started to spread throughout the ship. This corridor she knew, and it was the wrong place to be. The gangway ahead of her in the corridor dropped straight down into the area right outside of the main crew quarters. The smell alone was enough to make her turn around, but the groaning coming from below made her skin crawl. The worst part was that the only way down to the engine room from where she stood was through the corridor past the crew's quarters.

10 MUD ISLAND ASSAULT

From Mud Island we could see a blue and white ship coming straight toward us, but from the Beaver the view was slightly different. The ship that was on our horizon was heading for the coast slightly to the north of Mud Island, but there were shoals and sand bars along the coast that would stop it short of making landfall.

Kathy and the Chief were faced with a real problem just trying to get back into the shelter, but we already had our usual plan in mind. The Boston Whaler was safely tucked away in its own hidden boat garage on the southern tip of Mud Island, so we would take it out at night and head south to a safe enough distance to pick them up. The problem was that we couldn't communicate that to them. If we could, they could fly south, land at sea, and just wait for us to arrive.

The radiation levels had dropped to a level so low that it was barely reading anything on our hidden sensors, so we wouldn't have to worry about exposure. There were probably hundreds of people in our moat who had been fatally exposed, but there was nothing that could be done for them. After what we had seen them doing along the beach, I wasn't so sure we would have tried. The only thing worse than harvesting the crabs that had been eating their friends was cannibalism, and we weren't convinced that was beyond this group's level of thinking.

We all gathered around the dining room table for a group meeting to see if anyone could come up with some ideas in a hurry. Our designated radio operator, Molly, was at her post listening for anything on the radio. I looked around at the group and saw them looking at each other for answers. Jean, Tom, and Bus all looked at each other and at me as if they were waiting for someone to come up with something original.

Jean looked like the strain of thinking this problem through was going to make her have our baby before the day was over. Our two best planners were out there in an airplane, and if I knew them both as well as I thought I did, they had a plan but were trying to figure out how to pass it along to us in a way that wouldn't make sense to anyone who might be listening. That's when it I knew what we should do.

"We should anticipate the Chief and Kathy," I said.

All three of them looked at me expectantly.

"And exactly what do you think they're going to do, Eddie?"

Jean had a way of saying my name that could sound sweet and sour at the same time. She was frustrated because she was worried about our friends. They were so close to home, but outside was a floating city of sick people and a ship coming toward us. Both of those things were major obstacles to bringing the Chief and Kathy home.

I didn't answer immediately to give Jean a chance to think about the way she had answered me, and it paid off.

"I'm sorry," she said. "I sounded like a witch, didn't I."

It wasn't a question, so I just gave her a little smile. Tom and Bus stayed out of it, not wanting to get us too far away from the problem at hand.

"So, what do you think they are hoping we will do?" asked Tom.

"Well, when there's only one thing you can do, you should do it. They know the only way we can retrieve them is to pick them up down the coast at night, so we should go out through the southern escape hatch and launch the Boston Whaler. The current from the moat should carry us out far enough without us even having to turn on the motor. After we pick them up, we can use the motor to get close and then use paddles the rest of the way."

Bus was nodding at me as I talked, but when I finished he said, "Aren't you forgetting something? That ship will be here before nightfall, and I'm not entirely sure of where it will make landfall. It could drive right up the southern entrance to the moat for all we know."

"Okay," I said. "We can still do it in daylight. The boat people in our moat wouldn't even see us leaving. They don't have people in that end of the moat, and the beach is too far from the exit. It might even be better because the Chief and Kathy will be able to see us."

"We would have to move faster in daylight," said Jean.

The rest of us looked at her at same time and just waited.

It didn't take long for Jean to realize the three men were all giving her the same look.

"Mind if I take this one, Ed?" asked Tom. "It might keep you out of trouble."

"Be my guest," I said.

"Jean, you're not going with us. You're pregnant."

"You think I'm just going to sit here and wait for you guys again?"

All three of us said, "Yes."

Before Jean had a chance to start protesting, I saw Molly waving at us from the living room.

"Molly's got something."

We all ran into the living room at the same time as she was scribbling on a pad of paper. Molly was a bright girl, and she knew how to write map coordinates. The funny thing was that she knew how to write map coordinates before I did.

She handed me the top sheet from the pad and said, "It was Kathy. She didn't say anything except to stand by for instructions, then said the numbers. I recognized the first set as our location, so I think she's saying they're going to the second set."

Tom mussed Molly's hair and gave her a smile.

"Smart girl, Molly. Was there anything else?"

"No Daddy, she just gave the double click on the radio button."

Bus and I were already spreading out the map on a table while Jean was trying to get close enough to see. She was so short that her big belly was getting in the way when she leaned over the table.

Bus located the coordinates and traced a line from Mud Island out to the spot.

"Unless I miss my guess, that looks like the location of the ship that's coming this way. Why would they send us the coordinates to that ship?"

I looked at the coordinates and said, "No, I think the location is closer to us than the ship. Look at he depth markings on the map. It gets a bit shallow right there. I think they know we can see the ship coming, and that it may run aground before it reaches us."

"That's good to know," said Jean, "but did they tell us that for a reason other than to let us know we aren't going to have a ship drive up to our front door?

"Hard to tell," I said, "but if it stops short, we can wait until after dark to leave just as we said earlier."

Molly came into the dining room and handed us a new set of coordinates, but there were other numbers that didn't look like they belonged on a map, and they were followed by a set of coordinates that were inland.

Bus took a pencil and put a small circle at each spot. The first numbers were the same as the earlier set, and they did appear to be somewhere between Mud Island and the ship. The second set were south of the first mark and could be where the Chief wanted to land the plane for a rendezvous with us. The third group of numbers were sixteen, four, and nine. After a space, there was another set of coordinates, and when Bus drew the circle on the map, it was right in the center of Georgetown.

"They're telling us where to pick them up, and they're telling is to bring guns and ammo. The third set of coordinates is to remind us that Hampton is with them."

That was good news to me and Jean. Tom and Bus had never met Hampton, but he was a likable guy, and it would be good to have him with us. He was also a survivor if he managed to live through whatever happened at Georgetown and lived out in the open for as long as he had.

"The Chief and Kathy were armed when they left," said Bus. "They either ran into problems and lost their weapons, or they want us to bring more support in case we get spotted."

"There could be another reason," said Jean.

I hadn't noticed that she had left the dining room and was standing in front of the big monitor that showed a view of the beach. We all went to join her, and we could see what she meant.

The Chief had most likely gone to an altitude that gave him and Kathy a clear view of Mud Island without being heard from the ground. Given the amount of noise the Beaver's engine made, he must have gone up a few miles. From where they were, they could see what we were seeing outside through our security cameras.

The entire population of the boat city in our moat was trying to get to the beach for a look at the approaching ship, and it was obvious that they felt like it was their first chance to be rescued because most of them were waving their arms. Some had attached big sheets of cloth of various colors onto long poles and were waving them like flags.

I switched the monitor to a view that allowed us to see what was happening around the island, and we saw that the boats were already trying to get out of the moat at the main entrance to the north. Those that could get underway were turning in place to face outward, and we could see the people who had been living in the houseboat trying again to get our twin outboard boat to start. They had tried before without success, and they weren't likely to figure out what the Chief had done to disable it, but they were giving it another try.

The first boats got clear of the haphazard mess at the moat entrance and started out to sea. It was like someone got the cork out of a bottle, and a steady stream of boats followed. Some of the people on the beach began running back to the dock to try to catch rides on the boats, and some were dumb enough to start swimming. The crowd looked like it was going to go crazy, and there were far more people than we had realized.

Several of the boats that made it out of the logjam veered off course and came down along the island to the beach, presumably to pick up more people. That was their mistake, because their boats were quickly swamped by the desperate crowds. We watched as people fought with each other and then started shooting. People scattered, and some fell to the ground to die. No one considered what would happen next, as people continued to focus on the approaching ship.

The leaders from the houseboat had given up on our boat and were doing what they could to take boats away from other people. It looked like as many as six or seven men had leadership status, and they all managed to hitch rides with boats that were passing by. The camera view of the moat showed that most of the boats were under power, just waiting for their turn to get in line behind those that were leaving. Some of the boats that weren't under power either couldn't start or were being towed by other boats.

******

From a few miles above, Kathy was watching the events below through a set of binoculars and describing them to the Chief through their headsets. Hampton was doing the same from his window in the back of the Beaver, but Colleen was persistently tugging the binoculars away from him for a quick look.

They could see a steady stream of small boats, most no more than sixteen feet long, heading out to meet the big blue and white ship. It looked like at least a two hundred of them were at full speed as they passed the northern jetty. They could also see that the ship wasn't slowing down. It was on a collision course with a reef that was marked by a buoy, so the Chief knew that no one could be at the helm. If there was, they knew the reef was there, but they didn't care.

The Chief had seen ships run aground before, and depending on the speed of the impact, it wasn't a pretty sight. If there were living people on board who weren't braced for impact, they were thrown into bulkheads and often killed by equipment that wasn't secured. If they were topside, they were likely to be thrown overboard.

"Do you think it's safe to try for radio contact, Chief?"

"Wouldn't hurt. Those people in the boats are too busy to figure out where the radio broadcast is coming from."

Kathy keyed the microphone and said, "Unidentified vessel approaching the South Carolina coast at high speed. Be aware that you are about to enter shallow water. The buoy is located less than five degrees to your starboard bow."

They listened for a response for a few seconds, then she repeated the message. There was no change in course.

"Some of the lead boats are going to get to the reef before the ship. The wake will swamp them if they're too close," said Hampton.

There was a burst of static on their radio, and then a woman's voice came through.

"Unidentified radio transmission. I don't have you in my view. Can you provide location?"

The Chief and Kathy exchanged looks with each other. Neither of them could figure out what she meant by "view".

Kathy had a thought from her police training and asked the question even civilians understood from watching tv or using a CB radio.

"Negative if you're asking for our twenty. Hostiles in the area."

"Copy that," said the woman. "Plenty of hostiles here too."

That was what they had been afraid of. The ship was overrun by the infected dead, but at least one woman was onboard with access to a radio.

The voice came back before Kathy could ask more questions.

"Unable to reach the quarterdeck, so unable to pilot the vessel. As many as two to three hundred infected onboard. Unknown if others are alive, but doubtful. Cornered in radio room located amidships one deck below open cargo door to galley storage. Can you assist?"

It wasn't like the Mud Island survivors to say no to anyone who was still alive after the outbreak of the infection. If they were alive and unbitten, then they deserved to live. Kathy looked at the Chief before answering, and Hampton leaned forward between the front seats and grinned at both of them.

"We're in."

"Have you been infected?" Kathy asked into the microphone.

There was a brief pause that caused them to worry, but the voice came back and said, "Sorry, someone wanted into the radio room. Had to check the door."

"Unidentified friend, I have not been bitten, and I'm allergic to shellfish, so I have not been infected by the food.

Most of the crew ate the shellfish so the infection spread fast once it got started."

"Did she just say what I think she said?" asked the Chief.

"We all heard it," said Kathy. "It's time to introduce ourselves and let her know that we're at least going to give it a try. It's a good thing we already told our friends to bring more guns and ammo."

"Unidentified vessel, we can assist. Four friendlies along for the ride with three more inbound. I'm Kathy, and I don't think you'll have a hard time figuring out who we are since we will be armed, but be advised there are other unfriendlies inbound. Remain secure until you are sure it's us and not them."

"Thank you, Kathy. I'm Cassandra. Will remain secure, but please hurry."

"One more thing, Cassandra. People died after eating the shellfish. Did you mean crabs?"

"Ghost crabs and mangrove oysters harvested near Cameroon, Africa."

"Well, that explains what we suspected all along," said the Chief.

"Blue crabs," said Hampton. "I was wondering about that, too. Some of the people in Georgetown looked sick long before the town was overrun. I knew people were still crabbing after we closed off all of the routes in and out of town, but it bothered me when I thought about what was going into the water, so I didn't eat what they caught. I remember one guy saying that just left more for him."

"What about the rest of the food chain?" asked Colleen. "Do we have to worry about everything we eat, and why wouldn't cooking it kill the virus....or whatever it is?"

"We can worry about that later," said the Chief, "but for the time being we won't eat anything that doesn't come out of our supply room. Besides, you won't find crab dip on the table in our shelter, not unless you want to see Jean come unglued. In the meantime, I think we can break radio silence now. Things are starting to happen too fast for us to worry about someone hearing us."

Kathy keyed the microphone and asked Mud Island to respond. Molly answered immediately and asked her if they could see the beach. From a couple of miles away Kathy said they could see what we were watching on our security cameras.

People who had been shot during the fighting for the boats were getting back up from the sand and wandering into the crowds of people still waving at the approaching ship. The unsuspecting people toward the back of the crowd felt the bites on their arms, necks, and legs. The screaming started, but there was so much noise from the excited crowd that the people couldn't tell the difference between screams and cheers. Only a few people turned to look, but most of them just thought there were more fights. It wouldn't be long before the infected outnumbered the living on the beach.

"Molly, tell everyone to go now. There's a survivor on that ship, and we're going to try to help get her out of there."

When Molly told us Kathy had broken radio silence, and that the message was to go now, we started moving fast. The armory was just beyond the room that held our escape tunnel, so we all gathered there first. We had plenty of ammunition, M4's, M16's, and Glocks. We also each grabbed a machete and a pair of heavy duty work gloves. Backpacks were stuffed with ammunition until they were almost too heavy to carry.

I was glad Tom had been a professional baseball player because he had the legs for carrying that much weight. I was in the best shape of my entire life, but I was never going to catch up with him. The man was an absolute workhorse.

We gathered at the escape hatch, and Jean was waiting there for me. The look on her face said she was more worried about this trip outside than usual. She wrapped her arms around my waist and buried her face in my chest. She felt so comfortable against me that I could easily have stayed right where I was.

"You're going to be a father in a week or so. If you don't mind, I'd like for you to come back in one piece. I wish I was going with you."

"I plan to be here when you have our baby, so I'll come back in one piece and without getting hurt. I don't want you to be worry while I'm gone, but you know I have to be there for this."

There wasn't much else I could say except that I would be careful, and I expected her not to go outside while we were gone. She said something about no Russians in the moat, but both of us were thinking about the same thing. Going outside and surviving wasn't a sure thing anymore. We had seen a lot of bad things in the last year, but this situation looked wrong. There were too many things happening out there.

I gave Jean a long kiss then reluctantly let her go and went up the escape tunnel where Tom and Bus were waiting for me. The helpless look on her face was almost more than I could stand, and I could tell she was doing everything she could not to cry.

Jean watched me go into the tunnel then sealed the lower door behind me. I sealed the upper hatch as quickly as

I could, but I could still feel Jean standing below the bottom hatch as if she was right in front of me.

Tom and Bus checked to be sure the beach was clear at the southern end of Mud Island, and then we worked as fast as we could to get the Boston Whaler down to the water.

"Any radiation readings, Bus?" I asked.

"Nothing we need to worry about," he answered.

The motor started easily, and we headed out to the coordinates that Kathy had sent to us. We could see the blue and white ship in the distance, and there were so many small boats heading for it that we couldn't have guessed how many there were.

"How are we supposed to help the survivor on that ship with that many people trying to get there ahead of us?" I shouted over the sound of the motor.

"I don't know," yelled Tom. "Maybe the Chief has some ideas."

We were all watching the ship, but there was no mistaking the yellow dot that appeared in the distance behind it. The de Havilland Beaver seaplane passed behind the stern of the ship and gradually descended to the water.

******

Kathy radioed Cassandra one last time and told her to brace herself for impact. They could see that the ship was about to hit the reef, and there were at least fifty boats in the collision path. The Chief guessed that the people must have thought the ship would stop to rescue them, but even if the people on board the ship had been alive, it just wasn't something they would have done. Ships with living crews weren't likely to risk bringing the infection onboard.

From everyone's point of view it was a horrendous impact. The big ship slammed into the reef and was brought to such a rapid stop that it caused its own wake to catch up with it like a tidal wave. The wave passed the ship and crashed into the smaller boats that had gone to the port and starboard sides to move from the path of the bow.

Some of the small boats that had gotten there too quickly were swamped or crushed under the bow. Fewer than half of the original inhabitants of the Mud Island moat were left alive, and more were dying every minute as the big ship bucked with its stern higher out of the water than we could imagine it could go. When it dropped back down as the forward motion was completely stopped, it created a second tidal wave that rushed forward to claim a few more of the small boats that had somehow survived the first wave.

Inside the ship, Cassandra had gone to the forward bulkhead of the small radio room and laid her body against it as closely as she could. First she felt like gravity had changed from the deck to the wall, then she felt the room tilt until she was sure it was on its side. Then it was like an elevator changing directions, and gravity went from the bulkhead to the deck, to the opposite bulkhead, and then back to the deck again. She was tossed around like a rag doll, but the room was small enough to keep her from flying too far or too fast. She could only imagine what it had been like in the bigger compartments. The crew's berthing area was probably a big pile of bodies.

There was a vibration through the deck, and she was surprised to feel that the big screws behind the ship were still turning. That wasn't good. An engine that was pushing too hard to keep moving forward was more likely to catch fire when it overheated. If she could find her way out, she needed to start trying now. Fires on ships were a bad thing.

The cabin door was warped and didn't want to open. Cassandra looked around for something she could use to pry it open, but the room was too small to have anything useful, and for the first time since this ordeal had begun, she felt like she was going to panic. She could deal with anything except being trapped inside the little room.

She was just about to lose it when she remembered her meat cleaver. She pulled it from her belt and started working the sharp edge into the gap around the door. She kept telling herself to be patient so she wouldn't snap the blade in half as she pried. When the seal around the door was a little wider, she started to pull on the handle and pry with the cleaver at the same time. The door popped open and a tangle of bodies fell through.

Despite being pushed back against the bulkhead for a second time, Cassandra swung the heavy cleaver expertly. What had seemed like ten infected dead turned out to be four, and she delivered blows to their heads as fast as she could. She had to step on them to get out of the room, but there was no way she wanted to stay in there for one more minute.

The corridor outside the little room was just like the pile up on the door to the cabin, but most of the infected dead had been unable to bring themselves to a standing position. Cassandra hurried past them, stopping only when it looked like one was going to be able to grab her. She reached for the highest rung on a ladder that went up one deck and pulled herself free from the infected that were still trying to get to their feet.

Earlier when she had found herself with nowhere to go except down into the crew's berthing compartment, she had descended slowly and found that someone had done her a big favor. The steps of the steel ladder came down outside the door to the berthing area, and it was dogged shut with a fire fighting axe handle through the big locking wheel in the middle of the door. It was still in place as she went by, but the bulkhead had buckled and the door was ready to come off of its hinges. She climbed the next gangway quickly to get to the kitchen storage area. Her plan was to get to the open cargo door and jump. If she was as close to land as she thought she was, she could swim the rest of the way.

There was an odd feel to the vibrations in the deck, and she felt like the ship was moving sideways. Her first look out the cargo bay door confirmed her suspicions as she saw the turning screws were making the ship pivot around its bow. The ship was trying to turn sideways to the reef. That would be really bad news if the collision with the reef had opened a hole in the bow. She wasn't sure if the ship could pivot far enough to break free of the reef, but if it did it would start taking on water. Jumping from the ship wasn't going to be an option.

Her next look through the open door was down at the water, and she was surprised to see at least a dozen boats clustered only twenty feet below. There were men trying to throw ropes with makeshift hooks on them up into the storage area. One narrowly missed her, and she saw that it was a ten pound anchor. Whoever threw it that far wasn't someone she wanted to meet without a weapon in her hand.

When the anchor landed, its blades fanned outward and lodged around the steel legs of one of the heavy storage shelves. She saw the rope pull tight, and movement of the rope to the left and right told her someone was on their way up. It was undoubtedly the person who could throw a ten pound anchor that far.

Cassandra dove across the deck and brought the cleaver down on the rope. The weight of someone climbing the rope made the cleaver's job even easier, and it sliced clean through with one swing. The rope snaked out through the open door, and she heard loud cursing as the man crashed back into his boat. The fall wasn't likely to kill him, but it was one less thing trying to kill her.

She risked a quick look over the edge of the cargo door and was rewarded by a steady barrage of bullets. She didn't know how many guns there were, but it only took one. She got out of the way just in time as the next anchor flew past her. This one didn't hook onto anything and slid back through the open cargo door. Cassandra wished she had one infected dead in the storage area that she could hook the anchor to. They would be surprised when they dragged that back over the edge.

She laughed to herself, but the idea wasn't as bad as she thought. She looked around and saw that she had plenty of high places where she could climb to, and still have a clear shot at the door. She waited for the anchor to appear again, and she grabbed it before it could slide away. Whoever was on the other end of the rope must have been surprised to see the rope going into the opening of the ship instead of coming back out because they didn't try to stop it in time.

Cassandra ran over to the door to the galley and wrapped the line around the handle. As soon as it went tight she turned and ran for the nearest shelves and climbed to the top. She watched the line pull tighter, and just as she hoped, the door swung open. The infected dead that had chased her behind the serving line in the galley and survived the collision were tangled up against the door, and they fell through in a big pile.

There was plenty of noise at the cargo door because the first man was already halfway up the rope, and a second line had hooked onto the lip of the door where it met the deck. The men were cheering each other on as the first one got to the top and turned to grab the hand of the next man behind him.

They were both holding onto the rim of the door when their hands were bitten. The exposed flesh was ripped from their bones, and they immediately let go. They fell into the boats, taking people with them who had almost reached the top, followed by a rainstorm of bodies. The infected dead had reacted to the screams and didn't see Cassandra on the top shelf, and one by one they walked to the open door and then walked right over the edge.

Cassandra watched the parade of infected dead go by her until there weren't any more, and then she dropped down to the deck. She didn't see any activity over by the open cargo door, but she doubted she had done anything more than to delay the inevitable. Even if she managed to close the cargo door, she was likely to be shot making the effort. Her best bet was to escape to a higher deck, and she had at least bought herself some time by letting the infected come through the kitchen.

She hefted the cleaver in one hand, but she pulled her Glock from its holster with the other. If those people had managed to board from another part of the ship, shooting was going to be the only way to defend herself.

******

There would be time for a reunion later, but as the Boston Whaler bobbed next to the seaplane, I wished I could hug them all…even the Chief. He would have made a big deal out of that, so I settled for a few words of welcome.

Tom had managed to get control of the seaplane's wing just long enough to get the boat and plane into position to transfer to the boat, but he knew better than to hang on. The right wave at the right time, and he would have a choice between hanging on and losing his arms.

"Are we shallow enough to anchor?" yelled Kathy.

I gave her a thumbs up, and she let the anchor line go.

With everyone on board, I throttled up the engine and turned in the direction of the blue and white ship that was even now trying to power its way over the reef. I didn't have time to talk with everyone, but Hampton gave me a pat on the shoulder as he went by. He was trailed by a little strawberry blonde who gave me a smile and a pat on the shoulder where Tom had. I had to laugh even though I knew we were going into a really bad place in just a few minutes.

We came up on the port side of the ship where the reef made the water much more shallow than on the starboard side. There were several boats already lined up, and the people in them were trying to throw grappling hooks high enough to reach the railings. I saw one fly up in the air and come straight back down on the head of the moron who threw it.

"Those guys are going to kill themselves before we can," yelled the Chief.

I glanced back and saw him sighting down the barrel of a hunting rifle. He pulled the trigger and one of the men throwing an anchor threw short. He and the anchor both went into the water.

That brought the guns out on the boats, and shots were fired wildly in our direction. The people in the boats had made a lot of mistakes in one day, but opening fire instead of running was the biggest one. The Chief and Kathy were both deadly shooters, and their first few shots all hit their targets. Tom and Hampton had both moved to the bow where they could lay out to take aim, and they were also reducing the numbers in the boats. I was surprised to find Bus and the little strawberry blonde both doing damage, as well.

By the time we reached the side of the big ship, there were only a handful of people alive in the boats, and they were more than glad to leave. Our group stopped firing when it became clear that the other people preferred to leave, but instead of turning for land, they drove along the port side of the ship and tried to turn around the stern. The churning propellors took care of the small boats as they were pulled under in what looked like a huge blender.

We didn't know what was happening over on the starboard side of the ship, but we now had a clear port side to climb. The Chief was laughing at the attempts they had seen the people in the boats making. He produced a short piece of rope that looked like it had a big knot on the end of it. He called it a Monkey's Paw. He tied it to a longer piece of rope and expertly threw it over the railing on the first try. When it crossed the railing, he tugged at just the right moment, and the line spun around the top railing into a nice little knot.

The Chief went up the side of the ship with another rope over his shoulder and hopped over the railing. He tied off the second rope so we would have two ropes to climb and then dropped into a crouch to be sure nothing was going to attack us. We all got a chance to see that Colleen wasn't shy about joining in on the fight as she expertly went hand over hand up a rope. I turned the rudder over to Bus so I could start climbing with the others, and as soon as the last of us was climbing a rope, Bus pulled the boat away to a safe distance.

The Chief gave us a quick explanation of what he wanted to do, and told us he thought we were only looking for one survivor. He said that they had seen an open cargo door on the starboard side of the ship when they flew over it, so we should expect that some of the boat people would have gotten in through there.

When the Chief was done explaining the plan he asked if there were any questions, and I told him I had one. It was risky to ask, but I had to know something.

"I know we're doing the right thing by going in for one person, but I can't really put my finger on a reason other than that I would want someone to help me. Is there something else besides us being self-appointed knights in shining armor?"

I felt like a rat for asking, but I could see from the reaction of the others that they didn't mind the question. We didn't really need another reason, but it wouldn't hurt to have one.

The Chief looked like he was thinking about the answer, but then he just grinned and said, "No, that about covers it. Let's go find that survivor."

Kathy, the Chief, and Tom took off along the side of the ship in the direction of the stern. I went with Hampton and Colleen toward the bow. When the Chief had laid out his rescue plan, he explained that survivors on ships always try to go up, so search and rescue teams always start at the top. It made sense to me because you could always see the survivors on the top deck. The Chief also explained that the simple psychology was people also knew they could jump from a ship easier than they could dig a hole through the hull. The man had a way with words.

When we reached the bow, we found a big pile of infected dead still trying to untangle themselves from each other and from equipment. When the ship had hit the reef, they shot forward like rag dolls. Most of them had suffered some damage that was preventing them from standing up, and those that could stand were stuck in the twisted pile of bodies. It looked like a wrestling match with a lot of contestants.

We inspected the mess and decided it would be a waste of time to dispose of them, so we just located the ladder on the port side that went up to the next level. We had no idea if it was going to be the top deck or if we had another level to climb, but it looked like we had one more ladder to go.

On the stern of the ship, the rest of our group was delayed because the pile of infected was wrapped up around the bottom of the ladder. They had to carefully cut away almost two dozen grabbing, biting, and groaning infected before they could begin to climb. Once they were past them, they climbed the ladder and found a similar mess at what must have been a medical bay. Some of the infected were strapped down, some were tangled together, and some were wandering around.

By the time the Chief, Kathy and Tom got past the second landing, we had already reached our second ladder and climbed up to the vehicle deck. There were rows of Jeeps lined up the full length and width of the level. Some appeared to have been ransacked, but some still looked fully supplied and ready to send out on the next mission. It would be nice to be able to drive around in a sturdy vehicle, but roads were too unpredictable. You could be driving along a clear road for several miles and then run straight into a horde of infected dead walking right down the center line.

I didn't get much chance to look at the Jeeps because Hampton had a firm grip on my shirt near the collar. He yanked me off my feet and down below the row of Jeeps nearest to us. Looking between the tires under the Jeeps I could see several pairs of legs moving toward the center of the upper level.

These were not the slow, dragging legs of the infected dead. These were people who were moving forward with a purpose, and we had managed to come up on their flank.

Colleen tapped Hampton on the shoulder and pointed at something, and I saw that she had spotted an open gangway that came up through the deck from somewhere below. There were men climbing out of the gangway like spiders, and they looked like they were closing in on their prey.

******

Cassandra didn't meet with much resistance in the big galley of the ship because everything that wasn't fastened down was in a pile at the forward end, and it was a good thing that she didn't have to stop and fight her way through the infected dead because her pursuers had made it to the kitchen.

The boat people began fighting among themselves as soon as they found refrigerators that still worked and contained real food. There wasn't much, and even if it was a little out of date, it was still food. When the leaders of the boat people made it through the cargo door, they had a little bit of payback on their minds, so they began throwing people back out the door into the water until they restored some order.

Once they were back in control, they posted guards on the storage area and then ordered everyone else to go after whoever it was who had tormented them from the cargo door. They said no one would eat until they had the person who had dropped their anchors back on their heads, and they didn't think all of the infected that rained down on them had been an accident.

They all began piling through the kitchen door and across the galley, and one of them yelled that he thought someone had just gone up the gangway to the next level. The chase was on, and they ran like a pack of dogs after a rabbit.

Cassandra went up through the hatch at the top of the gangway onto the upper level and didn't slow down. The day was hot and sticky, and the sun was so bright that it hurt her eyes. She ran for the middle of the vehicle level with the idea that she could hold off enough of them with her M4 and her Glock long enough for the people on the radio to arrive.

It had occurred to her that she might get to the vehicle level and find a Jeep sitting on top of the hatch. She also thought the bow of the ship would have a spectacular pile of Jeeps on it, but the Mercy Mission ship had been an ocean going ferry until it was converted to a hospital ship, and the upper deck was lined with rows of cleats sunken in the deck, and each Jeep had been chained into place. She was grateful for that small favor, but she wished someone would have been smart enough to put locks on the gangway hatches. She could close them, but she couldn't lock them, so they wouldn't even slow down her pursuers.

She gave brief thought to the possibility of just shooting them as they stuck their heads out of the hatch, but there were two hatches on each end of the upper level. She couldn't cover two of them, so there was no way she could cover four. So, her best plan was to run as far as she could, shoot for as long as she could, and then jump from the port side of the ship if she had to. If the fall didn't kill her, maybe she would be picked up by her rescuers.

Cassandra ran to the middle and found a good spot to take aim at the people who were after her. When she was ready, she saw that a steady stream of armed men were at the far end of the vehicle deck and had spread out. She took aim at one and fired then immediately looked for another target.

******

From our hiding place behind the last row of Jeeps we heard the first shot and saw someone go down, but desperate people do desperate things, and instead of ducking and shooting back from the protection of the Jeeps, they started rushing forward as they shot toward the middle of the level. If it was our survivor who had shot at them, she was a good shot, but after the first few rounds she was too busy avoiding being shot to fight them off. There were at least thirty or forty people shooting back at her, and even though no more were coming up through the gangway hatch, I was sure there would be more below.

Hampton led the way and ran across the first row of Jeeps until he was roughly two thirds of the way across. Colleen ran behind him, but she stopped at the middle row. They both took aim, and I saw immediately how well they worked together. I moved over two rows until I could see the backs of the boat people going in the direction of the shooter. Hampton gave us a little wave, and we each found a target.

Cassandra had given up some ground because the wild shots were hitting her Jeep. She was surprised by how quickly she was being forced to retreat and was afraid she was going to have to jump after all. She looked behind her and saw there were only a few more rows of Jeeps, but when she turned to try to get off another shot, she saw the man she was randomly aiming at go down. It looked to her almost like his head exploded all by itself. Then two more fell, their rifles flying from their hands.

Her pursuers had nowhere to go, so they came straight at her. She saw that there were too many of them to shoot before they would reach her, but she didn't have a choice. She targeted one and shot him, but the man next to him got hit, too. This time the attacker flew backward instead of forward. She glanced over her shoulder and saw one of the biggest men she had ever seen, and he was sighting down the barrel of a rifle at the wave of attackers. After he shot one, he paused just long enough to give her a broad smile.

More shots came from behind her, and she turned the other way and saw a pretty blond and a tall, athletic looking man also shooting. They were outnumbered, but they had the discipline to stand still and find their targets while the attackers spent too much time dodging and running.

With nowhere to hide when the shots were coming from both sides, the last of the attackers tried to jump from the vehicle level. Some managed to jump far enough to clear the railings of the lower decks, but several hit the railings and then cartwheeled down to the water.

When the shooting stopped, Cassandra started advancing instead of retreating. None of the attackers had tried to hide, so they were able to do a clean sweep in a couple of minutes. Cassandra started to target three people she spotted who were all hanging back behind the Jeeps near the bow, but one of them yelled, "All clear," and waved his rifle over his head.

When the big man walked up to Cassandra and held his hand out to her and the others came in closer, all she could say was, "You people are good."

We all felt the massive vibration in the ship that seemed to make it shudder under our feet. The propellors were still trying to turn, but the engines had overheated to the breaking point. Far below us there were fires raging unchecked in the engine room, and the explosions were just barely loud enough for us to hear. The ship was sliding sideways along the reef, and it didn't feel like it was going to break free, but it was definitely going to do its best to sink. It was either going to be in one piece or several, and it was time for us to go.

The ship was leaning to the port side, and we went straight down the ropes instead of using our feet against the hull. Bus had shown some perfect timing by being under the ropes when we reached the railings. One by one we dropped into the Boston Whaler, and Bus pushed the throttle forward as the Chief came down last.

We were clear of the Mercy Mission ship when she had given up and broken in half. Between the explosions and the damage done when she collided with the reef, it was more than the hull could take. When it broke apart, the two halves slid away from each other and went separately below the surface of the water. The boat people inside tried to toss as much food as they could out of the cargo door, but they waited too long. The sinking ship collapsed onto them, and the suction caused by the two halves of the ship pulled the rest under with them.

Jean was on the radio with us as soon as we were clear, and she described a bleak scene on the beach facing the ocean. She was crying because she had seen the people falling off of the ship and didn't know if we were victims or winners. When she saw the Boston Whaler cruise up to the side of the big ship as it leaned over the smaller boat, she thought it would be crushed. Then she tried to count the number of people who slid down the ropes and just wasn't sure of how many she saw.

There was no one left alive on the beach or in the boats. Jean said anyone who got left behind was caught by the hordes of infected dead that were everywhere. She said she saw several people try to hide inside the houseboat, but someone had left the door open when it all started, so people had died and then turned inside. Our only choice for the time being was to go back into the Mud Island shelter through the escape tunnel, but that was fine with us.

We made a quick stop where the de Havilland Beaver bobbed on the waves and the Chief jumped over to the pilot side float. He powered up the plane while Tom and Hampton pulled in the anchors, and then we followed the plane as the Chief brought it closer to shore. It didn't take long for us to park it in shallower water and cover it with tarps. It would be safer hidden near the marshes until we could assess the situation back at the moat.

On the way back to the island, I saw Kathy and Colleen talking with Cassandra, and I stayed back to give them some space. I knew that Kathy was taking care of a chore that was important to our survival, and that was the inspection to verify Cassandra wasn't hiding a bite. A time would come when we would take someone in and find that they had been bitten, and then we would have to deny them entry into our sanctuary, but I really hoped it wouldn't be this time. She looked like she had been through so much already.

11 EPILOGUE

One of the really special things about owning a shelter like Mud Island is being able to show it off. Seeing the expression on someone's face when they see it the first time deserves a drum roll, but I have to be satisfied with just watching their eyes get big.

Petty Officer Cassandra Gibbs was no different, and even though Hampton and Colleen had seen a shelter that I wouldn't get to see for a long time, they were still impressed by our little corner of heaven. Hampton couldn't believe this was all practically in his back yard, and he said if he had built a shelter, he would have built it here, too.

We had landed the boat and easily pulled it into its hiding place since there were so many of us, then we slid down the tunnel to safety. Of course I had to be at the bottom to be able to see the expressions on the faces of the new arrivals. I almost missed it because Jean had me in a bear hug.

Colleen and Hampton were all smiles and big eyed, but Cassandra looked like she was going to come unglued. With her mouth hanging open as she turned in a circle, she very slowly said, "Oh, my God."

Everyone was introduced to Jean, and the two new ladies both had to ask her questions about when she was due, and of course they had to congratulate the father-to-be. Kathy said something in a discreetly low voice to Cassandra, and she gave her a nod. The two of them headed off in the direction of the showers so they could put the personal inspection behind them.

Jean chose that moment to put her hand on her big stomach and go, "Uh, oh."

Doctor Bus was quick to step in and start guiding Jean to our medical center. He had been expecting this to happen at any time and was just glad it wasn't when we were out rescuing Cassandra.

"You might want to let Kathy know what's going on, Chief. I need to take Ed with me, and Kathy wouldn't want to miss this."

"Can I come too?" asked Colleen.

"Of course," said Bus. "Tom, why don't you take Hampton up to meet Molly and see if he needs something to eat? The man could probably use a cold beer."

"Beer? You have cold beer?"

We all went in different directions, but the Mud Island family had grown. We would have to find a way to make due with what little space we had, but we would manage. I had gone from being a loner to having the closest family a man could have.

The next few hours seemed like days, but it was such a blur it could have been minutes. I wasn't really sure.

Kathy and Cassandra came back from the living quarters in a hurry and joined up with Colleen. They all helped Doctor Bus with Jean. I have to admit, he couldn't have had better assistants, and even though Jean was starting to say some really creative things about the labor pains, it was quite a festive atmosphere. The more creative she got, the harder they all laughed.

Someone said something about having a baby shower combined with the delivery, and they all laughed even harder.

They were all having such a good time in the little medical bay that the men, including me, were all left hanging around outside in the hall.

Between creative outbursts and labor pains, Jean saw me standing just outside the door and gave me a thumbs up.

"I've got this, Eddy. You can go take care of the guys. Besides, there isn't enough room in here."

I started to object, but another labor pain hit, and she yelled something about it being safer outside the shelter.

We all decided to get out while we could and went upstairs and wait for the big event, I saw Molly sitting sat the shortwave radio. She had the headphones on, but her head was aimed down at her feet. I could tell she felt left out.

I told the guys to save me a seat at the table and went over to Molly.

"Hey, girl. They could use a hand down in the medical bay. I think it will be okay to leave the radio unmanned for a bit."

"Really? Thanks, Uncle Eddy."

The smile looked as big as anything I had ever seen on the Chief's face. The headphones flew into the air as she dove out of her chair toward the kitchen. Halfway there she threw on the brakes, spun in a circle, and ran back over to where she had left me standing. I got a big hug, and then her black hair was practically flying out behind her as she ran past the kitchen table on her way to the lower levels. I noticed it was a little less curly, and she was growing a bit.

The guys were all having as much fun as the women down below, and when Molly blew past them at a dead run, they let out a cheer like she was winning a race.

Someone had gotten out the cold beer for Hampton, and one was waiting for me on the table. I don't know where he got them from, but the Chief produced a box of cigars.

"Here you go, Ed. When the good word comes up from below, you have to pass these out. It's bad luck to do it before then, so just have them ready."

Everyone lifted their bottles and held them across the table to clink them together in a toast.

Down in the medical bay, the women all got excited when Molly showed up. They made room for her up by Jean's head and gave her the main job of wiping Jean's forehead with a cool washcloth.

"Time to start keeping the language clean," said Kathy. "We don't need to be teaching Molly anything new."

Jean gave Kathy a grin while gritting her teeth and said, "Thanks a lot. I'll try to keep that in mind."

Then Jean proceeded to let out a string of words that rhymed with the more familiar terms.

We heard so much laughing coming from downstairs that everyone's eyebrows went up.

"Must be a funny looking baby," said Hampton.

It's really hard to breathe when beer comes out your nose.

That was the day Josh was born. The Chief tried to hide the misty eyes when he was introduced to my son and told we had named Josh after him. I didn't tease him this time. Besides, Jean would have put me back in the doghouse if I had. I just let the big guy have a private moment to deal with it.

As I was passing out the cigars, I looked at the calendar hanging in the kitchen and saw that it was the sixth of July, so Josh arrived right on schedule. Molly had herself a little cousin to take care of, and he sure had enough aunts and uncles to spoil him.

I could tell the Chief couldn't wait to start helping to make a man out of him, but first things first. The Chief had looked at the calendar, too, and he said it looked like we had about six months to plan for our next trip out of the shelter.

"Why six months?" I asked.

"It should be pretty cold by then," he said. "As a matter of fact, it will be freezing up north. We can talk about that tomorrow, though. It's time for you to be with your family."

I said good night and went down to the bedroom. Jean and I still had the master bedroom, but we agreed there would be too much traffic through the room for a new baby. For about the one hundredth time I wondered why my uncle had put the master bedroom in such an odd place.

An ammunition box had been converted into crib for Josh, and Hampton had even managed to find four legs to fasten onto the bottom. Jean had fallen asleep facing Josh in his new crib, so I slipped into the bed and snuggled up from behind her.

Jean sighed when I put an arm over her, and I felt a deep satisfaction. We had taken one small step forward to save the human race by Josh being born, and I knew that the fight for survival had really begun.

From the beginning I had been told to never leave the shelter once the apocalypse had begun, but we had learned something quickly. That just wouldn't work. We couldn't just watch the world die around us and do nothing. I knew that more than ever as I listened to Jean's soft breathing. I had been wrong to question our reasons for rescuing Cassandra. Whether it was one life or a thousand, every life was worth saving.

The Chief's little mutiny had been crazy to try on his own. That's why it was good that Kathy had rebelled along with him and snuck out after him. They may have been crazy, but they had saved the lives of thirty children and eighty adults. They might be stuck inside that shelter for years, but they would survive. They would live, and they would have more children.

Molly would be happy to keep them company on the radio and keep them up to date on the outside world. Now, there were children at Fort Sumter and Lake Norman for her to talk with.

That made our one contribution look smaller, but the baby sleeping near us was a symbol of the future that we were going to determine for ourselves.

I sighed happily along with Jean, pulled her a little closer to me, and drifted off to sleep.

ABOUT THE AUTHOR

Bob Howard (1951-) was born in New Jersey to an Army Sergeant from Ohio and a mother from Romania. He was moved from one Army base to the next, and before he began high school in Huntsville, Alabama he had lived most of his life overseas in Germany and Okinawa with brief stays in Maryland and North Carolina. He credits his imagination to his exposure to different cultures and environments at an early age. He began reading science fiction and fell in love with post apocalyptic novels. He still has an original copy of the first one he read in 1966, The Furies by Keith Edwards. He joined the Navy after high school and continued to move from one base to another, including a submarine base at Holy Loch, Scotland. He eventually stayed in one place when he got stationed in Charleston, South Carolina. He graduated with a BS in Psychology from the College of Charleston and married his wife of 32 years. His son still lives in Charleston, but his daughter has married and made a home in Ohio where the Howard family has its earliest known roots. Through the years he has had one burning passion that he has wanted to fulfill, and through The Infected Dead series he is getting to live that passion. Creating a book is something so many people want to do but never have the opportunity, and after writing these books he believes the sky is the limit. He plans to write for the rest of his life because it is enjoyable beyond his wildest dreams. As for the zombie genre, he saw Night of the Living Dead when it originally hit the theaters, and he believes until recently it didn't receive the attention it deserves.